To An

Enjoy it

Xavier Book 1:
Xavier Of The World

– CHRISTOPHER ABBOT –

An environmentally friendly book printed and bound in England by
www.printondemand-worldwide.com

XAVIER BOOK 1: XAVIER OF THE WORLD

Copyright © Christopher Abbot 2016

A catalogue record for this book is available from the British Library

ISBN 978-178456-327-1

FIRST PUBLISHED 2016 BY NU HUMANA PUBLISHING
An imprint of Upfront Publishing of
Peterborough, England.

For Mom and Dad

Acknowledgements

I would like to thank the following people for their kindness and help in allowing me to make this book a reality.

Steve Ashcroft for his unwavering belief and support over the last few years, my brother Tim for his 'Dunkirk Spirit'.

Factory Fifteen for their vision and work on visualising the universe.

Sascha Aktar for her help in editing this book.

Frank Jung at CAA for being a believer from the start and also to Aaron Lam.

All of my friends and family who have given their support and encouragement.

Duggie, the dog whose walks started all of this.

And finally to my wife Sonya for her love and support and to Frankie and Harry and Chloe.

I love you all.

★★★★★

The sun, the moon and the stars would have disappeared long ago...had
they happened to be within the reach of predatory human hands.
~ Havelock Ellis, The Dance of Life, 1923

Thank God men cannot fly, and lay waste the sky as well as the earth.
~ Henry David Thoreau

"In the long run a single-planet species will not survive...if we humans
want to survive as a species for millions of years then we must ultimately
populate other planets. Today that concept is barely conceivable but one
day there will be more human beings who live off Earth than live on it"
~ NASA Chief Michael Griffin

★★★★

★★★★★

Year	Event
1957	Sputnik is the first satellite to be launched into low Earth orbit.
1969	Apollo 11 - Neil Armstrong and Buzz Aldrin become the first humans to set foot on the moon.
2012	Space X become the first privately owned company to supply a cargo load to the International Space Station in low Earth orbit and signals the start of the emergence of private enterprise ventures in space.
2014	Contact.
2018	Combined EU Air Forces attack north African ports responsible for people smuggling into Europe. Military operations turn hundreds of thousands of migrants back towards Africa and the Middle East.
2020	New Cold War between the United States and Russia begins.
2021	Al Qaeda and the Taliban call end to hostilities with the United States.
2022	United States fire two nuclear warheads into targets in Northern Iraq and Syria in retaliation for a 'dirty bomb' detonated in Chicago.
2023	Russia, China and United States embark on First Arctic War over oil reserves. Using the 15 Naval Battle Groups in her fleet the US contain both the Chinese and Russian forces forcing a retreat. After a twelve month conflict the US again flexes its nuclear might. A Third World War is averted but the US strikes a number of cities around the world.
2025	Contact.
2028	Space A2Z become first private company to land on the Moon in partnership with NASA. China and Russia follow suit and a second space race begins.

Year	Event
2029	Collapse of the global banking system exactly 100 years after the Wall Street Crash sends the world into a continual cycle of violent civil unrest. Around the globe, politicians, bankers and the wealthy are singled out by mobs looking for someone to blame. Russia's oligarchs and many of Wall Street's bankers are tried and executed.
2032	Space A2Z become first private company to land on Mars.
2035	Massive breakthrough in Carbon nano-technology.
2040	Bio and solar energy replace fossil fuels as the most productive sources of energy.
2044	Birth of fusion power.
2045	Contact.
2047	First private space station is built by a conglomerate of entrepreneurs with the intention of developing commercial interests on the Moon and Mars and nearby asteroids.
2050	Major climate change sees a continent-wide drought and famine in Africa. A surge in mass migration to the north and south (now known as 'the African Flight') of the continent takes place. European nations use military force to protect their borders. What were once pitied as refugees are now seen as a scourge and are forced back to Africa or massacred.
2051	Worldwide migration ensues - Economic and climate changes see a mass upheaval around the world. Humanitarianism begins to be seen in the developed world as misappropriated logic.
2052	The Tragedy of St. Louis - the major American city is destroyed with over 100,000 deaths by a wall of tornadoes that sweep across the city caused by the climate changes affecting the world.

Year	Event
2054	First colony established on Mars by a coalition of nations and private corporations.
2055	First mining operation begins on Moon by Russian and American conglomerate.
2056	The United States of America and Canada form a Northern Alliance after a decade that sees the near death of the Union. The Northern Alliance, alongside the United Kingdom, Greenland Iceland, Norway, Sweden and Finland form a powerful union whose interests are not only for the planet Earth but also for space.
2060	Links are formed by scientists, private business interests and corporations to build the first colonies in space within the coming fifty years. They become known as The High Pioneers.
2064	First asteroid capture and mining operation begins.
2065	Contact.
2066	Extinction of many wild species reported due to famine or hunting. Ocean stocks are depleted and geneticists take samples for future storage. A global program of stockpiling DNA and specimens starts.
2069	100 years after the first moon landing, India builds its first manned space colony near to the moon.
2071	Russian corporations in collaboration with China build the first lunar smelters and rapid colonization of the Moon begins.
2078	Space propulsion technology rapidly advances allowing for the exploration of the outer solar system.
2084	The population of humans living in space exceeds 250,000.
2089	Morgan Baxter Laboratories develop the first Edu Imp technologies.

Year	Event
2091	Plans are announced for the building of the first Space Elevator to begin operations within the decade. Sites are chosen around the Equator to construct over fifty elevator bases.
2092	Android evolution begins with major advances in bio cybernetic development.
2093	North Pole ice caps melt flooding London and New York, amongst other cities.
2099	Dr. Charles Alexander formulates The Doctrine - the creation of ultra intelligent and super fast entities to run the day to day affairs of mankind whilst overseen by a politburo of self appointed advisors known as The Powers. Mankind's future on Earth becomes dictated by machines and Earth's failing resources.
2101	The Amazon forest is now a desert. Global temperatures soar by 10% and vast tracts of Earth become uninhabitable.
2104	In twenty years the population living off Earth increases to over five million. The figure is again set to quadruple within five years due to the successful operation of the first Space Elevator.
2105	Genesis - The official name of the newly designated colonies located in the Lagrange Point L5.
2106	Kremer Gracian is born in Biarritz, France.
2108	The Suffocation of 2108 - The worsening of weather conditions that culminates in giant wildfires, the great rivers drying up and vast tracts of land turned into desert. Droughts and famines ravage the planet. Typhoons and hurricanes batter cities and cause giant tsunamis. Various geo-engineering techniques prove ineffective which leads to the deaths of over a third of the world's population.

Year	Event
2109	Denton Amadeus elected by The Powers as the first head of Human Enterprises also known as Nu Humana. A solution to the crisis on Earth and for the first time a plan of action for mankind outside of Earth is drawn up. He mandates the evacuation of the entire human population from Earth.
2110	Declaration of Denton Amadeus. Legislation is drawn up for The Great Exodus to be carried out within the next fifty years signalling removal of all humans from Earth. To be relocated in the new space colonies of Genesis, Mars and the Moon. All colonies are to be populated by refugees from Earth and those that refuse will be executed.
2112	Gazelle Spa and Galaxie-Generale open Atlanterra, the first of the giant Space Elevators off the coast of Guiana. Over the next two decades, fifty space elevators are constructed around the Earth's equator.
2115	The Dearn Monroe asteroid is discovered in the Asteroid Belt. It is the biggest diamond ever found.
2119	Construction of over a thousand space colonies begins with many of the old nations of Earth building their own, alongside the newly formed corporations that have grown incredibly wealthy from the new opportunities within the solar system.
2132	Space Elevators around the globe constantly undertake the mass departure of whole cities and provinces. Everyday tens of thousands of people are propelled into space.
2133	The High Pioneers establish their own independent states within Genesis.

Year	Event
2135	Large scale automation has led to corporations becoming incredibly powerful. The rapid growth of android technology leads to trans-humans / androids becoming largely indistinguishable from humans. Due to public outrage trans-humans are given a distinguishing seal and a four year life span though many corporations ignore this dictate.
2144	New colonies established on Saturn's moons Tethys, Titan, Dione and Enceladus. Vast mining and refining operations are initiated. Ores, minerals and gases are harvested from Saturn, Jupiter and throughout the asteroid belt.
2148	The Loyal Order of Android Monks established by The Powers with the sole purpose of looking after the monuments of old Earth and initiate a program protect the remainder of species left on Earth. A secret agenda is drawn up that sanctions The Loyal Order to restore the planet back to its natural equilibrium.
2149	Populations on lunar colonies exceed 100 million people.
2150	Virgin Galactic opens the Branson Entertainment Crater.
2151	Eradication Squads scour the Earth to execute any stragglers of the Exodus or humans evading removal. Under the command of Kremer Gracian these squads form into a quasi religious faction that become the 'muscle' for The Powers. They call themselves The Shadows.
2160	Nu Humana announces that the economy of Earth and mankind is now entirely dependent on space resources and the colonisation of new moons and planets. The deadline for the removal of all humans from Earth is reached and a final warning for all remaining individuals.

Year	Event
2163	Terraforming of Mars begins as giant colonies all over the planet form.
2165	The Hives - an enormous group of space stations and colonies are constructed in the centre of Genesis acting as the home for the millions of displaced refugees from Earth. It soon becomes a ghetto and with new regulations and laws many try to seek refuge within an area known as Debris where the refuse and garbage of Genesis is dumped.
2166	Formation of The Air Authority in Genesis - the air rights of all human beings living within the newly formed area of The Hives is now overseen by The AA who, under the behest of The Powers, ensure that everyone works on The Arks in return for oxygen and shelter. Summary execution is sanctioned to control the society.
2172	A ring of asteroid forts are placed around the Earth and a force field activated to prevent anyone uninvited from returning to Earth. Known as The Celestial Gate it acts as a barrier and deterrent to every person that now resides in Genesis and the Moon.
2175	Educational Implanting or Edu Imps - Mind Uploading becomes popular throughout Genesis. The advancement is seen as normal, with distinct and significant divisions apparent throughout human society.
2184	Colonies established in the Kuiper Belt. For the first time mankind has spanned the solar system.
2190	Mars declares independence from Genesis and the United Colonies. First Martian War of Independence begins leading to a civil war amongst many settlers.
2195	After a bitter civil war, the emergence of the pro-Martian militia Knights Of Mars seize power and secede from the United Colonies.

Year	Event
2196	Commercial space industry is booming as trade between Genesis, the Moon, Mars and the other colonies rapidly increases. Production of colonies in Genesis grows and the populations of the Moon and Mars increase as new industries form.
2200	The Powers declare the Pax Humana. An empire that decrees to take mankind and human beings to every corner of the galaxy.
2202	The vast construction of Ark Light docks and the first Arks for travel to the stars are set in motion.
2208	The Powers pledge there will be more human life throughout the galaxy and provide the first glimpse at revolutionising inter stellar travel.
2212	First signs of environmental improvement on Earth after fifty years of human removal.
2222	The Loyal Order of Android Monks rekindle life in most of the devastated parts of the Earth. The Amazon rainforest begins to grow back. Sea stocks are approaching normal levels. Animals have been returned to their natural habitats and the air quality on Earth is back to pre 1700's level.
2245	The Powers return to Earth and headquarter themselves around the globe, building vast palaces and mansions from their wealth. Mankind's future is now being run from Earth, but there is now definitely no possible return for humanity to its home planet .

Year	Event
2256	The population of humans living in space exceeds 3 billion. Over 500 million people now call themselves Martian, with similar numbers living on the Moon. Genesis and the outer colonies account for the rest and for the first time in a century a population boom sees humans born in space about to exceed the last recorded Earth population.
2260	Completion and launch of first interstellar Ark. Odysseus 1 takes 200,000 humans to a new life in a new solar system.
2270	Within a decade, production of Arks increases from ten per year to twenty per year. Genesis and Ark Light docks work continually building these huge structures.
2278	Colonies across the mining colonies of the Kuiper Belt revolt and declare independence from Nu Humana. They are dealt with sternly by The Powers.
2288	Mars becomes the leading industrial planet within the solar system.
2293	Interstellar propulsion units for the new generation of Arks is unveiled. The ability to travel hundreds of light years within a life span becomes possible reviving a new surge in exploration.
2297	Earth becomes the home to ten thousand humans as rewards for service to families of The Powers. A new, privileged elite generation of Earthlings is allowed back to the planet under license.
2300	Genesis - The number of colonies and space stations constructed in this area surpasses one hundred and fifty-thousand and growing constantly.

Year	Event
2305	The Great Cathay Wheel - the largest man-made structure ever to be built - is completed. It is the home to over a hundred million people mainly from Chinese territories and controls much of Sino Space's ambitions.
2313	Earth returns to former glory as forest and oceans become filled with fauna and wildlife once again.
2322	Closure of all the space elevators - having served their purpose they are deactivated.
2334	Major revolt takes place on colonies throughout the Asteroid Belt. A battle for the space lanes threatens all corporate interests in the solar system. The rebels threaten Earth with an asteroid assault at Earth. Nu Humana negotiates a truce and a pact is made that creates certain autonomous rule for these outlying territories under the agreement of the Pax Humana.
2356	Gas refineries and cities are constructed on Jupiter, the giant gas planet accelerates the wealth and performance of the Pax Humana.
2375	First Ark arrives in Alpha Centauri after its hundred year journey. Colonisation proceeds but contact with the colonists is lost.
2382	Arks are continually being built and manned to all destinations throughout the universe.
2391	With the rise of the Edu Imp and mind uploading becoming a standard practice across the solar system, The Powers instigate a cull of all illegal implant manufacturers. Mind uploading is controlled by them alone and gives them the ability to program and control the populace.

Year	Event
2398	The wealth of operations in the Pax Humana allows for The Powers and The High Pioneers to share a lucrative pot. The corporations and operations that control the trade within the solar system reward many citizens within Genesis with luxury space stations for them to inhabit.
2409	Many of the Arks sent to parts of the galaxy have not been heard from and are presumed either lost or destroyed.
2427	Bhutan Kraldon assumes absolute control of The Powers and begins a dominant family dynasty.
2430	All of Earth's great monuments and buildings which have been preserved by the Loyal Order of Android Monks are re opened for The Powers.
2434	Mars completes the terra forming process and is now a verdant and productive planet. The vast geo engineering project has taken nearly 271 years to conclude has changed the culture and society of the planet.
2442	A tele-transporter is unveiled as the future of interstellar travel. It is hidden away after threats by Martian extremist militias wishing to take it over for their own advancement.
2450	Earth is cleared of all plastics and effectively decontaminated. The pollutants of the 20th and 21st Century are finally disposed of or have decomposed.
2477	Elson Kraldon takes over from his grandfather as leader of Nu Humana
2489	Establishment of the Seven - seven new Earth like planets have now been discovered and are ready for colonization. Calls for a return to Earth by the citizens of Genesis are rejected and agitators are executed. The Powers remain firm.

Year	Event
2505	Trade between all the newly colonised planets and moons thrives
2510	Nu Humana is in the ascendency, controlling every aspect of mankind's quest through the galaxy. Its reach is now in astronomical units rather than kilometers or miles.
2517	Drax Kraldon becomes the head of Nu Humana.
2534	Xavier Miro born.
2557	Tamarinsk IV Ark about to launch for Proxima Centauri from Ark Light.

Chris Abbot

★★★★★

1

Open Your Eyes

Open your eyes

Open your eyes

Swirling shafts of incandescent light cut through the high canopy of the forest and illuminated portions of open space. They seemed to be calling him towards them. Patterns danced on the floor around him, in motion with the beating of his heart. A single bead of sweat ran down his forehead and off the bridge of his nose. He paused for a second, taking in a deep breath of air that filled his lungs and briefly gave him respite from the burning sensation engulfing his whole body.

He glanced to his right transfixed as a nest of baby spiders scrambled over the carcass of a rat, devouring its bloated entrails in an early morning feast. There was no time to stop. Splinters flew in the air as a crack of bark flew past his ears - it was time to move on again. He was not alone.

Open your eyes

Open your eyes

He began running again, faster than before. He was relying on intuition. Slowing down was not an option.

The edges of his hands began to sting and bleed as he swiped away branches. The strands of vines and the blades of long grasses cut into them. As he parried the undergrowth away he left droplets of blood on the green. Stumbling down a small bank he came upon a stream. A small shoal of fish gathering in the shade of a large leaf that hung over the gently running waters.

All was still.

Translucent in the water, internal organs clearly visible, he could see the beating of their hearts. His own heart was beating twice as fast as these tiny creatures. He entered the swiftly flowing stream, the icy cold water filling his boots, rising up his legs and past his waist.

As he waded through the silt that rose, turbulent, swirling, ochre clouds surrounded him. The fish had dispersed and now viewed him with curious concern from the other side of the stream.

He heard an ominous rumble in the distance signalling the onset of another chase. He pushed himself through the water as it rose around his chest. His hands were soothed in the coolness of the fresh water. The overhangs of branches gave him some shelter but he knew he had to run. The rumbling was getting louder, with sounds like the trunks of trees snapping like twigs emerging from the forest.

Open your eyes

From the centre of the river to the opposite shoreline, he reached a silver sanded bank, the tracks of an animal embedded in the fine glittering grain. He wondered whether it had found its way home or perished before it could reach shelter. He took some deep breaths, filling his lungs with precious oxygen. From the stream, he ran through a clearing and into a wooded area abundant with bamboo plants. The dense foliage was almost impenetrable. He tucked his head down into his chest and continued into the deep vegetation.

Open your eyes

The humidity was overbearing now and constricted his breathing. The more he pushed, the more he felt like he was being pulled back. He stumbled forward, unsure of the direction he was heading, knowing that if he stopped, he would be done for. He gulped at the thought and found his throat tight and sore. He wished he had taken more water at the stream to stem what was now an unremitting thirst. He looked up towards a branch to see a python slithering back to his place of rest, oblivious to the drama unfolding below him.

Ping! There was a crack of bark as another projectile whistled past his ear.

Left or right? He had no time to decide.

Both were uphill.

His decision could be fatal.

Open your eyes

Something was telling him to go left.

He did not know why.

He stumbled over a rock and cursed, spitting out what little saliva he had left in his parched mouth before proceeding up the pathway. How did he know which trail was best? When another piece of bark exploded above his head, sending a splinter ricocheting into his shoulder, he followed his gut feeling. The track was steep. A large carpet of branches and leaves covered the brownish bracken floor as he scrambled over rocks and twigs.

The odour of old rotting vegetation filled his nostrils. It was part of the chain of life that kept the forest alive and the smell filled him with a sense of purpose. He was desperate for every breath now, lungs on fire, his muscles raging in agony. Every inhalation was painful and laboured. Yet he could feel himself getting higher on the wooded embankment and dared to look around.

Open your eyes

All he could see was thick forest. He wasn't high enough to see above the canopy just yet, but if he kept going up he was sure to be able to reach a better vantage point. The rumbling below intensified and he felt the ground moving. If he could make it to the top of the hill he would surely make his escape. Another bullet whistled past him. But why him? Why were they after him? For the first time since he'd begun to run, he felt fear.

He desperately yanked at exposed roots and dug in his heels and toes to make headway up the side of the hill. It felt like treading water, going through the motions but getting nowhere. He had to push himself that little bit harder, that little bit further, if he was going to make it and save himself.

He pulled himself past two large tree trunks and then mounted a rocky parapet. This granite outcrop was lined with deep fissures, perfect for gripping and excellent for climbing. He scaled the grey rock with a regained confidence. He pressed his bloodied fingers into the cracks and lifted himself bit by bit along the jagged stone outcrop, the mixture of dirt and sweat for once affording him some semblance of grip. Taking a deep breath he swung his legs out from underneath him onto the ledge.

He glanced back at the green roof of the forest and closed his eyes feeling the cold wet stone upon his face.

The feel, the smell, the taste, the cold wet stone.

It felt good.

Open your eyes

Open your eyes

Crack! Louder than before. The rock below him exploded and fragments of flint and stone flew in all directions. He hurled himself over the last part of the stone bulwark. There was another impact just below his feet that made him kick into the air, his heart pumping faster than ever.

Now, at the top of the forest he could see the canopy of stars. Stars straight ahead of him, thousands of stars, solar systems, constellations, galaxies all stretched out in front of him and he was running, running towards them, running for his life towards them.

A bang, this time to the left of him, made him stumble and lose his footing. He kept his balance whilst continuing to run toward the night sky. For some reason unknown to him he felt compelled, even drawn to the stars, as if they could provide him with sanctuary.

"I will be safe if I can reach them," he panted through his breath.

"I will be safe if I can reach them."

He repeated this mantra as if it would somehow protect him.

All at once he hit a force field, a wall of glass, a barrier to the sky.

He blinked for a moment, trying to take it all in.

Confused, he stepped back for a second trying to comprehend what had just happened.

He then ran his hand along the invisible barricade. It was solid and it was high. As he pushed against the surface, it seemed to push back. He placed his head on it; it was cool to the touch. He closed his eyes and collected his thoughts for the briefest of moments. The barrier was glass, solid and staunch and as he began to pull his head back he stared at an impression of his own blood and sweat smeared and imprinted on the translucent wall.

What was happening?

He looked around him and saw the horizon stretching for miles in both directions, a singular line that sliced his world in two. A frontier that encircled the forest as if it was contained inside a bowl.

Where am I?

He remembered being a child and someone having a terrarium, a small soil garden in a round glass bowl that he would gaze at for hours.

Out of nowhere a piercing, searing pain entered one side of his body and exited out the other. He winced, struggling to find his breath and staggered towards the boundary, breathless, tears filling his eyes.

This was incomprehensible. This had no beginning…

Open your eyes

Open your eyes

Open your eyes

Xavier Miro's eyelids sprang open.

In an instant they were wide apart, gazing glassily into the half light of his bedroom.

He had had that dream again. The nightmare which had been plaguing him for months. His sheets were soaked with sweat, he was disorientated and confused. He lifted himself up, his bare back peeling away from the bedcover as he stared vacantly towards the wall.

Open your eyes

Xavier impulsively uttered the first words of his day, "Open your…" and the subtle, phantom female voice ceased its relentless echo and faded into nothingness. As he focused on the void of his room, familiar objects began to take shape. He was safe…for now.

The curved walls and subtle recessed white lighting were testament to the utilitarian building techniques that had created his uniform sleeping chamber. The en-suite bathroom and glass fronted wardrobe, functional in design, began to form before him as his eyes adjusted to the light. He gazed to his left and the sealed window that was his companion. Its blue-white light relentlessly streamed in and illuminated the covers of the bed, defining his raised legs clearly, casting elongated shadows against the curvature of the walls. The room was bathed in a cerulean tint, the luminescence of which was so compelling that it forced any mortal to dream of its beauty.

Xavier had in every waking moment, as others like him, dreamt that one day he would be able to sample its air and water. That one day they would be allowed to venture on its soils and swim in its seas, smell its celebrated flowers and witness the extraordinary indigenous species that inhabited its many varied regions.

But this was just a wild dream; no ordinary man was ever allowed there.

Whilst he had once belonged to the indigenous species of the planet himself, he could no longer be trusted with venturing there, let alone living there, and so Xavier gazed from his porthole like every other person on the colonies, asteroids and distant planets; with a mixture of desire and regret at what was once their ancestral home.

These humans were a breed who would yearn for a planet they would never know, never discover, never take pleasure in its beautiful and unique vistas. These were the great, great, great, great, grandchildren and descendants of the human race who, generations before, had ruined and destroyed the most beautiful planet in the galaxy. They could only look with envious eyes at the world of which they had been deprived by their ancestors.

Xavier always awoke to the sight of his beloved planet, Earth.

★★★★★

2

The Cannery & The Hives

T rans-hab Unit 26-12-1739 CVT was like any other trans-hab, or trans-habitation capsule found in The Hives - a massive utilitarian housing project in the centre of an area known to the locals as The Cannery, because no matter what the size of space was, you were still living in a can. The egalitarian design of these trans-habs made it difficult to distinguish one from another, save for the hundred metre high letters and numerals adorning each of The Hives trans-hab units, spelling out its name and perimeter, preventing the tedious grind of journeying to the wrong block.

Xavier swiftly rubbed his eyes and face and began to come to his senses.

Members of the ancient Earth people had believed in life after death and reincarnation, that death was rebirth. He had been told by his friend Old Man Ray there was nothing to fear about death; that it was just a transition that happened to everyone. "We all die," Old Man Ray would say in his deep, rasping voice.

As he looked out of the window of his trans-hab towards the distant Earth the symbolic logo of Nu Humana based on Da Vinci's Vitruvian Man was embossed on the side of the Hive. It seemed to be stamped on most things.

Nu Humana, the all-dominant, omnipotent supremacy oversaw the development of mankind and its expansion into the universe, it governed everything that a person utilised from birth to death. It was there from the moment you took your first breath until after your final exhalation, when your body would be sent for recycling.

It provided you with a place to live, a life support suit to wear, a place to work and a common purpose; something that for so long had been missing from the human experience. Nu Humana actually allowed you time for leisure and reflection and most importantly, Nu Humana gave you hope. The symbol blazed out from the gunmetal grey surface of Hive 19-J-15 as a warning to the miscreants in the neighbourhood.

Xavier reached over to the side of his bed and grabbed a drink. He placed the straw of the sealed vessel to his lips and began to suck down the rich, vitamin-enhanced liquid that would act as his first food supplement of the day

"Screen on," murmured Xavier as the walls around him came to life, figures stepping out of the curvatures and re-enacting some kind of melodramatic scene in a factory where the characters were discussing the ergonomic potential of a wheat crop on the hydroponic installation they were setting up.

Whatever it was, Xavier didn't want it.

"Flip it!"

The room enveloped in flickering images from news reports, sports programs and music videos from all the latest Luna and Mars entertainment channels as it was every morning. Genesis had the best programs; the different cultures and mixes of people were so diverse that the TV shows reflected just about everything Genesis had to offer, including Can Com, which was one of the unusual and quirky dialects all the young kids seemed to speak, a mish-mash of Earth languages and space flight interfacing.

"Flick it!"

The walls seamlessly turned to a flame haired female reporter, styled in swathes of silver and black. Her eyes blacker than any black hole, drawing him in like a vortex.

"Welcome to Channel 999, Con-apt News for The Hives. Bringing you all the latest local, Genesis and interplanetary news as it happens here and around the system. This is Claudia Furukawa with a round-up of the news that affects you!"

"Claudia Furukawa is hot as hell," Xavier had a thing for female news reporters.

"The headlines, starting with inter-planetary news - The Martian insurgency continues today with bombs going off in three parts of Viking City, killing at least five hundred colonists. Authorities have blamed the explosions on the tensions between waves of the new colonists building new settlements in disputed territories who have been expanding rapidly through the Valles Marinares sector…"

Viking City...named after the first spacecraft to have landed on Mars. The early settlers of the red planet built a city around the site, invoking the spirit of legendary red-headed Earth men who had crossed the oceans of Earth in long boats thousands of years before .

A sound interrupted his thoughts and he swooped his hand.

"Who is it?"

"Zola,"

"How are you Zola?" with another hand motion he allowed the call to proceed.

"I'm good!"

The voice was young and sultry, and belonged to Zola Capello, Xavier's workmate at ArkLight Docks and girlfriend.

"Why can't I see you?" asked Xavier.

"Because I just stepped out from the Glo-Sho and it is too early Xavier, I look a mess and I am getting ready for work."

"So?"

She ignored his persistence, "So are we going out later?"

"Yep, where do you want to go? The Pleasure Dome? The Astral Apache? You name it I'll be there."

"I want to go to Debris," she said nonchalantly.

"Debris?" Xavier sounded surprised.

"Yes, really! There's a rave going on there that I don't want to miss."

"Unlike you to risk your life and liberty for a party in Debris," replied Xavier sarcastically.

"Well, I would like to go there!"

"Zola, you know they have checkpoints heading out towards Debris. I'm not sure we should go." Police activity had been strong in the last few months, targeting many of the ravers making their way from the Hives across what was known as The Divide.

"I know but there are lots of my friends going to the rave and I think it will be awesome," Zola insisted, not hearing a word Xavier had said.

"Okay," he uttered after a pause, " I have got to meet with Jericho earlier though."

"Fantastic!" said Zola, "I really have to run and you should get yourself ready and get to work."

"I am trying but…" Xavier attempted to put words to what he was feeling but Zola cut him off.

"See you later," with that the call ended and Xavier was again engulfed in images of Claudia Furukawa and the headline news, "Armoured biker gangs affiliated to The Kazinsky Burjit Mining Group and loyal to the Martian leader, Premier Templar, have caused friction throughout the Mars colonies recently and settlers are now demanding that counsellors from The Powers intervene in what has been a very bloody month for the Martian colonies; a full report coming up later in the program. Meanwhile, closer to home, demonstrations and minor explosions have taken place across a number of Nu Humana facilities in Genesis, though nobody was hurt or killed. The terrorist group Civilization is being held responsible for these outrages and the authorities are studying intelligence…"

He moved to the en suite and headed straight for the Glo-Sho. He glanced at the mirror, it was definitely time for a shave. The Glo-Sho door swivelled open with a hiss. As Xavier entered, a warm curtain of velvet light enveloped his body from head to toe.

Xavier could only imagine what drops of rain were like and yet the warm beams of light that surrounded him seemed to transport him to a place he had only seen in historical archives of the Earth, or in his dreams. The archives had shown him rain and waterfalls, all of which seemed so beautiful yet so alien. The gentle light glowed in a collage of colours, cleaning and refreshing every part of his body.

Water showers and baths were only for the extremely wealthy with the privilege of wasting precious water and had now for centuries been eliminated as an obsession of eccentric and uncultured earlier civilisations.

As Xavier bathed in the shaft of light he could feel himself coming back to life again as the refreshing currents encapsulated his body. He pushed his head forward and without saying a word an invisible mask surrounded his face and began to massage and remove his facial hair. He pulled back and rubbed his hands over his newly smooth face. Pushing the door open, Xavier returned to his bedroom.

Channel 999 news droned on, "Fighting continues on the newly discovered asteroid Centaur 1474 after Tigernaut and Dragonaut forces clashed over salvage and mining rights. Centaur 1474 is believed to contain in excess of 1.2 billion tons of pure nickel and, with many other minerals expected to be found on the asteroid tension has been high since the destruction of the Indian Prospecting Team by Chinese Dragonaut forces. General Juggi Khalsa, commander of the 6th Tigernaut Battalion, spoke of his frustration that Dragonaut forces had continued to dig in on Centaur 1474 even after reinforcements were destroyed en route. The Chinese Android Battalion was ambushed by Tigernaut forces en route to Centaur 1474, destroying all on board."

"Same shit, different day," muttered Xavier as he pressed the wall.

Spinning out, it opened to reveal a suit hanging neatly with boots and gloves opposite a selection of under suits. Xavier eased his athletic build into the under suit. It was an extra skin to protect him from the radiation, heat and extreme cold of deep space, which was worn under normal everyday clothes customised and adorned to show Xavier's own individual style. A life support system on Xavier's wrist operated immediately he left the comfort of his trans-hab.

As Xavier completed his final checks on the gauges and monitors of his suit, his attention returned to Claudia Furukawa. "…Sino Space, Mughal Space, Earth Corp and Nu Humana have announced the decision to build a hundred new Arks after the discovery of new life bearing planets in the Proxima Centauri constellation, just over 4.22 light years away. This is good news for Genesis and the famous docks of Ark Light. The latest Generation ship, Tamarinsk IV is due for completion imminently and this news can only bring joy to all the workers of Genesis and the prospective pioneers waiting for their place on one of the Arks and the new destiny that awaits them…"

"At last some good news for a change."

Xavier pressed a button to reveal his customised helmet which slid out of its protective glass cabinet with a swoosh. Picking up his helmet he bellowed out "Music." Instantly the walls of the room boomed to life as the news reporter slowly shrank back into the wall, a thumping bass line erupted all around as the sound of the latest import tunes of Scun Scum and Atoms 159, leaders of the Titan Moon Rock scene screamed out of the speakers.

With that, his hand touched a panel and he strode through the door into The Hives.

★★★★★

3
Granding On The Landing

Xavier took his usual seat at Nish-Kin's Noodle Bar on the landing of his block. He gazed at the people frenetically to-ing and fro-ing across one of the many landings of Hive 19 J 15. He unwrapped his chopsticks, out of habit wiping his sitting with the napkins provided and then placed his wrist over the reader which credited him with food and drink.

The strip was immense, with garish looking stores lining either side selling a profuse range of products and services to everyone and anyone. The central aisle was awash with food vendors under neon signs, street pedlars touting their latest wares and buskers balancing things, body popping or creating an incredible racket singing the latest songs from the Asteroid Belt while looking for a slot on Genesis Got Talent. Nish-Kin's Noodle Bar was a bit of an institution, the saying went, 'The food is great but the portions could be bigger!'

Xavier found Nish-Kin's a great place to eat and collect his thoughts before heading out to spray his graffiti or go to work, and was always comforted by the hot bowl of broth and noodles placed before him and began to contemplate the job in hand as he sucked down a mouthful.

"Do you need some more?" asked a squat fellow behind the counter, holding a ladle in the air.

Xavier shook his head and swallowed down a mouthful of piping hot dumpling then choked as from behind him the hand of his good friend Jericho Chong slapped him firmly on his back.

"What's going on noodle balls?" yelled Jericho, laughing out loud at seeing his friend choke upon his breakfast. Xavier coughed his last mouthful up, turning round to see a giggling Jericho, "I knew that would be you. You're an asshole!"

"I've been called worse but at least I know what I am," smiled Jericho grabbing the stool next to his buddy, sitting himself down and commandeering Xavier's drink.

"Are you heading to ArkLight?" asked Jericho.

"Yes, in a little while, I want to visit a work in progress on the way," said Xavier, "plus I need to swing by Kaiser's place later. See my pride and joy and pick up some paint and parts."

"Good, well I need to pick someone up!" replied Jericho, "I did a little deal."

"With who?"

"Oh, a friend," replied Jericho trying to avoid any more questions.

"Listen dude, I am not into taking friends along and you should know I am not into anyone knowing what I am up to. And you should be too."

"Relax, it's just a lady friend."

"Even worse!" shouted Xavier, spitting his noodles out, "Are you crazy?"

"Relax dude!'

Xavier fixed Jericho with a burning stare, shaking his head in disbelief, "Whenever we take someone with us accidents or incidents always happen."

"Oh you mean the time we had to hide from that security patrol for six hours and were hanging upside down under that carbon freighter?" Jericho sniggered, recalling a previous exploit out from the ArkLight Docks transit lanes.

"I am not laughing, Jericho. We are taking too many risks as it is, this shit will get us caught and our minds wiped."

"Our minds wiped if we're lucky," shrugged Jericho.

"Exactly! More likely we end up as a Boil in the Bag," Xavier seethed at his friend's bravado and folly, referring to the practice of some security groups who smashed the visors of people they caught causing their blood to boil in the space vacuum, "Sometimes, you behave like you have already had yours wiped!"

"Relax Xavier, you are with the master!" Jericho wheezed, sarcastically grabbing his throat mimicking his visor being smashed.

"Well, you do whatever you want to do, but I warn you it will come unstuck. There are too many drones and cams around at the moment. You get caught and we are as good as dead," Xavier returned to eating his noodles and shook his head.

Jericho proceeded to pick a dumpling from Xavier's bowl.

"You need to be vigilant, Jericho," Xavier scowled, "there are plenty of snoops mooching around Genesis, from the cops to the State Police, the ArkLight Transit Authority, the Air Authority, Corporate Revenue Enforcement, G-Loop Patrol, Earth Security I could go on."

Jericho rolled his eyes, "Not to mention the dreaded Shadows."

"Don't joke about that shit."

"Come on man, you're getting vexed."

"There are more jobs-worths, spy-cams and drones to make life difficult enough without..."

"More noodles?"

The conversation was interrupted by the Nish-Kin's cook offering another ladle.

"No, thanks," replied Xavier smiling before turning to Jericho, "you see what I mean? You don't know who's listening."

Jericho shrugged and quickly changed the subject, "The gantries are looking good, don't you think?"

They had recently left some pieces which had radiated out across the landings, making a big splash throughout the local neighbourhood. It had also been done at a price, as Xavier was sure they had been spotted by a drone and put his agitated state down to that.

Xavier nodded, annoyed that his breakfast was being ruined by Jericho.

"Morning my brethren!"

Xavier turned to see his foreman and mentor Old Man Ray standing behind him and Jericho, "Can I not just eat some food in peace," he coughed.

"I come in peace, dude," said Old Man Ray, his eyes darting all over the place. He gestured to the person sat next to Xavier to move along so he could take a seat.

"Do you know how important it is to have your own time and your own space?" asked Xavier as he raised his drink to his lips.

"Especially in a place like this!" said Old Man Ray not missing a beat, "Look at us! Millions of us crammed together in this vast conglomeration of colonies known as Genesis. All creeds and colours, breeds and nationalities working towards the Pax Humana."

Xavier shook his head and returned to his bowl of broth.

"I thought we'd see you down at ArkLight Ray, this isn't your usual hang?" said Jericho.

"Oh, I'm just strolling around spreading the word."

"You can get into trouble for that," replied Xavier, curtly.

"Well, you need to know more about your history boy!"

"History is banned, well Earth history that is," Jericho interrupted.

"Not if you get the right Edu-Imp it isn't," laughed Xavier.

"You see lads, the aspirations that have driven people to work have never really changed. Since man gathered together and hunted wild mammoths with flint spears to feed their mates and offspring, the desire to get a warmer, drier cave always led him to exert himself. The surroundings might be different now, but for time immemorial men and women have had to work, mostly doing things they don't want to do, for people they don't know and for reasons they didn't understand. It is no different now than it was in Roman times, medieval times, Georgian times or the early twenty-first century; the daily grind is still the same." Old Man Ray was a soap-box orator for anyone who cared to listen, a self confessed outsider and non-conformist in a conformist world. He wasn't everyone's cup of tea but Xavier had known him since he was young and enjoyed his eccentric nature possessing a knowledge and take on life that was rare in The Hives.

"You saying that Ray has reminded me we have work to do ourselves," Xavier took one last mouthful before getting up from his stool, grabbing his helmet and bag and thanking the chef for another fine dish.

"You're right Xavier, Vamos!" said Jericho.

"Come on dude, I will see you at the docks," said Xavier, placing an arm around Old Man Ray, "and be careful."

"You be careful Xavier! It is you who needs to watch your back."

Xavier stared at Ray then rolled his eyes, Ray was often prone to exaggeration, like when he said he'd been to Earth, Jericho always put it down to Ray being Ray.

Jericho and Ray turned and made their way towards the escalators and to one of the transit stations that were dotted all around The Hives ready to ferry the army of workers to ArkLight docks or the factories, mining works, refineries, chemical plants and hangars that combined with Genesis.

"You're an asshole by the way," Xavier shouted, grinning at his buddy.

Jericho smiled at him, nodding in agreement, "I know."

Old Man Ray looked back and waved at Xavier as he ran up some stairs then glanced back towards Nish-Kin's where he saw two cops speaking to the chef, "Watch your back son," he mumbled to himself.

★★★★★

4
High Rise & High Risk

The moon shone a brilliant white.
Orion's Belt flickered in the far distance and the constellations stretched out for billions of light years. Layer upon layer of tiny dots representing stars, galaxies and the incomprehensible depths of the universe.

A billboard reading 'Elrick & Lang - The Finest EVA Suits Known To Mankind' shone behind Xavier, who slipped in behind a service elevator for one of the ArkLight Local 79 Subsidiary Component Factories.

He then strode down Causeway 902318, one of thousands of spiral steel tracks weaving all over Genesis, connecting trans-habs and work units, acting as thoroughfares.

Xavier had read about and seen the work of an old Earth painter named M.C. Escher, who had sketched staircases and walkways that seemed to twist and coil in all directions but never really lead anywhere. It was as if Escher had been drawing Genesis all along. He looked carefully to his left and then to his right, making sure there were no spy-cams to witness his next movements.

"Space is the place," he said to himself, once again making sure he was not being observed. Then, pulling a canister from his belt, he shook it and sprayed resolutely the letters XVR. Taking another can from the other side of his belt, he made a deep red circle around the A, a symbol which had been banned for centuries, but now was appearing mysteriously all around Genesis. The symbol meant Anarchy, a word that had been erased out of the human language. It was a word that spoke volumes to Xavier and he wanted it to spark something in his fellow inhabitants in The Hives.

As he was spraying there was a dull metallic thud from above the causeway. He looked up but could see nothing. Another sound made him move to a portal window that looked down towards one of the Public Park and Observation Domes that were scattered around The Hives so people could feel like they were on Earth.

There was yet another thud. Finding an airlock covering and using a trick he had been shown, he pressed and twisted a latch and found himself in a small vestibule. Xavier checked his helmet and life support systems, then opened the other side of the airlock hatch and found himself in outer space. It really was that simple. He connected a life support leash from his belt to the outside and then descended a thirty meter slope from above the observation dome.

Xavier noticed water spewing from one of the countless pipes surrounding the Observation Hub, gushing into the cold vacuum of space and forming huge globules that floated away into the distance. This should have been checked. Misappropriation of such a precious commodity would not be tolerated by the authorities. The fact that water was being unnecessarily wasted would cause anger and outrage from the corporate chiefs of this sector.

Xavier gazed towards the millions of stars and galaxies that lay in front of him, each a world of their own. "We can't possibly be alone," he muttered, shaking his head, he wondered if other beings somewhere amongst those stars staring at his galaxy and thinking the exact same thing. A lone corporate freighter sailed passed him, its lights blinking, en-route and ferrying goods to a location on Genesis.

Xavier was alone.

He edged his way along a parapet and stared across to the other side. There was a sheer drop into infinity. Without the harness to secure you, a body would just drift off into eternity without a trace. Bracing himself, Xavier angled his body from the side of the colony and dropped a hundred meters down.

Before him was a landscape from Earth; buffaloes, elephants and giraffes roamed a plain, as birds soared down from multi-coloured skies and spiralled through technicolor mountains and clouds. Whales and fish leapt from sparkling blue oceans as jellyfish and octopi lurked below the waves. Scenes so rarified and exotic, in the confines of Genesis, could have only come from the mind of a maladjusted psychotic.

The sparkling silvery grey concrete surface that adorned nearly all the colonies of Genesis had now become a radiating, multicoloured expanse of reds, blues and greens. Xavier was proud of his artwork as he applied the Laz paint in the vacuum of space with style and composure, the laser and paint spreading across the slopes at a rapid fire rate glinting in the celestial light.

Xavier stopped abruptly. His mind was playing tricks, "What the…?"

In front of his very eyes, as if coming to life and drawing him into the panorama. He seemed to become enveloped by his production, and the animals started to move with vibrancy as if they were breathing in space, existing in the infinity and sentience of their surroundings. Within this milieu flowers appeared to move and Xavier felt a sensation, like wind upon his face, even though his visor was closed. "Am I on Zug juice?" he asked himself, as the intensity of the piece increased.

Xavier stretched out his arms and placed his hands upon the landscape that he had just painted. His body jolted as he felt himself trembling. Turning his gaze away, he caught sight of the billboard signs flickering and instantaneously the graffiti piece began replacing the commercials.

It was only the alarm of his oxygen supply beeping that snapped Xavier away from this extraordinary phenomenon. The telltale warning that he was down to his last twenty per cent of air registered in his brain and he gazed back at the piece, the billboards had reverted to how they had always been. He pulled himself up across his painting, walking up toward the safety of the causeway, which had now rotated countless times like every wheel and torus within Genesis to create an artificial gravity.

There was a jerk that sent Xavier flying forward spinning around, his arms flailing as he desperately tried to get a grip on the surface of the colony wall or any of the rails leading towards the airlock. The causeway was now above him as he dropped down and floated out into space. He pulled frantically on his safety line as it slid through his gloves, before yanking himself to a stop. He took a deep breath, now fully aware that he was using his remaining oxygen at a rapid rate.

For a few moments he seemed to hang motionless on his safety tether, incapable of movement. He then began to float back upward to the causeway. The whole colony turned again, the continual rotation of the colonies to create artificial gravity allowed him to grab a protruding handle that snapped him onto the side of the revolving tower and one of the service ledges that lined themselves in each direction. Xavier had barely enough strength to pull himself into a small sheltered opening.

"Blood!" It was then that he noticed what looked like a scarlet patch of blood forming on his chest. "This can't be good," he thought, not without alarm Xavier checked the life support unit on his wrist. He wasn't sure why but even in this moment, he could find it amusing that the unit reported he was alive and well.

"Machines don't lie, I guess," Xavier smirked to himself.

Another thud and then another. Blood, clearly not his own was smeared all over the causeway. He held himself close to the opening and tentatively pushed his head up to take a closer look as to where the noise and blood was coming from. A row of eight men stood opposite the leaking water pipe surrounded by what was clearly a group of Air Authority operatives in their blue uniforms and a bunch of local precinct cops.

A gang boss was rebuking his workers. Xavier could not hear what was being said and feared he would be seen if he raised himself any further from his bolt hole. He could sense that whatever was going on was not good.

His instinct proved right without any kind of warning. The workers were swiftly turned around without any indication of what was to come and were executed.

Nothing as simple as cold blood anymore they were boiled. '*Boil in the Bag*' just like he and Jericho had been talking about earlier. Each man had his visor smashed in and their oxygen supply ripped off. Xavier watched from his hiding place as the men clawed at the ground desperate for oxygen as their blood boiled in the vacuum. Their perished bodies hurtled into space. Some of the workers were still attached by safety lines and began to strike the causeway, creating loud thuds upon impact, before being cut away and sent spinning off into eternity.

It didn't matter how it was done.

It was plain murder.

Xavier cried into his helmet hiding his gaze from the horrific sight, hoping that he had not been seen by the Air Authority assassins. He had heard rumours of this type of atrocity but had never believed it, let alone witnessed it. He scrambled through the opening and into the airlock as the alarm for his oxygen buzzed at ten percent and continued to drop.

He closed the airlock door and sealed himself away as the hisses and gas exchanges balanced out.

There was a bleeping sound as the oxygen meter ticked away warning him that he needed to hurry. He could not speak, that would only waste precious air. In less than a minute he would be dead, as dead as those poor souls outside and he did not want that type of death.

A buzzer denoting the end of his oxygen supply went and Xavier knew it was all over. Just then the door to the airlock slid open and he tumbled into the chamber. He looked at the oxygen dial and hands shaking released his visor. It flew up in an instant, allowing Xavier to breath the recycled, and slightly fetid air of the Hives.

For a change, it smelt good.

★★★★★

5

The Initiation of Magnus Bowser

"What is your name?"

"M-M-M-M-Magnus Bowser," came the trembling reply.

It sounded unsure in itself, questioning if that really was his name.

Magnus Bowser had lived, it was safe to say, a very non-assuming life as resident of Trans-hab Unit 67 37 4904. It was true to say that The Clancy Spur was actually a more salubrious part of The Hives with its view of Earth and easy access to The Gloop, its mall and viewing bays. It was close to a number of recreation areas and residents there tended to work in the clerical and administrative sectors of American Asteroid Mining, one of the oldest asteroid mining corporations within Genesis. His life so far had been spent, like most residents of Genesis dreaming of visiting other planets in the known galaxies and then to one day settle on one of the newly colonised Earth like planets that had been discovered. To date though, the majority of his time on

Genesis had been spent analysing data retrieved from miners on a number of asteroids. He spent his days dissecting the gearing shift percentages needed to increase productivity on Outer Rim rock outcrops rather than local orbiting masses. These menial chores had left Magnus in search of more excitement in his dreary life. He had never really wanted to work in that particular field, but had been channelled towards the position after he had responded well to early Edu-Imp inserts on Advanced Asteroid and Molecular Geology when he was eight years old.

"Magnus Bowser of The Clancy Spur, I have an Earth-side view from my trans-hab and quite a ..." he stopped in mid sentence staring ahead at what stood before him.

Lucien Ferrer was attired in a tattered antique space suit, with its helmet visor closed. He leant forward towards Magnus Bowser and extended one of his leathery elongated and gloved hands towards him.

Magnus extended his, as if to shake it, but his was left in mid air as Ferrer's gnarled hand passed his and stroked the side of Magnus's cheek, causing him to stir uncomfortably and smile a stupid grin, that lasted all of a second.

"Magnus Bowser," retorted Ferrer, "what is it that brings you here today?"

"I wish to be a Shadow," muttered Magnus, cocking his neck to one side in an unconscious twitch.

"You wish to be a Shadow, do you," smiled Ferrer, "well, well, well, how amusing!"

Magnus nodded self consciously again, the fear he was trying to control quite obvious to anyone looking at his involuntary movements.

"That is an affirmative," replied Magnus, in an almost authoritative way.

Lucien Ferrer stared at him, his eyes looking deep into those of Magnus, "Why would you want to be a Shadow?"

"I want to live forever, do something more exciting with my life and…"

"Do you believe you are the right type of person to become a Shadow? Do you believe that you have as they say, what it takes?" Lucien questioned him smiling.

"Yes, sir I do believe that!" came the reply.

"You are an amusing little man," sneered Ferrer, as Magnus became more agitated, "tell me what you know about the Shadows."

Magnus coughed, clearing his throat before proceeding, "Well, the Shadows are said to be the remnants of the death squads used to exterminate any stragglers left on Earth during the Exodus. After carrying out their grim task on Earth they were stranded on Earth and became victim to an alien virus which was used to terminate any existing human DNA on Earth but leave all other living organisms unharmed, but due to an anomaly in the virus instead of killing the death squads it changed their molecular structure and left them in a state of suspended animation."

"Well done, Magnus Bowser you have done your homework."

"It is also presumed that Shadows are tied to Earth and unable to escape or leave there," Magnus paused for a second, "but I am not too sure if that is the case."

"Really and is there anything else you can enlighten me with."

"Well, sir," Magnus again paused, wondering if he should continue, "I believe you are over three hundred years of age!"

"I am older," replied Lucien Ferrer.

"Older?"

"Yes, Magnus, you could say that I created the Shadows."

Magnus blinked nervously, then attempted to speak before Lucien took hold of his chin and looked at him.

"Some of my best friends are Shadows...do you know Halucifer?"

Magnus shook his head.

"Halucifer is another incarnation of myself, the one that may help you become what you long to be."

Magnus was confused and did not know whether to shake his head or nod in agreement.

"So Magnus Bowser, have you prepared yourself for the process of becoming a Shadow?"

"I have sir, your holiness, your honourable self sir," mumbled Magnus.

"Magnus Bowser, can I ask you a polite question?" enquired Ferrer.

"By all means," came the reply.

"How on Earth did you find me?"

"I am not entirely sure," replied a confused Magnus, who seemed to relax at being asked such a question, "I really don't recall how I arrived here in such auspicious company. I mean it's not like you advertise."

"A comedian as well," Ferrer chuckled.

"I mean I had a dream that I was a Shadow and then I found myself here with you."

There was silence.

"This is not a dream still is it?" asked Magnus.

"I can assure you Magnus Bowser that you are not dreaming," Ferrer's voice now seemed to emanate from everywhere and the tone had significantly altered.

From the corner of his eye, Magnus Bowser detected some movement in what he assumed were long, dark drapes. He wondered if he had been the victim of a prank.

"Are you afraid Magnus Bowser?"

"No"

"Well, then you should be," Ferrer retorted, "you should be very afraid."

Ferrer then seemed to evaporate in front of him, startling Magnus.

What had been moments before a real person, visible to touch, now had become a kind of dust that hung in the air before that too disappeared.

The shifting drapes snaked along the floor.

Magnus could now hear nothing except for the sound of his heart beating rapidly inside his chest. Beads of sweat broke out on his forehead and he started to feel incredibly hot. He closed his eyes, hoping that by the time he opened them he would have actually been dreaming and wake in his bed with his head in a pillow. He pushed himself further into the chair he was seated on. A loud sound of wind rushing past his face alerted him to the very real feeling that someone or some…thing was close to him. He kept his eyes shut and gripped the arms of the chair. He had a burning sensation in his stomach, and he longed to move or better still, run. His eyes flew open, unable to bear not knowing what was going on. He lurched forward off his chair, as it crashed over on its side.

Lucien Ferrer was now no longer in the room, but there before him was a swirl of vapour and dust with red piercing eyes and the decrepit and decaying stench of death. Like fine threads of particles held together by a static energy they seemed to form the frame of something but what it was he could not make out. It was plainly not human, its shape altering and hovering before Magnus forming a wraith like apparition whose features were at first vague before gradually becoming more defined.

Magnus smiled. He felt a force pinning him to the floor.

"Magnus Bowser, I am Halucifer. Welcome to your death!"

Halucifer's hand reached out, his fingers extending like gnarled branches towards Magnus's eyes, piercing his face and gripping his brain. Halucifer squeezed and Magnus could feel his mouth open and tongue and oesophagus pull up. He felt as if he was retching, but nothing came out.

The fingers did not puncture the skin, it was as though they passed through it, leaving no wound just a spectral shadow around Magnus's face. The veins on his temples raised and began to burst, his eyes lolled back, sweat and tears on his face merging into a film on his face. He was lifted from the floor as an unseen force carried him into the air.

He could not make a sound, his body arched and contorted.

Halucifer, a phantasmic spectre hovered above him while Magnus's body writhed, dancing a dance of death.

The light and ambience of the chamber changed. Powerful shafts of silvery light engulfed them, Halucifer himself seemed to glow as energies sprinted from every recess of the room. Magnus could speak no more.

His memories flooded into his conscious mind, in this dark place, the memories of mundane events now appeared joyful, simple moments of a humdrum life were now celebrations of life itself. Eating lunch in the canteen with friends and colleagues, watching the Arks leave for their voyages to distant stars, the fanfares and parades that took place whenever an Ark was completed, even laying in his bed staring at the walls for hours had an appeal.

Magnus felt a little whimper come out of his mouth. His face was now contorted as it had become fear itself.

He was more frightened than he could ever have imagined.

He knew now with chilling certainty that the step he had taken was irrevocably set.

Darkness came over Magnus Bowser.

As he choked he felt the last life forces being sucked out of him like a sink emptying out into a plug hole.

And just like that Magnus Bowser was gone.

His body fell limply back onto the floor. Halucifer hovered around the corpse and like a black cloud enveloped the body as if inhaling the life force of Magnus. Halucifer inhaled more violently like a rabid animal as if ingesting the inner being and taking it to a place of no return.

He had swallowed his soul.

The once warm flesh of Magnus now turned cold and all life that had minutes before radiated from it, disappeared instantly leaving not the slightest hint that it had ever existed

The swirling wraiths converged behind Halucifer and encircling the body of Magnus, their eerie forms took shape and formed into Shadows, dreadful physical bodies that now took mortal form.

A low drone emanated from the Shadows, as the spirit of Magnus Bowser floated above his lifeless corpse, the sinister drone seemed to consume the spirit as it danced through them.

Halucifer stared at the lifeless corpse, leaning in close to the mortified features of Magnus.

In one fluid motion the Shadow of Magnus Bowser re-entered the corpse of Magnus turning the body into a raging mass of torment.

The Shadow was a ghost, the ghost a Shadow.

The remains of Magnus Bowser were removed from the chamber and there in its place stood Magnus Bowser. It had the shape of a human being, but was now just a vessel containing the dark spirit, every drop of virtue, kindness and integrity removed by Halucifer.

The skin was translucent like misted glass, and within it the swirl of dark forces and howling demons perceptible to the eye. The face was blank, like a marble sculpture frozen in a specific gaze. His body was bolt upright.

"I have a job for you," sneered Lucien Ferrer.

The creature that once was Magnus Bowser stared back at him, his lips slightly turning upwards in what could only be considered a smile. Boredom was no longer going to be an issue for Citizen Bowser.

★★★★★

6
Arks & Docks

ArkLight, the battalion headquarters of Nu Humana and home to the newest, and largest, interstellar fleet of spacecraft in Genesis: the Arks.

A row of lights extended before Xavier, positioned in multi-coloured rows alternating in red, green and yellow, magnetically pulling approaching vehicles into the docks of ArkLight. They seemed to go on for hundreds of miles like a technicolour carpet stretching into the blue-blackness of space. Although the framework of these behemoths had just been completed it would take probably another five years to have the Ark completely fitted and ready for launch into the farthest flung corners of the galaxy.

They looked like the carcass of an enormous dead animal, its bones picked clean by a myriad of creatures. Construction began with the skeleton which would be built and attached to the interior of the craft, before being covered in a steel skin for its onward journey. There seemed to be a continual supply of raw materials and a compliant workforce that revelled in the construction of such a fine and magnificent vessel. The fact was that when completed, there was a possibility that it would take the people who had helped construct it to begin a new life on a colony somewhere new.

This was all the encouragement a worker needed.

Signs and holographic notice boards hung in space, relaying and replaying propaganda and safety messages to the new arrivals at the docks. Buoys hovered at different points marking strategic spots for the traffic to turn, ascend and descend. Rows of site overseers and traffic cops lined the access route, corralling the workers into various parts of the giant craft. Automated Services and The Robot Corps vessels would dispatch and service robots that were required to do the mechanical and heavy duty work on the Arks.

Some of the larger robots were emblazoned with The Robotic Corps and Big Bad Technotrons logos, a nickname for the huge bulbous robots that welded and fused the keels of the gigantic craft together. Alongside these were riveter droids, as well as composite and structure robots that all held positions of responsibility in the assembly of these fine spacecrafts. Human and robot worked hand in hand. Thousands of workers were ferried on vast floating platforms from Genesis and disgorged into the bellies of the Arks.

A holographic sign read DF 118.

DF 118 was a gigantic dock constructed to house the Arks where Xavier often found himself. Whenever he looked at the Arks he wondered at the scale of these craft, their enormity was awe inspiring. These Arks, enormous in size and reminiscent of Leviathan were known as Generation Ships. Families would enter these vessels knowing that they would take the journey of a lifetime, never to return. It could take fifteen or more generations before they would find a possible planet or moon to inhabit and colonise.

"Good dawning citizen!"

A metallic voice greeted all that entered the Yards of Nu Humana docks in ArkLight. The sight of huge guns placed either side of the entrance and the heavily armed guards patrolling their observation towers and hanging from their armoured spacecraft or barricades was meant to intimidate all who entered. Security measures were there to make sure no terrorist attack ever took place, no industrial espionage occurred and no workers rioted. They never did. The formidable fortifications and daunting ensemble of military personnel clad in company regalia had been created to instil fear within the employees of Nu Humana. This had been ordained by The Powers.

Xavier joined a line of people approaching the intimidating entrance before them.

"Xavier Miro - 6-28-581."

A light drew across Xavier's face, scanning and recognising his features. "Proceed, Xavier Miro," came the female voice.

"Greetings, Citizen Miro," a smartly dressed trans-human supervisor said as Xavier turned a corner.

"Greetings, Citizen Cavell! How are you?"

"Wonderful, Xavier! We have a backlog to complete if you recall."

People greeted each other with salutations as they made their way to work like the commuters of Earth had done centuries before.

As Xavier stood in line he became deluged with holograms conveying the latest news and developments at ArkLight and the new Generation Ship.

Citizen Cavell guided Xavier towards a section where he would be transferred to the Edu-Imps sector of ArkLight. Xavier entered a cavernous sphere that glowed and seemed to possess no floor upon which to stand. Lights and liquid appeared around him, as a hologram of an attractive young woman was imparting information regarding the system Xavier was working on.

"Thank you for joining us, Citizen Miro. Please proceed ahead for Edu-Imp 11/17/Hypervelocity Conditioning Install-ation Program 56477- 609-HU."

"My favourite - another piece of data that every budding spacer requires," Xavier sighed, sarcastically. The truth was, he loved all the information he could get.

"Proceed," replied the hologram, oblivious to Xavier's tone.

"You look hot," cooed Xavier to the hologram, as his conveyor motioned him into the assembly hall. The hologram smiled politely as if conscious of the compliment.

As he swung round he saw the hottest sight in the whole of ArkLight...Zola Capello. She stood, hands on hips in a light green piped suit with white pads on her knees, shoulders and elbows. Her gloves seemed to accentuate the length of her fingers. She had long brown hair that shimmered crimson as it swished around in the light, her beautiful blue eyes piercing the hallway and engulfing Xavier in a haze. Her high cheek bones and natural beauty made her a real head turner within the docks and there was always an amorous young male trying to grab her attention. Zola worked in the Administration Section of ArkLight Docks and Xavier was smitten.

"Hey, Zola?" he called out to his significant other half.

"Xavier, you made it on time?" Zola replied, smiling, "You always just make it on time. Let me guess…breakfast at Nish-Kin's?"

"Yes, breakfast at Nish-Kin's as per usual, then a little confab with Jericho and Old Man Ray," Xavier motioned towards the line of people and the time it was taking to process everyone entering the yard, "what's going on here?"

"The security seems agitated for some reason," said Zola, as she looked down the line towards the entrance.

"Coming up to the launch of the Ark I suppose, they always get tetchy before a launch."

"You are right Xavier," replied Zola.

"Do you think Civilization are responsible for these bombings?" asked Xavier.

"I doubt it," replied Zola, "it's probably more to do with some Lunar separatist movement. I think Civilization are trying to do something positive that brings peoples' attention to the injustices going on here in Genesis." Xavier looked around at the line gesturing for Zola to keep her voice down as an overseer walked towards them, "Or it could have something to do with that announcement they are going to make regarding a special lottery," Zola continued.

"Lottery?" he asked.

"Yes, silly, the lottery, on all the billboards and TV?"

Xavier had met Zola way back at the academies. He didn't think her hair had changed in all that time and her eyes had always been mesmerising. They made a formidable team as kids, both as tough and as forthright as each other. It was Zola who was possibly the tougher of the two, Xavier thought. She was not one to suffer fools and was quite ruthless in her approach to life. She had been born into Genesis society with her mother and father both prominent members of Nu Humana who believed and followed the doctrines of Pax Humana to the letter.

Even so, Zola did not expect special treatment and she and her siblings had been brought up to respect every citizen no matter what their rank. Zola knew she had the looks and the intelligence to get where she wanted.

"So this lottery," enquired Xavier, "what's the big deal then? I mean, they always have them for Mars or a Generation Ship or win yourself a piece of prime Martian real estate - why are they pushing this one so much?"

"Rumour has it, the prize is a trip to Earth!"

"You're talking shit!" Xavier's eyes flew wide open, "Only the Powers are allowed to live on Earth, how come they're letting people visit Earth? The ban has been, what, three hundred years now?"

"I said it was a rumour. I don't know for sure, it's just what some people have been saying," replied Zola, "anyway I thought Earth was still all messed up?"

"Do you really think the Powers would live there if that was the case?" joked Xavier, "Like Drax Kraldon and his cronies are going to live in a radioactive sludge pool!"

"Your head is up your ass!" retorted Zola, "Just because you are always off painting the sides of ships and wheels with weird creatures."

"So we live in this steel and concrete asylum and they get to go to Earth because it is shitty! I don't get it!" said Xavier, shrugging his shoulders, "I mean, have you seen how beautiful and blue it looks?"

"Enough!" Zola snapped her fingers sarcastically, "I see it too but what are you going to do, right?"

Xavier had spent so much time throwing up pieces of artwork onto the sides of corporation vessels recently that he had no time for gossip, game shows or lotteries. He didn't like them anyway. It was always some gloomy contestant from some part of The Hives trying to win a place for their sick offspring on an Ark to Celestia or some other colony. He did like the shows where the contestants were so desperate to escape from being terminated by the Air Authority they would do anything to get more oxygen and save themselves. Those shows were a riot. Shows like '*Suck On This*' or '*The Seven O'Clock Knock*' however were uncomfortable viewing. Convicted contestants on '*Suck On This*' would get a call from Dr. Ignatius Perigord, the head of The Air Authority then fight over an air tank as a clock ticked down with a choice between oxygen or money. *'The Seven O'Clock Knock'* was just straight forward state execution packaged as prime time entertainment. Then he recalled what he had witnessed earlier and shuddered.

"I saw that piece you did on one of the outer rigs, it was beautiful, Xavier! I loved the flowers and trees that you did all down the underside and exhaust vents. They were sweet."

"Thanks Zola, just trying to spread my message in the best way I know how."

Xavier was proud of his art. It was something that had been in him for many years, a natural ability to draw and express himself through art. In his personal time he had taken a great interest in Earth paintings from the twentieth and twenty-first centuries, so he would purchase some illegal implants that told the history of early human street art and graffiti.

Xavier possessed a rarity of extraordinary value, an original Earth antiquity, a very fragile and battered picture book. Old Man Ray had, many moons ago, presented Xavier with this book that he claimed to have found when he was on Earth. Xavier believed Ray had concocted the story to make him seem somewhat mysterious. There was no doubting Ray was a little odd, but his gift to Xavier had been life-changing. Xavier had decided from that moment on to spread the message to the natives of The Hives. It was a secret, one only he and Ray knew about.

He kept it hidden away and out of view in his trans-hab. The book was entitled *'Subway Art'*. This ancient manuscript described 'graffiti' artists in a fabled and heavily populated city called New York. The book was so fragile now that Xavier could only look at it occasionally fearing it might disintegrate.

It told the story of how people the same age as Xavier, painted the sides of transit trains to express the vibrancy of this once great city. In particular it was a quote from a graffiti artist called Shy 147, who all those centuries ago stirred Xavier's passions and inspired him. It read:

'You just don't know how badly I want to reach my hands on a can of spray and touch my big train set in my yard and feel the voltage running through them trains while I paint my ghetto name on that iron screen for the people of the state of NYC to see and wonder on the art of the ghettoes and backstreets of our times'

The quote made Xavier feel so strong when he looked at his own neighbourhood; he decided that he, Xavier Miro, would make his own declarations to the corporations and to the people of The Hives.

Nothing had changed, there were still trains with brain-washed people on them blasting around from one place to another. Xavier knew he wanted the people of his time to witness his art. Xavier felt a connection as an artist with the kid who lived nearly six hundred years before him. He began to leave his mark everywhere. Some of his pieces came out as abstract works made to send signals to the minds of residents of the Hives in the sterile and clinical world they inhabited.

The corporations soon had teams of droids out cleaning them. Xavier kept going.

An ancient Greek word long forgotten kept surfacing in The Hives:

DEMOCRACY

Xavier had once found an Edu-Imp that had told the story of primitive man and how they communicated through cave art, explaining their lives in the most simple and rudimentary ways that sent a meaning to observers thousands of years later. Early cave painters were not only painting to leave a message, they were painting for themselves. It was something instinctual, an inbuilt feeling of expression.

Xavier felt that inner voice strongly and could not suppress it. His emotions could not be contained in a suit or a trans-hab, or in The Hives or Genesis. He was bigger than that; he was bigger than any corporation or power. He knew that he was not just here to just be a rigger at ArkLight and then disappear to some asteroid way off in the hinterland of another system, wearing a mask and breathing his own recycled breath and drinking his own piss.

Was that really the climax that awaited him, Zola and the rest of humanity?

The line towards the Edu-Imp Unit was decreasing quickly now, with only fifteen people before Zola and Xavier.

"So what you got today?" asked Zola.

"Some sort of aggregated hypervelocity installation program. You?"

"I've got some Biometrical Analysis Reports to complete, on life support systems in newly terra-formed mammals," replied Zola nonchalantly.

Xavier opened his jacket and furtively pulled out the old photograph he had taken from his closet in his trans-hab, "Take a look at this."

"What is it?" Zola whispered, as her eyes widened.

"It's going to be my next piece!"

"Who is he? What is that thing he's carrying?"

"His name is Duke, he was a surfer on Earth centuries ago. He used that thing to ride on top of the waves on the oceans there."

"Can you imagine that!" replied Zola, peeking up to make sure they were not being watched.

"I'm going to try," said Xavier, excitedly.

"What are you doing after you finish your shift?"

"Go paint I suppose or play Zaddonk...why?" Xavier winked, cheekily, "What you got planned?"

"Something you might find interesting," Zola winked back suggestively.

"Deal, let me know when you get done...call me right!"

"Move along," a voice bellowed from a corporate overseer behind, forcing Xavier to place the photograph quickly back into his jacket pocket.

"Be careful Xavi," Zola kissed him gently on his cheek.

"Second person to say that this morning," shrugged Xavier.

"I mean it. You can get into a lot of trouble with something like that," Zola smiled again at him as she entered the infusion unit where a headset framed her pretty face and an instantaneous flame seemed to encapsulate her for a couple of seconds. In that briefest of time, Zola Capello's brain was installed with all it required to complete her Life Systems Part 6785(2)17d-44 Biometric Reports Analysis and cleared her brain for entry into the Yards and Docks of ArkLight.

Xavier followed suit and was instantly familiar with Hypervelocity Installation.

"See you later, Zola," Xavier said, pulling down the visor to his helmet and wishing he could spend more time with her, the sweetest of spacers.

"You too, Xavi," Zola winked as her visor closed. Gently butting helmets together as a gesture of goodwill, they went on their separate ways.

As Xavier walked down towards the dock entrance he was blissfully unaware his movements were being tracked.

★★★★★

7

The Flying Carpets

S tepping from the Edu-Imp Unit and then into the Yards of Ark Light, the pair stepped into a new world.

Xavier entered a space of connected hexagonal plates that measured three meters across. As he placed his feet upon them, the plates seemed to register, come to life and secure him to the base. Gracefully, and with little effort, they separated from one another and began to lift away, rising and moving in different directions. They were nicknamed Flying Carpets, an allusion to the Arabian folk tales from old Earth.

These were work stations that transferred the user to his or her work place, their allotted spot on the vast Ark structure. As Xavier rose up he looked around at the enormity of the dock as it revealed itself. Like a large canyon, the dock seemed to dwarf the Ark that lay inside. Lines of Flying Carpets harried around the Generation Ship, each carrying an individual responding to the tasks they were given. Robots and mechanised welders crawled over the gigantic vessel's hull, seeking pre-determined areas that required their accurate attention. It was a symphony of construction, a rumbling ballet of mass industrialisation.

The Arks, as standard, were in excess of six hundred metres in width, a kilometre high and ten kilometres in length. They held up to a hundred thousand people, excluding those in suspended animation and frozen embryos that would be rekindled upon arrival at their destination. Animals and fauna were also taken, so the new arrivals had plenty of livestock to assimilate into their newly discovered surroundings. Seed banks and flora stocks, as well as bio forests and hydro gardens, were also assembled. The chasm was filled with all manner of workers, and trails of sparks seemed to spill from every available orifice of the enormous craft.

People moved with a combined purpose and unison, in a symbiotic and rhythmic dance alongside its gargantuan stature. As a parade of Flying Carpets hovered around an entry point, Xavier began to set out his measuring instruments and utensils for the hypervelocity analysis. A sonic bubble enclosed Xavier from the harshness of space making it much easier for the young spacer to work and move around.

He began to speak to himself in an unintelligible freeform speech pattern. This was the Edu-Imp beginning to take effect and trawl through the data, allowing segments to implant into Xavier's conscious mind and perform his designated mission at a given time. Although Xavier was aware of his surroundings, he completed this role as if under the influence of another being.

He was, in effect, brainwashed. The ability to solve virtually any problem lay within his mental grasp. The fact was he was under the influence of mechanical and artificial Artellect minds that churned out information, feasibilities and probabilities. 3-D images emerged from every side of the Flying Carpet showing him the internal workings of his task; Xavier approached them with relish, eager to begin installing the intricate mechanisms of the system.

Mind uploads had been popular for centuries, so with the introduction of mind scanning and the ability to tap directly into the brain and connect with all the synapses, neurones and electrical particles swimming around that incredible organ, people got hooked. That a user could not only accept and receive the information, but also be a part of the information, made things take a new turn. At first, mind uploads just imparted information from one user to the other, which allowed significant advances to be made in the teaching of people and brought new meaning to the term brainwashing.

Scientists had long understood the brain was a biological structure which acted in a binary way like a computer, and with the advances in technology one soon had the ability to read and understand how and why the brain operated in the way it did. It was also understood information received by the brain was stored forever, locked away in the unconscious somewhere, consigned to regions of cerebral matter, where it could repose for a lifetime and be totally inactive. Yet it could also be reactivated at any given point, and this is what made mind uploading and Edu-Imps so important. This was the

Golden Fleece. DML's or direct memory lifts were the Holy Grail of Edu-Imps. A DML Edu-Imp could make you feel like you were travelling back in time or journeying into the future. It was like being absorbed into the most realistic computer game you could imagine, an out of body experience second to none. If a scientist could control how this was switched on and off and how this indoctrination could be used upon a workforce then maybe they had the answer to all the issues which had dogged previous generations. A person could have any kind of personality, perhaps unsuited to work, but when the corporation wanted them to work they could then be switched on like a machine and sent to work to earn their keep.

Edu-Imps were created by Artellects; incredibly powerful computers that were capable of assimilating information more quickly than the human brain. Because of this, they had to be controlled. There had been a number of instances throughout history where the computers had overtaken their masters' authority and this had resulted in cataclysmic situations for the humans on Earth and elsewhere. From that point on, man had to be very careful what role the Artellects had to play. Man was smart, that was why he had been so successful. Yet by creating a machine more intelligent than him, he threatened his very own survival.

As it was, man still had the edge.

A machine was unable to carry out the procedures it had calculated but a human with an Artellect mind could carry out tasks that would have been unthinkable centuries before. They created the Edu-Imps, which used parts of a human's unconscious mind that were seldom used and, with a small discharge of information sent to the brain, man could do any of the activities that the Artellects had previously been better suited to. Frequently when a task was completed the expertise and capability vacated the recipient but for people like Xavier, that information and knowledge never left him. For this reason Xavier had become a fan of bootleg Imps.

These were illegally burned off of Artellects, making it possible to strip down the thrusters to a Rod in five minutes, or assemble an off-world hydrogen recall storage unit or even learn ancient Earth languages like German or Arabic. Some of Xavier's favourites were the Edu-Imps that taught him how to do zero gravity capoeira, paint like old Earth master artists like Rembrandt, Canaletto, or the Japanese artist Hokusai, all whilst rapping in Jamaican patois.

It was quite common for many youngsters to overload on Edu-Imps or even get corrupted ones that caused the user to have a burn-out or mind-wipe. This happened a great deal in The Hives with kids trying to better themselves using cheap Edu-Imps that sent the user swirling around uncontrollably before literally fusing out. Thousands of cheap corrupted Edu-Imps flooded The Hives imported from The Great Wheel of China. There were supposedly built in fail safes, so as to protect the most vulnerable user. Yet sometimes everything comes at a price, and of course the authorities did not want intrusive interlopers experiencing or seeing archival history from ancient Earth. Warnings and exposure to some of these

Edu-Imps sent some people into madness. It was thought you should be able to jolt yourself back into reality, just like a bad trip. Unfortunately this was not always the case, as your neurones became deluged with information and the authenticity of your experience became all too real. Soon your amygdala, the part of your brain controlling fear, would overload and you would basically frighten yourself to death.

Not a pleasant way to go at all.

Like a wall of stars, the Flying Carpets and their operators lit up the whole of the Ark, engaging themselves with the maintenance and construction of this Leviathan; a marriage of technology, human ingenuity and endeavour operating at breakneck speeds. The swift platforms scurried from one place to another, dodging one another as a seemingly endless supply from all across the solar system of raw materials continually fed the workforce.

Mass drivers from the Moon and Mars continually fired cargoes into space to be retrieved and hauled to the docks at ArkLight. Tankers carrying shipments from gas planets, freighters hauling ore from asteroids and moons in deep space; the constant trade and deliveries were continual and endless.

Xavier surveyed the impressive sight enveloping him, detaching himself from the thoughts he harboured about the corporation's motives for reaching distant galaxies. At ArkLight and within these docks he felt proud to be a human, to be a part of history and the great expansion of the human race to colonise the universe. He hoped one day he too would be able to make the leap into a new life in a new world.

One day that dream would be realised but right now, all that mattered was the building of the Ark.

★★★★★

8
Old Man Ray

Xavier was wriggling his nose.

"You have to control your urges, when you are wearing a space helmet," was the sugary sweet and slightly condescending voice on the commercial, "...something as insignificant as an itchy nose can be overwhelming in a claustrophobic helmet with the visor just centimetres from your face. Add to that an inability to scratch your itches and it becomes clear that mind control has to be the priority."

These were the problems that faced everyone who lived on Genesis. Xavier was now at the end of his shift, his nose itching and the briskness with which he had started his stint, when he first inserted the Edu-Imp, beginning to subside. The sounds in his helmet were now of commercials being played throughout ArkLight interspersed by yet another bulletin from Claudia Furukawa.

"Yet again, lottery fever grabs Genesis with millions rushing out and getting tickets for the chance to be on the next Nu Humana Ark, The Herschel VI, heading towards

Betelgeuse in the Orion constellation. A winning syndicate from The Star of David colonies was celebrating their good fortune that they would be taking their places and heading for a new life amongst the stars. Meanwhile, thousands have been joining in the party as they matched the numbers making them eligible for a place on the Tamarinsk IV expected to leave immediately. These last minute winners whooped with joy as they made their way to Terminal 19 for ferries that would take them to the immediately departing Ark. Simultaneously, people are bracing themselves for the Mega Super-Dooper Lotto that will see the winner get a chance to visit Earth. So Genesis, let's keep calm, keep working and most of all keep smiling! - Here's sports…"

Xavier was tingling; his concentration levels were now beginning to wane.

Edu-Imps had cut off points and Xavier felt that his mind was beginning to wander. The timing was perfect. Xavier turned to see a Flying Carpet hurtling towards him like a stray missile. He knew who was riding on it without even having to examine the disc any closer.

It was Old Man Ray.

There was something about Old Man Ray that Xavier just loved; his tatty, battered helmet and rough-shod boots, his life support suit that would have been condemned by others years ago yet was just fine for Ray. Adorned with his eccentric doodles that covered the entirety of his suit and ragged patches that looked like an old rug, Ray was a one-off, and so too was his good nature.

"What's up, dawg!" proclaimed Ray as he pulled alongside Xavier.

He was forever coming up with old Earth greetings that always made Xavier laugh.

"You dog!" he replied.

The thought of greeting someone using the name of an extinct Earth animal baffled Xavier but he joined in just the same.

"So they reckon this Ark will be completed very soon Xavier, and they are going to send her off to the Proxima Centauri galaxy filled with all those plucky, lucky souls who want to live in a utopian paradise," chortled Ray.

"You never have anything good to say about the Arks and mankind's venture to other planets," said Xavier.

"Because there is only one true paradise, Xavier and man was cast out of it. Sent from paradise and banished to the harsh cold element of space," Ray's white beard sparkled in the light of Xavier's workplace.

"A new beginning in Proxima Centauri is better than spending your life here!"

"How do you know it's a better life…you been there?" Ray barked, his eyes rolling wildly. "Have you been to paradise? Huh! Have you? … I have, I've seen paradise, felt it and smelt it, boy!"

"I would sooner take my chance on an Ark and see what happened than waste my life in this scrap yard," sighed Xavier.

"Life on an Ark!" exclaimed Ray, "You think a life caged in a floating sarcophagus is a life worth living? I can't believe it; I can't believe you're buying the lies, Xavier. Do you know man has messed up so many times but still keeps doing it?"

"Here we go again," replied Xavier.

"Don't you know anything, boy? We were banished. We came from paradise, we originate from paradise, we are descended from heaven and then we were cast out of paradise, banished from the Garden of Eden, because we sinned!"

"I haven't done anything wrong," Xavier blared, "blame it on those that went before you!"

"Damn!" Old Man Ray cursed, "Blame, yes blame…that's what they used to do back on Earth. Blame everyone else and never take responsibility; never accept that they had to answer to somebody and then what happens…you're gone!"

Xavier rolled his eyes.

"Xavier, this is important, something's going on, times are changing and you must be aware of it," said Ray.

"Don't you see, Xavier, they are conning us. That's right! Conning us! They are saying that we have to leave and go and find somewhere else to live, yet all the time they are living in heaven. They're living the dream, they are the dream. The Powers are the Lords of the Universe, they are the gods. Don't you understand…they are playing God!" Ray's platform was wobbling as he became ever more animated.

"What did I tell you Xavier? Use your talent to spread the word."

Xavier nodded in acknowledgment.

"You did those big beautiful murals, lighting up the pitch black depths…bringing light where there was once only darkness," Ray began to quiet down, the presence of a security interceptor a few meters away signalled Ray to calm himself.

"To hell with them!" he hissed, glancing over at the intimidating presence, "you are here my boy for something special. I don't know what it is, but let me tell you, you are not here to stand in ArkLight docks for Human Enterprises, wiring a hypervelocity unit whilst waiting to go to some smouldering rock in the Proxima Centauri. You are here to make these people think, Xavier!" Ray barked, motioning towards the jumbled mess of Genesis, which hung all around them.

It was an extraordinary backdrop to his extraordinary rant; the thousands upon thousands of colonies that glinted and shimmered in the sunlight as they hung against the black eternity of deep space.

"You know Ray, you are a pretty intense, dude!" smirked Xavier.

"Dude," laughed Ray, "dude, I love it, dude, dude, I love the word dude."

Xavier shook his head.

Ray was smiling now, "You know I used to be a Moon Dude?"

"Yes, I know," replied Xavier in a drawn out voice. Ray had told him everything fifty times over in the years he had known him.

"That's right, I was a Moon Dude, that's official, man. I was an original," Old Man Ray kicked his heels, unbothered by the security guards close by.

"That was fun," he continued, "we had our own crater, man, with a dome over the top where we had our own forest. And the trees and plants would grow hundreds of meters in the air because of the gravity, man. We had our own community, which was so much fun, man. It was *Sativaland*. It was awesome - totally far out! Thousands of like minded people living together in one enormous crater filled with beautiful plants and trees just taking care of one another. We lived in tree houses, dude, can you believe that? Tree houses! Do you even know what a tree house is? We were flower people dancing in the Earthlight, singing and whooping, down with nature and one another."

"I know Ray. You got laid a lot too, you've told me before," said Xavier, placating him.

"Yes, but it was beautiful…We had our own paradise and we stared at heaven every day," Ray began to slow down, "then, like they did on old Earth, people said you can't do that… you are having too much fun…too much fun! Can you believe that? You can be punished for having fun? So they came with their laws and their guns and they say 'no you can't live like that. No, you can't be that way, you've got to conform. Join the system. Get with the program,'…like they've got a program! Box you up and send you to Mars or The Cannery. Surround you with hard, clinical, regimented structures and brainwash you. That's what they do! That's what they do! And that's what they did."

Ray kept repeating himself, his eyes filled with tears and fury.

"Hey! Ray! It's okay. You need to calm down," Xavier could see the old man starting to weep as he recollected his past and the attention of the security guards added a little to Xavier being somewhat anxious. The security guards were a fair distance away now. They were there to police and provide order, but they were also there to eavesdrop and spy from time to time. Xavier wondered if they were being recorded.

"I don't care about those guys," said Ray, turning to the troops and pointing to himself. "They all know Old Man Ray," he said proudly.

"They sure do, dude," replied Xavier, patting him on the shoulder and smiling.

"What you up to when you finish here?"

"Oh, Zola has something planned for me," Xavier said smiling.

"Lucky boy!" Old Man Ray laughed, "She's a lovely girl."

"She sure is, but come with me Ray when we get some downtime and hang out. Let's go in the Rod and visit somewhere."

"Ah, Xavier, we should go over to Debris," Ray replied excitedly.

"Stop right there," Xavier said bringing his finger up to his helmet and covering his lips and signalling for him to be quiet.

"You're right. There are people I'd like you to meet…" Ray sighed. "Did I tell you I've been to Heaven?"

"Calm down now," Xavier again motioned his finger to his lips and Ray turned his Flying Carpet away, "Okay, okay. After work," and off he zoomed drawing the attention of the security with him.

"Shadows don't frighten me, Xavier," called Ray as he drifted away, "the Shadows don't frighten me!"

★★★★★

9

The Governor Titus Haq

K.C. Wang and her family had run the Politburo of Sino
Space for nearly thirty years with a cool and steady
hand. General Juggi Khalsa, the warlord-like premier of
Mughal Space, had overseen an aggressive dispute over mining
rights in the asteroid belt with their closest adversaries and
trading partners for the last two decades. However fractious
this conflict had been, full blown war had been averted.
Diplomacy had won the day.

As governor of Genesis, Titus Haq oversaw the many
factions, corporations and competing interests with
headquarters and bases in the region. Each of the major
colonies had their own business and spiritual leaders alongside
their respective military and political chiefs yet they all
consulted and reported to Haq.

Even the High Pioneer colonies, known as Independents
and fanatically proud of their autonomy were all represented
and had their say in what was a rumbustious free-for-all of
economic and political gerrymandering. Titus made sure that

everyones voice was heard or at least feel that the people of Genesis were able to have their voices heard even if it were just a sideshow. With the decisions being dictated by the corporate policies of The Powers.

Titus stood gazing out from his opulent apartment within the Governors Palace, a shining glass-like globular affair that commanded a view of the entirety of Genesis. His eyes and ears were fixed upon The Hives and ArkLight with its multitude of Generation Ships, all in various stages of construction, one day destined to leave their berths and head into the unknown.

"What is it about the Hives that fascinates me so much?" he asked, turning towards Carlos Zagrostine.

"They are all despicable!" came the reply, as he picked food from his teeth then flicked it from his fingers, "I am in agreement with Ignatius Perigord, the best solution for that ghetto is the complete termination of air and let the populace suffocate."

Titus looked at him shaking his head, "You are a disgusting individual, are you not Zagrostine?"

Titus was not appalled by his comments, but rather by his poor manners and etiquette and questioned to himself why this man was in his employ. Zagrostine shrugged and smirked then returned to his screen where audits for the various corporate interests flowed in an endless stream. Zagrostine was a heavily built individual and a financial maestro who had been part of the Genesis hierarchy for many years, reporting directly to the Governor who then in turn reported directly to The Powers.

"You have a point though, I suppose," replied Titus. "A workforce with nowhere to go can cause problems. You have to keep them occupied and living in hope that one day they will finally get the chance to find paradise."

"Why give people like this hope?"

"Everyone must have a dream. One day we will be able to leave Genesis and find new homes amongst the colonies," said Titus, gazing at a giant wall chart of the outposts, trade lanes and territories of the Pax Humana.

"Are you joking?' wailed Zagrostine, 'I love it here!'

"You love living in limbo?"

"It's all I have ever known. It's home for me and millions of others. We have a great life here. Everything you could ever wish for is within the assembled colonies of Genesis. It is the heart of the Pax Humana," Carlos Zagrostine may not have won any awards for his social etiquette but he was an ardent champion of the system in which he lived, "I've lived and worked in Genesis most of my life okay. I have been to the other colonies, including the moon and Mars but I do not care for either of them as they and their colonists do not care for Genesis and its inhabitants."

"You intrigue me Zagrostine," chuckled Titus, "how does someone with such an unrefined personality as yourself have such refined powers of observation?"

"Because I love Genesis. And it's not refinement, it's loyalty."

Zagrostine walked across the vast glass-fronted space and joined Titus as he looked from the large windows over the swathe of space, "Centuries ago on old Earth, there were huge cities known as 'melting pots' - New York, London, Shanghai for example, which were the crossroads for people both culturally and economically. Genesis is the same; it is a mixture of old and new and every culture that ever existed on Earth and every culture that has boomed since the Exodus is here. This is the greatest melting pot mankind has ever known. Why would you ever want to be anywhere else?"

"If I'd lived in Roman times, I'd have lived in Rome. Where else? Today America is the Roman Empire and New York is Rome itself," said Titus.

"Exactly, you quote the ancient Earth orator John Lennon," Zagrostine smiled.

"I personally like Genesis."

"Well, aren't you the lucky one," smirked Zagrostine, "to be able to choose between Earth and Genesis."

Haq had chiselled, noble features and he was young. Some said far too young to hold such a position as Governor of Genesis, but with an aristocratic background and the genetic stock of illustrious intelligentsia, he was a shoehorn into the position. His father, Alaman, had been a high level fixer for The Powers, one of the few entrusted with the secrets of State. It was unclear whether Titus was a clone of his father, but his conceited ability to rectify issues and problems had seen him land an executive position in his early teens, then oversee smaller trading colonies before being handed the role of

Governor. He was like a petulant Roman emperor commanding respect and accolade from a very early age.

"We should visit The Hives,"

"Why in Genesis would you want to do that?" Zagrostine
laughed.

"I am intrigued," Titus replied.

"Intrigued?" questioned Zagrostine, "by what exactly?"

"I want to understand what it is like to live in The Hives.
We are the elite, the patrician class. Who live away from the
mob, as our Roman ancestors would have referred to the
denizens of The Hives. We need to understand them."

Zagrostine could not contain himself and burst out
laughing, "Please tell me there is sarcasm in that answer."

"No, there is not," said Titus, "I would like to understand
what is going on over there."

"Are you after a cheap piece of ass?"

"How dare you!" roared Titus.

"I am sorry Titus. You need to head to one of the Pleasure
Asteroids for that," sniggered Zagrostine.

Titus straightened up, glaring at the rotund Zagrostine,
"Something lurks within The Hives. I can feel it, I have felt it
on a number of occasions and my consultations with Ferrer
have confirmed it."

"What do you mean?"

"I have recently had dreams about trouble within this
colony. Unrest whose catalyst is within The Hives."

Zagrostine nodded, "Well, that would be a breeding
ground for any kind of civil disobedience, especially with

Civilization carrying out attacks upon corporate property and perpetuating rebellion."

"How dare they call themselves by the name of Civilization when they wouldn't know the first thing about being part of a civilised society," replied Titus shaking his head in disgust.

"They are themselves a product of Nu Humana policy."

"They are bewildering I must admit. One minute they believe in democracy for all, then they want to abandon the quest for new colonies and return to Earth because they stupidly believe it is every human's right to return to Earth. Then they believe that Earth is a desolate wasteland, where life is unsustainable," sneered Titus.

Zagrostine shook his head returning to the large granite conference table in the centre of the room.

"Could you imagine if they were ever to find out the truth about Earth being a paradise once more. An Eden into which they were given no entry. There would be pandemonium, pure carnage."

"That is why Perigord is right. We must control the very air they breath," Zagrostine responded, while rummaging in his briefcase.

"It is the greatest secret ever. We have hoodwinked the whole populace and kept Earth for ourselves. It is the basis of our Pax Humana and is the basis for the development of the colonies. We have cheated mankind of their own planet. It is the most important secret and we need to protect it and in doing so protect mother Earth."

"You should be aware of this, it is something you need to see," Zagrostine pulled from his case a small metallic disc which he placed on the table, then waving his hand over the top. A set of holographic images sprang into the centre of the room from the box, "The feral mind of a feral youth."

"There's graffiti throughout The Hives isn't there," asked Titus.

"Yes, there is. Only these are different," replied Zagrostine moving the images on.

Titus walked from one side of the hologram to the other examining its lurid images intently. He was aware of the gangs that infested The Hives leaving their tags and scrawls delineating a gang territory or border on the landings and walkways; the usual scrawls and throw ups, but this was something entirely different.

"This graffiti…is of Earth!"

As one of the privileged class who had visited Earth, Titus knew exactly what he was seeing. Whoever they were, for he could not imagine one person doing this, they had replicated astonishingly realistic vistas of Earth. From its flora to its fauna to its indigenous tribes and moments from Earth's history - the graffiti was like an archive except painted on the walls of trans-habs, colony rings and freighters.

"We have seen this graffiti throughout The Hives and other parts of Genesis, it is also to be seen on the G-Loop and ArkLight," said Zagrostine, uncharacteristically solemn.

"In ancient days when men first travelled into the wilds of America, artists would send back paintings to benefactors on the East Coast of representations of what they thought the West was like. They were imaginary depictions created for the enthusiastic audiences back home. Fanciful visions made up by the artist to conjure intrigue and excitement of unknown places."

Some pieces contained slogans of dissent, others were questions to the reader in Can-Com, English, Mandarin and Russian asking them to explain how they felt about life in Genesis. Others were more dangerous to the regime, depicting Earth's violent history with images of conquistadors and armies battling.

Zagrostine pointed to the initials XVR and the name XAVIA and also the anarchy symbol which could be seen alongside a number of the images, "These are the only indications as to the identity of these people. I'm not certain what it spells out."

"It spells disaster!" came the sombre reply.

★★★★★

10
Dining at the Capello's

The dining room to the Capello household was lavishly appointed, with framed architectural drawings along one wall, then along the other images depicting what appeared to be a record of an attractive, exuberant couple attending important galas, balls and other prestigious social gatherings.

Dominating the room, though was a picture of the venerated leader and patron of the Pax Humana dynasty, the late lamented Bhutan Kraldon, looking down disapprovingly over the immaculate place settings and cutlery.

"Dinner won't be long," called out Amber Capello, a spritely fifty year old who glided around the kitchen of her apartment as if she might pirouette on stage at any moment as she had done in the many ballets she had performed. Her face and beauty belied her years for her behaviour and demeanour were still very much like a teenagers.

"Not a problem," grunted her husband Fabian from the other side of the luxurious executive suites. "I don't care how it comes or when it comes," he continued as he briefly looked towards the huge picture window. The apartment was located in one of the exclusive Earth-side trans-habs whose views gave an unrivalled and awe-inspiring panorama of the planet as it rotated, uninterrupted by anything but the odd Celestial Gate security outpost.

The Capello's could have chosen to live in one of the better colonies or one of the gated communities with the High Pioneers further away from the madness, so to speak. They could have moved out towards the moon or even the outer edges of the colony cluster, but their strong Party principles and belief in the Pax Humana would not allow them to do so.

Amber was also always in demand to dance in one of the many productions for the Nu Humana company which also dictated their place of abode.

For decades Amber had been the Prima Ballerina at the Red Planet Ballet on Mars and the ABC or Apollo Ballet Company on the moon. Her face as recognisable as Drax Kraldon or any of the Kraldon clan at best, or certainly Dr. Ignatius Perigord at worst.

She was a star.

Her pirouettes and leaps in low gravity would see her spring over fifteen meters into the air, an enthralled audience cheering on her every move. She was loved by her public, generating intense devotion from her followers.

The same could also be said of her husband, the revered engineer Fabian Capello.

Fabian was ten years older than his wife. His hair white and swept back and a pair of spectacles rested on the end of his nose. In fact, problems with eyesight had been eradicated through medical means centuries earlier, but Fabian loved the image of old inventors from history who always seemed to have spectacles perched somewhere about their person and so wore them more as an artefact from the past or to please himself than anything else.

"I will serve up when Zola gets here," Amber scurried around the dining table making sure the cutlery was all laid out correctly.

"Why don't you get a servant to do this Amber?"

"Because I enjoy being normal some nights."

"Whatever you say dear!" shrugged Fabian.

Fabian Capello, the man who had constructed many of the trans-habs throughout Genesis had also been responsible for some of the major civil engineering projects for Nu Humana including the tethering of the 415 Gales Paul asteroid then hauling it from the Asteroid Belt to Genesis and providing a significant supply of water for the inhabitants of the colonies.

A modest man with an inquisitive and logical mind, he had constructed an armada of powerful tug craft to grab, fasten then ferry this huge water laden asteroid through space. Although not a Power himself, Fabian commanded the respect of many in his society, especially the great scientific leader and Power, Elon Garibidian, with whom he worked very closely. The Nu Humana hierarchy always sought the attendance of Amber and Fabian for corporate gatherings and social conventions.

They were top tier, yet as a family they preferred to be private.

"It would be lovely if Brunel and Breeze were with us this evening," said Amber wistfully.

Their eldest child Brunel, had graduated from the Academy with distinction and had been rewarded with one of the most admired and honourable positions within society.

Fabian looked up at her and could see the sorrow etched in Amber's face, "As much as we may miss him he made a noble sacrifice for the Pax Humana. He is Chief Explorer and Commander of an Ark! He has gone to begin a new human colony somewhere for the good of mankind - we should be proud parents."

"I know…but I still just miss Brunel, my son."

"So too do I," conceded Fabian.

"And what of Breeze, will he visit us again?"

"It is hard to tell since he has been taken under the wing of Garibidian. He is helping to chart the galaxies at the Technical Astronomy and I believe the work he has undertaken there is of the utmost secrecy."

"Too many secrets," snapped Amber, "I just want to see my boys again."

"You will see them again soon, my dear," Fabian said kindly putting his hand on hers.

Amber turned back towards the kitchen, just as the front door opened and their beautiful daughter Zola walked in.

She was barely out of her teens and had been cited as a genius all through her classical Nu Humana education at the

Academy. She was an exemplary product of her education and upbringing, proving everyone was equal here in Genesis.

Which of course was not the case!

Zola and her brothers were of an outstanding gene pool, tutored by the best teachers and given a healthy balance of military, physical education and political indoctrination. A large dose of the right Edu-Imps added to that mix produced the most magnificent and distinguished alumni.

After playing Zaddonk in the courts with her friends, Zola looked exhausted and sweaty as she threw down her kit bag and grabbed a drink from the table.

"How are you, darling?" called Amber from the kitchen, "who won?"

"Hey mom! I'm good. Close game but we won again," replied Zola as she took a gulp from the glass. Zaddonk was played everywhere in Genesis and was a mixture of the old Earth games of soccer, basketball, Frisbee and mixed martial arts which, aided with jet-packs and close to zero gravity, made for a lively and frenetic team game, popular at all levels of society.

"How long will dinner be?" asked Zola.

"Not long. Be quick darling," Amber replied as she added the finishing touches to her meal.

"Let me just jump in the Glo-Sho," Zola said as she dashed from the dining room towards the bedroom wing.

Fabian looked up from his design documents and smiled at his daughter, "Hello beautiful, how are you?" he smiled.

She leant over and kissed her father on his forehead, "Hi Dad, I'm good."

"What's been going on? How is everything at ArkLight?"

"The usual,"

"The usual being?" asked Fabian, his face frowning in an enquiring manner.

"Well, things have been moving along really quickly on The Tamarinsk. I am being kept busy with so many different jobs that actually the usual is always unusual!"

"I suppose that makes sense." Fabian smiled, "Are you staying in after dinner?"

"No," came the blunt reply, "I am going to head out to see friends."

"Who? That gang at The Astral Apache?" asked Fabian sternly. It was obvious he disapproved of his daughter's friendship with her colleagues at the docks and people who he considered far below his daughter's status.

"Oh, by the way, Dad I wanted to say my living unit request has come through for my new trans-hab."

"I am really not happy about this," said Fabian, "you can stay here for as long as you like you know."

"I know, but all my friends are either being seconded to different places within the system or within Genesis, just like Brunel and Breeze. And everyone who got the grades gets the apartment for being a good citizen and contributing to the Pax Humana."

Zola walked to her bedroom and undressed, then stepped into the Glo-Sho as her father shook his head, the refreshing light cleansing and reinvigorating her.

"Leave her Fabian, she has grown up now," said Amber, placing her arm on his shoulder, "she can't always be your little girl."

"I know, I just don't like the thought of her leaving here," he replied solemnly, as he returned to his designs.

It was hard for him to let go of something as precious as Zola.

"Dinner will be ready in a few moments," Amber said, as she walked back towards the kitchen.

Stepping out from the Glo-Sho, her body tingling, Zola basked in the effects of the restorative purification lights.

Her body was then powdered and scented before she stepped into her undergarments and a mandatory figure hugging pressure suit. Many of Zola's friends wore suits with the breast and crotch areas detailed with designs and symbols, and Zola was no exception to the world of fashion. Sex was one thing the Pax Humana never interfered with and every young spacer wore them. She pulled on a pair of thigh length boots and put on her make up before striding back into the living area.

Fabian looked up at her, "You look stunning."

"Thanks Dad," Zola replied.

"Are you going to see the girls?" asked Amber.

"Yes, Mom!"

"And the guys?" Amber laughed.

"Yes, Mom!"

Her father glanced at her with a disapproving eye before asking, "Xavier?"

"Dad, there are things that you do that I don't approve of. So let's just leave it at that," said Zola taking her seat at the dining table. Despite himself, Fabian couldn't help admire the self-assurance his daughter displayed.

"We have always believed and supported the system. That the system will look after us. And we have always supported this doctrine since the Exodus, way before our time. It has treated us well and rewarded us for our devotion to that call. Is there anything wrong in that?" asked Fabian earnestly.

Zola looked straight at her father, "I hardly saw either of you growing up. I grew up in the Academy with the rest of the kids because you two were so devoted to the 'system'. Xavier and I have been friends since that time and all those people who you look down your nose at are products of this beloved system of yours too."

"I am not sure I want you to associate with someone like Xavier who is from the Hives and is just a rigger."

"Don't you talk about Xavier or my friends like that. They might live in the Hives and work in the docks or the pleasure domes but they are just as devoted to the Pax as you."

"My dear I know we committed ourselves to Pax Humana and the higher ups but we never neglected you."

"Really? Brunel could not wait to take up his position on that Ark never to return again. He could not wait to get away from here and you."

"Zola, that is unfair."

"And Breeze, I have not seen him in five years because he is committed to the Pax program!" Zola sighed.

"We all miss them but they dedicated themselves to mankind's advancement and with that comes a certain amount of sacrifice from all of us."

"You and Mom have done just fine, haven't you? Your executive suites, your trips around the solar system, your visits to Mars, hobnobbing with the great and good. Please don't you ever question my friends again."

"I worry about you Zola, that is all."

"Well, don't because I am just fine."

"You are young and reckless sometimes Zola, you need to be careful, our system has a way of dealing with those who walk a fine line and I do not want my daughter to fall into that trap."

Zola said nothing, but closed her eyes as if to block out her father's last comment.

Amber entered carrying a bowl of fresh food, the produce of one of the vast agricultural units on the outer edges of Genesis.

"Smells good mom!" Zola turned away from her father and beamed up at her mother.

"Doesn't it, darling!"

Amber placed the vegetables and Tunapia on the table.

Tunapia was a cross between tuna and talapia that seemed to have thrived in space over the decades of intensive cultivation techniques employed by many of the corporations.

Although nothing like fish from Earth it proved popular with everyone in Genesis and the Capello family were no exception.

"So what were you two talking about so heatedly?" enquired Amber.

Zola placed her hand on top of her father's and smiled, "Not much really Mom."

"Well, let's eat then," they settled down to eat with the images of the absent Brunel and Breeze hanging over them and the venerable Bhutan Kraldon and his grandson Drax.

★★★★★

11
Time Is On My Side

T ime is the strangest thing in space.
What is a second?
What is a minute?
An hour, a day, a week, a month, even a year?

The Earth rotates and orbits simultaneously around the sun which gave humans the twenty-four hour clock. Working from dawn and resting at night. It is the way we live our lives. The continual cycle of life in The Hives, the refineries of Zug, the docks of ArkLight as well as the thousands of asteroid mines in the solar system and factories throughout Genesis; this meant that people liked to party whenever they were afforded a break.

A trip to the Branson Entertainment Crater on the Moon was a popular leisure destination. As was a visit to a hydro forest. Playing sports such as Zaddonk and gliding in a low gravity cylinder was a fad, as was swimming in a water sphere; enormous zero-gravity swimming pools integrating the sensations of weightlessness and water. Of course there were the adventurers who would journey out to solar surf around Genesis, their burns and scars testament to the danger of this certain pursuit. Then there were the more laid-back and hedonistic pastimes at one of the resorts newly completed pleasure asteroids and casinos.

The average person just worked, happy to have something to occupy their time and keep their minds busy. Add to that the effect of the Edu-Imp which focused them on the task at hand and time flew right by. Xavier had been working at Ark Light for a year straight, with no breaks he could recall. Any free time he had, he spent drawing out designs to paint on the side of Arks and freighters or helping out in Kaiser O'Keefe's paint shop.

Within Genesis were hundreds of thousands of bars, clubs and eateries catering to this nonstop lifestyle. There were haunts all over The Hives. People were free to do what they wanted in their own time.

A crowd of around thirty or so people were huddled outside the door of The Astral Apache, chatting and talking. The neon bar sign was fashioned and reminiscent of New York bar signs in the twentieth century with the head of an ancient aboriginal Earth person as out of place as everything else you might find in the Hives. Opposite the entrance to the bar was a drop off platform for one of the many taxi and ferries operating in the locale, one of which Zola had used to take her from her trans-hab.

Zola strode through the entrance of the bar acknowledging a couple of girls as she entered and came to the long counter from which the barman Ortiz never strayed far. To one side of the bar was a gigantic window that looked over the Hives and its dizzying vertigo-inspiring view. There was a feeling of awe mixed with fear when gazing out at this enormous structure in which they were a part of. Every available space was filled with something; animal, vegetable, mineral. Everything was in motion, everything moving, turning and shifting.

The music in the Apache was still low with the mellow sounds of the Deano Kaminski Orchestra setting the mood for people to converse with one another before the breakneck sounds of one of the heavier artists to take over later on. In a cubicle near the window taking in the view were a group of six girls who all rose in unison and greeted Zola with hoots and hollers as she walked to their table.

"What's up, girls?"

"Hey space bitch!" called out Ilona Moonlight with her customary greeting. Her crew consisted of Ilona, Lola Love 18, She-La Carrere, Sebi Senagatu, Kim ToJe and Venus Hutton. All of these strong, energetic and beautiful women were regulars either at The Astral Apache or its sister club, The Cosmic Comanche. Zola placed her hands on her hips then gyrated in a way that accentuated her body before somersaulting in one fluid motion to the beat of the music.

"Nice!" winked Lola, before getting up and doing a move to the music too.

Lola Love 18 worked at one of the Pleasure Asteroids which were harboured within the Genesis conurbation. These were usually spent mining asteroids whose insides had been hollowed out and refitted into a casino cum hotel cum bordello. Convenient and debauched the local Pleasure Asteroids were another avenue for the citizens of Genesis to get their kicks.

Kim ToJe and Venus Hutton were friends of Zola from the academy and worked alongside her at ArkLight in one of the many Nu Humana subsidiary departments. They longed to be able to take an Ark to one of the new colonies possibly finding their Mister Right along the way, settle on a little plot of land and their have very own biosphere, just as the Pax Humana decreed.

Taking the small shuttle to the big Ark and seeing your descendants become the pioneer colonists on a new planet was what the Pax Humana was all about, but until then girls like Kim and Venus would have to make do with life within Genesis.

"Ortiz!" Lola shouted over, "Get some drinks sent over here will you!"

"So, whose going out?" asked Zola.

"Well, I am for sure," replied She-La.

"Going to get freaky!" laughed Sebi, clutching her crotch.

"I think Jericho and the guys are heading down soon," Ilona said, winking at Zola.

"Xavier too right?" said Zola.

"Yes, and Xavier!"

"Good because I need to get laid," she said not missing a beat.

The girls laughed and lifting their drinks simultaneously replied, "Deal!"

As they sat huddled around the table, behind them spacecraft glided past the windows of the bar outside, against the backdrop of myriad buildings.

"So how are the folks?" Ilona asked.

"Oh, fine. You know toeing the party line. Company people, are they not? Why do you ask?" replied Zola. Her background in the current climate required her to be wary of such a line of questioning.

"Sorry Zola!" replied Ilona, startled by Zola's severity, "I was just making conversation."

"I didn't mean to startle you Ilona its just that I try and live as independently from them as I can."

"I didn't mean to pry and sorry if I overstepped the mark, babe?"

"No - I am the one who should apologise," Zola moved over and gave Ilona a hug. "It's just hard sometimes living with them and their views. It can become stifling. They have such high and mighty opinions of themselves and look down on everyone else. They seem to forget that I was more or less left on my own for years."

"Your mom does seem nice though?"

"They are both nice," Zola paused a little unsure of what to say, "but they are just so for lack of a better word 'square'." She sighed, making the shape of a square with her fingers, the tension was broken with that and everyone felt it was okay to laugh.

"To be honest I'm surprised they let you do anything," confided Sebi.

"Oh they are fine about a lot of things and then can't stand me doing other things. It's a Pax Humana thing," replied Zola, knocking back her drink, "besides hypocrisy has always featured heavily throughout society, and theirs is no exception."

"Maybe they will get rid of parents one day and just take us straight from the womb," laughed Sebi.

"I have no doubt The Powers have looked into that as a very possible solution," Zola replied darkly but not without humour.

The room erupted with the sounds of Mining Munk Muzik. Zola looked up and saw the Space DJz had now taken to the stage and the place began to throb with beats and basslines. The girls jumped up from their seats with a chance to throw some moves. They had only been dancing a few moments when Zola caught sight of Xavier, Jericho and their crew silhouetted against the lights looking around to locate the girls. Zola gestured to Ilona and they walked over to them.

"So, where've you been boys?" Ilona asked.

Jericho was always the first to open his mouth, "Just hanging on the landing," he said while motioning her and everyone else towards the bar.

"What's it going to be then?" Ortiz the barman asked. As always, his sombre face as someone who had just lost a leg.

"Magic Mudge's all round brother Ortiz, and take one for yourself," a beaming Xavier laughed, placing his hand on the electronic slate for payment. Magic Mudge was a euphoric and slightly hallucinogenic drink served at The Astral Apache and Cosmic Comanche, incredibly popular with the clientele especially Xavier's gang. There was a cheer from the group as Ortiz smiled slightly, "That's generous of you Xavier, but you know I can't drink on the job."

Zola nuzzled into Xavier kissing him, "Look who's flash. What are you celebrating?"

"Aw, nothing," he shrugged, "just seeing you, I suppose."

"You know the saying flattery will get you everywhere right," Zola giggled.

"You look amazing!" Xavier could not take his eyes off her and her outfit, "Are you staying here or are you going to rave with us out in Debris?"

Zola paused for a moment, "We will be safe there?"

"Of course, you're with me…plus there will be plenty of people you know there. Even Old Man Ray."

As much as she liked to defy her parents, she knew that Debris was a whole different prospect than anywhere within the safety and security of Genesis. The journey itself from The Gloop and out across The Divide was monitored continually by security services who wanted to stop contraband and people crossing back and forth.

Lola walked towards them. "Hey, Xavi, honey, how have you been? Any more crazy dreams?"

"You know Lola, I had one last night. It was pretty terrifying. I was chased by some kind of…" Xavier broke off in mid sentence.

"You are always being chased, baby!" Lola replied giggling.

"He needs to stop taking those Edu-Imps all the time," said Zola,

"Taking too much of the Zug juice, that's what it is," laughed Ricardo, walking over.

"I ain't ever touched Zugbot mucus, man," scoffed Xavier. Zug juice was a highly hallucinogenic intoxicant taken from a symbiotic creature called a Zugbot found in the chemical refineries of Zug.

"Like you've done Zug juice Ricardo!" Ilona laughed.

"I have," he replied, testily.

"Well, then if you have, then maybe the problem is you never came down from it, you freak!" Lola and Ilona laughed.

"So who's going to Debris? They got some party there with the band Scun-Scum and all those mining munk freaks," Xavier turned to the group to see who was in.

"We'd go with you Xavier," said Lola, "but we have work. Got a special little gig on later all hush, hush!"

"Duty calls, know what I mean, Xavi," Ilona smiled, her beautiful face ready to grace one of the pleasure station portals.

"Xavier, what is it with you and Ray?" joked Jericho Chong, who had just walked in from the restroom. "I mean that man is out there, tripping for real. You and him got some kind of thing going? His head's so fried, dude."

"Yes, I heard they found places on Mercury that weren't as burnt out as that old dude," Ricardo wanting to get his two bits in.

With that, Xavier moved his arm towards Ricardo and without touching him sent him flying towards the restroom.

The gang went quiet.

"That's pretty cool, Xavier, I got to say," Sebi was the first to break the silence. "I have seen you do that a few times and that is well…impressive!"

"Xavier, you want to be sure The Shadows don't come after you with tricks like that," Zola said, shaking her head.

Xavier walked over and picked Ricardo up from the floor, "I've warned you not to mess with Ray. We go back that's all I'm saying."

"Sorry man," said Ricardo, looking up at Xavier with sincerity.

"No, I'm sorry man, so are we still going out to the rave later?" Xavier asked.

They touched fists and returned to the counter.

"I love you guys," giggled Lola Love 18. "Xavi's totally cool even if he says and does things I just don't get."

"You can say that again," said Zola.

They fuelled up on pre-party nutrition and hydration, splintering off into pockets of conversation.

Zola sidled over as Xavier finished his Yamp-E, a delicious fungus grown in the space farms and served with seasonal vegetables grown hydroponically in the same colonies.

"What's going on Spacer?"

"I want you to come with me now!" giggled Zola.

"Where are we headed?"

"That's for me to know, and you to find out," smiled Zola mysteriously.

"K-O-K Zola sounds like you have got your man," laughed Xavier, as he got up from his seat and back slapped his friends.

The girls said their good byes to them both and the couple left the Apache.

"We're going to head back over towards ArkLight," said Zola picking up her pace as they headed for a subway shuttle.

"What for?" asked Xavier, slightly bemused and believing he was on a promise, "I thought we were heading back to mine."

Zola paused and grinned, "You thought wrong!"

★★★★★

12

The History of The World Part 1

T he History of Earth is a tragic story but a true one.
Its rapid decline due in part to the ineptitude of
government, a global loss of ethics and the ignorance
of its people led to a moral then ecological decline.

Perhaps it had always been inevitable.

It had taken nearly eighty years since the first use of the
atom bomb before weapons of mass destruction were ever
used again. Some people celebrated, cheered as the missiles
flew over, saying it was the best thing that could have
happened.

On Capitol Hill a number of politicians were quoted as
saying, "There's plenty more of those missiles if you want
them! The taxpayer has paid for them so we might as well use
them!"

Sure enough, they got their wish.

Populations had exploded to an unprecedented level while
the natural resources were plundered without replenishment,

Earth could not support the huge populations as in the previous centuries without giving rise to conflict.

There was a need to control the third world populations, however drastic this strategy might be. It stopped the waves of uncontrolled and unchecked population growth and in turn the waves of immigration flooding the Western World.

It was a radical idea, but what the hell we have them and we paid for them so let's use them.

Radiation ain't that bad!

The clarion call for the extreme right became, "We've got nukes and we're going to use them!"

The twenty-first century was a turbulent one hundred years where conflicts raged continually and war was a fact of life.

What started as somebody else's war soon became yours.

Each regional conflict seemed to drag another nation in so that soon it became a world war without anyone realising it.

People are people, you cannot tell people to stop. You have to force them.

Eventually the space programs of the late twentieth century stopped as nations' pockets got tighter and the vision of space travel and colonisation became a thing of fantasy as opposed to a fact of reality. The beautiful dreamers who dreamt of space as the new frontier had viewed the vast expanse of space and the colonisation of it as a glorious vision for mankind. Yet they were branded as radicals and fantasists.

The death knell was sounded. The quest for space paused and instead was replaced with a quest for wealth in some quarters. Banks and corporations concerned only with making money for themselves and their clients created modern day slavery using debt as the shackles. These corporate financial houses created nothing but misery for the majority with a deliberate aim of keeping the riches for the one percenters.

Did they not realise the wealth and riches of the high frontier of space far surpassed anything they could make through trading derivatives?

This was futures trading!

It was left to the pioneers and the early spacers of the twenty-first century to push the boat out and led by a group of individuals who had been raised on the early ideals of space exploration, they proved it could be done.

Maybe the problems on Earth were the ones that needed to be sorted before journeying off into space, but for some those problems would never be resolved. And for them they were heading somewhere away from the mayhem...they were headed to space.

The nations of China, Japan and India pushed their programs, seeing the potential of building nations amongst the stars.

Despite war, economic strife, natural disaster the innate program of the human to procreate was undeterred.

War destroyed resources further and surges of people fleeing their homes and countries in search of better, safer lives in every direction created a whole new set of conflicts.

Choices become restricted and you find you have nowhere to go.

Things fall apart; the centre cannot hold
mere anarchy is loosed upon the world,
The blood-dimmed tide is loosed and everywhere,
the ceremony of innocence drowned.

~ WB Yeats - The Second Coming

Millions found themselves endlessly traversing the planet in search of home, being denied access to potential sanctuary as countries closed their borders. The turbulence of the 21st Century with its one hundred years of continual conflict and war-mongering seemed to go hand in hand with man's fascination of how technology could feed the war machine rather than his dreams of the stars.

As Earth's food stocks dwindled almost to a halt, both on land and sea. The human population experienced starvation. The sky was choking from the pollution of industry and debris from the global conflicts. The mutation of viruses and disease into undefinable strains while transmitting at alarming rates made the extinction of the species of homo sapiens and the animal species that co-existed with it a more than distinct possibility.

The Great Suffocate in 2108 was the culmination of two hundred years of ignorance.

It affected everybody.

Corporations and governments alike started to experiencing the results of centuries of hubris.

They had not listened or taken heed of the protestations as forests were ploughed down, seas polluted, animals hunted to extinction,

The mass graves may well contain their own children alongside those of the poor whom they had cared not one iota for.

The pollution of China, India, Europe, the Americas and of Russia and the African continent raised its toxic head and a billion citizens of Earth, an entire generation, succumbed to an untimely end.

Choked in a soup of shit. What a way to go!

This then was the point at which Earth having been ravaged, ceased to be a viable option and looking beyond the planet became an interesting proposition once again.

Those who had taken part in the wilful destruction of the Earth, now looked greedily at the glistening moon, Mars and even the asteroids with only one thing on their mind…profit.

It was now that they started to take notice and see what was beyond the atmosphere, to take an interest in life past low Earth orbit.

They could see the asteroids, the moon and Mars and they realised what they meant…profit.

What had been plainly obvious for some for over a century now began to make sense to the people in power, and plans were made to begin at all costs the leap into space that Neil Armstrong had spoken about one hundred and fifty years before. Each country now joined together and formed new corporations to exploit the vast resources that existed out in space.

Space Elevators began to be built all along the equator and those nations that could...did. Beautiful, magnificent structures stretching towards infinity, designed by the best architects and constructed by the best engineers. Like golden metal flowers, these life giving formations took to the skies, their solar panels glistening in the sunlight while the stem carried its cargo to the mechanical docking port in the sky before being ferried to its final destination.

Soon fifty elevators were constructed taking supplies, goods, food, water and minerals up into the heavens. War had accelerated technology and now the same technology engineered towards the murder of humankind was now being used to create new worlds.

The High Pioneers settled in an area known as Lagrangian Point 5. Unimpeded by the gravitational forces of the Earth and her moon they built their new homes. These colonies became ever popular with the new adventurer and began to form what became known as Genesis, a benchmark in the new human dream.

It was the dawn of a new human era.

In the beginning God created the heaven and the earth. And the earth was without form, and void; and darkness was upon the face of the deep. And the spirit of God moved upon the face of the waters. And God said, Let there be light...and there was light.

~ Genesis 1:1 The Holy Bible: King James version

Genesis was given its name from the first book of the Bible.

Faith became a powerful driver for the masses, not in the ways religion had before but everyone believed that they had to start again. It was as if an evangelical wave had swept over them and the chance to begin again somewhere new was all they cared for. They had to have another attempt at getting it right or they would become as extinct as the dinosaurs that roamed sixty-five million years before. Thousand year old differences were immediately settled and the race to create settlements in the stars began in earnest.

For the first time in a long time they were given hope and the person who gave them it was one of their own. A man born in the run down environs of Detroit with no hope. A man who worked his way through scholarships to West Point and then to Capitol Hill and the United Nations.

It was the great leader Denton Amadeus who emerged as the commander in chief of the world when an alliance of nations elected him as the man to rescue the planet from the brink of catastrophe.

Looking into the abyss it was Amadeus, a humble giant of a man who proposed the Earth be left to repair itself and that man be banished from the mother planet and, much to his surprise, the nations of the world agreed.

The people might not have, but then again they had no say in anything.

They would do as they were told and if they tried to stay on the Earth, they would be hunted down and killed or using a simpler method, canisters containing a poison that affected only humans would be used to clear the planet.

Genesis had begun with a few pioneers and some radical ideas. They had built early colonies in the Lagrange points then harnessed the solar energies of the sun and the mineral resources close at hand with a belief they were creating the future of mankind.

The momentum was unstoppable.

Rich untapped seams of mineral deposits on Mars and the moon and the bonanza of discovering every other month an asteroid that contained more metals and was more easily extracted than on Earth meant the human in space was at full tilt .

Wealth became unlimited to the corporations.

Space expansion had saved the Earth.

The sudden shift meant that man's expansion into space became the primary importance and the Earth became a secondary priority and so was left to heal.

Driven by the righteousness of their own cause of action in saving humanity and the mother Earth and spurred on by the strength of a global coalition working towards a common goal, The Powers as they became known, a faceless conglomeration of might and self interest turned their thoughts to one of the most important commodities that it had in abundance.

Humans, a breathing, breeding mass that needed to be clothed, sheltered and fed.

They could be sent to the corners of the newly constructed colonies around the solar system and become new markets to export products and services to and vice versa.

Mankind as commodity had a value.

Let's not kill it and eradicate it, let's export it. Let's take mankind as far as we can across the cold divides.

The Powers made a decision and plans were made.

The colonies on Mars and the moon could get on with their colonisation plans, they were easy to trade with and work alongside.

The High Pioneers and the intelligentsia were free to do whatever they wanted but the proletariat were to become the fodder of this grand experiment.

They just did not know it yet.

They could make their own craft, build their own future and for the first time play a real part in their own destiny.

Shape it and make it, it was down to them.

No more lounging around, no more sitting idle like back on Earth, the devil will make work for idle hands to do.

Not any more.

The hoi-polloi now had something to focus on, something they could aspire to.

For centuries they had been a population without purpose, a population without focus, now for the first time they could have their own say, work toward their own dreams, controlled by The Powers.

The ingenuity of man was marvellous.

If The Powers could remove the population of the Earth, then they could keep it for themselves.

A good deal.

★★★★★

13

Calvin Lacker

C alvin Lacker had an unassuming demeanour.
If you were to meet him in the line at the staff canteen and engage with him in conversation, one would be taken by his elegant manners and softly spoken nature. Yet, if you were to put this same man onto a podium to speak to an audience about his passion, you would unleash a man able to vocalise his powerful emotions and thoughts which would be considered dangerous and those of a radicalised firebrand. For the last few months this apparently demure soapbox orator had been using the art of diffusion and disguise to stay one step ahead of the powers that be.

The elevator seemed to descend for an eternity. Zola turned and smiled nervously at Xavier who seemed to be fascinated by the architecture of many of the buildings they passed before entering the shaft. She nudged him to get his attention, and he smiled back at her and nodded at the four other passengers on this apparently never ending ride.

"Where are we going?" Xavier whispered into Zola's ear.

"Be patient, you'll find out soon enough," she replied.

There was another couple besides them in the elevator. They seemed similar in age to Zola and Xavier and were dressed in ArkLight rigger gear. It was clear they worked at one of the other docks. There was also an older man who stared straight ahead ignoring all eye contact with his fellow passengers and also a teenager who smiled at Xavier as his eyes fell on him.

"Are you going to the rally?" he asked Xavier quietly. His voice barely audible to the others in the elevator carriage.

Zola screwed up her face warily at him but said nothing.

Xavier smiled then nodded in a friendly manner as the lift came to an abrupt halt. The young man smiled back, just as the doors opened onto a large gantry that led towards a cylindrical tower attached to the underside of DF118 dock. Contained inside was a secret vestibule which held around thirty people, many with their faces covered with visors from their helmets and bandanas. Many of these people were clearly workers at the docks, yet they all held their index and middle fingers over their left breast forming a C.

Zola too did the same.

The portico juddered slightly and then suddenly twisted and dropped ten meters before a door opened on the other side to a passageway into a large hangar and makeshift auditorium. There were thousands of people standing shoulder to shoulder.

Zola turned to him finally, "Surprise!"

"Wow!" said Xavier, "This is amazing."

"It can only mean one thing Xavier; the message is finally getting across."

Xavier was lost in thought for a moment, "What is this place?" he asked.

"It's probably one of the old propellant tanks or reactor hubs from a defunct mining vessel or ark," said Zola.

"No, it's too large, look at all the machinery and that plant over there," said Xavier, pointing north of the space.

Rows upon rows of industrial equipment was stacked on top of each other ready for shipping to a new moon or asteroid. An energetic manufacturing thrust had taken place in Genesis whenever a new mineral rich asteroid was discovered, but in the rush to create new products for the new colonies, over-production was rife and countless items of inventory had to be stored. The intrinsically wasteful nature of the Powers suited the people present just fine, creating makeshift viewing platforms for the assembled audience. From there a series of containers had been formed into an improvised conference hall and two cranes normally used for shifting equipment were now silhouetted by two spotlights which formed the temporary stage for the guest speakers.

"It's really massive...must have been forgotten by the authorities." As Zola spoke her sense of wonder reminded Xavier of a little girl, "I am always amazed at what you can find in Genesis if you look hard enough."

"I don't think the authorities ever forget anything though do they?" Xavier could not shake his sense of foreboding. Zola did not answer, trying to get a better view of the next speaker.

She took Xavier's hand as they swam through the crowd towards the front. Masses of workers in pressure suits sporting Nu Humana branding had gathered to listen to this workers rally.

Reaching the front she found the irrepressible Calvin Lacker about to make his speech. A tall, handsome and proud man with glistening wavy hair stood before them whose voice was clear and impassioned, "Thank you, ladies and gentlemen, for gathering here and caring enough about yourselves and your future to listen to what I have to say. You see the history of the world is sad and sadly true…"

There was a cheer from the audience as the powerful lilting tones filled the hangar.

"The history of the Earth is ours to question and ours to discover for ourselves, as we are the ones who have been born in this limbo destined to be here and never see the beauty and wonder of the Earth as our ancestors did for evermore. So we must ask ourselves the question? How did we arrive at this point? Why are we in a limbo? Who is responsible for this?"

"The Powers!" a huge shout came from the gathered audience.

"We seem to be part of a massive disconnect," Lacker paced across the podium pointing both hands in the air with an exaggerated manner. "Our life and our history began three hundred years ago when we all were forced to leave Earth and start a new life in the colonies of Genesis and the greater congress of the Pax Humana. It was Year Zero. Our ancestors the homo-sapiens were similar to us in look and physicality yet native to the planet Earth where we are native to space. So what is our future, what is our destiny? Have you ever questioned where you go next? Not as an individual, but as a society, that's the important question."

Lacker paused for a moment scratching his head, his dark brown eyes scanning the faces of the crowd then grinned, "They gave us a cosy, little trans-hab filled with every conceivable gadget you could ever wish for, they educated us en-masse in the life fantastic we were to expect in space. They 'gave' us a job; which was compulsory and to earn our keep but is it what 'we' desire? Have we ever been given a choice? So we get a trip to a pleasure dome or to the moon once in a while and if we are really lucky we get to go free on an Ark to an unknown destination of not our, but their choosing."

"Doesn't sound that bad to me!" shouted a lone voice from the crowd.

"Well, then friend, if you are happy and content with your life then you have got no need to worry and I'm wondering why you are here."

There was no reply.

"Here we are in ArkLight Docks. Do you actually know what we are building here? What we are creating? Do you really know what is going on in these colonies or for that matter on these Arks?"

Xavier could not help but be impressed by the man's passion and his speech.

"We have a hand in building them but where are they really going and what is the real goal here? Are you sharing in the bountiful supply of riches coming from all over this solar system and from the outer reaches? And why are we not allowed after three hundred years of living in these colonies to govern ourselves and have a say in our future. Why do we have a governor in the form of Titus Haq who has been placed before us as a puppet of The Powers? And why are we not allowed to return to Earth? They say they are protecting it from the ravages of mankind, that we cannot be trusted with returning there, but all it seems they want to do is keep it as their own little playground. Do we not know what's really happening? They will never allow us to return to Earth."

He paused, there was almost an audible hush that came over the crowd. He continued, "The venerated Drax Kraldon and his clan are given nepotistic rights handed down from generation to generation to oversee the safeguard of the planet and to keep the Pax Humana going forward. That kind of nonsense should have been abandoned centuries ago. These people aren't pharaohs, or monarchs, they are certainly not gods, they are men and women like you and I. Yet they are treated as celestial beings, why I ask you? Why?"

"This guy is pretty out there," said Xavier, as he turned to see Zola captivated by Lacker's oration.

"What if we all said one day, 'No, we will not take this anymore! No, we are not taking those Edu-Imps to program us to work on the Arks. What if we just downed tools and said we aren't going to be part of this system anymore!' What would they do?"

"Kill us and find others who will comply?" said a voice in the crowd.

Lacker paused, smiled and weighed up the retort, "Maybe you are right, but maybe that's exactly what they want you to believe. If you feel deep down that what you feel is right then…fight! If you have the strength of your convictions to be here and you feel the discontent thousands of others feel then fight! If you don't have then what are you doing here?"

"I'm with you Calvin, I'm with you all the way!" a voice shouted back, pumping his fist in the air.

Lacker raised his arm and punched the air then formed a C and covered his breast beating it, " Now imagine, if we all did that, if a thousand became ten thousand, then a hundred thousand, then a million? What if insurrection rather than blind compliance became the status quo!"

Lacker spat out his last sentence whipping the audience into a frenzy.

A cheer rose like a wave from the crowd.

"Do it people! Do it for Earth! Do it for yourselves!"

Xavier heard Zola's voice joining in caught up in the hysteria.

"We can show the people of The Hives an alternative way. The citizens of these places have been showing their discontent already. Have you seen the graffiti around The Hives of the scenes from Earth, of the animals and vistas and of the oceans and birds that used to live there?"

Zola grabbed Xavier's arm and squeezed. They gave each other a hug, "Shit, that's you Xavier…" Zola hissed in excitement.

"It stirs something doesn't it," Lacker continued, "it stirs something magical, something spiritual, it is mystical and powerful and above all it is hopeful."

Lacker crossed his arms and formed an X.

"Fuck!" cried Xavier.

"It's you, it's you," Zola was so excited she began to hold Xavier's arms up. A small crowd around them began to look at him.

"Stop it, Zola," Xavier said in a hand whisper. He was not ready for this.

"What are you embarrassed about? Your graffiti means something more than just a scrawl on a wall, you should tell him who you are."

Xavier shook his head, "No, no Zola, absolutely not."

"These are good people Xavier."

"I don't doubt it," he replied.

"It's our time and we deserve a right to be heard, the ninety-nine percent need to have voice and with you that voice gets a lot louder." Calvin Lacker walked from the podium to rapturous applause.

Zola grabbed at Xavier's arm before he had time to resist, "Come with me," she said firmly.

She directed him past the platform to a group of men gathered together talking to one another, "Citizen Rumbaquello!" she called, and immediately one of the group turned and stared at her smiling broadly. He had noble, discerning features and wore a black suit, "Zola!"

"Rumbaquello, this is Xavier,"

"Xavier?"

"The graffiti artist!"

Rumbaquello, looked at Xavier, it seemed appraising him, "I see. I must admit he is not what I expected."

"This is my friend."

"Who is this guy?"snapped Xavier.

"Sorry, I do apologise, I should introduce myself my name is Cort Rumbaquello, I have organised this gathering so we could hear Citizen Lacker speak."

"He was wonderful," said Zola enthusiastically.

Rumbaquello turned to Xavier, his apparent lack of regard for his appearance seemingly forgotten, "And you? I do imagine you found his words interesting."

Xavier shrugged.

"The artwork you produce around The Hives is quite unique…surreal to our eyes. Why do you do it?" quizzed Rumbaquello.

"Why? Who are you to ask?" Xavier was already tiring of being in the limelight, inwardly sending Zola dirty looks.

"I just wanted to know why you do it, that is all," said Rumbaquello, placing a hand on Xavier's shoulder.

Xavier calmed down , it was not a great start but seeing Zola's anxiety he decided to cool down. It seemed this man was important to her, "I do it because I want to be seen, I want to be known and I want the people of The Hives to see my work. That is all."

"But there must be something else to it!" Rumbaquello pushed Xavier again for an answer.

"Every artist wants to be seen and be heard. I am no different from any artist throughout history who has done the same, male or female, be they a Grand Master or an existential abstract artist or a graffiti artist, they do it for one reason to express themselves and they just do it."

Rumbaquello laughed out loud, ecstatic at Xavier's spontaneous response.

"It is like a shout I suppose saying to people that I exist, I am here," continued Xavier.

"And your passion and inspiration is quite formidable."

"My inspiration is that blue marble ball over there that we see every morning when we wake up in our trans-habs." Xavier felt Rumbaquello's enthusiasm allowing him to let his guard down but just a little.

"Yes, the little blue dot, the one we can see but never ever touch."

"The one that I am obsessed with," Xavier smiled at Zola with a look of growing admiration.

"Do you believe it is a haunted spirit world infested with the ghosts of those left behind?" quizzed Rumbaquello.

"What? The Shadows? It's complete mumbo jumbo Citizen Rumbaquello...I got that word from an Edu-Imp by the way,"

"I just wonder what it must be like to have lived there."

"I wonder too, I wonder what its like now…do you buy the lie?" Rumbaquello asked.

"The lie that it is not suitable for us humans to return there? No, I don't."

"It is good enough for the Powers though!"

"Obviously, they are Powers and they can live where they want."

"Your work is very powerful and brave Xavier, I should be honoured to introduce you to our guest," Rumbaquello turned from Xavier and Zola and tapped the shoulder of Calvin Lacker who had been standing just behind them.

"This, Calvin is the infamous graffiti writer in the flesh - Xavier Miro."

"Miro, your namesake was an artist centuries ago," said Lacker, with a charismatic smile.

"Yes, that's right Citizen Lacker how could I not have known of Joan Miro, he was a pioneer of political and abstract expressionism not unlike yourself."

Lacker and Rumbaquello laughed. Lacker turned to Zola, "And you are?"

"Zola Capello," she replied.

"Any relation to Fabian and Amber Capello?"

"Yes, I cannot escape the name," Zola frowned, "I am their youngest, Citizen Lacker."

"They are a wonderful couple, committed to the Pax Humana," Lacker said, with sincerity, "but we are a group who hold different views to those of your parents. We believe that the one percent need to listen to the ninety-nine percent to make up our own mind."

"I have had an interest in Civilisation for a long time," Zola replied.

"I am glad to hear it," replied Lacker, "and thank you for bringing your friend."

Xavier shrugged, crossing his arms to form an X like Lacker had done in the speech.

Lacker turned back to Xavier, "We have watched your work and it has given a strange sense of purpose and a tonic Xavier, it is not the sort of imagery one tends to see in The Hives, and yet you seem to be a company man. You work for the corporation, you are part of Nu Humana it says so on your jacket." Lacker pointed at the NUHU logo and mission badge identifying his work station.

"I agree with some of what you have to say citizen, but for many people they are just happy to have a place to live and a place to work. They don't always want to change what they've got. They are happy where they are at."

"So true, it is a complacency, they are given the loaves and games like all the civilisations that have gone before. "

"Can you blame them?" Xavier responded, "without it where would we be?"

"No, I understand your view but that is not the answer."

"We are free to do whatever we are told to do, that's how it works here, right?"

"I love that old school dogma," Lacker laughed, "you see what they have done?"

"We have a very short time here so you may as well live it as it comes, we are not eternal," replied Xavier.

"Oh you would be surprised Xavier, some people are still around from before the Digital Dark Age and the Exodus!" exclaimed Lacker

"And who are they?" Zola enquired.

"They are your enemy, they are all of our enemies. Because it is not natural for something to live like they do."

"So you are not the terrorists we have been led to believe," said Xavier.

"The old maxim of one man's terrorist is another man's freedom fighter. I am not a terrorist, I am not evil."

"So what is evil?"

"Evil is more sinister, when we do not perceive the threat it possesses and when it comes knocking with a smile."

"Like the Air Authority?"

"Yes, just like the Air Authority."

"But isn't this all some kind of fool's errand? You will never get to Earth...none of us will."

Calvin Lacker paused then clutched Xavier, "One of us might, Xavier, one of us might. Never forget what they sold mankind to get us to leave Earth in the first place...what was it?"

Xavier stared at Lacker blankly.

"One word...hope! You have to have hope young man. You have to believe that what is out there is better than what you have here. You just have to have hope."

Calvin Lacker embraced both Xavier and Zola, "You two be well and be safe and always keep your hope intact."

Zola began to cry, "I have hope, it is all I have."

"In the words of one of history's greatest men, Martin Luther King who centuries ago fought for the civil rights of his fellow humans, 'I might not get there with you, but I want you to know that we as a people will get to the Promised Land'."

Lacker kissed Zola on the forehead and turned back to Rumbaquello who smiled and escorted him back into the huddle of other people waiting to meet the speaker.

"I'll see you both around again soon," said Rumbaquello as he walked away.

Zola took Xavier's hand and guided him out towards a stairway which provided a route to the exits and elevators.

"That was pretty amazing," said Zola, her eyes filled with tears of joy, clearly overwhelmed at meeting Calvin Lacker.

"You know your way back pretty good."

Zola nodded then stuck out her tongue, then laughed, "I sure do, Citizen Graffiti King."

Xavier looked up and saw the young man who they had shared the elevator with passing by him in the opposite direction down some steps. He stared at Xavier momentarily and smiled, his eyes glazed yet possessing the slightest hint of anxiety.

"We should get out of here Zola," Xavier said with some urgency, he sensed something was not right and tugging at Zola's arm, he led her out to move more quickly. He pushed

Zola forward and stood behind her before looking quickly back in the direction they had came.

The young man was now stood next to Calvin Lacker and the group of people he was engaged in conversation with. Calvin noticed his presence and turned towards him and smiled. The young man smiled back as a glittering blue light emanated from his body. In an instant a terrific white light engulfed the activists and Calvin, who all seemed to shudder for a split-second before disintegrating. A ripple of air ballooned around them before travelling up and across the ceiling followed by the boom of an explosion. Xavier pushed Zola down to the floor as a sonic wave of debris ejected from the group. For a moment only, there was silence. Followed by the sounds of carnage.

The bellow of the explosion was now replaced by the screams and shouts of people injured and in shock. The dead, and there were many, made no sound. Xavier checked Zola and helped her to her feet.

"Are you OK?"

Zola was trembling and bleeding from a small cut to her forehead, "Yes," she replied brushing herself down.

"You have a small cut to your head but you will be okay," replied Xavier, wiping the blood away, "this place will be crawling with cops and security, we need to get out of here."

He took Zola by the hand, spotting a safety access hatchway which he knew would be their only escape and guided her towards it.

"Get your safety helmet on," demanded Xavier. Everyone in Genesis had a safety helmet with them in case of blowouts and pressure outages. It allowed the user a precious few minutes of air when an emergency happened.

"I can't go in there," Zola was panicked, "I am really scared of confined spaces."

"For real?" Xavier looked perplexed.

"Really, I can't!"

"Well, we are going to die then!"

Zola looked at Xavier and then at the hatch, "I need you to hold onto me tight as soon as we get through this hatch okay!"

"Fine. Done," said Xavier.

Xavier placed his own helmet on his head. "Just hold me tight Xavier once we're in there please,"said Zola as she closed her eyes allowing him to lead her into the small entrance which led into a pipe running alongside the elevator.

Inside the pipe Xavier wrapped his arms around Zola who was now shaking uncontrollably. Tenderly he made sure her safety helmet was clicked into place before looking up at the tube above him.

"It will either suck us up or suck us down," he kicked at a panel below him before reaching into his bag and pulling out a small firearm, a bolt gun from the docks.

"Okay, whatever!" said Zola, her eyes firmly shut.

"The panel's no use, it won't budge!" Xavier took aim at another panel above him, "Got to see if I can get that panel open." He kicked and shot at the same time but nothing happened. He realised he had only two shots left, so he attached his harness to Zola, "Hold on Zola!"

"Don't worry I'm holding on Xavier," she replied, in barely a whisper.

With one tremendous kick, he fired the last bolt skyward hoping that it would find its target. There was a tremendous shudder then a rumble below their feet and like a hose emptying all of its water in one go, suddenly they flew upwards and away from the destruction of the lone bomber.

★★★★★

Xavier lay in the bed of his trans-hab staring at the walls with the constant purr of the air conditioning units ringing in his ears, the words of Calvin Lacker racing through his mind.

His face and smile etched into his memory in the last conversation and moments before his assassination by the suicide bomber. Much as he tried he could not fully remove the distant and petrified expression of his killer and recalled their brief exchange in the elevator.

Could I have stopped him? Xavier thought to himself…not a chance.

In truth it had not crossed his mind. He had not known what was to occur but if he had known, surely he would have been able to stop the guy. Xavier was plagued by the fact he could not stop the deaths of so many. The bomber had been a boy, no older than sixteen years of age.

Where had he come from? One of the colonies or one of the academies closer to home? Wherever he had been raised who had been able to indoctrinate him so?

"Hey!" his thoughts were interrupted by Zola laying next to him.

"Are you okay?"

"Not really, that was so horrendous, I cannot believe what just happened."

"Cold blooded murder!"

"Calvin Lacker murdered before us…he has been an inspiration."

"It is just plain wrong! Nobody deserves to go out like that for saying what they feel!"

"Xavier, he obviously made an impression on you in just one meeting," said Zola, pressing his hand.

"I did know who he was, I was just never interested in what I thought he was all about."

"He was everything that you are about Xavi!"

"I know that now," Xavier said quietly, "I just never paid attention to what he had to say."

"Why?"

"I don't know, it seems so stupid now but sometimes isn't ignorance bliss! To question authority or worry about things."

"Happy in your bubble!" she sighed.

"You know Zola you are the one who has fought against your parents all the while and have always had a problem with the system and look where you have grown up?"

"I went to the same academy as you and work in ArkLight like you, I know."

"You have had the privilege of growing up in Valhalla, those beautiful executive suites of apartments and gardens. It's not exactly The Hives is it?"

"Well we aren't in Nu Venezia or one the High Pioneer colonies," snapped Zola, despite herself.

"You know you could have lived on a High Pioneer colony if your parents had chosen to, but they chose instead to be down with the Pax Humana and live close to the rest of us in a nice cosy apartment close enough to the ghetto to be 'of the people' though not in it!"

"Don't talk about my parents Xavier!"

"Why not? You're always slating them!"

"I do not," Zola paused, "okay I do but they are so much a part of the system and they like it here."

"Everyone else likes it here. Perhaps I'm actually happy with my life here? I've got food and I can eat, I've got clothes, we have stores to shop in, bars to drink in, places to go and spend vacation time. I have my souped up Aqua Terra and fly around the lanes and the G-Loop, I can hang out with my friends and play my music through my Bom-Barras sound system at full blast so you know I am pretty happy."

"But we are prisoners Xavier, we cannot leave here."

"I cannot leave here…you can!"

"What do you mean by that?"

"You could go to another colony or board an Ark whenever you wanted."

"But I don't want to do that...you want to go to Earth right?"

"Doesn't everybody?" Xavier pondered for a second.

"No, I don't think they do Xavier...most people are happy here biding time for an Ark even though they know they will never leave here, why would anyone want to go to Earth?"

"Why wouldn't you?"

"Earth is such a scary place!"

"Scary? What's scary about it?" laughed Xavier.

"You have to get past the Celestial Gate for one thing!"

"So Zola, a mesh of vehicle sized mines with laser guidance systems, high explosive limpet charges, thermo nuclear devices, laser cannons, interceptor strike craft, a network of sonic devices built to repel stray asteroids and space debris, a battery of fortresses containing over fifty-thousand defence androids and a thousand Earth Security Patrols armed to the teeth."

Zola could not help but break into a fit of giggles, "Is that all they've got?"

"I know right!" said Xavier, "Pussies!"

"We have everything we want here don't we?"

"Yes, we do but we also have a system that kills people and broadcasts it on TV gameshows," replied Xavier.

"But Xavier, you watch it!"

"Guilty as charged!"

"It is shocking entertainment and cruelty to poor people that my parents have also turned a blind eye to."

"State sanctioned execution…Air Authority, Genesis State Police, Colony Militias, Tigernauts, Dragonauts, Humanauts, corporate slayings, political slayings, drug rings, Implant gangs, pirate marauders, tearaway juvenile gangs…the list goes on!"

"And you like it here?"

"Zola, its the only home we've ever known. We have no way of knowing what's better!"

Zola could not help but laugh out loud, "You make me howl you know that."

She kissed Xavier.

"You can't please all of the people all of the time."

"You are crazy you know that…what you going to do now, spray some cargo ship or a freighter?"

Xavier paused for a second then looked directly at Zola, "No, with your help I can do something that will make those Civilisation people freak the fuck out! Something so big and monumental that every person in this solar system will see it. It will make their hairs stand on end and make Calvin Lacker a martyr and his death a turning point."

"I will do whatever it is to help you Xavier, you know that."

"The message I will send them will make them quake, I will show them what Xavier Miro can do," he replied, defiantly.

★★★★★

14
Precinct 4-52

P recinct 4-52 of the Genesis Federal Police held inmates who were seen more as a pesky nuisance than a real problem to the State or the Pax Humana. It was there to oversee hooliganism and delinquent youths mainly and the all too familiar domestic disturbances between warring families. Add to that, a little petty larceny and tipping off zoned out druggies to the Air Authority to be whacked for non-conformity, life for the cops here was no thrill. They could beat up low grade criminals, drunks or surly rapscallions giving them too much lip with no fear of any consequence . But basically, the place was a hang out for thuggish uniformed *shit-kickers* to flex their muscles and impose their bullying on members of the general public who they deemed out of order.

A detention centre adjacent to the precinct housed hundreds of transgressors who were kept for a short period of time for trivial matters in small cubicles, where they were either beaten black and blue or forced to listen to loud pounding electronic music continually, making them good for nothing by the time they left.

In the main block a garrison of licensed, badge wearing hoodlums cosied together eating Zug O'Noodles and waiting for any trouble that might arise. A bank of screens and holo-maps ran down one side of the main control room and monitored the movements of people going about their daily business. This had been the case for centuries. Hundreds of thousands of cameras watched every movement of the citizens of The Hives. It was true to say that for all those drones, spies-in-the-skies, closed circuit monitors and security systems, people still committed crimes and got away with committing crimes.

Officer Vigilant O'Donahue sat eating a large pot of noodles while dipping the remnants of his Sloppy Schmugs sandwich into a bowl of soup. His feet were laid upon his desk staring into nowhere, utterly oblivious to the comings and goings of the Landings on this section of The Hives. It was a quiet time now, just before the changeover in shifts, so he had let his colleagues leave early. Before some other team of social inadequates would come in and take over from his squad, and that was just fine with him. As O'Donahue took another bite from his sandwich, the sauce dribbling down the front of his uniform he was distracted by a powerful booming voice behind him, "What is your name officer?"

"Is that you Kenny, stop messing with me will ya!" he replied.

O'Donahue turned around to face whoever it was. He could feel his legs turning to jelly and his brain registering the high probability of a coronary thrombosis as before him stood the ominous presence of Governor Titus Haq and Carlos Zagrostine. He could also sense that they were not alone. O'Donahue shook his head and rubbed his eyes.

"What is your name man?" Titus demanded.

"O'Donahue, sir," he managed to splutter out.

"When did this start happening?" demanded Haq, gesturing to a video screen of a landing covered in local gang graffiti.

"What sir?" O'Donahue replied, placing his sloppy sandwich down on his desk and wiping his hands on his shirt.

"The graffiti around The Hives, you imbecile, Are you that stupid that you haven't noticed."

O'Donahue shook his head for the second time.

"Sorry sir I don't comprehend," he replied nervously, "We have had graffiti in The Hives for ages sir,"

"What do you mean ages? How long man? Be precise," Haq was impatient for an answer.

O'Donahue had been on surveillance duties for twenty years and took graffiti to be a form of boredom and gang demarcation for The Hives dwellers. If they caught someone red-handed then they would clobber them, but he had other more pressing things to deal with, like day to day life and trying to get on an Ark with the rest of his family.

"We have had graffiti all over the place for years sir, gang related, marking their territory…"

"No, you damned fool, this dissident, seditionary art, is a blatant call to arms you clot!" Haq placed a small box upon the desk which projected a selection of Xavier's artwork which Zagrostine had provided him with.

The officer looked at the images, "I mean this happens a lot sir,"

"It happens a lot!" Haq was incensed, "This is the 26th Century, we have the most sophisticated security systems in the history of mankind and you tell me that this happens a lot and you cannot track down and identify the perpetrator?"

As the images of Xavier's artwork flashed before them O'Donahue shrugged.

Haq banged his fist on the table, "How could this happen?"

"We have tried to track this guy down in the past," he ventured weakly.

Oblivious of the meaning of this artwork conveyed to the corporations.

"Really?" said Titus maliciously then turned to Zagrostine, "I need to speak with Ignatius Perigord about utilising the Air Authority in this sector."

"I will contact him immediately."

"Maybe, if we closed down the air supply in a few of these housing projects they might be persuaded to point us in the direction of this miscreant," snarled Haq.

Suddenly Haq turned around and with incredible force grabbed the sweating officer by the collar and threw him to the floor, "Now listen to this very carefully, tell all your crew of bullyboy cops to pull their fingers out and find this fucking graffiti artist."

"Sir," muttered O'Donahue, clearly terrified, "could I just tell you something…we have tried to locate the culprits in the past but nothing comes up from the database."

"Nothing? Well doesn't that make it even more suspicious"

"I know sir, I thought it was just a glitch."

"Everyone has a record don't they?"

"Not this guy!"

"Impossible…how can anyone live in The Hives without a file and remain undetected?" fumed Haq, "Is he being protected by someone?"

"I don't know sir, but we have nothing on file."

"Zagrostine, let's take a look at why there is no file on this person"

"Immediately," Zagrostine smirked, typing some notes into a small handheld device.

"Get up you piece of shit!" Haq pulled the grovelling and sobbing O'Donahue up from the floor and pushed him back on his seat wiping his hands on the remaining napkins on the desk.

O'Donahue gulped and nodded unable to even respond vocally.

Zagrostine grinned at him and drew his finger across his neck.

Haq glared at O'Donahue, "I need to introduce you to an old friend."

It was like something from a nightmare, two figures stepped from behind the Governor one clad in a black decaying space suit with its helmet still attached and the visor a swirling mist forming an unrecognisable face. The other was an equally terrifying presence, that of Magnus Bowser.

"This is Lucien Ferrer and his new wunderkind Magnus."

As well as being the Governor of Genesis, Titus Haq was also bestowed the role of Guardian of The Shadows, which his clone father had passed to him. It was one he relished and his alliance with something so dominant, affirmed his own capabilities. For many, the existence of The Shadows was seen as pure rumour, a remnant from a bygone era, a macabre leftover from the Exodus.

"You see, they are not just Earthbound beings!" seethed Haq as he turned to O'Donahue, "they have slipped Earth's coil and are very much here in Genesis."

O'Donahue tried to close his eyes but they sprang open again, "I'm... I'm... so sorry Governor Haq... please... please," he pleaded.

"That's more like it," Titus calmed a little, yet his tone remained menacing, "I should have you thrown out of an airlock and boiled alive. But I am merciful and want you to tell everyone you know that Shadows exist. Now I want this person apprehended immediately," he said, pointing at the screens showing Xavier's work, "or else I will have you all executed."

O'Donahue could not control himself, "Oh, you are so merciful...thank you Governor, for being so forgiving, we will find whoever it is...thank you," he tried to choke back the tears of relief as sweat poured from his forehead.

It had all happened in a matter of minutes. Lucien Ferrer and Magnus Bowser seemed to vanish and then Titus turned and left followed by Zagrostine, leaving a terror-stricken O'Donahue to collapse to the floor gasping for air.

Chris Abbot

★★★★★

15
K-O-K

G iant holographic letters spelling K-O-K sprang from the canopy of the famous Kaiser O'Keefe Body Work Shop as a testament to glitz and glamour. The garishly looking liquid, matter and gas signs designed by the one and only Xavier Miro performed a continual and diverse sequence of fluid motion advertising the renowned solar surfer and his wares.

Inside the entrance paraded a bevy of scantily clad girls, all beautiful and all wearing little but heels and the odd piece of clothing.

They received new customers to the showroom where an assortment of Rods were displayed, all resplendent and souped up by Kaiser O'Keefe and his consummate team of professional assistants. Many of his clients were workers back from smashing rocks and drilling holes for the last five years on an asteroid. The dazzling array of Rods sat gleaming for every discerning astronaut with time to kill and newly found bounty from spending time out on the Belt.

It was boom time out on the Belt. If you were prepared to haul your ass the couple of hundred million kilometres to get there, endure isolation, appalling working conditions, the risk of radiation sickness, possible cannibalism and inter-company warfare, then there was a fortune to be made. Hundreds of thousands of hopefuls would set off to seek their fortune and work for one of the mining federations based out there. The freezing depths of space seemed as appealing as a crack in your visor or an itch on the end of nose with your helmet shut, but the lure of prosperity was there for many. To Xavier, it seemed a long way to travel, even the fact that there were colonies of a few million plus didn't sweeten the idea of living in these remote locations for Xavier or for that matter his cronies.

The floor of the showroom gleamed underfoot, a sheer sheen looking quite treacherous and slippery with stubby little servo droids continually whirring round polishing every nook and cranny.

"Can I help at all?" asked one of the gorgeous hostesses cautiously, as Xavier and Jericho bounded across the floor dressed in rigger boots, workwear and harnesses, out of place within the confines of this gleaming spacecraft hall.

"No, we're fine!" replied Xavier, lifting his hand to rebuff her advances.

"Where do you want to go sir?" she asked again, a little more aggressively.

"Its fine. We're friends of Kaisers" Jericho responded. It was obvious from her face that she did not believe them, her rouge lipstick screwed up and she immediately signalled over two burly security men. Jericho and Xavier brushed past her with a polite cough as Jericho lied, "Ahem, I think you will find Kaiser is expecting us."

The two security men accompanied by a further two armed robo-guards appeared either side of them, "Your business here?" asked one of the guards, placing his hand on Xavier's chest and forcing him to stop in his tracks.

"I'm here to see Kaiser, I am Xavier Miro and this is my friend Jericho Chong."

With that the security guard relaxed his arm, "I know you. They're good, let 'em through," he winked, waving his colleagues off and ushering Xavier and Jericho from the showroom into the workshop itself.

Here, before them on hydraulic ramps were one hundred plus Rods all in different states of repair. Some were there to be remodelled but most were victims of collisions or debris strikes that were all too common on The Gloop and throughout Genesis. Panels were being cut away and new sections attached, automative repair crews jostled with one another and spare parts seemed to fly from crates towards pre ordained targets, to be fixed to the specific Rod.

Xavier and Jericho were recognised by many of the human staffers working in the shop. Robots and droids were there for all the heavy duty working but the artistic fabrication of metals, plastics and carbons could only be done by human beings together with the custom paint works where talents like Xavier's had come to the fore.

"Where is the big man?" asked Jericho to one of the body shop mechanics. From a doorway above the shop the frame of a huge man loomed, "I'm here kids!"

Kaiser O'Keefe was a big man, not only in stature but also in character. His presence commanded the room yet he was always able to laugh at himself with a little joke or a prank. Maybe that was why he was so popular amongst young and old of The Hives. For years ,he had been one of the most revered sportsmen in Genesis and had gained an admiring public with his daredevil feats of solar surfing, asteroid rod-rallying and lunar crater bob-sleighing. It was a miracle he was still alive.

Hailing from one of the trans-habs on the other side of The Hives, Kaiser O'Keefe was himself an icon and legend amongst the dwellers of Genesis. He was a tall, handsome, strong man, with jet black, close cropped hair and a roguish face. His athletic displays had found him many female admirers throughout Genesis after many years of wowing crowds with his daredevil displays. His initials, K-O-K, had become common parlance and part of Can Com speak. Kaiser would take normal Rods and make them into works of art, something Xavier could appreciate. A standard utility space Rod suitable for zooming around The Cannery would become, in Kaiser O'Keefe's yard, a souped up beast of engineering.

Kaiser's smile was warm and welcoming and his thick black hair was cut into a flat top. His body showed the wear and tear from his exploits but his arms and chest were still muscular in his white t-shirt.

"Welcome ladies, how can I help you?" his deep brogue returned and Kaiser gestured for them to come into his office, where there was a huge desk and comfy couches where they could flop down and relax, "Messieurs Miro and Chong. That could be a comedy double act you know," said Kaiser.

Jericho laughed as he took a seat, "Ha! Very funny!"

"I took an Edu-Imp the other night about comedic double acts in the early part of the 20th century, Abbott & Costello, Bing Crosby and Bob Hope but my favourite and you two are it…Laurel & Hardy!"

Xavier and Jericho looked at one another bemused then shrugged their shoulders.

"But we have more pressing matters to discuss - what a fine mess you've got yourselves into!" said Kaiser, his amiable tone now tinged with some displeasure.

"What do you mean Kaiser?" asked Xavier, concerned.

"I've had the police all over this place. Seems you guys did a piece of Graf over in one of the sectors where an undercover unit was operating, spy drones the lot, and you Mister Chong got ID'd."

"What?" Jericho was alarmed but played it cool.

"You ain't been picked up yet boy! But they are waiting, you mark my words," said Kaiser.

"Well, I haven't been picked up yet,"mumbled Jericho.

"You take too many risks boy, you're too loud and you are too flash!" shouted Kaiser.

"Look who's talking about flash!" snapped Jericho.

Kaiser launched from his chair and raised his hand to slap Jericho stopping only a few centimetres from his face. He would surely have broken Jericho's jaw if he made contact.

"I son, have earned the right to be flash!"

"I think we need to calm down here and just deal with the facts," Xavier said, stepping in-between the pair.

"The fact is, I had the police here looking for info on a Kaiser O'Keefe souped up Rod seen spraying a piece. They reported two rods but for some reason Xavier's never showed up on their systems just an unregistered one whose last owner happened to be flyboy here," Kaiser continued fuming.

Jericho pulled at his under-suit around his neck.

"That's right boy, I had those bastards here for two hours checking the workshop and going through stuff that I don't need them going through, you hear?"

"We hear you Kaiser," said Xavier calmly.

"All I need now is those Air Authority goons turning up and prying into who works where and who does what, you know you got a problem then. I am only here today because of my own hard work. I've stayed out of trouble! I don't need this heat."

" Kaiser, you have always helped me along the way and it is out of my gratitude to you that I did you paint jobs on the rods, so you know we would not want to get you into anything," Xavier said.

"Its true Xavier, you have always been a great comrade," Kaiser said, starting to calm down little.

"We built the most amazing rod in Aqua Terra and we have always had a great time hanging out and I am truly sorry to have put you in this position."

"Thanks Xavier but the truth is I have more than enough stuff going on behind the scenes here to get me whacked, so I need you guys to get this heat off me."

"I'm sorry to have to say what I'm going to say guys but I have a good life here and I just can't have any snooping from the authorities or any of that shit," Kaiser looked apologetic as he said the next part, "I don't ever want to see you walk through that showroom again. You hear?"

Jericho turned to Xavier who looked upset. After a moments silence he nodded, "Sure Kaiser, we totally get it."

"Now what is it you want today?" Kaiser was actually a big softy when handled right and Xavier felt he knew how to deal with him. Jericho sat quietly looking at the floor in front of him.

"I wondered if you could hook me up with some refills for Aqua Terra, I have a special piece I want to do and really put some of those jack-offs in their place."

"What you thinking?"

"Big!" replied Xavier, a smile spreading across his face, his eyes alive.

"I need some Edwards & Wayne multi-coloured laser matter spray with Chu&Chang Company liqui-mount and Do or Dye exploding pigment gas balls."

"Damn!" exclaimed Kaiser, "Is that all? You need to be coming and doing some work for me."

"This is a big piece, a special piece, this will wake people and shake people," Xavier's excitement was palpable, and as a result infectious. Kaiser could not help but smile.

"You're the man, Xavier!" he said, high-fiving him, "My man, you really gotta be careful or I'm going to get pinched, I mean it. You need to start being vigilant. Watch your back, at all times."

He pulled Xavier close to him and whispered, "Be careful of Jericho, he is careless, a total idiot at times and he takes too many risks. It's about being on your game, boy. Attention to detail is what counts and that means covering your ass."

Xavier pulled away and looked over to Jericho who was fumbling with his boots, unaware of anything being said. Xavier loved Jericho like a brother and loved his company. They had great laughs together and shared a mutual interest in girls and graffiti but there were times when Xavier just deep down knew that one day he would be let down by his friend.

"I've been working hard at DF118. We are nearing completion on this Ark and I have something special in mind," confided Xavier, "then the other night, Zola took me to one of those Civilization gatherings."

"What!" exclaimed Kaiser, "Are you crazy? Those things are fucking crawling with cops and snoops!"

"I saw the speaker Calvin Lacker!"

"They blew the fucker up!"

"I saw the kid who did it He spoke to me, looked me in the eye and then he blew himself to pieces."

"Xavier, this is some crazy shit."

"But the thing is Kaiser, before he was assassinated Lacker spoke to all those gathered about me...my work...he was talking about how inspiring it was."

Kaiser interrupted him, "Right, get the fuck out of here and do what you got to do but keep me out of that Civilization rebellion shit!"

Xavier nodded.

"Are you still having those dreams?" Kaiser asked, holding Xavier by the arms.

Again Xavier nodded.

"Well, keep them coming, because you are creating some crazy stuff out there!" Kaiser winked, "I've really heard it all now, your graffiti inspiring Civilization, damn. And hey it's okay to bring Aqua Terra round and I'll get her loaded up. No worries."

"K-O-K Chief!" Xavier replied. He knew Kaiser would load him up with what he needed and with his supplies sorted out he was ready to create a piece that would blow peoples' minds.

"K-O-K"

"Thanks Kaiser," said Xavier.

"No problem kid, but remember its really edgy out there. The Air Authority and The Hives police are jumpy. More so than usual so please be careful."

"You know I always fly straight," Xavier replied.

"Then just stay level."

Jericho jumped from his seat, "Are you guys finished yet?"

"Yes, we are," Kaiser straightened himself up and placed an arm around Xavier and then Jericho, gently pushing their heads together, "Now get the hell out of here."

As they turned to leave Kaiser called them back, "Hey I almost forgot, my man with the Edu-Imps on the Cathay Wheel discovered a really good haul. I have a gift for you," Kaiser walked to his desk, opened a black wooden box taking two phials from inside.

"Is that wood?" asked Jericho, staring down at the mahogany and ebony box.

"Yes, all the way from Earth," Kaiser then passed the phials to Xavier, "Here, take these!"

"What about me?" asked Jericho, upset he had not been given a gift.

"Sorry boy, nothing for you," snapped Kaiser, "these are for Miro only."

Xavier placed them inside his jacket and gave Kaiser a hug. "They will help with the dreams and with the visions," Kaiser said in his ear.

"They're Direct Memory Lifts taken from a donor's memory centuries ago and then synthesised for consumption. They are from your favourite era," Kaiser added.

"So nothing for me?" Jericho asked again.

"Again, no! Now really…get the hell out here!"

*****

16
Thanks for The Memories

Xavier loved the feeling moments before the Edu-Imp kicked in, the butterflies in his stomach and the warmth that seemed to overcome your body just as it began to hit. Edu-Imps worked on many different levels, making you either regress into the memory or connecting your synapses within your brain and making your cortex come to life. Ramming it, so to speak, with blueprints, templates and procedures for the end user to utilise. The British Library and the British Museum, The Louvre, The Met, Oxford and Cambridge, MIT and Harvard, Stanford, The Smithsonian and Berkeley were amongst a few of the great world libraries, museums and educational institutions during the 21st century who combined forces to amass the greatest database of knowledge known to man.

The gift from Kaiser O'Keefe lay in Xavier's hand, no bigger than a small pebble. If he held it to his eye and stared into the contents of the clear container he would see a crystalline liquid with a faint colour spectrum. These were regressive implants, a source of high entertainment and also, enlightenment to Xavier.

"So, you are giving me one, right!" Jericho pleaded.

"No man, I can't give you one of these," replied Xavier firmly.

"What the hell!" Jericho persisted. Xavier remembered what Kaiser had said. Even though Jericho was his best friend, they were for him alone.

"Kaiser obviously has his reasons," said Xavier, "I'm sorry dude, but he said not to give them to you."

"I cannot believe you are going to listen to that old man," Jericho spat with contempt, "I mean, what is it with you and these guys? Kaiser and Old Man Ray, it's unhealthy man!"

"Jericho, you are my dear and trusted friend. So too are Ray and Kaiser, do not for one minute think I would not want you to share this experience, but there is obviously a reason why you shouldn't take this, perhaps you could try to respect that."

"I don't get why you always seem to get the funky Edu-Imps from Kaiser and I just have to stand by and see you ride the brain waves," Jericho added petulantly.

"Cerebral curls are what we all want to ride but sometimes, like you know too well, they can be a bumpy ride," Xavier patted Jericho's arm. Regressive therapy had been a part of psycho-analysis for centuries and in Edu - Imp form it was not always guaranteed how they might affect the person. The memories could have different consequences for each and every one who took them. Fears and phobias lurked within every mind, and a strong state of health and mind was needed to ingest someone else's.

Jericho had had a couple of close calls in the past. This had caused him to leave Genesis for a while and work on an asteroid colony which itself raises all manner of temptations and vices. The outer colonies were the boonies for anyone from Genesis, but unless you were shipping to Debris permanently or could get a ticket to the moon and one of its colonies, then a few years breaking rocks could give you some much needed respite.

"Dude, Remember the incident with the dog?" Xavier gently reminded his friend, softening it by laughing, "That was crazy man!" Jericho laughed back at his friend, although his face showed tell-tale signs of anxiety.

"That's why you don't do them."

"I didn't even know what a dog was. Like who would up here?" Jericho shrugged his shoulders, unamused that Xavier was laughing.

"It was that tiny little terrier that was yelping."

"Dogs freaking out! Anyway I just got the wrong waves from some klutz who had a fear of dogs."

"We all react differently Jericho. Remember I had an incident with a dog once as well."

Jericho smiled a little, "Oh yeah, that's right."

"Look, I know you want to come on this one but who knows what will be there," Xavier continued to reassure Jericho, "just do me a favour. Watch out for me."

It was sometimes better to do the illegal Edu-Imps with somebody around so that if you did go taking your space helmet off or opening an airlock, they could help you. Jericho's episodes were attributed to very unstable Edu-Imps bought from pedlars out in Debris or by unscrupulous Memory Traders on The Cathay Wheel who copied them from copies allowing the built-in safety mechanisms to become obsolete. Jericho's fondness for Zug juice probably didn't help matters and living on The Hives for three decades would be enough to send anyone off their rocker.

Xavier had had hundreds if not thousands of Edu-Imps over the years but had never experienced a DML. Xavier knew he had the best of the best in his hands with grade A DML's or Direct Memory Lifts which were siphoned straight from the memory of the donor. They were the direct memories of the donor now synthesised into a liquid for a user to take. It was difficult to know exactly what that person would experience but for Xavier that was the thrill. Xavier sat on his seat looking towards Jericho then drew his tongue across his lips and smiled while counting down in his head…

Xavier was on a street corner of an Earth metropolis in the late twentieth century. He tried to get his bearings. He looked at the reflection of himself in a storefront window. He had now entered the stored memory of a person who had died probably five hundred years ago. Xavier forced himself to contain his emotions. He walked towards a news vendor who had newspapers, which Xavier recognised as an archaic medium of conveying information which he had heard of but never seen.

He could make out the old Earth-based English which had changed over time. The newspaper read 'New York Daily News, February 28, 1983.' He shook his head as the news vendor looked up at him, "You buying anything kid?" he growled at him.

Xavier became nervous. Could people see him as he was, as Xavier Miro, rigger at ArkLight Docks? He could see everything, up, down, sideways; there was no limit to what he could see or hear. These memories must have been grafted from them at a later date and banked in the Mind & Memory Depository of the Smithsonian along with millions of others.

A cry rang out, "Come on man. We're waiting for you!"

The shout came from a group of youths in their late teens, standing at the bottom of a set of stairs to the elevated subway. They began running up the stairs and Xavier followed. The youths ran and jumped a turnstile just as a subway train entered the platform. Xavier caught up and without any hesitation jumped into a carriage with the others. They were all laughing and dressed in what must have been the fashions of the day. Shell sneakers, jeans, caps and quilted body warmers, but no life support systems or regulatory space suits underneath. Xavier guessed his host must have been wearing the same attire and nothing too dissimilar, so sat down on a plastic seat adorned with graffiti. He could sense his heart beating a little faster. As Xavier examined the carriage and its passengers, it reminded him of being on the public Zoobs in

The Hives. The landings and trans-habs were all much the same, although you could tell certain differences like the air and space, but things did not feel too different. The graffiti left by the various gangs and artists throughout The Hives was similar in style. The letters may have been different and the language used varied as Can-Com was so popular throughout much of Genesis with the teens, but he could easily identify the early beginnings of this ritual marking.

"Who's going to The Roxy tonight?" a spotty Latino kid shouted at the top of his voice for the whole carriage to hear.
"Fab Five Freddy and Grandmaster Flash on the wheels of steel," said another turning to Xavier. Two of the youths were stood talking to one another. One carried a bag which contained cans of spray paint and the other held a box from which music emanated.
This is just like being back in The Hives, he thought.
"Hey Slice, we going to the same spot?"

"We're goin' a block before VC yard through our little hole and into the place to be, homes," Slice had chiselled features and wore his cap back to front. He started to jerk his body moving his hands and feet in a series of motions, "Pop that body…pop that body…I won't stop till I make my body pop!"
"Hey Skee! Show us how it's done!" Suddenly Xavier found his host leaping up from his chair as the sound of Boogie Down Bronx played. "Turn the ghetto blaster up," one of the crew yelled, as if it was not loud enough. The lyrics of the song filled the carriage and the host within whom Xavier was taking a ride then started to 'body pop' to the cheering group. Xavier

found his body jerking then without warning his whole body began contorting before he was almost flying up off the floor of the subway train.

Cool Johnski from the Freeze Force Crew
I came here to say a def rhyme for you
About the Boogie Down Bronx, it's a one of a kind
It's the place to be; it's a state of mind
But the guys out here, they really are crookin'
They snatch gold chains when the cops ain't lookin'
But what can I say? It's the place to be
It's where I stay in reality
So listen close and you all will hear
About the devestatin' body rocker of the year
Boogie Down Bronx, Boogie Down Bronx, Boogie
Boogie Down Bronx, Boogie Down Bronx, Boogie

As the doors to the subway train opened the crew ran laughing down the stairs and out onto the street. Yellow traffic lights hanging above the street changed from green to red above their heads as they dashed across a near deserted highway towards a large chain link and mesh fence.

Old boxes, sheets of cardboard and newspapers covered a small hole in the security perimeter which the crew crawled through on their bellies. They were in a yard where all the subway trains for the New York transit were stored overnight. The carriages all appeared to be grey and black in the night sky.

"Whose holdin' the paint, yo?" cried Slice. The host's memories were gradually trickling into his mind. Xavier realised his host name was Skee 22 and he was with a graffiti crew called the Bronx Yard Kings in the early 1980s in the city of New York. Through the memory influx he learnt that New York had been one of the main metropolitan areas of old Earth before it was flooded and abandoned in the 23rd Century, as he had already discovered. Xavier could still have his own thoughts even though he was in his host's mind and memory. Who was this Skee 22 and how had he come to have his mind copied and his memories stored? Xavier also found himself wondering how Kaiser O' Keefe was able to get such powerful uploads and implants.

"That's Krylon paint I got there, man!" said Slice, needing an audience, "Come on, keep up dude!" He was finding the clarity of this Memory Lift was immense. He was right where the action happened and it appeared that he was actually conversing with the subjects as opposed to being a passenger along for the ride. Someone had really ramped up the cortex connectivity and the biological decoding systems had been fully accelerated, giving the user a one on one experience. Xavier wondered if another person taking the same DML would have the same experience?

"Fuck yeah!" Xavier shouted and within minutes they had the holdall open and were busy sifting through the canisters of paint. Xavier was unaware which person was speaking, him or his host.

"Over there Skee, take that one," one of the crew shouted.

"Do the characters Skee, do the characters man! You're dope at that shit!" said Slice, his legs already straddling the sides of two carriages and beginning to line out his piece.

"Yeah, do the lizards or Cheech!" came another voice.

He picked up some cans and began to nervously do the first outlines. Xavier did not know whether he should do it or whether his host was already doing it for him. He wondered if he could influence his host and bring a piece of 26th Century spray art to the rough streets of the broken Bronx of the late 20th Century.

Whatever he did, his host seemed to oblige or vice versa. What started off as a lizard like cartoon creature seemed to take shape before them.

"Yeah, man that looks dope!"

"Those Vaughn Bodé characters are a trip man! For real!"

Skee or Xavier or whoever he was then took another two cans to fill in. He could feel how cold his hands were getting in this star-filled night.

One of the crew kept look out and checked his watch as the others painted. The hours went quickly and the Bronx Yard Kings only had a limited amount of time before the next shift of transit cops with their K9 units came on a circuit patrol of the rolling stock.

"Come on man, we got to get going!"

Xavier did not know what he should do or what would happen. Now he began to fill in but jumping down he searched through the bags of paint to find as many colours as he could carry. Then it was as if he took over his host in a strange and extraordinary interaction.

He started to spray in a style so furiously and artistically the rest of the crew stopped what they were doing to look at him at work.

Slice shook his head in disbelief "What the f…"

Xavier was busily spraying a Hives-style piece on a subway car in the twentieth century and the crew had never seen anything like it.

"Way to go Skee, that is some badass shit you are doing there."

"How you doing that, man?"

"That shit for real!"

Xavier sprayed with lines and dots and bursts and flashes leaving the rest of the gang gob-smacked watching silently as he finished his piece. The lizard had had a Xavier style makeover. Xavier had used his 26th Century spray skills and brought them to the Bronx. The image was unlike anything the crew had ever seen before.

"Skee, you were like possessed man! That shit is dope!" Slice said, his eyes taking in the amazing multi-coloured piece before him. There were shouts in the distance and then the sound of something that Xavier or his host dreaded…the barking of dogs.

The crew scrambled together the cans of paint and began running towards the hole in the fence. Xavier could feel his heart pounding, the fear starting to take over. He had to keep running just like in his dream and get away from the approaching dogs barking viciously that pursued them. In front of him, the members of the crew pushed their way through the hole in the fence as the dogs and their handlers ran down the tracks in pursuit. Xavier was the last to get through and could hear the dogs charging, getting ever closer. He thought he felt their hot breath around his ankles as his arms finally went through the hole, his heart feeling it was about to explode when he felt Slice and the others pull him through.

"Fucking dogs right!" the face of Jericho Chong stood before him laughing and looking impishly concerned, "You okay?"

Xavier looked at the familiar surroundings of his trans-hab and smiled. "That was wild!"

"Looks it, dude!"

Xavier held Jericho by his arms and stared into his face, "Let's go paint."

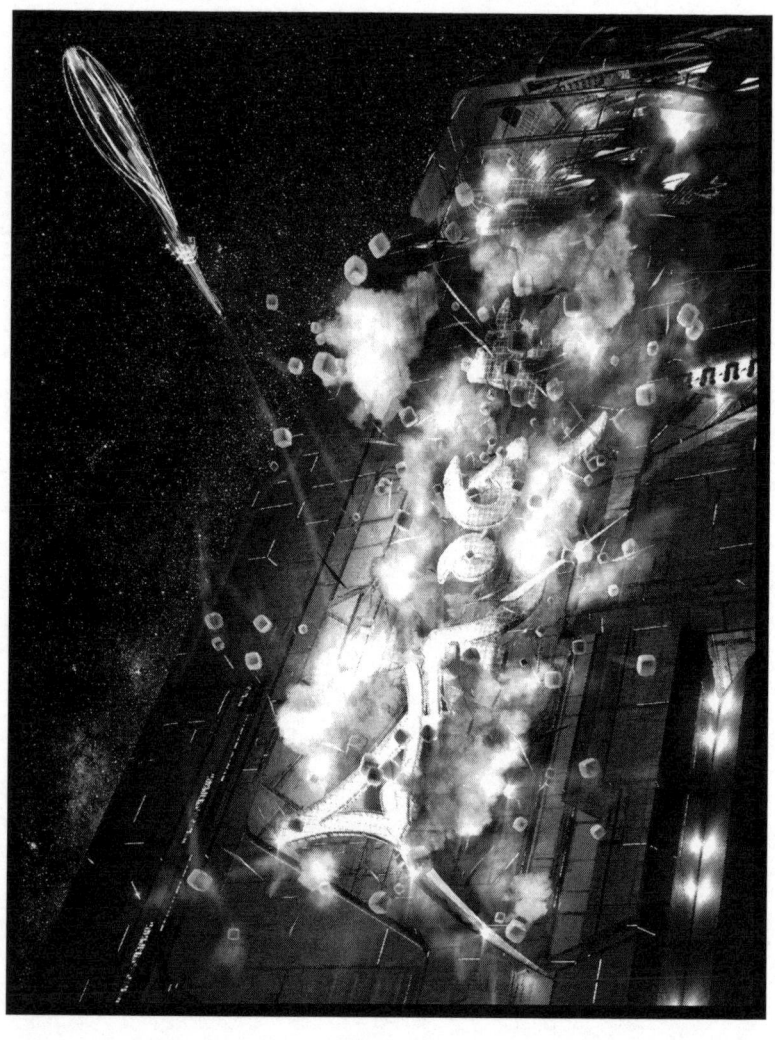

★★★★★

17

Tagging The Tamarinsk

"Greetings citizens, this is Claudia Furukawa at Bay DF118 ArkLight for the launch of the Tamarinsk, the latest Ark to leave the famous space docks of Genesis. All final checks are complete as we now await ignition, and for the great craft to emerge from her hangar. Gathered here today are thousands of people to send the mighty Ark off on her maiden voyage of discovery into the system of Proxima Centauri, taking mankind where it has never been before and spreading the spirit of humanity to new worlds and galaxies, creating the Pax Humana…."

Jericho Chong flew past Xavier, screaming "Let's do this!" into his headset.

"Hell yeah!" replied Xavier.

For the launch the security perimeter had the same defence systems found in most Nu Humana sites. Heavily armed ArkLight guards were supported by Nu Humana personnel endlessly monitoring the comings and goings of the workforce as well as the provisions and supplies required.

Normally it would be impossible for ArkLight workers to gain access to such an impregnable facility out of hours and during such a sensitive time but Xavier and Jericho were not challenged once and Xavier liked that. They passed the perimeter with an ArkLight Docks security team waving them through causing Xavier to smile and then they were finally into the yards of ArkLight, snooping around, the cloaking devices which they had fitted for their next task shielding them for the time being from any unwanted attention from ArkLight security or drones.

They passed down one of the illuminated keels of The Tamarinsk Ark that was nearing completion before its epic journey into the unknown. In the last few months hundreds of thousands of people, from adults to embryos, had been led or placed two by two into the belly of the great craft. Some would remain as DNA and embryos frozen for specific points in the journey, others would monitor the ship and live the rest of their lives as caretakers of this precious cargo until its destination end.

After proceeding down the keel for two kilometres, Xavier called over to Jericho, "This is the spot."

"Perfect," said Jericho.

"Go to the right of me about a klick and work diagonally from me, Jericho, and…" Xavier paused, " keep a look out for guards, will you?."

"You got it, Xavier," Jericho's Rod Warp Child descended and began to pull up near one of the engine exhausts, "I'm going to do my piece here," he continued.

"Be careful then, in case they decide to run an unplanned check of that engine...you might end up crispier than a booger in a solar surfer's helmet," joked Xavier, all too aware his friend had passed his suggested spot and was now dangerously close to the vent. That was Jericho for you.

Xavier turned Aqua Terra to face the steel of the Tamarinsk and cracked his neck on each side. He did this every time, it was his ritual. He extended his hands as if to play a piano and stretched and loosened his fingers. An array of screens appeared at either side of him. He placed his hands into what appeared to be floating gloves which were held out in front of him. He closed his eyes.

Aqua Terra moved slowly towards the hull of the Tamarinsk and from the front fuselage of the space rod, two doors opened with a whirr. Out of them came two nozzles that contained a magnetic paint and the supplies from Kaiser. These nozzles, combined with a laser, applied a coat of paint to a metal surface even in a vacuum.

Aqua Terra connected with Xavier. Firstly, a sensory implant reader ran a sequence locking them into the artwork. The piece was outlined with spaces and the basic design was mapped out in front of Xavier. Small rockets built into the fuselage of Aqua Terra tilted the craft in small bursts allowing her to manoeuvre in any direction. Aqua Terra seemed to glide in one flowing motion as Xavier controlled her and the designs flowing from within his mind. The Edu-Imps which originally alerted him to the different styles of graffiti writing kicked in, and the artwork began to take form.

Xavier began thickening the edges so his graffiti piece would become recognisable. Xavier was so close and Aqua Terra moved so smoothly and quickly alongside the Ark that he could not make out how it would finally look.

He knew it would be a beautiful piece, but at this moment, he had to use his better judgment to make sure things were right at this stage. His perspective was a blur as the Laz-Can operated at a high speed, changing colours, nozzles and flow, pushing the Rod to its absolute limit.

The cockpit of Aqua Terra was illuminated by the light of the design emanating from the control panel. He was looking at doing a relatively complicated piece, around three kilometres in length, so he needed to make sure that the drift of Aqua Terra, his speed and calculations were all correct. This was a serious undertaking. He had to be sure he was focused at all times.

"You are here with Claudia Furukawa for the launch of the Tamarinsk Ark. In the audience today are many dignitaries from the collective corporations that have helped contribute to this fine Life Ark enabling us all to enjoy human life in new territories, making mankind's presence known in all the developing worlds. As well as being shown throughout Genesis and the collective colonies, the launch is being broadcast live on the Moon and the outer colonies and asteroids that make up our great union of colonies. The Powers have sent their blessings from Earth for the safe and secure voyage to Proxima Centauri of the Tamarinsk, that the freedoms and glory of humanity is being taken to new planets so mankind can prosper and call the cosmos its own…"

With deft gestures, Xavier's hands, eyes and brain worked as one. He and Aqua Terra became symbiotic, Xavier was in a trance, a puppet master controlling his craft. It was all about the details and before long Xavier began to fly along adding the final strokes to the steel canvas. Time and experience had taught Xavier the maxim sometimes less is more. His pieces were always on a   grand scale but they contained what he believed necessary to get his message across to the population of Genesis. He was always in awe of how each composition came to life. The magic never ceased to enthral. The contours and base colours were all done and the lettering needed his attention. The nozzles were a medley of colours, altering the spray at such a rate that huge areas were covered in a matter of minutes.

The creation was complete. Xavier thought of all the impresarios who had gone before him, whose legacies had left such lasting impressions on human civilisation. He thought of Picasso, Da Vinci, Warhol, Rembrandt, Frida Kahlo, Canaletto, Van Gogh, Monet, Lempicka, Dali and his own namesake: Miro. Earth civilisation had given birth to so many artists whose ideas and visions had influenced the human spirit, inspired by what they had seen, to go and create art for themselves.

For a moment Xavier saw himself as a link to the long chain of artists from antiquity to now, to this moment, to him Xavier Miro and this leviathan of a spacecraft as his canvas. He hoped through his work his peers might feel that they, too, were important and they, too, had a voice. What had happened on Earth? What had happened to society? What had happened to the culture of a planet that, for thousands of years, had pushed itself forward creatively? Had human civilisation become so dumb that art and expression didn't matter? The force and power of art had been forgotten, it seemed to Xavier. The sheer majesty of the greatest works of art was now ignored. Art had been abandoned.

What was left? The High Pioneers and the Powers had continued to prosper in their own private worlds, but there were no museums or galleries in The Hives. How had humans ended up living in controlled, sterile and homogenised worlds, as subjugated and oppressed populations almost in the same way as they had five hundred years before?

Xavier felt as if something was painting through him. The colours, the shapes of all sizes, vivid and lurid hues told a story. Xavier was buzzing, pulsing along with Aqua Terra.

"...with the countdown commencing and as we await the tugs to pull away the protective structures that encase the Tamarinsk Ark, we can only dream of what lies in store for this great craft on this truly memorable journey in the history and advancement of human civilisation..."

The Tamarinsk was fully loaded with its cargo of living human beings and frozen human embryos used for artificial insemination on a new colony. Its voyage through the local 'neighbourhood' and the new planets awaited all those on board.

He had left his mark all over Genesis for all to see but this was different. Xavier had never done anything on this scale and never on anything as prominent as the Tamarinsk Ark. It was his Magnus opus, his Sistine Chapel. This was Xavier's masterpiece.

Aqua Terra moved to the bottom corner of the piece and Xavier signed it: XAVIA MMDLVII.

"Claudia Furukawa, anchorwoman for Channel 999 is live to ArkLight as the countdown reaches T minus 5 - 4 - 3 - 2 - 1..."

As the customary speeches and celebrations commenced, the Leviathan slipped from the dock. The Ark had been encased in an enormous holographic shroud obscuring Xavier and Jericho. Crowds gathered on viewing platforms and from the observation decks throughout Genesis cheered as sections of the Tamarinsk were unveiled. Shafts of brilliant light illuminated the craft's infrastructure as it was unveiled from its mooring and the gleaming steel and Nu Humana crest and logos glittered as the beams flickered up and down the drive units. Excitement grew from the cheering spectators and viewers watching from their trans-habs as the stasis and freight modules of the Ark were revealed.

Then everything changed. Not only on the Tamarinsk but for Xavier. It was as if time had stopped. A colossal piece of graffiti stretched along its entire hull. Earth in all her glory, animals and beasts so extraordinary looking to the residents of Genesis. Historical events depicting epic scenes were extended in vast panoramas documenting the conquistadors of ancient

Earth terrorising Aztec warriors, Eradication Squads during the Exodus subjugating fleeing citizens. A mixture of jackboots and jackals running amok in a technicolour tableau that was the mind of Xavier. The gasps were audible even in space. It would be a moment engraved forever in his mind. It was also an image that sent reverberations throughout Genesis.

In front of the assorted dignitaries, heads of corporations, scientists and the billions of citizens all over Genesis, the Moon and Mars, Xavier's colossal graffiti was splashed alongside the great Ark. Carlos Zagrostine turned to see Governor Haq's face turn almost purple with rage, "Find Xavier now!" he bellowed.

"This is Claudia Furukawa at the launch of The Tamarinsk Ark and to all you viewers in your trans-habs throughout Genesis we are witnessing the most amazing scenes as what can only be described as truly monumental graffiti adorns the side of the Ark which is destined now to travel through deep space. This is quite astounding; the images we are seeing are created by an artist known as XAVIA, whose work I have seen all around The Hives, it depicts mesmerising views of what we can only assume to be visions of Earth…"

★★★★★

18
The Seven O'Clock Knock!

Xavier opened his eyes and for the first time in what seemed like an age, felt refreshed from his sleep. He walked over to his bathroom mirror and took a long look at himself. He noticed his eyes no longer appeared ashen. His mind was clear.He had slept without any event. No dreams, no visions and most importantly no nightmares.

"Maybe I will ease off the Edu-Imps," he told himself concerned he was overdoing the knowledge. He entered the Glo-Sho feeling every beam of light penetrating his skin, refreshing him inside and out. He put on his clothes, things felt good. The buzzer to his door sounded and he looked at the monitor next to his bed. It was Zola. Perfect.

She smiled at the camera that scanned the outside of the trans-hab. Xavier buzzed her in.

"Come and join me in the boudoir," Xavier called.

"I am not here to fuck you, Xavier! I am here to fucking kill you!" Zola, her face contorted with rage, screamed like Xavier had never heard her scream before.

"What?" Xavier was mildly puzzled but still in his bubble of post graff euphoria.

"You used my security passes for ArkLight last night didn't you?"

"What?" a perplexed Xavier replied.

"This is serious Xavier. I am in big trouble."

"Zola, honestly my love I don't know what you are on about?" Xavier said, feeling helpless in the face of Zola's wrath.

"Who do you think you are?" Zola continued, her face contorted with anger.

"Zola!" Xavier grabbed her firmly but gently as she ran towards him raising her hand and clenching her fist to hit him.

"Xavier, I don't need to tell you but on the off-chance you weren't involved there was a major security breach at DF118 and a piece of two kilometre long graffiti appeared down the side of the Tamarinsk Ark, you hear me? The Tamarinsk Ark!" she started screaming again.

Xavier smiled, inwardly. The thought of his giant piece on the side of the Generation Ship as it hot footed its way to Proxima Centauri amused him.

"You used my security clearance and passes to enter the yard last night. This is a serious breach."

"It wasn't me!" Xavier pleaded.

Zola's teeth were gritted, "Don't make me hit you! Else I will damage you and it will hurt."

Xavier grabbed her by the wrists, "Calm down baby!"

"Don't baby me!" Zola was incandescent with rage, "Do you know what this means?"

There was silence.

"This is a major and I repeat major humiliation for the corporation and the party and they are going to want to know how some dumb-fuck graffiti artist managed to break into a top security military dock yard and desecrate something Nu Humana and the rest of those bastards pride in so much," she paused for a moment, "in fact you had better run."

"What?"

"I mean it!" she screamed out loud.

"Morning folks, this sounds like fun!" Jericho popped his head from beneath the covers of the sofa in Xavier's front room where he had been sleeping.

"Did I hear someone say breakfast at Nish-kin's?"

"No, you did not hear anyone say breakfast at Nish-Kin's, because you and your stupid ass friend here are part of the problem, and you will be lucky to get some raw sewage swabs when the authorities have dealt with you."

"Zola chill. It wasn't us!" replied Jericho nonchalantly, he turned away and looked to the wall, "TV on," he continued.

Instantly a hologram filled the side of the apartment and characters from a sitcom filled the room.

After going quiet for a moment, Zola said, "I trusted you Xavier. I've championed you, supported you. Loved you."

"What are you on about Zola?"

"The access codes for entry into the docks, could have only come from me. They can only be traced to me. I am the Security Administration Officer, because my mom and dad are

187

party apparatchiks and lauded by the Powers and all those corporate head honchos."

Finally Xavier spoke inadvertently admitting his guilt, " I never meant to hurt you Zola."

"I will be held to account for allowing you into the docks, maybe I will be accused of being an accomplice. I will be investigated along with my family," continued Zola.

"But I have not taken anything from you Zola. You have to trust me."

"You can vouch for me also," said Jericho as he flicked through the channels.

"Then something has alerted the security department within ArkLight Docks that I am the person who gave you access. But I never did." Zola's eyes filled with tears as the enormity of what could possibly happen began to play on her mind. She walked into the living area and sat at the end of the sofa from where Jericho still lay sprawled. "Somehow they believe I gave you an access code into the docks and now the whole of The Hives, of Genesis, of the fucking Pax Humana has seen your graffiti plastered across an Ark."

"Pretty wild, huh!" smirked Jericho.

"You can joke but someone is going to get boiled here, and it's probably me."

"What have I done?" said Xavier. He felt the floor slipping away from under him and sat down heavily.

"You have used my I-D, whether purposefully or accidentally to gain entry into ArkLight during a period where no unauthorised person was allowed, and you have painted your graffiti all over the biggest space ship in the solar system."

"We are going to be Mind Wiped!" he said quietly, holding his head in his hands.

"Who cares!" said Jericho defiantly, as the theme tune to Channel 44's ratings favourite *Suck On This* started on the Holo TV. A sublime intro alluded to the fact this was a *Hives Special*. "This should be fun!"

Air Authority goons appeared from nowhere it seemed, to give unsuspecting victims the dreaded *'Seven o'clock knock!'*

Dr. Ignatius Perigord was joined by the creepy presenter Saville Hall, who glared at the camera, "Welcome to *Suck On This* where only the most slovenly and loathsome people need apply. So where are we today…"

Jericho stared at the images before him and the normally busy and crowded landings . He noticed all the shuttered shops down the landing, the deserted cafes and food stalls were empty. Then he noticed the neon sign of their beloved eatery Nish-Kin's

"Damn! We got locals!" said Jericho, his throat tightening as the images of the landing hit home to their location.

Xavier looked at the Holo TV with disbelief, "That's our landing."

The screen cut to an all too familiar hallway.

"The Air Authority are outside on our landing."

"Is that us?" Zola's face changed to one of horror, "I told you, I told you."

On screen, the camera flicked from door to door, playing a cruel and taunting game before settling on a doorway exactly the same as theirs, "That's us!" Xavier cried, as he gathered his helmet and personal belongings. Jericho scrambled towards the door as Zola began to dial the PIN number, "Damn!" she shouted, as the PIN refused to register.

Xavier grabbed his blaster, aiming it at the door. Jericho held up his hand and shook his head shouting at Xavier, "Ricochets and shrapnel could do more harm than good."

Xavier then threw it in his bag and joined Jericho and Zola. Here he demanded the keypad and punched in the numbers.

"9-3-6-3-4-9-4"

Nothing.

"We are locked in."

Terror gripped them.

Again nothing.

But Xavier kept punching in the numbers in frustration.

"We're running out of time," Zola urged.

The landing was obviously in a lock down situation and tenants all down the landing would be doing the same, he thought. Minutes went by and the panic increased until with a familiar hiss and click the door flew open and they fell out onto the empty landing.

There were no guards outside, no Air Authority. They looked at one another in disbelief. It had not been their doorway. After a few moments of staring blankly at each other, Xavier began to laugh. Then Zola and lastly Jericho. The fear had passed in a vapour of glorious relief - for now. Fifty meters down the landing a commotion was taking place, as a group of residents gathered around an Air Authority cordon outside his neighbours the Balthazar's, who had unfortunately been greeted with '*The Seven O'Clock Knock*'.

★★★★★

19
A Sharp Intake Of Breath

Trans-habs usually had a numeric code which patched you into all the facilities and services necessary within the confines of Genesis. The basics of life were provided for - heating, lighting, water and air were all supplied via the corporations to your very own home, the trans-hab.

Trans-habs were cozy affairs with a living space and a dining room, a recreation room and dormitory for whoever slept there, a Glo-Sho to wash in and suit room to store helmets and suits when you returned from being outside.

Everyone was expected to work and contribute to the goal of 'human expansion'. The very thought that you might not do so was vilified. Retribution was quick and cruel. There was a 'three strikes and you're out' policy in effect. A repeat offender, who was not contributing in the way that a corporation deemed satisfactory, was dealt with within forty-eight hours.

They had a big choice to make:

a) Find another trans-hab or unit outside of Genesis that might take you, and there was no real chance of that.

b) Buy a ticket on one of the Arks, unless they were scheduled to leave on one, of which the chances were slim.

c) Jump a freighter to one of the mining colonies, which was like being sent to an isolation unit only worse.

d) Try and emigrate to one of the colonies on the Moon or Mars, which was virtually impossible.

e) Take the fifty-fifty (the shuttle that ran towards Debris) and take your chances there.

f) Or take your chances with Dr. Ignatius Perigord and an audit from the Air Authority, which usually ended in death.

Within every trans-hab was the AA logo for the Air Authority. It controlled that most vital of requirements in space, air to breathe. Air was a benefit in space, not a right. Beneath the logo were lights that assured you that you had not transgressed.

Red, amber and green.

You always wanted that light glowing green.

For instance if you had developed a problem with non attendance then a 3-D hologram of Dr. Perigord would appear before you and read your name and rights, before dictating the following:

"I, Doctor Ignatius Perigord, have been ordained by Powers greater than you under the Statutory Trans-hab Health Act of 2376 paragraph sixteen, code 21-11-55.

In conjunction with your governing corporation, industrial partner to which you have been assigned (insert corp. /

industry), with your pact with Nu Humana the code that covers and binds us all while living here in Genesis.

And with the agreement of the Officer Commanding ~ The Hives Residential Domain and the consent of the Genesis Peoples' Congress, I issue the ultimate command.

You have forty-eight hours to remove yourself from these premises and seek refuge with an alternative sanctum.

You have by your actions, or lack thereof, been disengaged from the freedoms afforded to you of refuge and shelter and to act as a committed member of this society.

You are no longer a welcome citizen of Genesis or The Hives therefore you are banished forthwith either to seek shelter elsewhere or face termination.

This executive command is irrevocable and not subject to appeal and the process of air termination is effective immediately."

With those words twenty-five per cent of the available air supply would be extracted from the trans-hab, just to get the point across. A buzzer would sound and a clock would begin the countdown. Death-by-suffocation. A particularly nasty way to meet your maker. A slow and lingering end, your life sucked away by a faceless, nameless remote operative in an office many miles away.

For the dwellers of The Hives, the termination would be broadcast. A potential public execution would, from time to time, cause a flicker of interest from the other residents. It was a severe sentence for a problem workforce and one that was repeated on a regular basis.

It was a tough gig if you liked to lie in bed most days. In Genesis, and especially in The Hives, audiences would tune into Channel 44, the Nu Humana propaganda and motivation station, for another of its grisly broadcasts meant to keep the workforce performing efficiently through the 'stick' method.

★★★★★

The sad and forlorn figures of Johnson K. Balthazar, his wife Noleen and their two children Dermo and Damo stared pathetically towards the camera that were to make them stars for a micro second as the winning candidates of '*The Seven O'Clock Knock*'.

"It has been found that you are guilty of the heinous crime of work evasion and, in turn, non-contribution to your corporation and fellow citizens. You have been offered fair alternatives which you have failed to take and so for this crime I recommend the penalty of death."

The voice of Doctor Ignatius Perigord filled the room, as the quivering Balthazar family stared at the hologram of the Air Authority supremo which appeared before them.

"You have been given a number of warnings about your apathetic approach but have chosen to ignore them."

The Balthazar's huddled together as the hologram turned into Doctor Perigord standing before them in person. His presence filled them with dread and they began to shudder with fear as Perigord rattled off an ordinance explaining the reasons why the Balthazar family had run out of options and were about to be terminated.

The camera quickly cut back to a grinning Saville Hall staring at the desperate family before noting to the audience at home how disgusting the crime of lethargy was. Like a ghoulish look through the keyhole, viewers were allowed to gaze at the final moments of fellow citizens while mocking their personal decor.

The Balthazar's looked at one another in bewilderment, unsure of the unfolding events.

"You are to become an example of what happens to a person when they do not partake in our system of fairness and rights because of selfishness, indifference and idleness, which impacts on not only the citizens of Genesis but also on the members of your family too," commanded Perigord.

"B-b-but my wife and children have been ill," spluttered Johnson.

"You know the procedure and you know the limits of what is acceptable Mr. Balthazar," replied Ignatius Perigord.

"But what about my children?"

The camera scanned the overweight and sickly looking pair.

"What about them?" the reply was blunt.

"You can't just execute them. They have done nothing," begged Balthazar.

"Exactly! They have done nothing!" came the cold blooded retort.

It was clear the two children would not make it in the harshness of space and they would either come to harm themselves or, worse still, harm others.

In the Genesis era, a program of physical profiling had been instrumental for centuries.

"They are life unworthy of life," Perigord snarled as he surveyed the family.

"They do not deserve to die like this," pleaded Johnson.

"It is unfortunate, but I see no alternative in this case. You are not right for the Pax Humana program we have in Genesis and I cannot see you and your family as anything more than a burden on our privileged society," Perigord continued, "really, you have used all your opportunities for a corporation, colony, territory or planet to shelter you."

"We have never had that opportunity. We are simple spacers, I beg you Doctor Perigord."

"Do not beg. It is pathetic in this day and age. You have been given fair and ample warning to seek sanctuary and you have failed."

In his last moments, Johnson Balthazar seemed to transform from a put-upon family man to a defiant rebel. "The writing is on the wall, democracy for The Hives. Long live Xavier!" he yelled out belligerently to the surprise of his family and perhaps even himself.

"The writing is on the wall?" a quizzical Perigord enquired, "repeat what you just said!"

"The writing is on the wall people," Balthazar straightened himself and looked directly into the camera before continuing, "rise up and long live Xavier!"

"I can pass but one sentence. Death by asphyxiation," Perigord punched Johnson to the floor and stormed out of the trans-hab followed by the preening Saville Hall.

Noleen screamed.

The children burst into tears.

"There needs to be some kind of appeal?" wailed Noleen, as the holographic image of Perigord returned before them.

"No appeal. No clemency. No mercy. Forthwith, the sentence is to be carried out immediately."

The sheer chill of Ignatius Perigord seemed to permeate the room. The doors were sealed and the lights in the trans-hab dimmed leaving only the red glow of the Air Authority beacon as the countdown began. The red light began to flash followed by the other lights all turning red. The family began to panic, their terror broadcast to the inhabitants of Genesis that wanted to watch this dreadful spectacle. Then the first red light went out.

Around the refineries and docks a number of workers looked up from their duties to watch the final moments of the Balthazar family being broadcast on giant screens before returning to their tasks. The people of Genesis were unfazed by these public executions, the last moments of the Balthazar family were broadcast to an indifferent populace busy toiling away around the assorted space stations. The majority of people had received the message, unfortunately the Balthazars had not.

Light two went off and the wife and children huddled together as a horrified Johnson threw himself at the screen, tears streaming down his face begging for mercy.

It echoed the evil pogroms in history when races were massacred due to their ethnicity.

"You cannot do this. It is not human."

"What would you know about being human?" Perigord retorted, reminiscent of a game show presenter baiting his contestant.

Lights three and four were on and then off within seconds. The final red light blinked once, then twice to signify the beginning of asphyxiation. A buzzer rang injecting even more fear into the poor souls of the Balthazars; it indicated the process of execution had begun. A vacuum created a pressure inside the trans-hab. Following three further flashes of the red light the oxygen began to be extracted from the unit.

The cruel and ghoulish entertainment commenced and it was apparent death was encroaching. As the families' death throes faded from the screen, the symbol of the Air Authority replaced it with the slogan:

There is no excuse for laziness. Be part of the system or the system will take you apart.

The screen stayed locked on the slogan for a moment before returning to the sponsor's logo and the rest of the day's programming.

★★★★★

20
Crisis A Gwarn!

"**D**o you people have no sense of compassion?"
"This is a travesty of justice!"
"Don't you thugs have any feelings?"
"…these people have been ill!"

It was unusual for the residents of The Hives to be so vocal following what had become a routine Air Authority termination. Normally the discontinuance of air supply might bring a few jeers from members of the public who felt some empathy with the person but more often there was total apathy to the subjects' plight and fall from grace. The citizens of Genesis were till now mostly desensitised.

On the landing of 19-J-15 the mood was like never before. What would ordinarily have been deserted landings soon became filled with citizens actually affected and angered by what they had just seen on their screens. Ignoring the imposed lockdown, residents streamed from their doorways and surrounded the Air Authority and local police cordon which circled the Balthazar's home.

Agitated, the neighbours chanted, "No more executions, no more pain!"

Doctor Ignatius Perigord, dressed in his official uniform fresh from the Balthazar's trans-hab stood in person witnessing the demonstration by the local community. He turned to one of his subordinates, "I would terminate the air supply for the whole block if I had my way."

The subordinate nodded, "We can."

"How would we do it?" Perigord continued.

"It is a simple process sir," the subordinate looked at the shouting mob then at Perigord. "We have air manufacturing plants attached to The Hives and major refineries within the Genesis Loop. Tankers are replenishing the plants daily and every four weeks there is a supply changeover."

Perigord smiled a cynical sinister grin, listening with glee to the details of affecting mass genocide.

"You know as well as I do sir, that it only takes a small amount of time for the atmosphere levels and environments to change."

"Yes, no time at all really. Look into it," grinned Perigord, mulling over the plan of action.

"We change the air supply and regulate the reserve, so as to control the populace. My office as you are aware sir, oversees this process. We can also make sure they are compliant via chemicals pumped into the supply."

"Compliant…yes, that sounds good. They certainly are not compliant at this moment," Perigord said, as he stared at the baying horde.

★★★★★

Xavier spoke first, "The Air Authority are at the Balthazars. Damn! I know them, they are a nice family."

"I know them too," Jericho said, " those people are good people!"

"Lets go back inside and see whats happening," Zola walked into the apartment and stared at the screen. They stood watching silently. It all seemed to happen so fast. Four lives taken by the touch of a button, two of them children.

Zola began crying and Jericho punched the walls, "Wait do you hear that noise outside?"

They rushed outside to see the totally unexpected crowd rallying for the Balthazar's. Before they knew it Jericho was gone.

"Murderers!" Jericho began shouting in the midst of the melee. Soon the crowd began chanting with him.

An Air Authority spherical drone circled above the security officers, its cameras in seconds scanning and comparing faces in the tumult. As the phalanx of officers pushed so too did the crowd.

Zola tugged at Xavier's coat, "Xavier!" she demanded, "We have to go, let's get the hell out of here."

"Jericho!" Xavier tried to shout to his buddy above the din.

"This is bad for us. We need to get out of here. He's made his choice."

Instantly, within the screen of the drone, a symbol flashed bright red and alerted Genesis Federal Command which in turn notified the Air Authority team at 19-J-15.

As the drone once again flew over the crowd, Xavier and Zola ducked down shielding their faces from the prying camera and then huddled behind the crowd.

"Keep down," shouted Xavier.

Jericho's face was processed within microseconds and the previous sightings of him and his rod Warp Child throughout The Hives and ArkLight Docks came flooding back in a frenzied blur on the screen.

Apprehend & Arrest

Apprehend & Arrest

The words began to blink upon the screen inside the helmets of the Air Authority enforcers. Suddenly the drone locked upon the face of Jericho. A red laser beam targeted his face, marking him for extraction from the riotous crowd. Jericho was spitting with rage. Engrossed with the demonstration, unaware of the imminent threat to his liberty which his friends were witnessing unfold before them.

In a split second a snatch squad broke from the barricade and grabbed at Jericho. Despite being caught unawares, his sharp reflexes still allowed him to evade them and twist out of their grasp.

"Get away from me copper!" Jericho shouted, baiting the AA thugs.

Jericho managed to wriggle free of the flailing arms of the snatch squad and twisting on his heels, spun out of the grasp of the oncoming heavies. Xavier looked across at the commotion and called Jericho's name as he watched his friend break free and run down the landing towards the airlocks and causeway for 20-K-16.

"Get out of here Jericho!" Xavier said as the drone pursued Jericho, its laser never once leaving the sprinting runaway.

"We need to go now!" Zola screamed as she pulled Xavier towards her in desperation.

Jericho looked back towards Xavier.

For a moment, Xavier saw the flicker in his eyes before two of the snatch squad tackled Jericho to the ground. Within seconds, two other guards had grabbed Jericho's flailing arms and legs while another ran towards him. His head was kicked repeatedly, until he was rendered unconscious.

Xavier ran in the opposite direction. Zola looked back only to see a group of AA goons bludgeoning Jericho and firing from close range taser guns and sonic restraints. Jericho's body contorted as wave after wave of sickening blows rained down and pummelled his body. She felt a wave of nausea rise up. Must keep running.

They made their way towards the public hangars of the block. The gravity of the situation hung over them. Xavier's actions had produced consequences of such great magnitude and with such tremendous speed - it was difficult to process. Those Air Authority officers were not the type of people who helped old ladies back to their trans-hab when they were lost.

There was nothing nice about them.

What would become of Jericho? The way he was being beaten he would be lucky to survive a trip to the Confinement

Block. They might just take him to an airlock and flush him out into space.

Nobody would be any the wiser.

"Xavier we need to split up," Zola said quietly.

"What are you on about?"

"You have to get out of here and make it to Debris. Find Ray. He knows people who will help you. You need to get away or the authorities will kill you," she paused for a second, "I need to make sure my parents are OK and find out about the security clearance at ArkLight."

"I can't let you do that on your own!"

"You can and you have to," she continued, "they murdered Calvin Lacker, we saw it, we were there. This is what they will do to us. We got away by the skin of our teeth but the people are rising, they are not going to take this anymore. They look at your graffiti and it says something to them. You will soon be a fugitive. It's only a matter of time till they figure out who XAVIA is."

It was the truth. He could not possibly stay in The Hives or return to ArkLight. He was now on the run.

"But…"

"Just go Xavier!"

Xavier looked at her beautiful face. She was so damn strong and so sharp. Back at the academy it was always Zola who could whip up a plan from nothing.

"I will be fine and will meet with you somewhere, you know that," she said.

"Maybe on Earth, one day," Xavier laughed.

Zola smiled, "Maybe."

They kissed one another, "Be safe, Zola. Be safe."

"You need to go now Xavier," Zola said quietly, turning away and walking up towards the Landing

"Get gone," she shouted, throwing her arm up without looking back.

Xavier headed to his hangar and to Aqua Terra.

He liked being a fugitive.

★★★★★

21
A Town Called Debris

*D*ebris was a mess.
A monumental mess.
It was the perfect hiding place for a fugitive.

It comprised two hundred miles of floating junk, the detritus of The Cannery, the flotsam and jetsam of humanity suspended out of sight of the High Pioneers and away from the corporations. Millions of tons of mined asteroid rock were trawled and deposited after all the ores had been extracted, then spat out here and jumbled together with fragments of derelict Arks and twisted, crumbling colony structures. The docks where they had once been built would be dismantled and dragged through space to be cast away from prying eyes. There was always a need for somewhere to send your unwanted dregs.

In the case of Debris, this included people and so it had grown and developed into a vast twisted outpost of large scale settlements. For some, it was a rough diamond - a dark star.

Anything that had passed its sell by date or was no longer of any use in Genesis was carted out and jettisoned into space to find its way here. The continual construction sites and docks produced scrap aplenty, parts of Debris would have keels from starships protruding where they had been towed and abandoned leaving the inhabitants to scurry all over the wreck, looking for something that could be recycled. Toilet units, sink units, waste disposal units, in fact anything with the word 'unit' on it could be found here. Within the confines of Debris were salvaged spacecraft and tankers that had been turned into townships, old space freighters, tug boats and liners, container craft and tankers were all to be found entrapped in this tomb; one giant wrecking yard connecting with another and then another, seemingly continuing forever. The vast interiors of these Leviathans transformed into colonies of their own, interlinked with one another and created by a faithful community who had, in turn, set up their own fiefdoms to rule and oversee their subjects.

A flotsam *favela* of sorts, governed by outlaws and with its own rules and customs, Debris was home to pirates, scavengers and vagabonds, a wild and dangerous place where you had to keep your wits about you. It was also the home to many who simply did not wish to conform to life in Genesis - the persecuted, the abandoned, those escaping the reaches of the corporations and the Air Authority, people who did not wish to be part of the Nu Humana experiment.

For a visitor Debris was a dangerous and deadly place. Those who lived there however, had to call it home.

The spirit of the Debris residents was legendary. They seemed to have a *joie de vivre,* a shared passion for celebratory music, salvaging the junk around them and utilising and working together free from the clutches of the big corporations in Genesis. There was danger always lurking in Debris even when venturing towards these environs, but that was Debris for you. Convoys of Pods would converge together from Genesis, employing security guards to protect them as they traversed towards the rubble and steel remains. The asteroid colonies scattered throughout the system seemed to have an uncanny knack of making hypnotic, pounding beats with voluptuous vocals and carousing chants which whipped up listeners into a frenzy, the craze for Mining Muzik never seemed to diminish. When played at a party, people would lose control, their bodies swirling in wonderful arabesque shapes while whooping and chanting becoming a mesh of bodies spellbound by the sound.

A Debris party was epic.

You would find yourself dancing alongside some of the hardest miners and most dangerous pirates, mutineers and mercenaries, as well as a few Cannery Kids and *colonistas* from some of the more exclusive colonies. Whenever a major rave took place, a truce would be declared. The pirate scavengers would take time off from their plundering activities and any hostilities would cease until after the event. The *Debris Detente* as it was known came into full effect. The reason for this cessation in hostilities was simple. Pirates like to party and dance to the sounds of the vast array of performing artists to be found in Debris like Scun Scum, Klakto, Crater Face, Bilge Pipe and the rising starlet of the mining scene, Minnie Rall. Add to that the potent serum exuded from a Zugbot and you were definitely up for a great night out.

Zugbots were cyborgs, an amalgamation of droid and genetically deficient clone discharge that produced small and pitiful creatures. They should have been terminated in the lab, but as always, some sick bastard saw a way of making money and crafted a cybernetic breathing apparatus allowing them to work in conditions a normal human could not withstand. They worked in the harsh confines of space and in time the Zugbot had become impregnated with the powerful toxic chemicals discharged from these industrial installations. Something within a Zugbot's DNA changed the chemicals into a highly psychedelic secretion emanating from their skin. In the cold of space, the Zugbot performed its duties efficiently and without distraction. Life expectancy for a Zugbot was low but in a society that gleefully watched the suffocation of others as entertainment, a Zugbot's quality of life was no cause for concern.

Xavier had always loved them.

Zugbots were used to clean out the pipes and tunnels of the chemical plants and refineries of Polluto and Zug. Polluto was the nickname for a gas refinery that processed captured gases from enormous clouds in deep space that would be transferred to Genesis to be processed and used in the construction of Arks or for use among the colonies. There was no shortage of gas anymore. Barges laden, tail to tail, with cargo or rubble en route to Debris were illuminated by the flashes and flames that shot out of the refineries as excess gases flared into the ink black cold of space.

As they waddled along the outside of the giant ducts of the refineries or giant exhaust pipes, they seemed almost to exhibit a cheery dolefulness as they carried on cleaning and fixing blockages, occasionally being caught by a blast of supercharged gas exuding from the pipes which incinerated them to a crisp. They were popular mascots on pirate ships probably faring better overall on a pirate vessel than on a cleaning team. Taken from the vacuum of space, a Zugbot would perspire in a warm room causing the toxic mucus contained under their skin to ooze. It could be seen radiating off the Zugbots - a fluorescent orange and purple that sparkled as it rose into the atmosphere. Some pirates would wipe the mucus on themselves, sending them into delirious, euphoric and transcendent states of mind. The more adventurous would even ingest the secretions which would send them into a metaphysical state where they would travel back to the moment of the Big Bang as though they were a part of it.

This had now given birth to the adoration of the Zugbot by the pirate gangs who would treat their favourite Zugbots like revered deities. It was said that every Zugbot's mucus was different and varied in potency and effect and so Zugbots were traded between gangs. When exposed to the mucus, people often went crazy and it was deadly if you were exposed to it for long periods. This probably explained why most of the pirates were complete lunatics. In Debris, certain Zugbots were associated with certain gangs. Hovering podiums or 'temple floats' built by pirates, adorned with sound systems, dancers and chanting buccaneers reciting mystical incantations, competed with one another at the Debris bacchanals. Zugbots no longer just graced the vessels of pirate ships, but also the legendary bacchanalian celebrations in Debris.

★★★★★

The journey from The Hives had been relatively easy. Xavier had managed to collect Old Man Ray from his favoured drinking establishment The White Star Bar, an old converted defence satellite. What it defended, nobody was quite sure, but it had now become one of The Hives hang-outs frequented by dock workers from ArkLight, stumbling in after a hard days graft. They were a grizzled and gnarly bunch, shouting at one another above the din of the music and using its low gravity to bounce from one conversation to the next. Most of the regulars there were tough old riggers destined to end their days either at ArkLight in some hideous industrial accident or in this particular hostelry.

Xavier did not want to hang around too long. Luckily Old Man Ray was more than ready to leave with him.

He finished his drink shouting, "Let's have it!"

Then placed his helmet on as the other riggers shook their heads and carried on drinking. He walked towards a row of tubes that descended towards the parking lot. With a quick program as he entered, the tube guided itself out to allow you to embark your chosen craft upon its arrival. Xavier expertly guided Aqua Terra towards the tubes, calling Old Man Ray who tapped some digits as the tube swung across and sealed him within the airlock. In a matter of three bleeps and four whirrs the tube had connected to Aqua Terra and Old Man Ray was shot down and into the Rod signed, sealed and delivered. He sat down in the seat next to Xavier his face beaming.

"You should have seen it Xavier," Ray was excited, "it was incredible. It must have been a top buzz. I cannot imagine what the Powers thought when they saw that graffiti all down the side."

Xavier grimaced, "Yeah! It was quite a trip," he said, the fate of Jericho and Zola lapsing back into his head.

"They will be okay Xavier. Mark my words," Old Man Ray placed a reassuring hand upon Xavier's arm.

Xavier remained silent, staring at the controls and displays of Aqua Terra and making the calculations for flying to places like Debris. He turned to Old Man Ray, "I could see real fear in Jericho's eyes."

"They put fear into everyone. They use terror to suppress us. It has been used as a tactic for aeons. They want you to fear them, man. Or fear something!"

"Not anymore," stated Xavier, "not anymore...all that's over Ray."

"I will put you in touch with some people who will help you on your way."

"But what about Zola?" asked Xavier. He couldn't help thinking about her.

"Zola is a big strong girl," replied Ray, "you mark my words. She will be just fine."

"I know she's got the brains but will she have the balls?"

"She's got balls Xavier, don't you worry about that!"

Xavier said nothing, trying to put his mind to the journey at hand.

"Seriously boy!" Old Man Ray continued, "Centuries ago, during a regime known as the Soviet Union, the common people would drink vodka, the traditional drink at that time, and toast one another with the words 'I drink to protest!'" He put his hand on Xavier's arm, "I think that is what we need to do now."

Xavier cracked a smile, "You really are one crazy old dude, but I have got to say, I could definitely use a drink."

Old Man Ray laughed, "I thought you might."

★★★★★

22
A.C.A.B

T he room was bare and dark apart from a single gurney containing the near lifeless body of Jericho Chong. His chest seemed to strain with every laboured breath he took and what could only be described as a pitiful wheeze as he tried desperately to fill his lungs with oxygen. His left arm hung limply from the side of the stretcher and the pitter-patter of blood droplets ran down his fingers to form an ever-growing puddle upon the floor.

He was surrounded by the same six burly thugs who had beaten him unconscious. They glared down at him impervious of his pain and suffering.

"Officer O'Donahue, you seem to have captured one of the reprobates responsible for covering the walls of Genesis with their dissident ramblings."

The eerie stillness was interrupted by the theatrical entrance of Titus Haq.

"And by the look of him you seem to have killed him!"

"I did as requested sir!" O'Donahue barked. He stared at the governor. His pupils seemed dilated and his chest puffed up still pumped up on the adrenaline of beating someone to a pulp.

"He looks good for nothing apart from a trip to be recycled and then incinerated."

Haq was joined by Ignatius Perigord and Carlos Zagrostine, who gazed at the prostrate body of Jericho and then at his assailants, "They seem to have had a liking for this poor wretched family."

Perigord glared at Zagrostine, "I am not sure if they liked them or whether they just dislike us."

"So Ignatius, what are we to make of today's unrest?"

"It seems as though the family had been struck down by some strange illness after a recent trip to The Cathay Wheel. They were unable to work and some of their neighbours covered for them but they don't seem to have logged it into the system and somehow we were alerted to that Landing."

"You were alerted to that Landing?" Zagrostine questioned, demanding more information.

"They were deemed to have been unfit and unable to work and so too their children. And so termination was considered the best option," Perigord replied.

"But this was the same trans-hab block as the dissident graffiti artists," Haq said, "Is that just coincidence?"

"Yes, sheer coincidence," came the blunt reply.

"And what of this graffiti artist Xavier. Xavier Miro?"

"Again, he seems to be popular."

"The strangest thing is at work here," Haq said, "How has a person in such a high security position, a person who not only has a trans-hab, social security number and identity pass not been identified before?"

O'Donahue shrugged, "He is not on any files that we have."

"How can that be? How come not one of us, not one security operative has been able to actually identify and locate who this person is."

"What about the girl?" Zagrostine interrupted.

"Her name is Zola Capello."

Haq smiled, "Capello? Not the daughter of Fabian and Amber Capello? How is she involved in this?"

"She works in the Security Administration Office for Nu Humana at ArkLight Docks."

"One can only assume that her relationship with this Miro character has led her to foolishly allow him access into the yards."

Titus studied an array of images now projected onto one of the walls of the room.

"Quite extraordinary!" he continued, admiringly.

"Why has she been so stupid as to align herself with these low-lifes?" Zagrostine questioned, "It will only destroy her family and its proud position and reputation."

"What fools these mortals be!" Titus stared intently at Zola's profile.

Thousands of images suddenly leapt from the small container placed on the floor and projected on to the wall of

Zola, Xavier and Jericho from the tens of thousands of cameras and face recognition devices scattered throughout the Hives and Genesis. It was a document of their lives, images from their childhood and through the academies. It flooded out from the box like a torrent, as if their every moment had been captured alongside that of everyone else for processing. Somewhere a phenomenal computer program sifted through the billions of hours of captured data from around the colony and compiled a snapshot of them in a matter of minutes.

"I still don't understand. Why have we not been able until this moment to identify Xavier Miro?"

"Perhaps because we have not looked."

"Or have not cared."

"It says he comes from the Hives!"

"We would have found him for sure if we had his data," O'Donahue piped in.

"It make no sense," Titus smacked his hands together, "this man has been protected from the inside."

"And what of this Jericho Chong?" Perigord asked Titus as they walked up to the stretcher and gazed down at his bloodied face

"Now he does for sure come from the Hives," smirked O'Donahue, "I have known about him since he was a juvenile and from time to time as an adult before he skedaddled to some mining colony on Ceres in the Belt."

"You saved your own skin by capturing this felon today O'Donahue but there is a bigger conspiracy going on here and ·one that we need to remedy immediately."

"What do you suggest?" asked Perigord.

"We need to eliminate this dissident and all of his associates with extreme prejudice before things get out of hand."

"And what of this good-for-nothing Jericho Chong?"

They stood around the gurney staring at the near extinguished body of Jericho Chong, one time graffiti artist, miner, dock worker and lover of Nish-Kin's noodles, before Titus broke the silence, "Maybe my old friend Lucien Ferrer might be able to help and we could have him in our gainful employ!"

★★★★★

23
The Powers That Be

L ife can never be fair.
There is always an oppressor to an oppressed.
There is always a have, alongside a have-not.
There will always be the powerful and the powerless…

The evening sun was full and intense. Its warm golden-orange beams lighting the low wispy clouds and making a spectacular red and purple sky. The meeting had been scheduled for seven that evening with most attendees arriving early to take in the beautiful setting. The fresh summer air and the cooling breeze had all the makings of a memorable evening.

There had been an old saying about this city, *'Paris is for lovers'*, but there were no 'lovers' here.

A flotilla of majestic air yachts, their sleek lines and observation booths hovering close to the tower, their berths in mid-air waiting for their owners to disembark.

This gathering at sunset was being held in the ancient Earth city of Paris on the viewing platform of one of old Earth's most iconic European buildings , the viewing deck on the top floor of the Eiffel Tower.

This beautiful structure had been kept intact and preserved by The Loyal Order of Android Monks. They had made sure these great monuments and triumphs of human engineering had been treated with the love and respect they warranted. They hoped they would still be there in another five hundred years.

Paris, like London, Rome, New York, Florence and all the wonderful cities of the world had been kept and preserved and their contents logged and itemised. Whether these ubiquitous 'future generations' would ever get the chance to live on Earth again was not of consequence. The Pyramids, the Great Wall of China, the seven wonders of the ancient world and the twelve wonders of the modern world were all protected.

Various crews from the Loyal Order were stationed in all the main old cities and numbered in the hundreds of thousands. Their task was simple; after the expulsion of humans, nature rapidly took over and within a matter of months, entire cities were covered in plants, weeds and flora.

Water and unregulated growth turned these cities into jungles. Buildings becoming festooned with vines eventually destroying the structure. Not every building was preserved but those deemed to be of significance and importance were ring fenced and the marauding vegetation and animal life kept at bay. Teams repaired then maintained, and sometimes even relocated buildings such as London's Big Ben Tower, St.Paul's Cathedral, Rome's Vatican, New York's Empire State Building, the Shinto temples in Japan, St Basil's in Moscow and the Wat Arun in Bangkok .

These monuments were cleaned and illuminated in the evening, with elevated moving walkways connecting them so that dignitaries and the Powers could visit them without having to venture into the wilderness that encroached the rest of the cities. Much of central London had been kept as it was and acted as the central offices and bureaucratic headquarters for a number of the large galactic corporations. A very enviable gig for anyone within the hierarchy of a corporation. It was the same in Washington DC. where the White House II (the previous one had been destroyed in a terrorist attack in 2034) and the Lincoln Memorial were protected and preserved. In the rest of the city wild animals roamed free. The artefacts of Earth including buildings had become regulated and controlled. They became museum pieces for the most powerful people in the known galaxy, for them to show or hand down to their families. The marvels of humankind and the beauty that had been achieved on old Earth, when man's knowledge and imagination was channelled and applied to creativity rather than destruction, had now become mere playthings for the rich and powerful.

The Loyal Order of Android Monks had created theme parks of sorts in many of these cities, showcasing the architecture alongside the wild animals that roamed and lived within the city boundaries. From time to time, they would have to cull and temper the deer and other creatures that had made their home here but that was just to keep equilibrium and order. Earth had become a zoo, a private jungle for the Powers to go on safari in.

They could act out their fantasies in their private Gardens of Eden without fear of banishment and without the prying eyes and indignation of the multitudes from Genesis. Not even the wealthy Pioneers and *nouveau riche* industrialists could experience this unless they had been welcomed into the gang.

This was strictly invite only.

The jungles and deserts had too been returned to the teeming abundance of centuries before where the animals roamed free, without fear of being hunted by the greatest biped mammal, the homo sapien. Large parts of the Sahara had actually now been reclaimed by the jungles and forests which existed there thousands of years before, and the Amazon had become a vast sea of trees and vegetation covering the entire continent. Rumours abounded that some of the indigenous tribes had escaped the mass human expulsion and were now lost within the enormous jungles.

The Earth was alive again and the air that filled the skies now was of the purest kind. Free from the pollution of centuries before. Forests were filled with animals, butterflies and bees fluttered around, flocks of birds crossed the skies and the calls and cries of nature could be heard in the woods and on the prairies.

The natural balance of the mother planet had been restored.

The white air yachts were now all moored and their passengers began to disembark, assisted by a group of white attired robots and loyal servants. The servants were made up of families who had been in service with The Powers for generations. They attended to every need and ordered the robots to ensure each attendee was safe and well provided for.

The final yacht of Senator Ronson Fleming reached the observation floor and as its covered gangplank extended, a rush of activity took over as the guests were escorted into the comforts of the deck. The room was filled with comfortable leather sofas and a number of modernist old Earth statues. It was opulent but not excessive. Exquisite vintage wines and spirits were on offer as well as Earth grown fruit juices. The once forgotten activity of cigar smoking was being indulged in by a number of guests on the balcony that ran all around the room.

Here were twelve of the most powerful people in the known galaxy.

They were not nicknamed 'The Disciples of The Gods' for nothing.

A casual observer might think they had stumbled upon a group of opera aficionados or vintage car enthusiasts rather than men and women who controlled every breath taken by what was now 'humanity'. Some of them were suited up businessmen, looking every inch the tycoons and merchant princes they were. There were mega industrialists, manicured and immaculately dressed, sharing small talk against the backdrop of the most coveted view in Paris during old Earth times.

Drax Kraldon, a tall, handsome, white haired man, with a perfectly manicured beard and piercing green eyes was a commanding presence. As head of Human Enterprises now known as Nu Humana, Kraldon was the man who had overseen the destiny of mankind for the last forty years. This was no small feat and one he executed with a ruthlessly cool efficiency.

This evening he was playing the cordial host to the Genesis governor Titus Haq accompanied by Carlos Zagrostine and a selection of moguls. These men and women made up the board of EarthCorp which along with Nu Humana had trail blazed everything and anything to do with deep space exploration. EarthCorp was a front for a vast number of conglomerates that channelled their efforts and finances into discovering new Earth-like planets to conquer and colonise before exporting the joys and benefits of the old planet to the systems beyond the Kuiper Belt.

"Welcome one and all to our little *soiree*"declared Drax, as he raised his glass.

They saluted and turned toward their host, "It is good to see you all here on this most beautiful of evenings," his arm swirled at the sight of the setting sun and the illuminated Trocadero glowing amongst the dense green vegetation.

Below him monuments and buildings became bathed in a golden light and the areas took on a fairy tale semblance. The rest of Paris was too quiet, all human life that had made this city so vibrant now eliminated. The Seine was sombre. Periodically it was embellished by light, but apart from that there was no movement. Like a museum at midnight after everyone had gone home, the city had an eeriness about it. The squawk of birds, the roars of hunting beasts and the cries of the prey being caught, were the only sounds to break the air in the distance. There was speculation regarding small pockets of human life who lived in the shadows of the cities and wilderness alongside the Shadows. For anyone born and brought up on Genesis to have witnessed this spectacle of Paris at dusk would have been astounding, but for the hierarchy here gathered, even though the night was gorgeous, the sights, sounds and smells were quite routine and normal.

"Nothing quite like Paris in the springtime I was once told," Dmitri Illeyenich, head of Ruski Lunski quipped.

"Very true, Dmitri," chuckled Ronson Fleming, swigging from a large cut glass tumbler of whisky. As the Controller of the Moon, Fleming knew Dmitri Illeyenich well and was aware that he was a man of substantial means. A fearsome businessman, tough and entrepreneurial, wily and intelligent, Dimitri was a man whose jokes you laughed at even if they weren't amusing. Ruski Lunski had been a major coloniser of the moon and its mineral wealth had made the Russians powerful and wealthy. The old rivalries between Ruski Lunski, Sino Space, Genesis Space Technologies and American Astroid Mining had recently caused a number of confrontations and skirmishes Ronson Fleming had had to pass rulings on. Added to this, a surge in migration due to the desire of millions of colonists who wished to reside and work on the Moon made the place more volatile than ever. Then there was Felix Keeto of Pan Universal Industries, who relaxed with a cigar and a two hundred year old brandy expertly created by The Loyal Order. Next to him were General Juggi Khalsa, head of the Tigernauts, leader of Mughal Space and the respected Professor Aldous Hoffman, responsible for the education policies, doctrines, historical revisions and mind manipulations which took place within Genesis. Dieter Rodriguez from Orbital Systems and Primo Mietsu of Crux Industries responsible for much of the research and development in the colonies, shared a joke, "I have never seen so many people that hated each other so much gathered in one place."

They chuckled heartily.

It was true. The people gathered in Paris were great rivals, but like all businessmen before them worked together well to ensure their interests were protected. With them, the head of Sino Space, the Cathay Wheel and other Chinese interests around the solar system.

K.C. Wang. She like her father before her, ran these enterprises with great foresight but also with an iron fist. Next to her was the famous Doctor Garibidian, responsible for the construction of the Arks. He was also developing the next stage of mass human transit in the form of the colossal tele-transporter, Project GK-IV, being constructed in L4.

This evening he would present his plans to all present.

Premier Templar of Mars, had not made it in person but his holographic image mingled with guests regardless of the fact he was 225 million kilometres away. Political tensions were at boiling point on Mars. Rumour had it Premier Templar was about to begin purging his opposition.

They looked like a group of middle aged men and women holding onto power. Never to be shared while holding onto secrets no one would ever uncover.

And they were.

A multitude of advisors stood nearby taking notes and relaying messages to the minions that did the bidding of The Powers. These were the people who ran the human empire from the collective conglomerate headquarters around the solar system and beyond. It seemed ostensibly a social event but this was how business had been conducted for centuries; informal get-togethers followed by a dinner and a shake of the hand. There were other families living on Earth, maybe fifty-thousand. They too had power and controlled industries and technologies, yet all were sworn to the secrecy and code of the Pax Humana.

However the twelve assembled here and their entourages were the decision-makers whose judgements affected the lives of everyone and shaped the destiny of humankind.

"So…what are you going to do then?" roared Ronson Fleming, "I have got too many of you people coming into the lunar territories as it is, getting all aggressive."

"You people! Who do you think you are talking to?" snapped Dmitri.

"Dmitri, Dmitri, its time for some tough talk on this matter," Fleming replied, "Ruski Lunski are bringing in more and more people to the moon and we cannot cope. There needs to be a clarity as to how this is handled."

Around the room the heads began to talk business, "We need to get more steel from the moon Fleming," asked Felix Keeto.

"I need you to sort this asteroid problem out with Khalsa," Drax Kraldon turned towards K.C.Wang.

"When are we getting the next Ark away Doctor Garibidian?" enquired K.C. Wang, fixing her gaze firmly on him, her mind working out calculations which she could pass back to her team.

"The Tamarinsk Ark will be leaving presently, Madam Wang. It is departing from ArkLight as we speak, I believe. Then I will tell you about our future projects," he replied.

"I look forward to that, Doctor Garibidian," she smiled.

"We have those mining colonies at full production," Drax Kraldon said, proudly.

"How are the Proxima Centauri calculations looking?"

"They have found over four billion tons of helium three ready for harvesting," Professor Hoffman replied.

"Jupiter's moons are at full capacity," beamed Rodriguez, sampling more hors d'oeuvres.

"We received the tech reports from Zamyatin...excellent prospects!" chimed in Mietsu.

For an hour they exchanged a vociferous banter, sometimes straight faced, sometimes joking, shrugging shoulders as they got things done. Everything recorded to be noted and executed as executive orders.

"So Titus what's the story in Genesis? The people there seem to be problematic at present?" rasped Drax.

"There is no problem on Genesis, Drax. There is a little unrest within the Hives but nothing to worry about," replied the governor confidently, wiping his mouth and ignoring the furore of the room.

"We need to crack a few heads that's all," Carlos Zagrostine could not help but pipe in.

"But from where we are productivity is dropping and there is a great deal of discontent," retorted Drax.

"People are starting to lose faith in the system, they thought they would be away from Genesis and heading to the promised land. As it is they are stuck in Genesis building Arks and only one in twenty is ever getting the chance to leave," Haq replied.

"We need to get those Arks away, that's what we need. We are being overwhelmed with people on the Cathay Wheel and that can only lead to trouble," Wang interjected.

"That is a problem!" Doctor Garibidian remarked.

"It is a problem we need to deal with sooner than later," snapped Zagrostine, whose paunchy little face seemed to flush bright red.

"Can't we do something about this? I mean I thought we had this under control!" asked Senator Fleming.

"Speak to Perigord, he should be able to sort this mess out," Juggi Khalsa stirred in his seat.

"We need to drastically change policy here," said Dmitri.

"You do realise this don't you," Primo Mietsu.

Haq remained silent, his face showing no emotion but a disdain for all of those gathered here.

"That is why we are having such problems on the Moon," said Fleming.

"And we have this immigrant tide wanting to come to Mars and I won't have that at all," barked Premier Templar, "we have enough problems as it is; a near civil war at present and our people will turn on any new wave of settler. Of this I am sure...as I will sanction it."

"Let's have a few executions from the Air Authority, that should keep them in line," said Professor Hoffmann loudly, taking a large gulp of wine from his glass.

"What is a few hundred executions going to achieve? We need a radical rethink on policy. Sino Space is full to capacity. We are building Arks as fast as we can and we all agree we have the raw materials and the manpower but the time it takes to build these arks is too long," said Wang, her frustration apparent.

"It's naturally frustrating, They are going Can Crazy being stuck in space for so long – we promised them new worlds and planets...a new life,"shrugged Keeto.

"Which *are* out there," Doctor Garibidian noted.

"But we can't get them to those planets in time," Primo Mietsu contested.

"I have made some calculations and we have just too many people," interrupted Professor Hoffman.

There was silence.

"That has always been the case," General Khasla replied.

"So what do we do?" said K.C.Wang

"We need to control the population in the Hives for a start," interrupted Haq.

"It will save us air supply," agreed Zagrostine,"in fact we could do with taking the Hives out altogether" Zagrostine said.

"Turn off the air supply?" Drax Kraldon shrugged, aware of where the conversation was headed.

"Get Perigord to sort something out, he likes killing people," Premier Templar laughed.

"Excuse me, but we need people too," Dieter Rodriguez said , getting up from his seat.

"We have wars to fight, we have colonies to build, markets to create and we also have...the *other* problem," Khalsa countered.

Silence again.

The other problem.

"We can't just exterminate our own people," questioned Wang, "or can we?"

"It would be a final solution to one of mankind's enduring problems...sustainability," answered Hoffman. "We have always, throughout mankind's and Earth history, had to deal with the rise in human population and the depletion of food stocks and natural resources, which in turn creates civil unrest, which then leads to pestilence, war and destruction."

"May I just add, Professor, this is all off the record," Kraldon interjected. "This has been contained to date because of the environment that people find themselves in...space.

What we have on our hands is something which will only get worse."

They spoke about the lives of millions of people as if they were insects in a container. They cared for them as a storekeeper cares for his stock. The people in the Hives were expendable, another commodity to be bought and sold, traded on the whims of the twelve gathered there.

"What are you saying?" asked Hoffman.

"We absolutely need to control the population," said Kraldon, abruptly.

Fleming and Templar both nodded.

"We need them to breed, but controlling the population is a tricky subject, unless a dramatic move is taken," Keeto replied.

"If you feel we need to take such drastic action, so be it," Illeyenich said.

"Don't be so hasty," Juggi Khalsa interrupted.

"The human," began Drax Kraldon, stretching out his fingers and pacing around the room, "is the most important asset that we have. We will protect the human."

Murmurs came from the twelve as the sun finally set below the horizon.

He continued, "As a unit of commerce, we need to exploit them.We are here because of humans and we, too, are humans. Let us never forget that. We are after all Nu Humana."

There was a polite applause from the guests, including Titus Haq who followed Drax's every move.

"Combined, we are the most powerful force in our galaxy. We are here collectively to export humanity to every corner of the known galaxy, take our people and our way of life to colonise wherever we choose and take whatever we want...whatever it takes! We have advanced more in three hundred years than mankind has ever done and that expansion has brought us wealth, privilege and knowledge beyond what we could ever have imagined. We are the force to be reckoned with; we are the greatest organism that has ever evolved."

The room erupted in clapping and back slapping as they cheered on their leader.

"Now, we have the power over life and death, billions of beings are under our control, something which we can and should not take lightly. We must use the human race in its most efficient way to build Arks and take journeys to colonise distant planets."

Drax paused, then looked towards Doctor Garibidian. "Elon here, has been working tirelessly on the next chapter of our evolution. The mass particle teletransporter Project GK-IV will enable whole colonies to be teletransported to the farthest reaches of the galaxy. This technology is so advanced and secret, it must be kept within the confines of this room. Doctor Garibidian, please, enlighten us."

The esteemed scientist was a man whose looks belied his years. He stood and turned to the assembled guests. "I cannot stand here and listen to your ravings about how to decimate the population of Genesis because of some protests or unrest in the Hives. We made promises that we need to deliver on. I understand along the way there is sacrifice. All of us gathered in this room have made forfeits to get where they are today. The future, like Drax just pointed out, is to keep the human race stable and then transport them throughout the 'local neighbourhood' of galaxies. Mankind's advance will be rapid and the returns substantial. Project GK-IV is near completion with the first tests already done. It is located in a militarised zone of the Langrange Point L4, with the utmost security. It is protected like Earth is and everything there is for our eyes only. I believe that in the next two years we can begin to make real changes in how we send humans to new worlds and revolutionise the history of mankind."

The room was silenced as the doctor returned to his seat and finished his speech.

"In the future it may be necessary to reassess where the human race is headed and how we are to move forward. I, for one, am not an advocate of genocide but if needs must…"

Drax Kraldon looked at the faces as they stared back at him, "I concur with Doctor Garibidian, I do not believe that it would be in the best interest to annihilate our workforce in the Hives. It seems somewhat radical but the future of the human race is more important than the discontented utterances of the present proletariat who are securely contained a few hundred thousand miles away."

Drax took a mouthful of iced water and gazed for a few seconds out across the rapidly darkening landscape of Paris before addressing the group.

"There has of late, been a little bit of imbalance and instability throughout the Hives," he paused, "you have all met Genesis governor Titus Haq before. Maybe he could shed light on the situation we find ourselves."

Titus smiled at the guests and nodded appreciably at Drax, before stepping forward and commanding the centre of the room. Titus Haq was a lot younger than the gathered clan. He wore a black uniform with the insignia of The Shadows on the chest and possessed a commanding presence.

"I have watched and heard from you all today and I will begin by showing you something," Titus began. "Something that has happened while we have been seated in this room."

He motioned his arm and the lighting dimmed slightly as a holographic display took centre stage. It was The Tamarinsk Ark leaving the docks of ArkLight emblazoned with a mural kilometres in length along its side. Xavier's murals daubed around the wheels and spheres of Genesis and The Hives - graffiti pieces, depicting images so unfamiliar and bizarre to the citizens of Genesis. The letters XVR or XAVIA, which he made no attempt to hide, indicated who was responsible. There were enormous murals of oceans filled with fish and jungles packed with animals, ancient structures such as the Pyramids in Egypt and Chichen Itza, with alien beings dancing and flying around them. There were significant historical moments depicted where humans and aliens had cohabited. Also the defacement of corporate logos and messages that questioned the authority of The Powers.

And again, the word Democracy and the symbol for Anarchy.

"What is this?" demanded Dimitri.

They stared again at the images of the giant Tamarinsk Ark, the pride of Nu Humana, The Powers and the united corporations of Genesis. Leaving the protection of the docks of Ark Light, heading into deep space with its hull covered from fore to aft with a graffiti piece that featured chains being broken, people rioting and images of conquistadors being garrotted whilst children play in glorious fields.

Enormous letters spelt out:

BE EXACTLY WHAT YOU WANT TO BE - DO WHAT YOU WANT TO DO!

Drax stood, open mouthed, as he watched the scenes unfold before him of the images painted along the Arks side.

"This is treasonous Titus," Felix Keeto declared.

"Treasonous and damaging to all of our plans, it is causing all manner of problems," Titus replied, "what this has created within the Hives are murmurings of discontent that we have to attend to immediately,"

"Titus, I see the name XAVIA, tell us more about this person," queried Drax.

"We have finally identified the person as Xavier Miro. He is from a trans-hab in The Hives and works as a rigger in ArkLight. Little is known of his whereabouts, he seems to have appeared out of nowhere. We have observed and monitored the situation from afar rather than arrest or remove him. We know he is a product of our academies and work details, he has never been brought to the attention of the Air Authority and remains incognito."

"I would hardly say this is incognito, Haq!" shouted Senator Fleming. "The kid is spraying graffiti all over the place and called for anarchy and democracy and then does something like this. That is hardly incognito."

"There has never been any record of checks for him. He seems to exist but not exist. He has a job, a trans-hab, a girlfriend, a Rod and a social life but we do not know who he is or where he is from," retorted Titus Haq, himself confused by the mystery that surrounded Xavier. It would be unheard of to think that someone could live within Genesis for a number of years without them being noticed.

"We just see his graffiti and the name XAVIA. It is as if someone has removed all records from the system and allowed him to exist outside the system."

"There was graffiti in ancient Rome," said Dieter Rodriguez quietly, "graffiti is something which has existed for millennia. What is one man doing that others aren't?"

"There are many gangs and people leaving their marks on the side of a wall but none that make them three kilometres long with messages spouting democracy. These have meaning!" exclaimed Haq. "They are meant to destroy the very being of The Powers and question our authority!"

"It comes with the territory, does it not?" asked Felix Keeto.

"I agree you will always have some kind of lone voice or insurgent demonstrating against authority," continued Haq.

"Sir, as you are aware, we can find and execute hackers or anyone using electronic communication almost immediately, even psychic terrorists can be easily identified and caught. But this man has chosen an almost prehistoric form of conveying his message and spreading his dissidence throughout the Hives and it seems he has remained undetected due to this."

A number of the guests shook their head, a belligerent Dimitri Illeneyich was fuming.

"I am sorry Haq, but are you trying to say that you have made this journey to Earth to see us because of a graffiti artist when we have the lives of billions under our control."

Titus stared at Dimitri, contemptuously, "This man also has an aura like nothing I have ever witnessed before. He has something ghostly about him, he radiates an energy that confounds myself and Halucifer. The problem is these dissident messages…this inflammable graffiti is being used as subliminal propaganda to the people of the Hives and believe me, it is working. It is creating a cult within the Hives and people are questioning why they are there and how they got there."

"So what is it saying exactly?" Primo Mietsu interrupted.

"If you would let me finish," Haq began, angry at the ignorance and arrogance of The Powers around him, "you have the luck, shall we call it, to have been born into privilege and so have found yourselves living on Earth controlling the fortunes of others. Xavier Miro, is saying quite simply, that there is an alternative to this system. He is telling the masses that there is a paradise close at hand… Earth," Haq paused briefly nodding his head, "yes...your private Earth...he is preaching that, ultimately, The Powers will lose their control."

For the first time, the twelve most powerful people in the known universe squirmed.

"Why have we not been able to stop this sooner, Titus?" Illeyenich demanded.

"Why are we getting all excited about some kid? Take him out and kill him!" Templar screamed, "I have far more important issues than this."

"This is just a damned graffiti artist! You are the governor...sort this out!" shouted Ronson Fleming.

"Is he working alone?" asked Doctor Garabidian.

"I believe that he works alone most times and also with an accomplice who we have in our custody."

"Is he aligned with the Civilisation movement?"

"No, I don't believe he is and we have taken measures to curtail any influence from Civilisation in the colonies."

"I heard - you have removed the figurehead Calvin Lacker," responded Drax.

"We used an external agency to carry out that operation. We are monitoring the situation but within a short amount of time a new figure always replaces the old," replied Titus.

The comment seemed barbed and directed towards Drax.

There was an uneasy silence between Drax and Haq.

"Where is he now?" asked Kraldon, politely ignoring the uneasy hush.

"On his way to Debris," Titus responded, sneering, "he is someone that we need to either educate or exterminate,"

"They are the scrawls of a foolish young man, nothing more!" flickered Premier Templar his 3-D link breaking up .

"The scrawls of a foolish young man can influence the many. I do not think we should ignore this," Zagrostine puffed on his cigar

"What shall we do?" asked K.C.Wang.

"Haq?" They all turned towards Titus.

"I engaged the services of Ferrer and his Shadows," Haq answered.

"No, not yet," Hoffman declared, "use an external agency and make sure we are not implicated."

"I have the perfect team for such an operation, Torruk and the Ganglion militia," said Senator Fleming raising his hands, as he turned to one of his advisors.

"They are certainly capable and callous enough for such a mission and for the right fee will do the job without any questions," Titus replied.

"Do you believe it such a threat?" Dieter Rodriguez breathed deeply.

"Who cares anyway," said Fleming, "we are The Powers."

"Messages like this cannot be tolerated within this society. The man is a threat to the fabric and must be taken out," Titus exclaimed

"Go do it," came the reply.

"You are the governor of Genesis, Titus and we entrust you to deal with this matter effectively and swiftly. Keep me informed of any developments," Drax commanded. Titus nodded towards Drax and then gestured to Zagrostine to join him, before turning and leaving from the room as the light returned and the moon began to light up old Paris.

"Right let's get back to proper business, Proxima Centauri and our interests across the Kuiper Belt" commanded Drax Kraldon.

"At last," sighed Dmitri Illeyenich, "I can't believe we were talking about some kid and his graffiti." And with that they began to talk about the opportunities that abounded them in the reaches of outer space.

"Ladies and gentlemen, let us eat," Drax Kraldon stated, standing up and ushering everyone towards a beautiful laid out dining room.

The stars twinkled in the dark blue sky as moon beams shone over the Eiffel Tower illuminating a concerned looking Doctor Garibidian and Drax Kraldon who were deep in thought.

"This Xavier problem – is it really that bad?"

"I think he believes he can save the world," Kraldon replied, "first, let's see if he can save himself."

★★★★★

24
What Fools These Mortals Be!

T he Capello apartments were silent as Zola made her way through the front door into the dimly lit hallway. Only the hum of the air conditioning system could be heard as she swiftly made her way to her bedroom. Zola grabbed her belongings, throwing them into a large travel bag. She grabbed her helmet and a few family mementoes from a drawer; photos of her parents and of her brothers, alongside a picture of her and her friends playing Zaddonk in one of the Rec-Halls. She felt a sob rising in her throat and quickly placed her hand over her mouth, muffling the noise and placed a few more trinkets into the bag.

"What's the rush?"

Zola jumped back, startled by the voice. The shape of her father was silhouetted against the doorway.

"Uhm!…No rush," she said a little too quickly.

"I told you that nothing would come of socialising with that crowd. I knew it would end in trouble," said Fabian, solemnly, "We cannot even begin to foresee what trouble lies ahead for us all now."

"Oh Dad," cried Zola, "I didn't mean any harm to you or mom. You know that."

Fabian walked over to her and cradled her in his arms kissing her hair as he had done when she was a little girl, "I know," he said.

"My dear Zola, '*Shall we their fond pageant see? Lord, what fools these mortals be!*'"

"Puck!" Zola said smiling.

He nodded, "You remember? I used to read to you from *A Midsummer Nights Dream,*" he said gently.

"Yes, I never realised you were reading forbidden Earth literature!"

He just gathered her belongings from the bed and placed them in the bag. "I have already been approached by the authorities asking about your whereabouts Zola."

"What did you tell them?"

"My darling Zola I told them the truth," Fabian smiled, "I have not known your whereabouts or comings and goings for many years. You come and go as you please, you are your own woman."

Zola smiled despite the tears streaming down her face.

"You must get away from here," he whispered.

"Where?"

"It's not safe here. You should try and get on an Ark or a freighter somewhere."

"What about Brunel or Breeze?"

"Yes, your brothers do have contacts and friends within the intergalactic shipping lines, but they're both uncontactable. But I am not convinced that you should go through them, in any case."

"I just don't know where to start, Dad!" Zola said, in desperation.

"You have to start somewhere, Zola. It is just not safe for you here."

"What have I done?" she said quietly.

"Yes, you have done something very dangerous my dear. You have decided to have integrity and follow your conscience. That is all...you have been honest."

Zola burst into tears again, Fabian held her by the arms and looked into her eyes, "Stop this crying at once," he said, "I cannot remember the last time I saw you cry. You haven't cried since you were a child sobbing after losing at Zaddonk and now you shed tears...it is too late to start crying now." Fabian's voice croaked a little.

"But I did not want to bring trouble to our door," Zola said, continuing to sob.

"It has happened now Zola, and we will deal with it. Come now," Fabian wiped her tears with the palms of his hands and zipped her bag shut.

"What about mom?" asked Zola.

"She is fine, working, doing what she does best, a talk show I believe. She is unaware of all this furore."

"You need to call her."

"I have already, though I said nothing about what has been going on."

"Oh mom!" Zola burst into fresh tears at the thought she may never see her mother again.

"Zola, I am telling you. You need to go now before it is too late. Get away from here. Debris is too dangerous, Mars is too far, maybe the moon. Maybe one day you may get the chance of going to Earth."

"Earth? How?"

Fabian chuckled, "I used to dream about going to Earth every night when I slept as a little boy. What it must be like to have walked centuries before on her deserted beaches feeling her winds against your face, or through her woods and forest. As I got older I realised I would never be able to do that. Maybe one day you may get the chance but for me those dreams are gone."

Zola stared at her father.

"I have questioned for many years my own convictions about Pax Humana. I have witnessed things which I have not agreed with but I did what I thought was best and kept my mouth shut," Fabian continued sternly, "I always believed that mankind's place was amongst the stars and for the greater good, we should expand to frontiers new. Yet, at what price? It has been a regime that has treated both myself and your mother well. You and your brothers have wanted for nothing, you have had the best Nu Humana could offer."

"I did what I thought was right," Zola said, a spark of defiance returning.

"We all believe what we do is right, but now you will find out whether you were wrong," said Fabian obstinately.

"Father you are just brainwashed by them."

"Zola, I love you. Never mind me. You must go, now."

Fabian was all too aware of the consequences of opposing Nu Humana or the other corporations. He knew that the fall from grace that would beset him and his wife would be swift and he wanted Zola to be far away when it happened.

Zola picked up her bag.

"Zola, you have harboured many secrets from me over the years, so I am sure you will work something out. We brought you up to be a survivor."

She wiped her tears and strode to the door. She gently kissed her father one last time on his cheek.

Fabian stood impassively beside her as she opened the front door and stepped away.

"Zola, I used to see Xavier's paintings scattered around Genesis. And used to think about what he painted for the people. I, like yourself, had access to Edu-Imps and memory banks unlike many of the residents of The Hives. So I know the secrets of history, the Digital Dark Age and of The Powers, but I kept my mouth shut," Fabian paused, "for too many people who have attempted to change their world, it has ended in calamity not only for them but for their cause."

"So you do nothing?" Zola stood nonchalantly.

"Trying to find a better way, fighting for personal freedoms, replacing one system with another, only for the new one to become as corrupt as the previous one. Be careful what you wish for Zola, for it is endemic of mankind."

"I love you dad," she said before giving her father a hug. She feared she might never see him again.

They stood there for a while unable to let go.

"I love you too Zola. Be well my child."

★★★★★

25
Dumpo And The Rave

"**A**re you sure you know where you are going?" Old Man Ray asked Xavier.

"What?" said Xavier looking around at the derelict spacecraft and boulders of Debris as they proceeded deeper and deeper into the interior of the menacing zone.

"The place changes so quickly now. I am not so sure," replied Ray, sheepishly.

"Great, just great!" exclaimed Xavier, "The last thing we need is to be lost in Debris with who knows what lurking around every corner."

"We'll be fine. Nothing will hurt us," said Ray.

"You don't think we look just a little out of place in an OK 3000?"

"Listen son, if they had wanted to kill you, they'd have done it by now."

"Very reassuring," Xavier replied, checking that his personal sidearm was with him.

Aqua Terra proceeded cautiously, penetrating what Xavier assumed to be the interior of a disused freighter. Lights from little settlements and private homesteads, attached to the sides of depleted asteroids, illuminated the way. Refuse was everywhere, ensuring it was incredibly dangerous to fly through Debris. The region lay across what was known as The Divide, an area separating the Genesis colonies from the abandoned wastage and discarded vessels that made up this wilderness. Even with the many protective shields and deflectors that were fitted to Aqua Terra, Xavier still fretted about the paint job on his beloved Rod, although he knew that was the least of his worries.

"Now, I used to come here with an old timer called Ducky Clarke. An absolutely crazy man many moons ago and as far as I am aware, the place is still here and so too is Ducky!" said Ray.

"Well, I hope so, for your sake," Xavier said lightly.

Old Man Ray fixed his eyes on Xavier, unimpressed.

"I'm kidding!" Xavier said by way of apology. Upsetting Ray was not the best course of action, he knew that.

They entered a vast cavernous expanse that resembled the hulls of countless vessels which had been turned inward to form cathedral-like chasms.

"That's the place!" cried Old Man Ray, pointing to a glowing yellow and green beacon in the distance.

"I knew it would be here! I knew it," he said, "see boy, my memory is not that bad after all."

There was a flurry of activity. Rods and craft appeared, many heading straight up to a glowing light at the very top of this gigantic chamber; an endless procession of gallivanting spacers. The G's kicked in, Xavier pulled back on the controls and Aqua Terra ascended vertically, forcing Old Man Ray into the back of his seat. Thankfully he was strapped in or he would have shot out of his chair and into the ceiling. With a slight rotation, Xavier guided Aqua Terra towards a narrow entrance that seemed to be the entrance for the other Rods. They entered a large hangar with four protruding gantries where Rods could dock and disembark. Two robots approached from the gantry, lights flashing so as to direct the Rod into a waiting bay.

"Don't tell me they have valet parking in Debris," sighed Xavier, shaking his head.

"You are always having a pop, young man. There are some very decent people who live in Debris. Many of them better than the brainwashed toe rags you find in The Hives, let me tell you!" Ray replied, firmly. "You don't need to park here anyway, Xavier. Let me show you where to go. We're on the guest list."

It seemed people were arriving from all over Debris. Bus parties, barges, couples on the back of space-bikes, mechanised trucks, personnel vehicles; every type of transport imaginable.

"Where to now Ray?" asked Xavier.

Ray gestured to the right and Xavier turned his rod. As they got closer a large steel door slid open revealing a loading bay with a pipe that automatically descended over the hatch of

Aqua Terra. A red light flashed momentarily before turning to green.

"We are good to go, boy. I told you I knew all the right places."

"Yes, I hear you Ray."

With that, the harnesses of the seat restraints opened allowing them both to get up from their seats. Xavier placed his sidearm inside his jacket, just in case, while Ray fumbled around with his bag making sure he had all his necessities. Old Man Ray was always forgetting things, so he had to go through an elaborate routine wherever he went, checking every pocket and compartment to make sure he had not lost anything.

"Sends me mad this does," he said furiously, rummaging through his bag, "I hate living in space sometimes."

"You should be used to it by now," said Xavier.

"You never get used to it. It's not natural, is it? I'd like to walk around in the nude if I had the chance, but that ain't going to happen! I remember back in the good old days in *Sativaland* where we would all walk around naked, free to do as we pleased in our domed environments amongst the plants, going from one tree-house to another, gazing at the glorious Earth and wondering what she would have been like centuries before we were banished."

"You Moon Dudes," shrugged Xavier, nonchalantly, "You're all a little freaky if you ask me."

"Freaky! We sure were freaky! We were damned Moon Dudes! What do you expect?" Ray spluttered in excitement, "You look at mother nature every day of your life knowing you will never be able to get there. Watching those oceans in the distance is enough to turn anyone freaky. You can see it, but you can never touch it. You see boy, you've all been brainwashed. You have all become conditioned. They do that to you, these corporations, and The Powers who control them. That's how they want you to be. It's your planet too, you know!" Xavier recognised an Old Man Ray rant when he heard one, and said nothing. Ray paused briefly and took in a deep breath.

"Don't forget to bring your helmet," said Ray sharply, pointing at Xavier's helmet that had been left on his seat.

"We expecting trouble?"

"This is Debris, Xavier. You never know what to expect!" Ray said sternly.

He then tied his long white hair back with a multi-coloured band, attached his helmet to his rucksack and taking a small box from his pocket, proceeded to take a pill.

"What are those for?" Xavier asked again.

"My heart, son, my heart," replied Ray, as he led the way.

They walked up the exit pipe and into the gantry. Xavier turned to Ray, "Will Aqua Terra be okay? I mean nobody is going to touch her. Are they?"

"Aqua Terra will be perfectly fine here, Xavier," Ray said reassuringly. "You will be well received and looked after."

They passed a large menacing group of security guards and robots.

"I told you, there are a lot of good people in Debris. People who are here to help others. People who do not need to hear the messages of The Powers; people who have stepped out from the shadows."

Ray then turned to face Xavier, "Xavier, you are a young man, but you are also worldly and wise in many ways. Listen to those around you and listen to yourself. Your dreams are messages from somewhere. Understand them and share them. There is always danger, but you have to face it. You do anyway; everyone does. Every day you leave the confines of your trans-hab and enter the docks you take risks. I am an old man now, Old Man Ray they call me, I remember when it was just Ray. Time goes by so quickly. We are just molecules in this great, enormous Universe, but you are special, trust me, you are a different set of molecules from the rest of us."

Xavier tried to speak but Ray held his finger up, "Don't say anything, let's rave!"

They walked down a corridor filled with revellers whose excitement was palpable. The atmosphere was jovial and polite, and there was an air of expectancy. People were greeting one another, telling jokes and catching up on gossip. Old Man Ray would nod to each group and smile his gentle smile, acknowledged by everyone as he made his way through the throngs.

Xavier followed at his side, aware of all the gentle adulation and respect Old Man Ray was receiving. Moon Dudes were well loved all over Genesis. Seen by some as a relic of a bygone age, they were admired because they had endured and found a sanctuary on the moon centuries before, discovering an oasis for humans in desolate conditions.

Old Man Ray had lived on the moon throughout his childhood and Xavier did not know why he had come to Genesis, but ever since he could remember, Old Man Ray had been there; guiding him and instructing him as he began working at Ark Light. It was Ray who had explained to him the origin of art on Earth which had begun when men had entered caves and left paintings upon the walls that depicted wild animal life they had seen and hunted. He had explained to Xavier that those images had been created for their own enjoyment and for the enjoyment of others. They did not *have* to paint on the cave walls. They did it for their own pleasure and entertainment. Xavier had taken that on board and felt it had lot to do with his need to spray the walls of The Hives and the great Arks and freighters. He was inspired by the old Earth dwellers of urban areas who, once upon a time, created visual art for the people of their slums that had in time become a worldwide network of art that connected certain artists and cities. Like the cavemen he had initially done it for his own amusement. Now, it seemed, people in The Cannery believed he was writing especially to them sending covert messages. For Xavier, it was still very much about seeing his work on the sides of structures, large-scale. As they entered the foyer of the party, Old Man Ray was greeted by a rather over-excited man in what looked to be animal furs.

"Hey Ray, my old man, it's Slobbo!" he shouted, in a strong Russian accent.

"Wow! It's Slobbo Grenzky!" said Old Man Ray, greeting the large, moustachioed man with a pretty intimidating presence.

Slobbo Grenzky was the premier rave promoter in Debris. He was from one of the Ruski spheres on the Moon side of Genesis and had worked for many years in one of the craters owned by Ruski Lunski, one of the biggest aggregators of moon rock. Lunar dust was important for the development of Genesis and especially in the construction of scores of early spheres where it had been used as a preventative measure against the radioactive rays that journeyed through space from the sun. From time to time solar winds full of radioactivity would penetrate parts of Genesis, killing thousands. Because of this a three meter defensive rock-screen was placed around the wheels and spheres insulating and protecting inhabitants from the harmful rays. This had elevated the owners of the Ruski Lunski corporation to the status of trillionaires.

Slobbo had worked his way up from being a lowly miner to a wealthy executive within Ruski Lunski, before taking an early retirement and living in one of the High Pioneers colonies. He had procured a beautiful Solar Yacht and had more time to indulge in his passion for Mining Muzik by throwing outrageously popular parties in Debris. Slobbo had used murder and extortion to make his way, which by the look of Slobbo came as no surprise to Xavier. He was now a ruthless assassin. Having built up from the odd hit on rivals and troublemakers before turning it into his core business. And why not? He was good at it and plus there was money in it.

Within a couple of years he had become the most dominant figure in the moon aggregated-rock business. His employers now worked for him and his competitors…well, they were all dead.

He stood before Xavier and Old Man Ray in what looked like synthetic animal furs, a forage cap and a brilliant diamond necklace that could only have come from one of the asteroids in the Kuiper Belt. It seemed to be surrounded by what looked like dried ears.

"What's going on guys? Old Man Ray, you're looking keefer my man! Old Moon Dude!" said Slobbo in his heavily accented English.

"Can't complain, Slobbo. Still crazy after all these years, know what I mean. The place looks fantastic by the way. Looks like we could be in for some fun," said Old Man Ray.

"You know that I always have the best parties and especially when I have the company of friends old and new."

Old Man Ray turned to Xavier, "Sorry I have not introduced my friend. This here is Xavier Miro. He is a very dear person to me."

"Not a problem Ray, a dear friend to you is a dear friend to me. It is my pleasure." And with that, Slobbo immediately took Xavier's hand in his meaty palm and led him into the rave.

"Let me get you guys a drink," he said, signalling to a beautiful waitress. "So what do you think? This is all mine. The greatest rave in the known galaxy," he said, with a sweeping gesture. "This is what I do and I love it. No more mining in some shit hole for me. I like to party; party like no one else has done before. Existential!"

Slobbo's enthusiasm made Xavier smile, wondering absently what he had meant by his last exclamation. The three of them walked together into an auditorium that seemed to extend infinitely. A waitress brought over a servo droid with three large glasses of champagne. She smiled and the droid whirred as the drinks were raised towards them.

"Xavier, have you ever had champagne?" Slobbo enquired.

"Can't say I have but I think I've heard of it. What is it?"

"My friend, it is the drink of the Gods!" Slobbo's voice was full of power and authority, "You see my friend has a vineyard factory ship on the High Side of Genesis. Champagne is made from grapes and he makes it like they used to on Earth centuries ago. They called it Genesis Cristal."

They chinked glasses and Xavier felt the bubbles in his glass go up his nose. It was a strange sensation.

"Tastes good" Xavier said, experiencing a warmth spreading in his chest.

"*Spasiba*," replied Slobbo laughing. "Come with me. Let's cut through the dressing rooms."

He pulled Ray to his side, "I have been listening to some fantastic music from Earth, from centuries ago. We pulled some Edu-Imps you had told us to listen to, great stuff, like James Brown, Parliament/Funkadelic and Sly and The Family Stone, thanks old friend!"

"Happy to help Slobbo."

Slobbo thumped Ray on his back, his eyes rolling, "What were those people on?"

"I dunno, but I have to say this is delicious!" said Ray, helping himself to another glass of Slobbo's champagne.

"I am glad you like it," said Slobbo. "Here, come with me," he said ushering Xavier and Old Man Ray to a VIP area decorated in the style of a lunar bedouin tent.

A group of Slobbo's heavies and body guards formed a protective cordon for him and his personal guests to keep at bay the unwashed, uninitiated and uninvited. Only the beautiful and esteemed of Slobbo's crowd were allowed access here and Xavier felt quite out of place in these luscious surrounds of party central. Slobbo signalled for more of his champagne to be brought to them from one of a troupe of girls that stood quietly and demurely to the side of the area.

"Ray, so wonderful to see you again. You still look ancient," Slobbo joked, pulling at his cheek.

Old Man Ray smiled but was not really smiling. "Slobbo, I remember you when you were swinging around in your old man's ball bag. Then you were doing hits out of Apollo City for the Lunski Bratva."

"Relax Ray, we all have our secrets, right?" Slobbo said apologetically. Despite the camaraderie Xavier picked up an undercurrent of tension between them. Old Man Ray took Slobbo's head in his hands and kissed him on his forehead winking at Slobbo.

"And you Xavier? I believe I have heard of your name before," Slobbo turned to the young rigger.

"Really?" Xavier wondered in what context. He sipped some more of the champagne.

The girl who had greeted Ray and Xavier as they entered the Thunderground sidled up to Slobbo, trying to get his attention.

She was extraordinarily beautiful, and she may as well have been naked as her party outfit did not amount to anything more than a few pieces of polite tape placed strategically. Xavier smiled trying not to look.

"The free and easy lifestyle of Debris eh?" laughed Ray. "Able to dress and behave as you want, when you want."

"It ain't so bad in Genesis Ray if you are my age and know where to look," grinned Xavier, "but I will take a piece of that all day long," indicating ahead where a group of girls, painted head to toe in silver and gold, prepared themselves to go out onto the dance floor. They were sprinkling glitter on their naked, airbrushed bodies, laughing and giggling at one another. Their luscious hair was adorned with flowers from one of the hydro gardens.

Xavier took a step towards them when they started running over. He moved out of their way to avoid being trampled.

"Ray! Ray! Ray! It's Old Man Ray!" The girls were jubilant and planted kisses all over him.

Xavier nearly choked on his champagne. Who was this man? This was Old Man Ray, the cranky loony Moon Dude from ArkLight Docks, rigger and grinder on the Tamarinsk Ark. Now he was being greeted as though he was Jett Jensen.

Old Man Ray pulled himself away from the amorous advances of the glittering girls and deflecting his embarrassment, turned to Xavier, "This is my good friend Xavier Miro."

A tall red haired girl stepped forward with blue lightning make up on either side of her eyes, she winked at Xavier, "Hi, Xavier Miro. I love your work," She planted a kiss on his lips. "My name is Keki Lascaux. Welcome to the Thunderground!"

"You know my work?" Xavier nearly choked on his bubbles.

"We all do," said Keki.

"That's very interesting," Xavier replied, dumbfounded.

"Let's get interesting later…" She winked and grasped his hand tightly before kissing him.

Slobbo burst into laughter, "She's got you Xavier!"

"Those girls will chew you up and then spit you out," Ray declared. "In the best possible way of course."

"You know what they say," Slobbo added. "Those that know…know!"

"Strictly for the hardcore. Only for the headstrong," laughed Xavier.

"You got it boy, those old sayings are so true," said Old Man Ray.

"Come and join us," Keki's friend suggested. They sat on a row of huge cushions around a small table as a warm and gentle ambient tune played.

"So, what are those things you paint Xavier?" asked Keki.

"What are those thing I paint…hmm!"

"The things you paint on the sides of The Hives and colony walls."

"They are animals," Xavier answered finally.

The girl seemed unsure of what he meant.

"Earth animals. They used to inhabit that blue dot we look at every day."

"I see! And what are the other things?"Keki enquired.

"They are scenes from Earth. That's what the planet used to look like hundreds of years ago," said Xavier.

"And as a matter of fact what it looks like today, this very moment," Old Man Ray interrupted.

"Wow! Beautiful!" Keki said, sidling closer to Xavier.

"Some of the characters I do are the indigenous tribes that used to live there," Xavier continued, "like we used to."

"Isn't it funny how we look at Earth every day in the distance knowing we will never get there. And funny to think that we once came from there?" said her friend before getting up and joining the rest of the girls, leaving Keki alone with Xavier and Ray.

"It must have been like that on Earth centuries ago when people looked at the moon and dreamt of visiting there," Keki continued.

"You are from the Moon originally aren't you Ray?" enquired Keki, pouring more drinks for everyone.

"Don't get him started on that," said Xavier, hurriedly stopping himself and changing tack. Ray was easily offended. "You know once upon a time, the moon was not touched by human hands. It was perfect. A perfect environment. Then man arrived from Earth and left his first footprint, then a tyre track, then left his first pile of garbage, then left for a while," he paused momentarily. "Came back again and then never left."

Old Man Ray stared at Xavier as he spoke so passionately. He also saw how intently Slobbo listened to him tell the history of a place they both knew so well.

"Now it looks like a planet full of garbage! Nobody respected the fact that once it was a unique environment, unpolluted and untouched. No! They dug holes, mined the ores, built their cities and that perfect wasteland of rock, became a dumping ground for us humans."

"Sad. It seems we always do the same thing?" said Keki astutely, with an understanding beyond her seemingly young years.

"Some people have done well out of the trade of mineral rights on the moon," said Slobbo.

Keki leant in towards Xavier, "Xavier, there are so many people throughout Genesis who love the messages you send. How do you find inspiration?"

"I'm a dreamer, just a dreamer," he coughed. "I will tell you this, I have always had feelings about being on Earth and felt energies which are particularly strong right now. I know it sounds crazy but I think I have been there."

"Really?" sighed Keki, staring intently at him.

"Well, I do a lot of Edu-Imps too," Xavier laughed, feeling an uneasy intensity developing between Keki and himself, as she hung on his every word. After all there was the matter of Zola.

"You should speak with Slobbo," Keki leapt from her seat and turned to the big Russian.

"Yes!" shouted Slobbo, "I am the King of The Edu-Imp, you know young man! Any unsanctioned Edu-Imp you have been doing has usually had my mark on it."

"That's right!" Old Man Ray piped in.

"Really?" Xavier replied, with genuine amazement.

"Whatever you want I can hook you up?" Slobbo said, proudly.

Xavier shook his head at the prospect of a new supplier of illicit Edu-Imps.

"Let's put it this way I have my fingers in a lot of pies. What do you like?" Slobbo asked.

"I like all sorts…20th and 21st Century mainly. Straight-Up-Imps, Liqui-Hitz, Cerebral Curls even DML's."

Slobbo laughed, "A connoisseur I see. I take it you have a good source."

Xavier smiled, "I like the Edu to be educational if you know what I mean. Historical Earth is my personal favourite. Anything that I can learn from, anything with a twist," he said careful not to give up Kaiser as his main supplier of Edu-Imps.

"OK, well leave it with me, and I will get you some of the best there is," Slobbo nodded and smiled pouring himself another drink.

"K-O-K," said Xavier, excited at the prospect of a new source of Edu-Imps.

"Would you like to try some of this?" asked Keki, opening a small golden container, her elegant fingernails glinting in the light.

"Sure, I guess…but what is it?" Xavier asked peering into the mysterious box.

"Oh man! You want to see the Big Bang?" Slobbo beamed, his face lighting up.

"The creation of the universe is contained in that little vial," chortled Slobbo. "Let me tell you!"

"This is Zug mucus, straight off the back," said Keki, "It's from Dumpo!"

"You do know who Dumpo is, right? Property of one heavy bunch of pirates who happen to be my good, good friends," Slobbo was proud of the fact he had such connections, not that there was any doubt that a man in his position had access to pretty much anything.

"She is here tonight," said Keki reverentially, revealing her veneration of the old Zugbot.

"The Ha! Ha! Matey's look after her. She is a freaking divine-being to those guys. They will murder people to protect her. They look after her well."

Xavier had heard how the pirate gangs kept Zugbots on board their ships

"I know who she is," Old Man Ray acknowledged.

"From time to time they give me some of her mucus…pure mucus. The finest mucus you can get. Incredible stuff," Slobbo grinned excitedly and nodded at his guests, "it is like receiving an offering or blessing from a god.

They say she has magical powers and that the mucus contains stardust from another galaxy."

"Transcendental stuff you know, c'mon try some," Keki coaxed Xavier gently.

Old Man Ray looked at Xavier and then the golden container as if it held the key of life to the universe. Maybe it did.

"Let's do some, man!" an eager Slobbo snatched the container from Keki. A haze of kaleidoscopic colours swirled around above the box from the glittering crystals inside. It looked like a huge ball of candy cotton twinkling amidst them.

"Woah! Looks good, take a whiff!" said Slobbo.

Xavier and Keki politely waited for Slobbo and then Old Man Ray to inhale the multicoloured mirage. Next Keki took a long inhale of the vapours. She immediately lay down on the cushions, closing her eyes.

"Here Xavier!" Slobbo beamed, pulling what appeared to be a small golden dagger out which he twirled for a few seconds in the air, capturing the hallucinogenic candy cotton substance as it stuck to the sides of the blade.

"You can only use gold," he said, as the treacly material bonded to the edge, "it is the only material in which it can be stored and used. Don't ask me why!"

He looked as if he was conducting an orchestra with a baton when without warning, he lunged across at Xavier, seizing him and pinning him to his seat, "Here boy. Try some of this!"

"Hey man! What're you doing?" Ray cried out.

Slobbo used his body to barricade Xavier. He pinched his nose, forcing him to open his mouth before wiping the sides of the dagger containing the mucus across Xavier's tongue. Keki began mumbling something. Xavier began to shudder.

"Just relax," Slobbo crooned as he released him from his grip.

"What was that for? That's some strong shit for him!" said Ray, concerned for Xavier.

"He will be fine!" countered the Russian as he sat back down.

Xavier's eyes lost focus and he sat motionless leaning on the wall.

"So what about you Ray?"

"Hand it over," said the Old Man not batting an eye.

Slobbo placed some on the old man's tongue, "Thank the pirates for this!"

He then let Keki lick off some more of the nectar from the dagger. He then took a larger bit for himself, putting some on his tongue and snorting another piece from the tip of the dagger. Once again he laughed uproariously.

Xavier looked at Ray looking back at him, and then to Keki and Slobbo, as they all began to disintegrate into another time and space.

Their bodies contorted at the same time and then they were gone. Gone into oblivion.

Chris Abbot

★★★★★

26
THUNDERGROUND

THIS IS A NEW LANGUAGE
THIS IS A NEW LANGUAGE
THIS IS A NEW LANGUAGE

T hunderground.

The repeated chant beckoned everyone towards the huge dance floor. It became apparent to Xavier that the Thunderground was an old power station and military hangar which had been converted by Slobbo and his cronies into a vast discotheque. It must have been three hundred years old but was still safe and serviceable. It was not as big as any of the contemporary space stations which could be tens of kilometres in length but it was still vast. An Island One series, around five kilometres in diameter, it had been salvaged by Slobbo, resealed and made safe and habitable then converted into his own personal pleasure palace.

The main section had three floors with the main floor open to the heavens and entrances which opened up the other floors. It rotated at one revolution per minute to maintain gravity, but as you got closer to the centre of the sphere you would enter zero-gravity. Here, revellers would embark on zero-G dancing. Huge bubbles of water that partygoers could dive into, shot out of cannons. The assortment of characters ranged from shamanic pirates out of their minds on Zugbot mucus who floated along on temple podiums, pioneer colonists losing it amongst the scum of Debris, Scun Scum groupies who followed the likes of Crater Face around the solar system, ravers from The Hives who zoned out in Debris for a few weeks before returning to work on the Arks and *nouveau riche* mining prospectors with their wives or girlfriends flashing their riches to the Debris locals. Anyone who wanted to be free of the shackles of The Cannery and embrace hedonism were to be found here.

Many partygoers were dressed like mythical birds, celestial beings or star signs, their fanciful costumes replete with wings that allowed them to swoop down from weightlessness onto the main dance floor. The majority of people came in their protective atmosphere suits, customised, as was the fashion, with Cannery regalia fixed to their helmets and pads and with patches and badges denoting the station or sphere from which they came.

All of these wanderers and travellers were now dancing together to the sounds of Crater Face, who were performing a set of mining anthems and beats. They were all united by one cause - transcendence.

Crater Face, dressed in full attire, twisted around the stage as their latest track, 'Approach and Identify - Recognize Me And I'll Shoot' boomed through the arena.

Lasers swathed the audiences in ever changing glows. The place was alive - the mass of dancers becoming more and more lost in their primal trance. Here the tribal instinct ruled. Here they were not governed by the restraints and limitations imposed on them. Here, was pure freedom.

Zugbots floated on raised hover platforms, their hallucinogenic vapours cascading into the atmosphere. Surrounding each Zugbot were a cluster of pirates wearing protective masks so as not to overdose on the intoxicating fumes, ensured the attentions of the excitable crowd did not trouble their charge too much. The Zugbots shuffled from left to right entranced by the music and unaware of the hysteria they were creating around them. A ceremony would take place sporadically where a pirate would scrape some of the mucus exuded from the Zugbot and offer it to the crowd.

As the drum beat kicked up a notch, sharpening like knives, the hypersonic sounds became a force field. Xavier was lost in the intensity. He could just about make out Old Man Ray surrounded by a throng of young Canners and ravers from Debris. He was jerking his body to the beat shouting from the top of his lungs, "It takes the old ones to show the young ones how to do it!"

Xavier had no idea how he had gotten to the dance floor or even to Debris. In this moment he knew nothing.

Ahead of him, Xavier could make out one of the platforms used for the Zugbots coming towards him. He saw the mighty Dumpo, sitting upon a dais. Dumpo was as legendary in Debris as Old Man Ray seemed to be, a large rotund Zugbot with a tough, light-green leathery hide, bedecked with beads and necklaces from top to bottom. Dumpo had over decades made her name as the notorious party Zugbot because of her seemingly inexhaustible, streaming supply of hallucinogenic mucus that blew out of her and vaporised in the air. Dumpo was fiercely guarded by her shamanic pirate gang, The Ha Ha Mateys!, who danced around her and revered her as a fantastical deity. They delighted in the preposterous names they gave themselves, whilst their lewd and effusive gestures to one another delighted onlookers. The Shiver Me Timbers, The Debris Devils, The Black Holies, The Immortal Souls, The Bandit Queens and The Celestial Scallywags, resplendent in their flamboyant garb, acknowledged one another with flourishing bows, jigs, swearing shanties and full blown pagan idolatry.

"Beware, Xavier, beware! Keep your wits about you!"

Xavier froze. Where had the voice come from? He was sure he hadn't heard it with his ears. Overhead, Dumpo was gliding back. Xavier could see her descending, her skin green and gold like a lizard from one of his murals. Old Man Ray was grinning and bowing. Dumpo was now floating away. Xavier could have sworn she was looking right at him. Revellers shrieked with delight as she discharged a glistening rainbow cloud of her precious elixir. The pirates whooped with joy.

Keki Lascaux was standing in front of him. She kissed him hard and then pulled away. Xavier's body was jolting as the rhythm of Crater Face now turned to that of Scun Scum and the hit 'Drill Me, Master, Drill Me!' mixed with 'I Smell Gas, Here's My Pipe!'

He had no control. It was as if the energy of the music, the elation of the people around him was inside him, moving him, lifting him, lifting him…lifting everyone.

Zero gravity. His body was in the air. Everyone was in the air. Couples embraced airborne arabesques, Old Man Ray hung in the air, his arms open wide.

From somewhere he heard the words, "Let's start as we mean to go on! Let's start as we mean to go on!" as Scun Scum's vocal filled the air.

Below him Keki was floating up towards him, her arms outstretched. She was radiant. Her hair a floating luminous mass.

He was reaching out, pulling her towards him. They were kissing. He felt they were as one body.

She was whispering, "I cannot think of anywhere I would rather be right now."

Above them the vast expanse of space, glinting - the deep blues of Earth in the distance. Xavier felt he was exactly where needed to be - at this moment, in this place. He did not know if he spoke it.

Keki embraced Xavier wrapping her legs around his. They spun through the air, hurtling as one, swirling and laughing deliriously. Their arms flailed to the music, their legs and bodies entwined. Xavier felt he was immersed in her hair floating out like a protective mask and her perfume which seemed to engulf him. He heard her giggle as if very far away and then Xavier was lost. Around him people seemed to be swimming in and out of enormous suspended spheres of water, rolling, spinning and wheeling through the air.

Keki gestured Xavier towards the water. Their mouths connected again, her beautiful blue eyes seemingly staring into him. From the corner of his eye he thought he saw a blanket of small red droplets. Keki was looking right at him, her eyes boring into him. A tear rolled out of her eye floating up. Red droplets were materialising all around them. Still her blue eyes looking into his. She appeared to be quivering.

He heard himself calling her.

Keki not responding.

Keki's body going limp, flittering like a silk scarf. Her beautiful eyes still open.

★★★★★

27
Ganglions

E verything had seemed to be in slow motion before. Now it had speeded up as stark reality engulfed him.

Xavier could only have imagined what his face looked like as a mixture of horror and shock. He saw the face of Slobbo transform as the big Russian realised what had happened, his eyes bulging out of his head.

The lifeless body of Keki Lascaux, dancer extraordinaire, a girl so full of love and life fell from Xavier's arms. She spun slowly, floating away as if performing a morbid ballet, a trail of red blood bubbles trailing from the back of her head like a scarlet tail. Xavier reached out towards her, trying desperately to grab hold of her, as a red mist appeared to the right of him and then to the left. The music was still pounding and the flickering strobes animated everything around him. He kicked his legs to propel himself away as two more bodies drifted where only seconds before they had been revelling. Xavier watched their screaming partners as he floated, tears welling up in his eyes. Xavier felt a strong hand upon his forearm and a sharp tug as Old Man Ray and Slobbo pulled him towards them under the shelter of a large steel stanchion.

"Ganglions!" Slobbo screamed, as a group of these creatures, mutant mercenaries, came careering through the terrified crowd, shooting and bludgeoning anyone in their way. They were grabbing anything they wanted.They seemed to be heading straight towards Xavier, Old Man Ray and Slobbo.

Xavier felt frozen. Slobbo began to shake him.

Ganglions came from a mining colony near the Outer Rim, victims of a radiation outbreak a century before which had left them no choice but to interbreed. They had become a savagely violent band of mercenaries who sold their services to the highest bidder. They would prey on lone freighters which had lost their way in the Rim, and it was rumoured they would cannibalise the poor souls found on board.

Old Man Ray slapped Xavier hard across his face.

"Xavier," he bellowed, "we need to move! Now!"

"Keki?" Xavier mouthed.

"She's dead, boy."

Xavier flinched and looked again to where they had just been. The ecstatic revellers were now panicking and looking for cover as Ganglion marksman took crack shots as they tried to flee. Their costumes billowing out as their bodies spiralled down once shot.

Red clouds of blood replaced joyful dancers.

The party masks now death masks.

The costumes ghostly shrouds.

"Fish in a barrel!" shouted Old Man Ray. He turned to Slobbo who had now managed to retrieve Keki's lifeless body. He was carrying the controls for the sphere purposefully.

"This scum is going to pay for this outrage," the Russian screamed, his face and neck red with rage.

With the flick of an emergency switch the sphere suddenly kicked back into life and began to rotate again. Gravity returned and thousands of revellers fell unceremoniously to the floor. Gruesome piles of bodies were growing all around the room, as bodies fell upon other bodies. The sound of bones cracking and gravity taking over filling the room with screams, shrieks and sobbing as they struggled to get away. The scramble for survival had begun.

They hurtled towards the decks trampling one another in a desperate bid to flee. All the stories about the risks of partying in Debris were about to come true. Within the space of a minute, the euphoric highs of thousands had been replaced with sheer terror.

"We have to get out of here! Now!" bawled Old Man Ray, pulling Xavier up from the floor.

Shots still flew in all directions killing people as they clambered to find the exits. The protective windows were built to withstand the odd blast from a gun but a continual barrage spelt death. Ruptured shields would mean being exposed to the vacuum of space and being boiled alive through hypoxia.

"This is an outrage. I will torture the perpetrators till I find out who is responsible," Slobbo raged, "we have an amnesty.

This is murder. All the top pirate crews and their chiefs were here. Not one would break the code."

"This is not the work of pirates," replied Old Man Ray, "this is far higher up. This is an organised hit."

"I am going to kill every last one of them," retorted Slobbo, as his bodyguard passed him a couple of firearms, "I do the murdering around here."

Xavier felt his mind clearing. He crouched down and pulled his sidearm from his jacket.

"Not yet boy!" said Old Man Ray, laser bolts and shrapnel flying in all directions. He placed his hand firmly on Xavier's arm and stared into his eyes and repeated himself solemnly, "Not yet!"

Slobbo looked at the young rigger and shook his head.

"You may have a lot to answer for," he said, "perhaps, I should have been more wary of you and what you represent, but for now, keep your head down."

With that, Slobbo strode steadfastly towards a group of sheltering pirates.

In a haze of Zugbot hallucinogens the pirates turned as one.

"It has nothing to do with us!" they cried.

"They're Ganglions," said another.

"I saw their leader, Torruk, earlier and thought it strange for him to be here. Amnesty or not, he does not come to these parties. He is one of the vilest and most terrifying of men! He would sell his own mother."

"He did sell his mother!" another pirate shouted.

"I believe you. We'll get to the bottom of this later but for now we are going to have to fight this mutant scum," Slobbo roared.

"If that seal goes, we are all done for. We have to take these Ganglions out and now. No mercy! Except Torruk...I need him alive. I need to know who ordered this," Slobbo said, the last part in a voice laced with pure revenge.

"Torruk may have no morals but this is suicidal - to take on the pirates of Debris at a party thrown by Slobbo Grenzky! It makes no sense!" declared one of the pirates.

Slobbo may have been big and had a penchant for wearing synthetic animal furs, drinking champagne, dancing with a bevy of girls and throwing lavish parties but he was not a man to be trifled with. The scars across his body paid testament to that. He was a generous host and he loved the people he called his friends, be they corporate men, pirates, prophets or poets. He had battled and fought for everything he had and he certainly was not going to let a bunch of mutant gunmen ruin his party and take his life and the lives of his friends. He had also seen the beautiful body of Keki float past him. She was one of his favourite girls. He had a niggling feeling that Xavier was the cause of this. But for the moment, he had other things on his mind.

Turning to the assembled pirates he shouted, "No more hiding. Let's go hunting!"

In one fluid movement the group, led by Slobbo, jumped out screaming like interstellar buccaneers from behind the stanchion, towards the bewildered Ganglions. In the mayhem that ensued, they joined as one with the other pirate gangs, with the sole intent of killing or capturing as many of the mercenary Ganglions as they could. Slobbo had always been good to them, always treating the pirates with respect and welcoming them to his parties on the condition they lay down their weapons and disputes whilst under his roof. They were going to fight for Slobbo because of this respect, something which was not easy to find in Debris or on Genesis.

"You stay here and wait for us to come back," Old Man Ray said, staring directly into Xavier's face.

Xavier looked at him, his face cold and unresponsive. A chill ran through Old Man Ray as he looked at the young rigger. Xavier held his sidearm close to him, savage acts and brutal killing taking place around him. The pirates' experienced hand of vengeance began to wreak its deadly touch. Callous butchery was now the order of the day as revenge, in its most cold and violent form was dished up.

The freighter upon which The Ganglions arrived was boarded and any mercenary that was captured alive was to be bound and forced to lay prostrate upon the deck.

"Who is your leader?" shouted the pirate Gratt The Brat, his mouth foaming from Zug juice and his body covered in battle scars and tattoos.

"Torruk," a terrified Ganglion gave up his name without hesitation.

"Good for you," said Gratt the Brat and with that he smashed a large cudgel over the Ganglion's skull. The sickening thud sent the other Ganglions quivering in terror.

"Torruk is not a Ganglion, he not one of us from the Outer Rim, he is from Debris," said another, even more grotesque Ganglion.

'Where is he?' demanded the burly presence of Fazza, the most psychotic of The Ha Ha Mateys!

"He is over there!" replied one of the Ganglions, motioning towards a pod that was preparing to leave the sphere. "He has fifty of us all heavily armed. They will not come quietly!"

"Oh you're right about that. They will come screaming!" said the battle scarred pirate Fazza, and with that he severed the Ganglion's head from his shoulders.

The Debris Devils and Immortal Soul pirates surged towards the Ganglions and attacked them with their bare hands, joining Slobbo and Old Man Ray. Their small group was in a final charge towards the bandits.

"We will eliminate them one by one!" cried Slobbo, as he led the charge.

With explosions all around them Slobbo and Old Man Ray charged forward firing. Three Ganglions disintegrated before them.

"Boris, grab this!" Slobbo threw his laser rifle to his personal guard and drew a shimmering, jewel encrusted cutlass from its sheath and slashed the head of a Ganglion clean off.

Xavier was still standing on the sidelines, his sidearm drawn and down by his side. Finally he lifted his arm very slowly and deliberately and pointed it at the head of a Ganglion and fired. The Ganglion's body dropped to the floor, a dead weight. He fired again at another and another, all clean head shots. Old Man Ray turned to see the young rigger striding methodically through the remnants of the dance floor executing any Ganglion in sight - injured or alive.

"Grab the boy," shouted Slobbo, as he watched Xavier continue on his lone trail of destruction.

Slobbo's security guards ran to seize Xavier. There was something strange surrounding him, an aura, a force field that seemed to ensure no-one could get near him. Xavier fixed his stare on Slobbo.

"Do not force me to hurt you," Xavier said.

Confused, Slobbo nodded, looking over at Old Man Ray who looked equally confused.

Slobbo Grensky, the most generous benefactor in Debris, was also the most feared of all those who operated within Debris. He had not built his reputation on being kindly to his enemies or showing mercy to those who crossed him but he was genuinely unnerved by Xavier.

The fate of Torruk and the rest of the mercenaries was sealed.

They made their way towards the pod where Torruk was holed up. A salvo of rounds flew in their direction from the weapons of the cornered mercenaries.

"Burn them out!" declared Slobbo, "but I want Torruk alive."

A pair of pirates carrying a flamethrower ran forward and fired a blast of burning liquid towards the pod.

"What about the protective sphere around the Thunderground?' shouted Old Man Ray, "won't the flames from the pod damage the seals?"

"We will cut the pod loose when the time is right. I know what I am doing!" Slobbo roared, and with that the pirates and Slobbo's men swarmed towards the escape pod.

Torruk would have been better off taking his own life. The barrage and ferocity of the assault by the pirates meant the mercenaries had little to no time before they were overrun. Torruk was dragged flailing like a wild animal from the escape pod. A mercenary since childhood, Torruk had dark features and close cropped hair and a vicious scar running from his temple to his jaw. His eyes were red and wild. He screamed obscenities in a Outer Rim colony accent at the top of his voice, spitting a vile tirade towards his captors. The remainder of the escaping Ganglions were slaughtered mercilessly as they cowered from the vicious onslaught of the pirates,wailing unintelligible laments in their own language. The escape pod was soon jettisoned and sent colliding into a junk container floating along in Debris.

Torruk's hands were quickly bound behind his back, "On your knees scum!" bellowed Slobbo. Torruk complied, he seemed to know the gig was up.

"I am Slobbo Grensky," boomed Slobbo at the Ganglion leader.

Torruk spat a mouthful of blood towards Slobbo, falling centimetres short of its target.

"Make your peace with whoever it is you make peace with Torruk, You are not going to be alive much longer," said Slobbo, in a perfectly calm but sinister voice.

Torruk was facing Slobbo, Old Man Ray and a hundred shamanic pirates hungry for revenge. A sight that would put the fear into the most hardened and violent criminal. Xavier stood behind them, his eyes fixed on the rogue, Torruk.

"Who is responsible for sending you here?" Slobbo asked with deadly calm.

The mercenary leader made no sound. He offered no recognition that a question had even been asked of him.

At that moment, the wild-eyed captain of The Debris Devils stepped forward and drawing the most fearsome of daggers, shrieked at Torruk, "Death by a thousand cuts or do I cut out his heart?"

The rest of the Debris Devils took up the chant "A thousand cuts, a thousand cuts!"

For the first time Torruk visibly trembled at the prospect of being sliced alive piece by piece.

"Put him in the pot, matey!" said Horror McGrath, leader of The Immortal Souls, "I'm feeling peckish."

"Put him in the pot, put him in the pot!" the new chant started up as hungry, drug-addled pirates; frenzied and possessed danced around the Ganglion leader.

"If you answer me, I will be merciful and quick. If you don't answer me, I will leave you to them. It's your choice," said Slobbo, leaning into the reticent mercenary.

Torruk first looked up at the hulking sight of Slobbo, his scarred and battered face etched with rage, then at the tattooed, mangled features of the baying pirates who had began pirouetting with one another and singing space shanties. He knew either way, his fate was confirmed it was just a matter of getting it over and done with. He decided to take his chances with Slobbo.

"Titus Haq recruited me. They wanted Xavier Miro at any cost. I had seen the XAVIA tags around Genesis but I had no idea who he was or why they wanted him. They just told me that they wanted him dead and that I should use whatever force necessary, 'Take him out. We don't care about the rest of the Debris scum.' That is what they told me. I didn't know this was your territory. I was told to kill everyone if needs be," Torruk confessed to the giant Russian killer.

Old Man Ray turned to Xavier, "Who'd have thought it…they fear you, Xavier."

"Whatever you have done and whatever you are, they are willing to destroy many lives for you," Slobbo said solemnly, "you have something The Powers fear."

"I created a piece of graffiti on the side of an Ark about to be launched and they come and kill innocent Keki and all these people?" Xavier was spluttering, shrieking with rage. He pushed Slobbo aside going for the mercenary leader.

"No! I'm going to kill this piece of shit! I'll kill 'em all!"

Slobbo's men blocked Xavier's way to Torruk.

"Take him away from here," he gestured to his men, "they will take you to people who will shelter you for a while. It is too dangerous here in Debris and to be quite honest, I've had enough of you," Slobbo said to Xavier.

Old Man Ray turned to Slobbo, "Thanks my friend. Trust me. This boy is worth protecting. I know. I am sorry this has happened. I am sorry about your people."

"Old Man Ray, take care of yourself. I do not feel we will see each other alive again, friend."

"Perhaps, Slobbo this is the beginning of the revolution we have longed to see. I will go with him now, but..." he said turning to Xavier,"Sorry buddy, then you're on your own. I am way too old for this shit."

Slobbo laughed heartily, "Ray you are a funny bugger. Look after the boy then. For The Powers to do this - he must be special indeed. Don't worry about me." He lunged forward and Old Man Ray stepped back and then Slobbo grabbed him, giving him a bear hug.

Xavier and Old Man Ray left the scene of carnage escorted by a group of Slobbo's security guards. Slobbo saluted as they left and then turned towards the prostrate Torruk. Torruk looked up at his captors, resigned to his fate. The pirates were sharpening their knives.

"So? What are you waiting for?" he snarled, turning to the pirates. His mirth of a moment ago replaced with pure rage.

Slobbo declared with a wry smile, "Dinner's up!"

With that, Torruk was hauled away into the darkest recesses of Debris by the pirates, his blood curdling screams echoing through the ghostly interior.

★★★★★

28

Zola Powered

Z ola was wired. Unable to sleep for days, she was now jacked up on adrenaline, cortisol geared for fight or flight. She had never felt this vulnerable and alone, cosseted in the warmth and love of her family, her friends, protected as she had been; Zola now was facing a chasm. She had tried despite her father's admonitions, to contact Breeze. She and her brothers had been close, but they had gone their way, fully ensconced in the Nu Humana patrician corporate fabric, and she a different way.

"Diametrically opposed now," she thought grimly.

Breeze was part of a top-secret project under the guidance of Dr. Elon Garibidian, the brilliant visionary and scientist, who had become a Power, entrusted with the preservation of mankind as a species. Brunel was part of Nu Ark Lines ferrying humans to far off moons and planets. She had tried to contact Breeze, he did not answer. Instead the impersonal automated voice of the answering droid, telling her she was now being transferred to Nu Humana Command. She knew then, she would never speak with them again. Not as long as she was tied up in all this.

Her friends Lola Love 18 and Ilona Moonlight could do nothing. She had to keep them out of it.

"Kaiser," she thought, "Kaiser O'Keefe."

She could go to him…she could trust him.

Avoiding all forms of public transport she took a few local taxis in an erratic pattern. She kept her head bowed and found herself within a short amount of time standing below the distinctive sign reading K-O-K. Unnoticed she slipped into the showroom. Kaiser was talking to one of his many adoring female entourage, his arms swirling through the air as he demonstrated one of his all-time signature Solar Surfing moves.

Zola, her sweatshirt hood over her head cleared her throat. Kaiser looked over his shoulder and saw her. He strode over and to her surprise scooped her up in his arms and bundled her into the back of the showroom.

"Zola! What are you doing here?" Kaiser seemed frustrated.

"I had nobody to turn to!" she replied desperately, tears welling in her eyes.

"Zola, you should not have come here. I am under observation myself. I know from the inside, that they will not stop till they find you and Xavier. I have had them down here asking questions already. You of all people know they just need an excuse to bust my balls!"

"I don't know where to go Kaiser, I cannot go back home."

"No!" he said firmly, "You cannot go there."

"Shall I try and get on an Ark?"

"Ark! Schmark!" Kaiser said dismissively. "You don't want to get into one of those crates."

"But where then?"

"You started on this mission with Xavier and you need to be with him. He needs you."

"But where is he? Debris? Take me there."

Kaiser shrugged, "Zola I cannot take you there. And Xavier would not want me to do that. It's not safe for you…a girl like you."

"A girl like me!" Zola scowled, "What do you mean…a girl like me?"

"You know what I mean…no, you need to get to the Cathay Wheel. You get there and I have people who can help you."

Zola paced up and down like a caged panther.

"Look Zola, you have to make a decision. Jericho is dead. And your parents are pretty much…" He paused trying to be as diplomatic as possible. "Your parents are not going to be able to help you out of this one."

"I thought it would be better for me to be on my own. I told Xavier to run and get as far away as possible…become a fugitive," Zola said, "I thought I could look after myself and that in turn would help Xavier. I turn around and he's already gone."

Kaiser laughed, "Zola do you see what thinking did! That's guys for you!"

"Right! What do you know?" Zola sighed, jokingly.

Kaiser grinned and held his huge arms outstretched consolingly, "Give me a hug!"

Kaiser gave Zola a hug and a gentle peck on the forehead as she sniffled.

"So, can you get me to the Cathay Wheel then?" Zola asked, taking a seat on one of the sofas.

"I cannot take you myself, but I have transport going every few days back and forth, Imps, parts for Rods, that kind of thing. And I have people there who can look after you for a while. You just have to be low key. Head down…know what I mean?"

"Oh, I can do that," Zola reclined back, kicking off her boots, "you don't mind do you?"

"No, sure you go ahead."

Zola fluffed up a cushion and placed her head down.

"You want to eat?"

"Nope I just need to sleep."

"K-O-K Zola. Get some shut eye, I'll will make some calls."

No sooner had she shut her eyes, she was instantly asleep.

Kaiser looked at her; serene, beautiful in that moment but a whole heap of trouble.

He had faith in her. She would be alright. Better than that, she would survive.

"Whoever lands you, Zola is a lucky man. But boy! Is he playing with fire!"

It was time for him to make a call.

★★★★★

29
Without A Song

"This is Claudia Furukawa with Channel 999 news for The Hives…in dramatic scenes today, the legendary and much loved ballerina Amber Capello was arrested by Genesis security forces acting under the direction of Governor Titus Haq, on orders placed by Nu Humana. Her husband, the respected and notable Chief Engineer Fabian Capello has already been placed under house arrest while authorities investigate a series of security breaches at ArkLight Docks which has seen cultural and moral terrorism occur. Authorities have also launched a Genesis wide manhunt for their daughter, Zola Capello who is wanted for questioning. This was in connection with the acts of vandalism committed during the launch of the Tamarinsk Ark. Security forces today issued the following all points bulletin to all of Genesis enforcement agencies to be on the look out for citizen Xavier Miro, who is wanted in connection with serious acts of vandalism throughout the colonies. These subversive and inflammatory actions have forced a clampdown on all gang-related graffiti activity throughout The Hives. An alert has been issued throughout all transit routes from The Hives and checkpoints have been established along the Gloop so expect delays…Xavier Miro is said to be responsible for seditious comments and graffiti and incitement to cause disorder including the recent paint attack at the launch of the Tamarinsk Ark. He is said to have been assisted by citizen Zola Capello. Here's Kristen Holz at Genesis Federal HQ with members of the Nu Humana investigation team…"

Uniformed officials stood in rows looking out into the battalion of television crews and reporters. Reporting was strictly controlled by Nu Humana but a growing band of journalists eager to question the protectors of the State were pushing the barriers with the recent turn of events finally unable to quietly accept the continual bullying of the public by their overlords.

"How do you react when acts of dissidence like this take place right under your nose?" asked reporter Kristen Holz.

"Come on Holz," replied a belligerent Carlos Zagrostine, "you know the routine. Acts of vandalism and terrorism will be dealt with in a judicial manner but will receive extreme penalties. We will not tolerate anyone, and I mean anyone allowing the cultivation of these ideas and the shielding of these perpetrators. This is not a turf war or gang-related. This is an attack on the very fabric of our society."

"With regards to our society, Sir. Why do you think the perpetrator has taken such a stand?" asked another reporter from the throng.

"Ignorant and hysterical disobedience is what I call it. The Pax Humana has been in existence for centuries now and every citizen has been sheltered and protected by Nu Humana and its corporations. We do not look back ladies and gentlemen, we look forward."

"But sir, Don't you think the graffiti asks certain questions about our history that..." The reporter was cut off mid sentence, "I think you are giving far too much credence and coverage to a lone vandal. We have had to deal with atrocities carried out by the group that call themselves Civilisation in recent years and I do not believe the actions of one man need to have such a high level of media interest. You are playing into this hooligan's hands. I repeat to you, when these culprits are apprehended they will be dealt with to the full extent of the law and so too anyone who has collaborated with them in their tasks."

"What about today's arrest of Amber Capello and the house arrest of Fabian Capello?" asked a hack, from the celebrity channel GMZ.

"Can you confirm that their daughter is also being sought by authorities?" enquired another.

"I cannot talk about ongoing operations but what I can say is that Nu Humana allows people to rise rapidly through the ranks and fulfil whatever their ambitions are. Politically or business wise, creatively or academically, this great institution we belong to allows us all to prosper as individuals. Amber and Fabian Capello are no different."

"With the greatest respect but this sounds like a propaganda exercise."

"The Pax Humana offers opportunity to everyone, but it must be understood that rank is there to be awarded, and when certain people break the rules, to be taken away as well. Anybody and everybody will be held to account if they conspire against Nu Humana. Our retribution will be swift and…final."

Fabian Capello switched off the holo-TV and collected his papers, arranging them neatly as he always did before retiring to bed. He sat for a moment at his desk and looked at the photographs of his sons Brunel and Breeze, resplendent in their uniforms and also of Zola as a small child of six or seven held in her mother's arms. He kissed his index and ring finger touching each of their photographs with the two fingers. They had had some wonderful times together as a family. He rose from his desk and walked to the living area. Fabian Capello, still an imposing figure despite his age, poured himself a large drink of rare brandy from an illuminated cabinet. It had been a gift from the Powers. The brandy was four hundred years old. It was a thank you to the man whose engineering skills had helped forge the modern world.

He swilled the brandy around his mouth and gulped it down. Then poured another glass and repeated his actions.

He walked to his front door and exited his apartment. He then took the elevator down to the foyer of his exclusive apartment block. The servo-droids and porter saluted him as he walked past them. Two security guards got up from their seats as he strolled out towards one of the fashionable landings of this chic habitation zone. Fabian signalled to them he was going to take a stroll in the private and exclusive hydro garden opposite, which was for the sole use of residents of his block.

The gardens were fairly large and densely planted with all manner of greenery and trees. Railings and small walls were embellished with pretty hanging flowers and the perfumed air filled Fabian with a sensuous delight which forced him to close his eyes and take a number of deep breaths. He gazed up at the dome above him and the darkness of space. The lights of other colonies blinked in the distance to one side like stars twinkling, and before him, taking centre stage was the fantastic view of the blue pearl called Earth.

He had aways dreamt that one day he would have been able to feel the wind and rains of the planet on his face, to sample its clear and pure air and drink its wonderful water. He strode down a small path that led to a pool filled with ornamental fish and took a seat on a small blue stone bench where he and Amber had spent many times together. He gently caressed the seat where she had sat and gazed across the pond, his head full of beautiful memories of them together.

The words of an old Earth song filled his head, one he and Amber had loved from a time when love and emotions, however complicated, were free.

I'll never know what makes the rain to fall
I'll never know what makes that grass so tall
I only know there ain't no love at all.
Without a song.

In the distance, the two security guards had entered the garden and were watching him closely.

After a few minutes, Fabian got up from the bench undetected as the guards were conversing amongst themselves. He walked across a glade, his hands touching all the leaves and flowers of the amazing plants grown in this artificial environment. He came to a thicket which marked the perimeter and eased himself through the foliage to an access walkway at the edge of the dome. Furtively looking over his shoulder, Fabian knew what he was looking for. He found a latch, pulled at the lever and entered through a small door closing it behind him.

He was in an airlock a small porthole gazing out towards Earth. Safety overrides and security systems had been easy to undermine for a man like him. With his eyes fixed on the swirling white cloud patterns above the oceans of Earth, all those hundreds of thousands of miles away, Fabian tapped away at a keypad, lifted a lever and waited as a warning message flashed and a thirty-second countdown started, signalling the unlocking of the airlock.

He closed his eyes and thought about the love of his life - Amber.

A second later the door flew open, sucking Fabian into the vast void of space.

*****

30

The Average Touring Munk Band

P eople don't tend to say too much when they are in shock, distressed and just plain wiped out.

The power of communication had evaded them. They were battered and bruised, ragged soldiers returning from a very unorthodox battlefield. Xavier and the members of Scun Scum journeyed away from Debris, away from the slaughter and mayhem they had witnessed and been part of at the Thunderground.

Being involved in one of most violent episodes in Debris nightlife history, with him being the intended target of brutal merciless brigands, was taking its toll on Xavier. He stared into space, his eyes glazed, deep in thought. He was removed from his companions in the room. The Average Touring Munk band travelled from gig to gig, being revered on every side of the solar system. They would usually have been hard at work partying until they reached their next destination but they were currently recovering from being completely traumatised by the events that had just unfolded.

Their tour vessel was impressive and the success and fame of playing Asteroid Mining Music around much of the known system had brought them a lavish lifestyle and every *accoutrement* their success could buy. The artists comprising the A.T.M.B, Scun Scum, Crater Face and Minnie Rall were known throughout not just Debris but the whole of Genesis, as well as on the Moon and Mars. The party for Slobbo had been a thank you to the mighty Russian for his early support and his appreciation for good mining music. Now they were sneaking out possibly the most wanted man in Genesis history Xavier, Old Man Ray and Aqua Terra on their tour vessel, away from the not just any Ganglion stragglers who may not have got the memo, but the Powers themselves.

The vessel was a gleaming golden craft with a domed observation deck and six different floors on which the musicians were provided with every provision and had every need attended to as they hurtled through space from one gig to the next. Xavier sat in one of the huge and luxurious armchairs overlooking the hot tub in the recreation part of the ship, his mind absorbed with thoughts of Keki. Why did an innocent bystander like her have to lose her life because of him? He also thought of Zola on the run. Would Zola understand if he told her? He wondered whether the moments he had shared together with Keki were wrong. He felt a rage and fury inside him like never before. It was a feeling that came from a source deep within him. Keki's untimely death was the proverbial straw that had broken him. What he felt now was a desire for revenge, for justice, for all the wrongs made right. Zola's life had probably been destroyed now. Jericho's was over. And here he was careering through space - where he didn't know and for what? Some graffiti?

He banged his fist on the table he was sitting at, unaware he had even done it. Minnie Rall fumbled with her drink and coughed, shaking her head at Xavier. He looked up, he sensed he was being viewed, judged, summed up. Nervous conversation ensued around him. The musicians were perturbed by the carnage in Debris; perturbed too, by his presence. The irony of his situation was apparent to him. Under any other circumstances, travelling on the tour ship of his heroes would have been the single most unbelievable thing that could happen to him, in his life.

"What the fuck!" said Kleb The Pleb, "I mean what the fuck just happened?"

"I was just happy my drinks rider was all there," cried Minnie Rall, pouring herself a large drink. "The performance had been going well till those horrible green fuckers arrived."

"Those horrible green fuckers happened to be vicious mercenaries from the outer belt with serious anger issues?" Crater Face couldn't resist.

"Those Ganglions who murdered everyone around us?" Minnie began crying. "You know I don't mind people zero G dancing, doing Zug and flipping out. But I draw the line at them fucking exploding around me on the dance floor!"

Crater Face, whose face resembled that of the dark side of the moon and whose manner was, at best abrupt, was the creative force behind the awesome chanting patois hit '*Zunga*

Dang Dang Dang! Zunga Dang Dang Dong!' It was based on the reverberation of a drilling platform on one of the distant mining rigs. It had become a smash hit throughout Genesis.

Crater Face glared at a solemn looking Xavier, "We think we're hardcore, dude, but you my friend are too hardcore!"

"Xavier Miro, what the fuck have you been up to?" asked Scun Scum musician Cack.

Xavier shook his head, he found it difficult to utter words. He spoke as if reading a rehearsed speech, "I am a rigger in ArkLight Docks. I am also a graffiti artist. I created a piece on the side a launching Ark."

"Dude, we know who you are! We want to see this 'art' that has started a fucking war!"

Xavier opened up his bag and pulled out a small pad that opened up and projected a hologram of his latest works he and Aqua Terra had completed. Crater Face and Kleb The Pleb's seemed mesmerised.

"Honestly, I couldn't tell you what it all means, but it's sure pissed off a lot of people," said Xavier quietly, aware suddenly of feeling very, very, tired.

Hieroglyphics and dancing aliens married with elephants and lions, dinosaurs and flying saucers in landscapes of old Earth that looked wildly out of place here in the depths of space.

"How can something so beautiful, create so much trouble?" Old Man Ray's deep voice spoke for the first time all night.

"Yeah, for you guys. I'm not that happy with you guys being here to be honest," Minnie Rall said, "but hey! I was out-voted as per usual, and so make yourselves at home."

She poured herself another drink, her make-up running down her face.

"Well, you are saving our lives," said Xavier.

"We have friends who will help us along the way I am sure," said Old Man Ray, reassuringly.

"Nice, great, you have friends. But you know what they say, 'A friend in need is a friend you don't need,'" Minnie Rall was now stumbling with the alcohol.

"I disagree Minnie. The saying is a friend in need is a friend indeed," said Cack.

"Look, I'm happy to have you aboard and along for the ride. We'll make sure you get where you need to go, safe and sound," Crater Face said, glaring at Minnie. "She's been through a lot. She's not herself," he added apologetically.

Xavier nodded, "Thanks, under any other circumstances, I would be overjoyed. I worship you guys!"

"Try and get some rest, Xavier. For now at least, you're safe."

Old Man Ray stood up, "Fellas, this has been a long day for all of us. I haven't slept since I don't know when. You don't mind if I jump in there do you?"

He pointed to the heated pool area.

"Go ahead," said Crater Face.

Old Man Ray walked over to the pool and began removing his overalls and space suit.

"A water pool, what a bloody luxury," he said, easing himself into the pool, "Anyone care to join me? The water's lovely."

He looked back to see Xavier enveloped in the plush body of the luxurious chair. Minnie Rall staggered away as Kleb The Pleb threw a cover over the chair he had sat down on before departing to his suite. A few minutes later, three groupies giggled and undressed to their underwear before joining Old Man Ray in the bubbling pool. Cack and Crater Face walked up towards the viewing gallery to gaze out at the thousands of colonies stretched before them, each one part of the Genesis conurbation. The tour vessel headed towards Nu Venezia, leaving the memory and carnage of Debris in the distance.

*****

31
Dragonaut Borders

Sino Space or Dragonaut guards as they were better known were not, by reputation the friendliest of characters. Their border patrols and colony security were notorious, they were some of the most unpleasant people who ever donned a uniform. Smiling was not part of their makeup and there were certainly no awards for politeness and geniality.

Every vessel, including the one Zola Capello found herself stowed away on, going in and out of the Cathay Wheel had its cargo checked by these Dragonaut guards.

Zola sat in a vestibule set back in the hull of a midsize colony-transit freighter used to run short haul cargo between the different colonies. Her journey from The Hives had taken a long time. Longer than expected. She wanted to get off the freighter. Kaiser had arranged for a handler to meet her. If it wasn't for Kaiser…she tried not to think about it.

A young deckhand, no older than fourteen, with slicked back hair and a manner three decades his senior ushered Zola from her seat and informed her of their imminent arrival at the checkpoint.

"Lady," he said, condescendingly, "we are about to go through inspection."

Zola nodded and collected her belongings. She was escorted down a series of corridors all dimly lit and into a suspended animation chamber. The room consisted of twelve coffin-like units resembling tanning beds with clear plastic lids arranged down two walls. Above each Sus-An chamber a panel of lights blinked in a series of patterns

"In here?" she asked, slightly perturbed.

The deckhand nodded.

"Look I am not very good in confined spaces," Zola pleaded.

"I thought you said you were from The Hives?"

The deckhand lifted the lid to one of the chambers.

"Look, I…I…I…"

"Just get in there and do as we say and you will be okay," said the deckhand, pushing Zola towards the unit.

The deckhand nodded, encouraging Zola as she crept towards the Sus-An chambers.

Zola looked at the slightly soiled mattress and a single black hair glaring up from the pillow in the chamber, and looked back at the deckhand, "I'm not going in there."

"Look, are we doing this or what?" said the deckhand testily.

Zola closed her eyes for a moment, then she climbed into the unit. Her heart racing. Her breathing quickening.

"Can you knock me out? Give me an anaesthetic or something, please."

"I can't tranq you. It's too late," he replied, becoming increasingly agitated, "we're going to get to the checkpoint soon. You gotta settle down."

"But can't you...!" Zola stopped mid sentence.

This was it. This was the moment, just her alone in a box. She took a few deep breaths. She had to ride this one out.

"That's it girl, deep breaths! Close your eyes and deep breaths."

The deckhand closed the lid and pressed a button sealing the chamber. Immediately he typed a false log and record, bringing up a fictitious set of monitor readings. Since he was a small child he had been part of this people smuggling outfit, taking human cargo to new lives in new colonies and to new opportunities. His crew had a good track record. The other crews were routinely boarded and often dumped their 'cargo' along the way like space junk. They were well connected and knew Kaiser was a man of his word. The deckhand walked away shaking his head. He may have been young looking but he was worldly wise. He had a feeling about this consignment. He hoped it was a good feeling.

Shortly, an inspection team of five Sino Space guards and their supervisor boarded and made preliminary checks of the crew and cargo lists. The Black Betty had done this trip thousands of times and a set of Sino Space monitor droids were released and sent scurrying on board to scan for alien shipments and other life forces along with any hidden contraband. The Black Betty's lading bills were checked by the supervisor once, twice, thrice. All was good. The crew members stood in line as a member of the boarding team winked as he walked past them, his regular supply of Martian whisky guaranteed. There was an air of business as usual with everything present and correct as the droids returned from their inspection routes.

"All good here," came the reply from the supervisor, "we will not keep you. You can be on your way."

The guards turned to leave and then it started. What sounded like a muffled voice and someone pounding for dear life emanated from one of the rooms song the corridor.

"What is that?" asked the supervisor.

"Nothing?" came the reply from the first mate, his face showing signs of consternation.

The banging continued, the crew fidgeted nervously and tensions mounted as the guards looked at one another. The muffled voice sounded a lot like a woman crying out for help from the cordoned off Sus-An chamber.

The supervisor looked at the guard who had inspected the area, "I thought you said you had checked this area?"

"I did,"the guard replied, looking very worried,"I checked the logs and scanned it…nothing came up. There is nothing to report."

"Well, there is obviously something to report now!" demanded the supervisor, to the ashen faced guard.

He stormed towards the Sus-An chamber and banged the button to the side of the unit from where the banging was coming from, to a reveal a hyper-ventilating and near hysterical Zola Capello begging to be let out.

The officer grunted in Mandarin and then in Can-Com and unceremoniously pulled Zola out of the chamber by her collar.

"We have ourselves a stowaway," he declared.

He took a closer look at Zola's sweating, tear-sodden face while scanning her with a handheld recognition kit, "She's not just a stowaway…she's wanted. Very wanted!"

"Zola Capello, you are under arrest by order of the Governor of Genesis, Titus Haq for crimes of treason against the Pax Humana."

★★★★★

32

A Gondola In Nu Venezia

The canals of Nu Venezia stretched out as far as the eye could wander. A series of locks controlled the levels of water between two adjacent channels. Canals and waterways formed an important part of the infrastructure of the Torus colonies in space. For one thing, the canals were an ideal way of transporting goods and communicating with other people. They were also pleasant to live amongst.

Nu Venezia was the home for many of the descendants of The High Pioneers, the original settlers of space who had built their colonies to resemble idyllic locations on Earth; they replicated the names and locations, stocking them with everything they could no longer find on Earth.

The steel circles of the colony wheels had a couple of channels built into them that would act as waterways, all important to the lifeblood of the colony, they affected the atmosphere and the climate. On either side of the canals were terraced villas, *palazzos* and apartments, their balconies covered in flower baskets; jasmine, orange blossom, magnolias and bougainvillea fragranced the air. Xavier was overwhelmed by their powerful bouquets; he had seen them via Edu-Imps. The one thing his imagination could not provide were these delicious fragrances detected only by his olfactory senses.

Beautiful hanging gardens with palm trees, orange groves and orchards of fruit trees filled recreational spaces. Children played in paddling pools and splashed about in fountains. Stairs connected the terraced levels and cycle paths that ran alongside the canals and waterways allowing people to jog or run for miles on end. People exercised running up and down the steps and stretched out on the lawns. Little quays were festooned with multi-coloured lilies, iridescent in the changing light of the colony, sparkling like gems. Small robotic animals joined the waterfowl, floating along, patrolling and cleaning the water of any foreign objects. The fresh water was teeming with fish, and robot lifeguards were stationed at various points to observe and protect the inquisitive wader or swimmer who may get into trouble while playing around in the water.

There was a relaxed feel to Nu Venezia. Mothers dressed in colourful flowing robes tended to their children in a warm and languid Mediterranean-like climate. The rays of the sun were monitored and timed by mirrors and advanced pioneer technology, to create perfectly blissful days lasting all year round. Only five kilometres above their heads, the inhabitants were protected by a gigantic plastic canopy shielding them from the perils of space and the harmful rays of the sun, allowing them to live and love in a perfectly controlled environment, tuned to one setting - harmony. It appeared that the settlers here actually believed they were living on Earth, even though the colony was over three hundred and fifty-thousand kilometres away from Earth.

Like the rest of the dwellers in Genesis, they too at one time longed to return to Earth, but unlike the others, they had forfeited that dream a long time ago. Nu Venezia and the other pioneer colonies were a haven for anyone who lived there, created by the visionaries of the twenty-second century.

These pioneers used their knowledge, passion and foresight to create such utopias in space. They operated as independent territories from the rest of Genesis, individual city states like Venice or Florence on Earth. They traded commodities but their main export was knowledge. They traded knowledge with the corporations in return for being left to run their autonomous provinces away from the grasp and influence of the space conglomerates.

The majority of the scientists, physicists and biologists were descendants of the High Pioneers and were now twenty or so generations into developing their own worlds, both physically and spiritually. Their aspirations were not to find new planets or Valhalla in some distant galaxy. They had already created their own paradises and were happy enough to live there amongst the stars, protected by the corporations and, of course, the private militias they employed to provide security and protect them.

Gondolas glided back and forth, as well as paddle boards that took to the water. The occasional barge loaded with goods gently meandered along the watercourse. The barges were laden with freshly grown produce; vegetables, fruits and herbs from little markets and settlements that circled around the colony. Life in Nu Venezia and the other high colonies was good, really good. They wanted for nothing and ran their states with a righteous and vigorous zeal. They worked hard for what they had, and outsiders were not generally welcome. Most visitors were treated with suspicion.

Rings appeared on the surface of the water as a sudden shower, programmed to sporadically occur during the course of the day, refreshed the environment. People scurried across the many bridges and sought shelter as the light downpour refreshed the terraces and parks. A small jetty jutted out slightly into the waterway and a set of stairs led up to an imposing villa where a group of small children played on the terrace, oblivious to the rain.

A voice beckoned over and over, "Come in. Come in. Get out of the rain."

Xavier was enjoying the rain as it hit his face. He had never experienced such a sensation, artificial or otherwise, droplets of water were not an everyday occurrence for someone from The Hives. The odd sensation of water hitting his face, at first gently then with increasing force splashing and refreshing his face and saturating his clothes was exhilarating. He felt so alive. He stood there transfixed as the rain fell and washed over him.

"Come in. Come in. You will get soaked."

The voice was familiar and within seconds of entering the inside of the villa it became apparent to whom the voice belonged.

'As My Sphere Turns' had been a show which had run on Genesis TV for decades; it was the pits. Yet it was by far the most popular soap opera in the colonies and told of the lives and loves of the inhabitants of a fictitious sphere called Elysian Fields; their aspirations, infatuations, ambitions and desires had been the daily diet for millions since its inception.

It was meant to reflect the lives of people on Genesis and the dreams they held of becoming new pioneers venturing into the unknown to colonise new planets. The cast were stars all over Genesis and the lead actor, Jett Jensen, could be seen on billboards and holograms all over the many hoardings and stations of Genesis. Jensen's other show was 'Into The Galaxy'; the story of human adventurers as they established colonies in new star systems. With his blond hair and roguish good looks, Jett had an all American look about him; his face was to be seen on commercials for everything and anything you could imagine. This allowed him to travel wherever he wanted, where he was the guest of honour at many of the swankiest parties held by the rich and the powerful throughout the system. He was known by everyone in The Hives, as well as the High Pioneers in their spheres; loved and loathed in equal measure.

"What a drongo!" Xavier would often say when zooming past one of the billboards with his face staring out. "I just don't get why people like him! I hate him."

"He's easy to dislike," Jericho would say.

Now, from within the villa, the familiar voice called Xavier and beckoned him towards shelter against the unannounced shower. Old Man Ray led the way into the living room where Jett Jensen stood casually dressed, smiling his big welcoming toothy smile.

"Ray, welcome," Jensen said, embracing the old rigger, "It's been too long. I hope that you are well."

He turned to Xavier and extended his hand to him.

"It is a real pleasure to meet you, I have heard so much from Ray and others."

Xavier acknowledged him warily.

"Pleasure," he replied.

Jett Jensen knows me? He thought to himself.

Bemused, Xavier sat down and made himself comfortable as a droid busied itself tidying around them. The surreal events that had transpired on Debris and the journey on board the tour vessel had left him drained; he was devoid of energy, of the ability to speak, to think. He had managed to sleep most of the way, and now wasn't sure what to do with himself. Xavier and Ray were poured glasses of freshly squeezed Nu Venezia orange juice. It tasted so delicious Xavier was compelled to ask what it was.

"It is grown in our very own orange groves here in Nu Venezia. You could see the citrus trees as you walked up, couldn't you?"

Xavier had never seen a citrus tree and the closest thing he could recall coming anywhere close to freshly squeezed juice was a synthetic brew he got in The Hives one day purporting to be from a Hydro Garden.

The taste of this juice was like nothing he'd ever experienced.

Again, he felt alive.

★★★★★

33
Jett and Civilization

"Technology was the key," said Jett, as he took a swig from his glass.

The light, surrounding him from outside, seemed to make his body glisten.

"The technology has always been there, Xavier. We are the most ingenious of mammals and we have advanced rapidly. It was only twelve thousand years ago that you can honestly say human civilisation started and barely five thousand years ago that we began to keep any record of our experiences."

Old Man Ray nodded in agreement, "It's incredible to think we have come so far in such a short space of time. Some creatures take millions of years to develop and evolve, yet the human civilisation has done it in less than twelve thousand years."

"It has been less than four hundred thousand years since man walked upright from the plains of Africa and migrated across Earth."

"And look at us now," said Xavier

"Yes, look at us now...confined to living in The Cannery in space," Jett replied.

"Yes," Xavier answered, "but you have it pretty sweet here Jett. Just look at this place!"

They gazed out of the terrace as the last drops of the shower splashed upon the tiles. "It's beautiful, like a paradise in the bleakness of space. It's not like being in The Hives,"he continued.

"No, it's not to be taken for granted, but it's not Earth either," smiled Jett.

"They made a mess of Earth and we've had to pay for that mess," Old Man Ray said.

"We made no mess," said Xavier, "it was those bums before us who messed everything up. They were the ones that ignored the warnings."

"That's not really fair," said Jett, "you can't blame the entire global population for the mismanagement of the planet."

"Well, someone got it wrong!" Xavier exclaimed, agitated. There was always an excuse, it was hard to pinpoint who was to blame.

"Sure, someone did, but to blame the whole population is not right. The one thing man can be held responsible for is not listening, for turning a blind eye and then passing the buck. When one does it they all do it and end up blaming one another."

"Collective responsibility I think it's called," replied Ray.

"Well, whoever, whatever, however. It was a disaster," exclaimed Xavier.

"Then they set off on this rapid race to the stars and that was it," Jett continued. "The problems on Earth became unsolvable; it began to spiral out of control."

"Yet at the same time they began to reach for the High Frontier," Old Man Ray said, making himself cozy in a large chair, pouring himself a hearty drink.

"How did that happen?" Xavier asked.

"Well, actually it's surprising you ask because your graffiti speaks volumes about what happened?" Jett replied.

"You really think so?"

"The thing is it is really easy to forget that the Powers who control Genesis and these corporations are just like us. They are human."

"So, how did the corporations advance so rapidly in the twenty-second and twenty-third centuries?"

"It goes back to technology. When Watt discovered steam power the world changed. When Carnegie was able to mass produce steel that changed the world and when Edison invented the light bulb that changed the world," Jett replied, "just like Professor Kairies Arnold and the carbon nanotube allowed us to create the space elevator and Doctor Choi Lang who invented the fusion engine. Technology is responsible for the transformation of the world."

"Mankind makes great leaps with or without technology," added Old Man Ray.

"Yes, mankind does, but perhaps they are helped along when the time in evolution is right?"

"The Powers are controlled by other powers?" Xavier walked around the room. He couldn't for the life of him think how Old Man Ray and Jett Jensen could possibly know one another.

"Yes, far more powerful than we can imagine. I worked with a group that I'm sure you're familiar with, Civilization. Their research suggests the corporations of the old Earth nations made some kind of deal with an alien race." Even off screen Jett was a thespian, speaking eloquently.

"For what?"

"Technology! Man began the slow but necessary pursuit for the stars and there seems a distinct possibility deals may have been struck, cabals may have been formed."

"What kind of deals?" persisted Xavier.

"The technology that has taken man to the stars is not man's alone. This knowledge has come from other sources, sources which had an interest in not only us but in our planet... alien sources."

"So, who did these deals?" Xavier had to know more, know all of it.

"Since the Digital Dark Age, information on all of Earth's history has been limited. We have scant information and records to go on and Edu-Imps can only give you so much information on the past. I dare say you've done your fair share of those," said Jett, smiling at Xavier.

"You could say that," said Xavier.

"Xavier, your graffiti is unnerving for the authorities It contains far too much detail for them. It gives away too much."

"Who did the deals Jett, and for what?"

"Deals were done with governments and corporations on Earth that enabled them to fast forward into the solar system and beyond, whilst the world plummeted into a spiral of destruction."

"I don't get this. What was their gain?"

"Who? The corporations? They had everything to gain. The Powers and their capitalist minions were able to make fortunes from the vast wealth of minerals on asteroids and new planets. Their ability to travel the galaxy and harvest gold and diamonds, hydrogen and helium. Harnessing the new found technology has allowed them to master the world and they have only just begun."

"The raw materials these corporations have access to is incredible," said Ray.

"I believe the raw material that is most important to them is us…" Jett said.

"Us?" exclaimed Xavier.

"Humans! They need humans. They have a captive population, and they need *us* to populate the universe."

"Why?"

"Because, Xavier…" Jett paused, "we are successful. We have proven that on Earth by evolving so quickly. We are the most adaptable beings in the Universe, and the Universe is a vast place."

"Even though space has been a relatively new habitat to man we have rapidly adapted to this new frontier," said Ray, pouring himself another drink.

"That's all very well, but we didn't do a great job on Earth now. Did we?" Xavier said wryly.

"Yep, that's for damn sure," agreed Old Man Ray.

"Oh Xavier, Ray," said an impassioned Jett, "Earth is stronger than we know. She is not as fragile as we might think; she will not go down without a fight. She is in a better state than she has ever been."

"The human is the weak link," said Xavier.

"Correct. For all its fantastic attributes, it has a number of inherent faults which cannot be changed."

"What are those?" asked Xavier.

"Emotion for one," said Old Man Ray.

"And an inescapable capacity for self destruction and the destruction of others!" Jett responded.

"For all of their advances, mankind cannot seem to use these advances for the benefit of all."

"It seems to only benefit a few, right?"

"Right!"

"I am afraid we have the same old story permeating human civilisation - the rich getting richer while the masses are kept occupied with structures of work, life and entertainment," Jett continued.

"Is that where you come in?" said Xavier, sarcastically.

Jett nodded.

"No doubt about it. Yes, that is where I come in. Jett Jensen, performer of mind numbing garbage and kiss ass man to the man! Thanks!"

"You're welcome."

A selection of food had been brought into the room and Xavier suddenly ravenous took full advantage of the spread. He turned around and said to Jett. "Look, all I know is this. My name is Xavier Miro, I live in The Hives and occasionally spray graffiti. I work at ArkLight and am assigned to Nu Humana and Human Enterprises. Until very recently, like a week ago, I was pretty satisfied with my lot. I had a job, a girlfriend, friends and a pretty rad Rod called Aqua Terra. I was happy. Then I sprayed some bad-ass graffiti on a major Ark called Tamarinsk and here I am."

Old Man Ray sat listening to the young rigger and smiling.

"All I wanted to do was go to work, keep the Air Authority from knocking on my door and work my quota. In my off time, I liked to hang out, try to get laid and spray the sides of buildings, show people who Xavier is with his XVR tag. And then I wanted to someday board an Ark and get to some settlement or newly discovered planet and settle down with a wife and be a human being."

"You sound like the corporate dream, minus the graffiti," laughed Jett.

"Unfortunately it's all I've ever really known, right?"

"It's all many people know, but I'm pretty sure you realise now, it's not the *only* way. You need to go to Earth Xavier see for yourself. It is the only way…trust me."

"Oh yeah! Nice one, trust you! I don't even fucking know you!" Xavier exploded, immediately regretting it. Jett was a friend of Old Man Ray's and deserved his respect.

"Whatever you're doing, Xavier it's scaring the Powers. You're making the people of The Hives think!"

"Yeah! Thinking is bad for you," quipped Old Man Ray. "I've only just learnt to do joined up thinking."

"Xavier, I am a member of Civilization," declared Jett.

"Oh, so you're a terrorist now?"

"No, I am a person who believes there is a better way."

"A better way…a better way…what is this 'better way'?"

"Of course there's a better way than being subjects in a tyrannical reign and Civilization is the key," Jett straightened up, proud of his admission. "In the 2530s, Civilization was a dissident group responsible for demonstrating against the corporations. This led to rioting around The Hives years before you were born, until they were wiped out in a purge by the Shadows."

"I thought they had zoned in on you guys and wiped you all out, one by one,' said Xavier.

'We took some collateral damage, but we never really went away. We licked our wounds, we re-grouped and enlisted new members.'

"Is that a fact? Well, I met Calvin Lacker on the very night he got blown to shit!" said Xavier.

"You met Calvin Lacker on that dreadful night?"

"I went down with my girlfriend Zola Capello and he spoke about my graffiti and how it had a message. I thought the guy was crazy!"

"Xavier, you were with Zola?"

"Do you know Zola?"

"You will be surprised at who are members of Civilization."

"It seems everyone has been looking for the truth, or something..." Xavier spoke quietly now, thinking of Zola.

"Everyone!"

"Then I, Xavier Miro, resident of The Hives, citizen of Genesis, worker at ArkLight assigned to Nu Humana and occasional graffiti artist hereby declare that I am going to Earth!" said Xavier defiantly.

Jett's expression was solemn, "A good decision Xavier Miro. There is something about you. I feel strongly that you going to Earth is exactly what needs to happen. Not just so you can find out the truth for yourself but for all of us."

Xavier nodded, "Okay...so now...how do you two propose I do this?"

Xavier was grinning.

"Head towards The Cathay Wheel."

"Uhm!...Correct me if I'm wrong but that sounds like an incredibly bad idea!" Xavier felt the sheer absurdity of the decision he had made was giving him new energy.

"The Cathay Wheel harbours all sorts of people including smugglers of every description who know the space ways between here and the moon better than anybody, they will be able to guide you."

"So what then? I just turn up unannounced and I will get taken care of."

"Trust me Xavier, and you have to trust me. There are people who have access codes and charts to get past the Celestine Gate and its security."

"Who?"

"That, I cannot disclose at this time. But someone who has been monitoring your work is looking out for you."

Even Xavier's bravado could not stop him from being taken aback by this new information.

"This shit is crazy!" He said after a few moments of silence, looking to Old Man Ray.

"You have your craft Aqua Terra in the bays ready and waiting for you. The band were good enough to bring it along."

"Really?" Xavier looked over at his old friend again, "You coming?"

Old Man Ray had a glint in his eye, "You kidding? Wouldn't miss it for the world."

"I have had my people fuel and maintain your craft," Jett continued, placing his drink upon a small table and escorting his guests to a side door down to one of his private hangars.

"Your dreams have taken you this far. Xavier, now go the whole way and find out what more there is."

"I have lost a lot of people already Mr Jensen and I'm not sure what exactly it is I am looking for but here I go," Xavier replied, as he and Old Man Ray walked towards a pristine Aqua Terra.

Jett paused for a second and looked into Xavier's eyes. "The truth, that is all."

"Hey," Old Man Ray turned around, "I owe you Jett, old friend."

★★★★★

34
Maybe Just Maybe

U nrelenting piercing light bleached the walls of the cell
and everything within it. There was no place to hide
from the glare, She closed her eyes, it was her only way of
escape. She sat with her legs huddled close to her and her head
pressed into her knees, eyes squeezed tightly shut. She sat on a
concrete bench rocking back and forth. She had given up
trying to keep track of time.

The handover from the Sino Space guards had been swift
and Zola's repatriation and extradition followed. She had said
literally nothing to her arresting guards apart from the
confirmation of her age and name. She had been moved from
one stark federal building to another and had been hounded by
one Dragonaut interrogator after another. She was blindfolded
and yelled at, and now she felt numb. Now, being alone with
her thoughts was making her feel insane. First she thought that
she had been set up by Kaiser and the crew, but then why
would he want or need to do something like that. Then she
ruminated over her parents, her brothers; images streamed

continually into her mind with no cessation. She worried about what would happen to them. Would the retribution for her acts be exacted on them? Most of all she thought about Xavier. Zola wanted to know his whereabouts, what he was doing. She felt a sob rising…was he even alive? The one thing she did know was that she was on her own. There was no cavalry coming to rescue her, no knight in shining armour - these walls spelt her fate.

She had not yet seen the faces of her captors, and so could not be certain where she was. A droid brought her food at intervals and surveillance cameras watched her every move. She ate, she slept, she breathed, she paced around the cell and they watched. The commode was in the corner of the cell. They watched.

"Prisoner Capello, stand immediately and take two paces forward," boomed a metallic voice through the cell.

The silence was broken.

She stood up slowly, her eyes squinting in the light and placed her feet on two templates marked on the floor and her hands on two templates on the wall. In one fluid motion a clear plastic screen bound her to the wall and spun her round and she found herself on the opposite side of the cell. The restraining screen released itself and she was ordered to take a position to her right away from the footplates. She bowed her head as she complied.

"Prisoner Capello turn around," the metallic voice requested.

Zola turned round to find Governor Titus Haq stood before her.

"My, my…what a beautiful creature you are!" he proclaimed.

For once in her life Zola was speechless. All sorts of sensations flooded her being, none of them good.

"Come…follow me," said Titus and he walked towards a small interrogation room where he gestured for her to take a seat at a table. Her eyes watered and fluttered as she turned to adjust to the change in the lights. Zola shuffled towards the desk, taking a seat and thought it best to look down towards her feet and not engage with the Governor.

There was a few moments silence before Titus enquired facetiously, "My dear, is it my charming good looks?"

She did not answer.

"Zola, I am sorry about your father. He is the innocent victim of a tragic set of circumstances."

Zola blinked in the lights. At the time of her arrest she now recalled someone barking this information out, but till this moment it had not registered. It simply couldn't be true. Zola was silent. Still not looking up, she asked tentatively, "My mother?"

"Distraught about her husband and her little girl but…she is a tough cookie isn't she?" Titus grinned, it seemed all a big game to him.

Zola seemed to smile for a brief second at these words. Even in the mouth of a monster, they were true. Amber was a woman of incredible grit.

"I need to be like mom," she muttered, not intending to be heard.

Titus smiled, "Yes you do. She is a very strong and driven woman. I like to see that in the old ones. A survivor...don't you think?"

Zola nodded uncertainly.

"Just like you Zola," Titus reached out his hand and placed it on hers.

"Why have you kept me?" Zola asked, raising her head with tears streaming over her cheeks. She didn't even notice Titus' hand.

"Why have I kept you? What do you mean?"

"Why have I been kept alive?"

"I can do anything I like with you Zola," Titus whispered, menacingly. "I don't have to answer questions like that. Remember that."

Zola looked at her hands wanting to pull hers away desperately.

"You are a lovely, pretty young girl of good stock, but you have been mixing with the wrong crowd and look where it has landed you? Wearing a bright orange prisoner's jumpsuit...a mere convict."

"Why did you not have me killed?"

"I usually kill the ugly ones first."

"That's a joke, right?" said Zola, finding her voice as her discomfort rose.

"It's not a joke Zola. I could have had you killed quite easily, eating vacuum like your poor father, who by the way did not deserve to go out the way he did."

"What do you mean?"

"Oh, of course you don't know do you? Your father went out in the style of a good old Roman patrician. So as not to bring shame upon his family or the senate, just like Seneca. Your father had a sense of status and duty. He knew where he stood in the Pax Humana and how the system had helped him and how his spoilt little girl had ruined it for him. A good man your father," said Titus still smiling.

She stared down at the table.

"You have not answered my question?" she said shortly.

"I do not have to tell you. I could have had your mind wiped and re-indoctrinated but in a way you are far more interesting to me alive than dead."

"Just tell me this then clearly. Is my mother okay?"

Titus stood to his feet, "Your mother! What a lady! She's still got it hasn't she?"

Zola wanted to punch Titus but kept her gaze to the table, "What do you want me to say? That she is a very attractive woman?"

"She sure is. And she has passed all those beautiful genes on to her baby girl…but you should be asking yourself Zola where this leaves you?"

"I've been asking that. You're not telling me," Zola risked his anger, as her anger rose.

"It leaves you in deep shit Zola!" Titus snapped, "Allowing your stupid friends access to prohibited areas of ArkLight Docks. Letting them paint their garbage alongside corporation property. Sending out misguided and inappropriate visions and mindless nonsense to a crass public."

"Xavier believes in something..." she ventured, knowing Titus would not appreciate her loyalty.

Titus looked at Zola as if he was pitying her, "Belief is a killer. It is of no use to the general public. They can believe what they want but we do not encourage it."

"I did not give him access."

"You gave him Edu-Imps."

"I give a lot of people Edu-Imps it is part of my role and my job."

"It is part of our role, to monitor where those Edu-Imps go to and you messed up."

"I did not realise," Zola replied blankly. She didn't have much hope for herself.

"You did not realise!" he screamed.

Titus stopped and straightened his uniform then leaned into Zola, "This Xavier Miro is a thorn in my side. Do you want to know why?"

"Go on, tell me."

"Because he does not exist."

"I have no idea what you're talking about."

"We have no record of him. The strangest thing about this man is that we have no prints, no DNA, no records, no images, no face recognition, no iris or voice recognition. Nothing."

"I don't understand?" said Zola, furrowing her brow. Titus walked around the desk looking into the corners of the room trying to decide which pieces of information to confer.

"He has a trans-hab, he went to the academies, has a job, his security number is 628-581-922 and he has friends but he does not have any records or data files. He has no history."

"Seems appropriate in a society where history is banned," Zola could not help herself.

"History is not banned. It is controlled!"

"I have not tampered with his files, if that's what you're getting at."

"Well, someone has. Because Xavier Miro does not exist and that my dear is impossible."

Zola smiled, "Wow. This really bothers you, doesn't it?"

Titus was not amused, "We know everything about everyone."

Zola shrugged. Zola, the real Zola was back. When all your worst fears come true, perhaps there is nothing more to fear.

"You need to start thinking Zola," he bellowed.

"Or else?"

Titus poured himself some water and placed a glass in front of her. She did not touch it.

"What do I do with you Zola? Do I leave you to rot in one of these cells?"

He walked up behind her, standing still breathing on the back of her neck. She felt her skin crawl. "Or should we send off your mother on some freighter and let her perish on some rock in the middle of the asteroid belt... would you like that?"

Zola was quiet. There was no point letting him see her emotions.

He continued, "Because I'm thinking there's probably more I can do. There's your brothers, Brunel and Breeze?"

She tried desperately to give away nothing. Inside, was in emotional overdrive.

"Brunel is on an Ark and un-contactable and Breeze, the clever one, is on a top secret assignment for Nu Humana," Titus continued, "so I cannot imagine he would want to have anything to do with you. You are the shame of the family Zola."

Zola could contain herself no more. She jumped towards Titus spitting at him, "Leave my family out of this."

"That's more like it Zola, show some spirit. You are such an amazing product of the Pax Humana. Shining examples of all that is good with our system. You are from an exemplary family of excellent standing who have achieved all that is possible within our society. Your brothers are forging the new future in the Pax Humana. You should too!" declared Titus.

"I said...leave my family out of it!"

Titus grabbed her arm with one hand and her face with his other, "You have a couple of options open to you Zola. The legacy of Fabian and Amber and the fate of Brunel and Breeze now rest with the decision you make now. I cannot see why you would choose to make the wrong one."

"What do you mean?"

"I am giving you a break Zola. I do not wish to see a girl like you, with a family of such a social position become common criminals for the likes of someone who does not even exist."

Zola felt the fear rising as Titus increased the pressure.

"An error of judgement we can perhaps overlook," he said in oily tones as he released his grip, "you are a vibrant product of the best of our academia. You could be a shining light of the Pax Humana, a role model for all the girls working within Genesis… a beacon."

Time was running out, and Zola made her decision.

"We wouldn't want to see you shuffling around in a cell with your brain zapped doing sexual tricks for the guards now would we," Titus said slyly.

There it was. Zola surpassed her nausea as he walked towards her and stroked her cheek. It wasn't hard for her to make a decision.

"I am going to give you the chance of a lifetime!" Titus ran his fingers through her hair and pulled her towards him, "You are going to show them, show everybody, me included what it is to be Nu Humana."

She stared at the governor, as she prepared herself for what she was going to do. Her life depended on the next few moments, pulling off the act of her life. With that she leaned in to kiss Governor Titus Haq intensely.

"Thank you," said the Governor.

These were times of war, and she was a soldier on the field of battle.

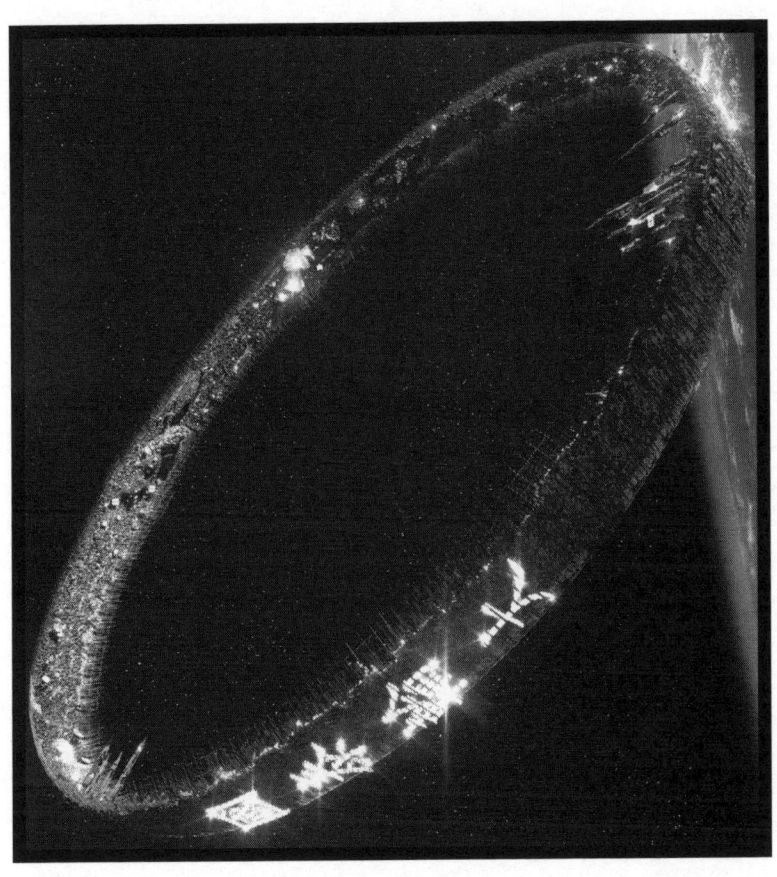

★★★★★

35
The Great Wheel of China

T here had been no goodbyes. Xavier and Old Man Ray had set out to make the dangerous leap across to the Great Wheel of China which dominated the eastern part of Genesis. Aqua Terra was enabled to make short trips around Genesis and the colonies, and the journey to what some referred to as The Cathay Wheel and even to the Moon was well within its range. The sight of the Moon and Earth in the distance made the voyage a beautiful one as they looked out of the windows of Aqua Terra pondering the fates of Zola and Jericho.

It did not take long after they had crossed the border perimeter into Sino Space for Dragonaut Guards to make themselves known. From out of the depths the inky blackness and the glow of various floating satellites a squadron of fighter craft came from all directions.

There before them lay The Cathay Wheel, the largest man-made object ever to be constructed and home to two hundred million human beings. Within its confines people were conceived, born, reared and educated. The Dragonaut interceptors were small and agile fighters with the ability to dart about at incredible speeds. They could detect if human life was onboard and so had yet to fire. Xavier began to tap furiously at the controls, setting new commands into the onboard computer. A warning flashed on a screen in front of Xavier:

★★★WARNING★★★
YOU ARE NOW IN SINO SPACE TERRITORY
YOU HAVE NO CLEARANCE
REPORT BACK OR FACE THE CONSEQUENCES!

"Nice welcome," said Xavier, "good timing, Aqua Terra."

"My orders were to power down," the voice of Aqua Terra's onboard computer chimed, "I cannot be held accountable for your predicament," it continued with what sounded very much like sarcasm.

"No, you cannot... but can you get us out of here?"

Aqua Terra was a fast moving ship but the interceptors of the Dragonaut Guards were meant to meet their mark. Once they were targeted onto something, that something would be intercepted, no matter what occurred to thwart them.

"No, sir I don't think we can lose these beauties!" said Old Man Ray, shaking his head from side to side.

"Garbage Exhaust Chute! Lima Three Ten Four!" Aqua Terra blared, moments later, identifying a means of entry into the giant torus.

"Set your course," Xavier shouted.

"There is an outlet above Lima Three Ten Four that will give you access to the orbital habitat. Be aware that there are garbage crafts present at the exit," said the Aqua Terra computer sounding pleased with itself.

There were other Chinese colonies within Genesis but this was by far the largest and most densely populated. Tens of millions of people lived here, cramped together on top of one another. Every bit of available space turned into living quarters in skyscrapers teeming with life; it was like The Hives only inside a giant ring-shaped space station. Lines of traffic streamed in all directions; such was the frenetic pace and activity of The Cathay Wheel. The policy of mass migration wasn't happening. Here, like The Mughal Space colonies, The Hives, The Star of David, The Star of Bethlehem, and El Cielo Entre Las Estrella favelas, millions of people were waiting for a day that would never come. The day they would board an Ark and be taken somewhere else.

Xavier steered Aqua Terra down. She wheeled round, up past a row of garbage vessels lined up to remove the daily tens of thousands of tons of waste to be shipped across to Debris. The area was full of activity. Scores of waste gangs and space tatters flew in all directions looking for scrap to scavenge or pilfer.

"These guys are going to start firing soon!" exclaimed Old Man Ray, as Xavier deftly manoeuvred in between the hundreds of craft and small vehicles outside the refuse chute.

"They had better not mess with me!"

And with that, Xavier did a complete one eighty turn, heading straight through two shocked refuse operatives in full grabbing apparatus loading a transfer station. Aqua Terra passed into a loading bay and hundreds of suited workers scattered in all directions as they flew low through stacks of containers that were being loaded by robots onto conveyor belts. There was a flash of light on the starboard side of Aqua Terra. Before any alarms sounded, Xavier realised Sino Space were firing warning shots.

"I thought you said they wouldn't dare fire?" yelled Old Man Ray, as the blasts resounded through the cabin.

"I didn't think they would with all this activity," said Xavier, "damage report Aqua Terra?"

"Deflectors on, nothing to report," replied Aqua Terra. Her sensors registered an opening on the port seal that could provide a means of entry into the interior of the Cathay Wheel. It was large enough to pass through and a temporary gel seal had been draped across the entrance. The gel foam seal was used in construction projects; it was an interim measure, used to cover cracks or projectile damage that were all too frequent in Genesis.

The interceptors dropped back. Getting Aqua Terra through was an incredibly delicate manoeuvre. These seals were for objects no bigger than a person. Taking a craft through was no mean feat. As Xavier pondered the best angle of entry, his mind was made up quickly, as another barrage of fire rained above Aqua Terra, the fluorescent flares twinkling inside the cabin urging Xavier to make haste.

"C'mon!" urged Old Man Ray, watching the Sino Space Dragonaut interceptors bearing down on them.

"Give me a second," said Xavier, as he punched a command into the panel at his side. He slowed the craft down. At the right speed you were able to pass through the protective sealing gel without causing damage to yourself, the sphere or its inhabitants. Xavier dropped the power momentarily on Aqua Terra's thrusters and the gel enveloped her. It took all of his guile to guide the small Rod through the viscous material and he knew that he could be spat back out into space if he got it wrong. Xavier gently nudged the controls and Aqua Terra eased her way with a satisfying pop as it unleashed from the syrupy sealant.

The vast magnitude of the Great Wheel lay before them. The largest colony structure ever created. Essentially a bright red rotating drum, it contained numerous cities, suburbs and biomes for its inhabitants. It was elegant and futuristic while looking with pride to its past - its heritage and origin. The wheel had a different creed to The Hives. Aqua Terra descended past a huge stanchion that attached the main body of the wheel, below them clouds covered the vast megalopolis. The Cathay Wheel was so large it had its own weather system. It was a place where everything was artificial. It had become necessary to create an artificial world to house the hundreds of millions of refugees from Earth.

"It's strange to think man could create a fabricated environment with its own weather system, trees and wildlife yet could not look after the planet Earth," muttered Old Man Ray, gazing at the sight below him.

They descended into a world where the scale of man's progression and ingenuity had come to pass. It was like the cities of Hong Kong, Shanghai, Guangzhou and Peking had been combined; the entire colony teemed with human life. Parts of the wheel resembled ancient Imperial China, yet transported three hundred thousand miles from Earth and a thousand years into the future. Pagodas and palaces were laid out with courtyards and steps with thousands of tower blocks surrounding them, all emblazoned with banners proclaiming the long march to the stars and the Sino Space emblem.

People were playing Zaddonk, soccer and even mah-jong on the rooftops. Some were doing tai-chi or reading. Xavier noticed there were no green spaces anywhere. Residents hung out clothing to dry on a thousand balconies, others were eating food at floating food trucks and conversing. There were other colony wheel structures within Genesis but none anywhere near the scale or ambition of the Cathay Wheel. Most of the colony wheels though followed a similar design. There was a central waterway which allowed for waterside development, communication and the transport of produce by barges. Here, that ideal had been replaced by a crowded canal of barges and junks that fought for the right of way with other vessels in the shipping of goods and people to all parts of the Cathay Wheel. A rail line followed the same circular path as the waterway, with its carriages brimming to capacity with passengers. They entered and exited at various stops around the wheel.

Thousands of flying tuk-tuks, hover bikes and buses crisscrossed, missing each other only by a hair's breadth.

The bustle and charge of human life, of individuals - millions of them, going about their daily tasks echoed throughout the wheel in an unceasing almost deafening buzz normal to the residents of this colony. Any space that was not filled with human life was filled with a billboard or hologram stand advertising a dizzying array of products and services. Huge symbols and letters marked out areas and sectors, and gigantic red banners and flags streamed from the buildings. The faces of the leaders of Sino Space and the Great Cathay Celestial Republic stared down at the populace from holograms and posters.

The spiritual leader, San Chun Li, smiled graciously and K.C.Wang, chairman of Sino Space, looking enlightened and committed to the technological advancement, reciting mantras to anyone who could be bothered to listen.

Aside from San Chun Li - the divine, spiritual leader and master of the martial arts - Panda Panda were actually the most famous faces on the Great Wheel. These were a pair of modified, cybernetic pranksters: a slapstick TV duo of cloned and genetically modified talking pandas that got into all manner of scrapes and loved to have a sing-song at the end of their show.

For a split second, Xavier grinned as he recalled the two black and white bozos trying and failing to put Edu-Imps into one another. The moment was broken with a buzz in the cockpit and voices reverberating around his head.

"Xavier…I think we lost them," came Old Man Ray voice on the communicator.

"Think again," replied Xavier.

In front of the craft were one hundred interceptors in rows three deep, their lights flashing, their armaments on display. A message came over the com. It was the head of security for The Great Wheel of China.

"You have illegally entered Sino Space Territory and The Great Cathay Wheel. You shall be escorted to a Sino Space security dock. You will follow us immediately and comply with all of our orders."

"Something tells me he means it Xavier!" said Old Man Ray.

"Do ya' think we will get to see Panda Panda?" asked Xavier.

"Stranger things have happened!"

★★★★★

36
An Audience With San Chun Li

A gong sounded as they entered a large courtyard escorted by twenty armed Sino Space guards. After landing at the security dock, Xavier and Old Man Ray were frisked and questioned by a senior official. Much to the official's disbelief, as well as Xavier's, they were informed that they were to meet with San Chun Li.

San Chun Li had been the definitive symbol of Sino Space for over a century, a politician and spiritual leader who encouraged the people of Sino Space to embrace the history and culture of the Chinese people. A one time soldier, kung fu master and businessman, San Chun Li had been deified by the people of The Cathay Wheel into a beacon of hope and fortitude in these dangerous times. His likeness was everywhere in The Cathay Wheel and it was believed by many that he was immortal.

From the courtyard they entered a corridor where down one side were a row of pillars, each twenty meters tall made of white marble lining the space for over one hundred meters.

Parallel to this ran a channel flowing with water into a range of pools filled with golden carp. Xavier looked down at them. Thousands of orange and golden koi carps which to the inhabitants of the Cathay Wheel symbolised abundance. He had never seen anything like it before.

Steps led them down the entire hundred meter stretch and before them a spectacular multi coloured and bejewelled doorway was opened. They were ushered into a large salon, shafts of light streamed in from the ceiling. Incense burned from the backs of sculpted jade dragons and flower baskets hung from the ceiling filled with red hibiscus and white chrysanthemums creating a luscious, almost overpowering, aroma. The figure of a man stood by a huge window, his back turned to them.

Xavier looked over at Old Man Ray who seemed to have gone pale.

"It's going to be okay Ray...trust me," said Xavier, reassuringly.

Xavier wasn't sure why, but a calm had come over him.

"You really have a gift, Mr. Miro," San Chun Li declared, turning to greet them, "You are not a simple vandal that's for sure. It is apparent you have an important message you wish to convey."

Xavier said nothing, instead he smiled recalling the enormity of the graffiti he and Jericho had left along the side of the Tamarinsk Ark.

"Well, as far as viewings and ratings go Mr Miro, you are something rather special. Do you know what you have just achieved?" asked San Chun Li, exhaling smoke from his vape pipe.

"No sir, I do not believe I do, your honour," Xavier replied.

"Please, Mr. Miro, you do not have to call me 'your honour' I do not need to be venerated or revered. However, it is true I am your senior and also a master of many arts, so your respect is appreciated."

He paused briefly, "If you must you can call me Master or Sir. In fact, Sir is sufficient."

"Yes, Sir," Xavier ventured, respectfully.

"You have become in a very short period of time, Public Enemy Number One to some, but to the people of The Hives and The Cannery you are now a hero," San Chun Li continued.

"I never intended that to happen," Xavier replied.

"Mr. Miro, as you may be aware I am the spiritual leader of the people of The Great Cathay Wheel and of the Chinese origin people who have settled on Genesis and the outer colonies," San Chun Li said, inhaling the fumes from his vape pipe. A gust of smoke then masked his face for a moment before clearing.

"People are free to do what they want, within the limits of our controlled society. We do not allow anarchy within our colony and we cannot condone dreadful or dissident behaviour that goes against what we believe is right. This is the liberty that we hold dear. These are the freedoms every generation has held dear since the dawn of government." The smile had left

San Chun Li's face as he delivered the last sentence, "People will go to work whenever they are told, do whatever they are told to so long as they are fed, housed and given some basic freedoms to enjoy in their spare time; be it eating, sleeping, shopping for goods or making love. That they can do whatever they want, whenever they want just as long as we have told them that they can."

San Chun Li smiled a smile that did not reach his eyes, "These are the lives of countless millions of people, Mr. Miro, however the majority of people do not really want to do very much, let me tell you. The majority of people are idle and lazy, they will fall by the wayside, be thrust out and eventually removed. They are not driven like you to seek out answers. Unlike you, Xavier Miro, knowledge is not their pursuit."

He poured a glass of water, gesturing his two guests to join him at the window that overlooked the great megalopolis, "Take a look. Life here is difficult at the best of times, but the human spirit for a few can be sometimes tenacious. We try to find the best in the situations presented to us."

San Chun Li paused inhaling from his vape pipe, again blowing a huge cloud that once again momentarily covered his face, "I am sure you are aware how difficult life can be living in space. In fact, living in space, where there is no space to live in. Everyone scrambling for a little room...look at this, how does one care for one's soul?"

They gazed out toward the countless buildings containing millions of people and watched as hovercrafts flew above the skyscrapers of the colony wheel. San Chun Li motioned back towards the room and to the servants that stood waiting.

"Ray, if you wouldn't mind, I would like to have a few words with Xavier alone."

Old Man Ray exchanged a quick look, "It's okay," mouthed Xavier.

An attendant stepped out from the periphery and led Old Man Ray away to a seated area, offering him refreshments. He had relaxed considerably, impending doom seemed to have drifted away, for now.

Xavier asked, "So, what am I doing here? Jett Jensen said if I headed to The Cathay Wheel I would be able…"

"You really don't know, do you?" San Chun Li cut off Xavier in mid-sentence.

"The Powers? Who exactly are they?" asked Xavier.

"Mr. Miro, you are getting ahead of yourself," smiled San Chun Li, "generations ago, the governments and the people of Earth made terrible mistakes and unfortunately, they keep making them. It is nothing new, they have been making them for millennia, some call it evolution. It was a mistake that would have terrible repercussions for you and me and the millions upon millions of people that live here in Genesis, on the Moon and even the colonies on Mars."

"You don't say!" said Xavier.

Xavier straightened as the old gentleman stared at him.

"The decisions that have been made, and are still being made by a small handful of people, affect the lives of billions. There is a belief the people of Genesis should live a certain way. The reasons for which even I have no say. We had to leave our mother planet, the place that bore us and we have been banished forever. Imagine that Xavier? Our punishment for destroying the planet that gave us life... is a life of limbo in the emptiness of space."

"I understand what you mean," said Xavier, surveying the madness of the wheel outside.

"Do you Xavier? I think you are clever but I am not sure you fully understand the ramifications," continued San Chun Li, "Are you aware of Adam and Eve and The Garden of Eden? The books of the Old Testament?"

"No sir, I am not."

The old master stroked his chin. He inhaled deeply, exhaling a cloud of blue smoke.

"Five hundred years ago, there was ignorance of what the future of mankind would bring. Everyone lived in the present, unsympathetic and inconsiderate of their actions. Those generations never believed that the way they lived would have such a great effect on their descendants centuries later. Nobody cared. Millions upon millions died of famine, nuclear war, biological disaster, disease and pollution. This proved to have very severe consequences for everyone involved."

"Bad management, you could say," said Xavier.

"What they thought wasn't their problem became everyone's problem, so much so it even came to the attention of beings far away from Earth, who worried about us as a species. Our ancestors created a world that could no longer be inhabited, forcing their descendants to live like this...in an incessant psychotic purgatory," San Chun Li waved his arm across the skyline.

"So how are we here? What happened?" said Xavier, brow furrowed as he gazed out towards the mass of life.

"That, you will have to find out for yourself," he poured himself some tea from a beautiful antique pot adorned with flowers and a mountain scene of Earth. "Xavier, these things have been put in place for a reason, by people and beings far more powerful than you and I."

"Beings?"

"You, Mr. Miro. You are making people think. The Powers don't like that. A person does well not to think too much. Those controlling the masses benefit from the peoples' lack of thought. So, when suddenly they start to think and you're the reason...well, you can understand…"

They walked back through the courtyard.

"I know this might sound like everyone who dreams, but I truly believe I am here for something special," said Xavier, scuffling the flagstones with his boots.

"Oh, believe me, Xavier, you are!" replied San Chun.

San Chun Li stopped and altered the brim of his hat then narrowed his eyes at Xavier.

"What do you think you will achieve, Xavier? Do you think you will change anything? And in that case do you believe people want change? There will always be a minority who want to change things, that has been the case throughout history. The minority opposing the majority and that age old and infernal problem of democracy!" San Chun Li's voice was raised now, "There is no democracy Xavier, there never has been."

"I don't have the answers…sir Mr. Jensen said that someone had the ability to get us past the Celestial Gate and to Earth," said Xavier trying to end the conversation and get to the main reason he was there.

"You really are no more than a vandal and a common criminal who should be handed to The Shadows or the Air Authority for termination. I cannot have you executed."

"Executed?" Old Man Ray, jumped into the conversation. He had been listening for a while.

"Old Man Ray!" San Chun Li turned, looking intently at Old Man Ray, "Join us!"

Taking Old Man Ray's hands into his own he looked at the backs of them before turning them over to the palms, "Who is the older of us? You or I?"

"By the looks of things, me," answered Ray, cooly.

"Yes, I think you are older than anyone here could ever have imagined aren't you?" said San Chun Li.

"Age is an irrelevance," replied Old Man Ray, "would you not agree?"

San Chun Li paused for a moment, holding his gaze at the Moon Dude before smiling then turning, "If you return to The Hives, they will kill you both. It is only through my intervention that you were not killed by the Dragonaut interceptors. Sino Space does not like brigands arriving unannounced in its territory but fortunately for you, I knew you were coming."

"How?" said Xavier, shaking his head, "Thank you."

"It is not I you need to thank. You have friends in high places."

"Higher than you?" said Old Man Ray.

"Yes, indeed Mr. Ray, there is a 'higher than me'!" San Chun Li said with a nod.

The old master signalled to an attendant to bring over a tray of engraved sake cups and a bottle of warm sake which were placed before them on a small table. He then passed them to Old Man Ray and to Xavier and then took his own.

"I rarely make toasts but I thought this occasion warranted it. What you are about to embark on Xavier with my help is a journey truly worth celebrating."

Xavier looked at his friend. They exchanged a glance. Neither of them sure what 'journey' San Chun Li was talking about.

"A toast!" said Old Man Ray. Xavier toasted without knowing what they were toasting. Just as his cup touched his lips, Ray grabbed it out of his hand, "Not you boy. You're the designated driver," he said jovially.

"Pardon me," Ray emitted a burp, winking at San Chun Li.

"And now," their elegant host said, putting his hands on their shoulders, "it is time I send you on your way."

Taking Xavier's hand, San Chun Li placed a small card written in Mandarin and Can-Com English before closing Xavier's fingers around the card. He then muttered a few words to some waiting guards. "I promise you both safe passage from here to wherever you choose. You may take some time here within The Cathay Wheel but then you need to continue your journey and see where it takes you. I think you will be surprised. You have humanity and humility Xavier, which are wonderful traits to have. You have many more things to do and achieve before you can rest so take it while you can. You may just be here to save us!"

"That's what you think?" Xavier looked at him disbelievingly, "With respect Sir, I have no super powers."

"You have belief, the greatest power of all. You have the power to change us all. Who knows, perhaps your morality will lead to your immortality," San Chun Li looked away gesturing for them to go, "they will take you now."

He raised his hand and nodded at the guards.

Xavier and Old Man Ray walked with the Sino Space Guards and shook their heads, puzzled but glad to not be incarcerated, or worse, dead.

"Here!" a Sino Space officer escorted them towards a doorway that led towards an outside bay. "Mr Miro," the officer spoke in perfect Can-Com English, "your craft will remain here. We assure you it will be safe. You have ten hours available to you in The Cathay Wheel, then you must return to hangar 212 and leave Sino Space territory without hesitation." He pointed them towards a doorway and the turmoil of the streets outside, urging them to leave.

Xavier looked at the card San Chun Li had given him. It was an address. He then looked at the mayhem before him and smiled at the officer.

"So…what do you want to do?" asked Old Man Ray.

Chris Abbot

"Let's go for a walk!"

*****

37
A Walk In The Cathay Wheel

Market stalls nestled together endlessly, every spare vestige of space seemingly taken. The sheer magnitude of the Cathay Wheel could prove daunting to a new-comer; the pace was frenetic set against a backdrop of pure cacophony. It was dizzying to look up at the canyon of towering structures stretching up along the wheel of the colony.

Xavier looked back where he had left Aqua Terra. He had no idea where he was going. He had an address on an antique postcard. They had pointed him in the general direction now he and his faithful friend Old Man Ray faced the unknown again.

"Psst…," Xavier heard it first.

"Hey, come here," the voice was more insistent.

Xavier and Old Man Ray saw a teenage girl standing in an alleyway beckoning them to follow.

"Come," her voice was urgent.

"Who?" asked Xavier, "Who is after us?"

"Everyone!"

They followed the teenager through a network of side streets. People sat on benches lost in different conversations. Industrious looking men and women prepared street food for the throngs of pedestrians, releasing intoxicating aromas as pans sizzled. Xavier was feeling apprehensive.

"Where are you taking us?" Xavier asked.

"Don't ask me questions," said the teenage girl firmly, "you want to get past the Celestial Gate don't you?"

"How the hell..." Xavier was flummoxed, "How the hell do you know?"

"Everyone wants a bit of you Xavier, but luckily you have a lot of people on your side and wanting to help."

A small courtyard opened before them with steps at the far end leading into another courtyard then another. The maze seemed to go on endlessly. People milled about attending to their daily lives. Fresh laundry was hung out on balconies above them. Xavier wondered if he would find his way back. Old Man Ray seemed to be mumbling and behaving in an erratic and confused manner. Xavier believed it to be fatigue.

"Hey Ray, you okay?" Xavier mouthed.

"Never better," came the reply.

"Well, tell me if you need to rest."

They came to a shopfront, its window filled with teapots of all shapes and sizes and the paraphernalia for making tea.

"In here quickly," the girl urged.

The store was filled with boxes and a couple of low sitting tables for tea ceremonies. A small doorway led down a flight of stairs and into a smoke-filled office looking out over a small loading bay.

The teenager pulled two chairs towards a desk, "Please. Do take a seat."

Xavier and Old Man Ray reluctantly sat down as requested, "I try not to smoke other people's smoke," said Ray, to a hooded figure sat on the other side.

"You are friend of Slobbo Grensky are you not?" the voice was female.

"Yeah, I guess you could say me and Slobbo go back."

"It is not a test, just a question."

"Then you have your answer," Old Man Ray replied, bluntly.

"Kaiser O'Keefe sends his regards too," the figure turned to reveal a middle aged woman, her head covered with a veil and a cigarette hanging from her lip, "My name is YangYang."

The teenager motioned around them and poured tea from a glass teapot.

"We're fine thanks," said Xavier, "I'm tea'd out!"

"No offence YangYang but my friend and I are tired and have had ample amounts of tea, so if it is okay with you then we can just get to the point. Why are we here?"

YangYang smiled, "That is fine. No offence taken!"

"We have had a very long and eventful journey and...well, as I said...patience is getting low."

"I am just a conveyor of news Xavier from back in the Hives."

"What's that?"

"Your friend Jericho was badly injured by the Air Authority."

"I know, I saw it myself."

"It is not yet known whether he is alive or dead"

Xavier, his face impassive, looked directly at YangYang, "And Zola?"

"Kaiser placed her on one of his ships and tried to get her here," said YangYang sipping her tea, "you don't mind me do you?"

Xavier shook his head, "Then what happened?"

"During a routine stop by a team who were supposedly on Kaiser's payroll they found Zola. There was nothing they could do but to report it and take her prisoner."

Xavier brought his head to his hands and wiped his face, his mind swimming.

"We do not know her whereabouts now but she was taken from custody here in the Cathay Wheel almost immediately and returned to Genesis."

"Do you know how she is?"

"We have informants within Sino Space security who told us she was processed and shipped back to Genesis at break neck speed directly to Federal HQ for interrogation."

"Will she be mind-wiped?"

"Xavier I do not know," YangYang said mildly.

Old Man Ray looked perplexed. His eyes seemed glazed.

"YangYang I need to go, my friend here does not seem well."

YangYang passed Xavier a small ampoule, "Your friend Kaiser sent me a message and told me to give you this."

"What is it?"

"It contains the old smugglers routes to Earth. This is a highly prized Imp and he insisted you have it. It will get you through parts of the Celestial Gate and perhaps all the way to Earth. You will still have to get past parts of security, but this will plot your route."

"I am going to Earth!" Xavier said, as he looked at the small ampoule in his hand.

"It seems that way," replied YangYang.

"Does it work?"

YangYang stood and looked out of the window at the loading bay, "Let's say it is tried and tested. Your friend Kaiser is well connected with our operation here."

From the corner of his eye, Xavier's attention was drawn through the window to the rear wall of the loading bay where he could see what he thought were a group of masked raiders entering. Xavier grabbed his bag and then clasped hold of Old Man Ray's arm.

YangYang turned as if in slow motion, "Get out of here," she screamed.

The furious sound of gunfire emanated from the bay as the room began to shake. Splinters of plaster and plastic flew through the air. An explosion blasted through the room and the window overlooking the loading bay shattered, covering YangYang in fragments of glass, the force sending her crashing across her desk and into a wall of cabinets at the other end of the room. The ampoule he was holding from YangYang had been prised from his hand by the blast and now rolled on the floor with thousands of fragments. Xavier plucked it from the floor and without giving it a second thought swallowed the contents and made his way towards the door.

"Let's get out of here!" he shouted. Old Man Ray was reeling from the explosion.

It was obvious that YangYang was either unconscious or dead but he had no time to check and his immediate thoughts were of saving himself and his buddy. He stumbled forward to help Ray out of there. He spotted the teenager beckoning him towards her.

"What's going on?"

"Who knows? Maybe rival gang, always fighting, maybe territory dispute!" the teenager said, nonchalantly.

"Is that your mom," Xavier gestured towards the motionless body of YangYang.

"Nah!" said the teenage shaking her head, "Just bitch I work for."

Xavier shook his head, "Okay well…whatever. We need to get the fuck outta here!"

The teenager ran ahead and gestured them to follow her, motioning with her hand to stay low. They followed the teenager through the rubble of the building as the sound of gunfire echoed close behind them. Xavier began to think that perhaps it had just been luck, but bad at that, that had played a part in this internecine feud between rival factions, but it was just a little too close for comfort for him. Someone could have been trying to kill them. Small, metre wide gullies strewn with garbage and litter separated the buildings and the three of them pushed their way against the vast amounts of rubbish that had built up over time

"I don't even know your name," Xavier said as he followed the young girl.

"No need to know."

The gully opened onto a dank, dirty alleyway. People were shooting up or passed out. Some ate, some were huddled together. At one end of the alley a street could be seen which was opposite to the end of the block from where they had come from. Safety at last, Xavier thought.

"Thank you," Xavier said, to his guide, again, "I would still like to know your name."

The teenager smiled, "Okay then, my name is..." she stopped mid-sentence.

Without warning a figure stepped out in front of the teenager. A thud was heard as her body juddered and crumpled to the floor. Before they could do anything a voice called from the semi darkness and the shape of a cloaked figure stepped forward.

"It's the Shadows!" screeched Old Man Ray.

"Keep your mouth shut old man! I am far from that."

"Why did you do that?" asked Xavier, looking down at the collapsed body of their guide.

"You should not worry about what I did to her," came the reply, "worry about yourself."

A face revealed itself. Piercing green eyes sparkled like emeralds, surrounded by thick jet black hair. There was an air of self assurance and authority in the voice and the manner.

"Is she alive?"

"She will be fine. Don't worry. She is unconscious not dead. She was leading you to another gang. She will come to in a few moments and scurry back to whoever will pay her next."

"Who are you?'

"My name is Captain Jagz Powar!"

"I have heard of you," said Old Man Ray "You are a Tigernaut officer."

"Was," Jagz replied, "I see you have experienced a close call with the smuggling gangs of The Cathay Wheel."

"What just happened there?"

"Triads or Tiandihui. That's gangsters to the layman - fighting over turf, drugs, money, people, power - they smuggle …every illicit product including Edu-Imps that make their way to any colony in Genesis as well as here…they are behind it."

"Triads?" asked Xavier.

"Ancient organised criminal gangs who came up from Earth centuries ago and set up shop here and on Mughal Space. You have them in the Hives but they operate mainly from The Great Wheel."

"You were a Tigernaut officer aren't you an enemy of Sino Space? Is it safe for you to be on The Cathay Wheel?"

"My business here is private but affects everyone who lives here and the colonies of Genesis."

"So what has that got to do with us?"

Jagz pulled Xavier and Old Man Ray out of the alley and into a doorway,"What you just witnessed is nothing to what will happen if I do not stop these gangs."

"What does this have to do with me?"

"Organised crime has always smuggled between the various colonies including my own Mughal Space but we have something far more sinister and deadly going on."

"What's that?"

"Ganglion gangs have been trafficking for years but they are merely guns for hire. Someone with much more influence is behind this, someone has given them a passage to Earth."

"To do what?"

"Smuggle ancient artefacts and animals from Earth to The Cathay Wheel and beyond. There is a highly lucrative market in these artefacts and the black market is booming in pre-Exodus Earth made goods especially anything natural like wood or animal hide. The danger for the colonies is many of these artefacts contain Earth borne bacteria which will decimate perhaps annihilate whole colony populations. It is a treacherous business and if not stopped could endanger everyone within Genesis and I mean everyone."

"Who would do that?"

"Other than the Powers and very trusted custodians, few have such access and all of the space elevators are no longer in use or were destroyed…you I believe may have the key."

"I have the key?"

"A Ganglion gang has tried to kill you and yet you have escaped and made your way here."

"I think that was just good fortune."

"I think its more than luck Xavier, you have been given access by someone or something to get you through the Celestial Gate."

"And who sent you?"

"I work alone. Nobody tells me where to go or what to do," said Jagz Powar emphatically.

"I am going to get to Earth one way or other," said Xavier, "I have no idea how I can help you but if I can I will."

"If you are able to get to Earth then I need to find out how contraband is getting here from Earth to The Cathay Wheel," Jagz paused as he pulled across his cloak, holding his hand aloft then waving them along. "Watch your back, there are many who want to help you but there are plenty who would like to see the back of you."

"What about the girl here," Xavier looked down at the guide who was now beginning to revive from her state of inertia.

"She will be fine, I will make sure of it. But you need to go now!"

Xavier and Old Man Ray looked at one another, "Our time is running out and we need to get back to our craft."

They looked at the labyrinth of buildings before them and shook their heads, "Do you think we will be able to make it back to Aqua Terra in time?"

"If you are planning on making it to Earth, Citizen Miro, then I am sure you will be able to find your way through the streets of the Great Wheel," Jagz said, "follow your instinct and your gut and you will arrive safe and sound."

Old Man Ray and Xavier had begun to walk towards the tallest structure they could see in the distance before Xavier turned back towards Jagz, who was now watching them from the dark recesses of a doorway.

"Thank you," called Xavier, "as the old astronauts would say *'Godspeed'*"

Jagz acknowledged them, "Godspeed Xavier, Godspeed," before disappearing in the depths of the enormous megalopolis.

They walked for what seemed to be hours through the streets of The Cathay Wheel, Old Man Ray tiring with every step he took. He said nothing, just focused ahead on each stride as Xavier guided them at every turn towards Aqua Terra. The walls of the government buildings adorned with images of K.C.Wang, Lin Fan Zhang, San Chun Li and other Sino Space officials came into view.

"Never a fucking taxi when you need one is there," Old Man Ray smiled, clearly in pain.

They walked to their craft unchallenged by any of the Sino Space guards and climbed back into Aqua Terra and pulled their harnesses over them.

"This is one sweet ride. Good to be sat back inside you," laughed Xavier, before turning to Ray, "Pretty far out! huh?"

"Just go! Let's get out of here!" demanded Old Man Ray, sweat pouring from his forehead.

"What's up with you?" Xavier asked, he could plainly see that Ray was in some kind of trouble.

"I am dying!"

"Dying!?"

"Xavier, I am an old man; older than you can imagine and I have been away from the moon for too long. I need to return to my people on the Moon," Old Man Ray clutched his stomach gritting his teeth.

"What's going on Ray?" Xavier's face was filled with concern.

"I would have loved to come to Earth with you, but you will have to do that part on your own boy. I need you to take me to the Moon. Take me back to the Moon Dudes and they will heal me."

Old Man Ray smiled at Xavier, then passed out.

Xavier flicked a few switches and the craft came to life and began her ascent, swirling up through the stately buildings of The Celestial Palace and The Great Cathay Wheel.

He looked and saw Old Man Ray fall in and out of consciousness, as they were joined by four interceptors there to escort them out of Sino Space.

A hologram of Panda Panda, wearing overalls and programming an initiation sequence for a proton thruster, was being broadcast from a skyscraper and below him a multitude of people moved as one as they performed some ritual exercise together.

From his window, San Chun Li gazed up and watched as Aqua Terra and her escort rose up into the air and out of the colony.

"The winds of the heavens shift suddenly; so does human fate....Godspeed Xavier!"

★★★★★

38
An Errand For The Pupil

Titus was slumped across a red sofa staring through the large window looking out across the amalgam colonies of Genesis and The Hives. Surveying all that he controlled was a tiresome job and he reached over to a bowl of fruit recently brought from his family's gardens on Earth. It was hard for him to make up his mind and his hand hovered over the colourful shapes before him.

"Have you ever tried fruit grown on Earth, Zola?" He looked at her, as he took a bite from a glistening red apple. The juices ran in rivulets down either side of his mouth. Zola did not reply. She was sitting at the other end of the lounge, her eyes distant, her mind elsewhere.

"Come," Titus said, handing her a piece of fruit, "it's delicious, I love apples!"

"Do you think I have never eaten fruit before, Titus?" snapped Zola, as she grabbed a grape and popped it in her mouth, "There...you happy? I've had better...the ones from the vineyards close to Nu Venezia are pretty good."

Titus coughed, "I have tried produce from all over Genesis and though it is good, it can never compare with fruit from Earth."

"Whatever!"

Zola was finding it difficult to fully veil her hostility towards Titus. To save her mother and her own life, she was playing this game with him. It was a dangerous game she was playing and and she had to be more careful. Sex was Titus's weakness and he was known to go to great lengths in order to play his debauched games. Zola shuddered at what he might have in store for her.

"You look stunning by the way," Titus said, leering at Zola who no longer wore her standard issue space suit and ArkLight fatigues. She had to wear a figure-hugging dress courtesy of Governor Haq revealing her every contour. Her hair had been styled and flowed over her shoulders, unrestricted by the confines of a space helmet.

"When do I get to see my mother, Titus?" Zola asked, reigning in her vitriol.

"All in good time Zola," Titus replied, "all in good time."

"You promised that I would meet with her," she replied, as evenly as she could muster.

"Act in haste and repent at leisure," Titus sneered. "Your mother is fine and you will see her soon enough. In the meantime, if you'll excuse me I have to speak with someone about some unfinished business."

"And what shall I do?"

Titus motioned towards a glass-fronted swimming pool and gymnasium with views out towards the colonies of The Cannery.

"Make yourself even more beautiful, for when I return," he leered.

He made his way to the door bowing his head at Zola before turning and heading down a dimly lit corridor into an antechamber at the end.

"Monsieur Ferrer, we have a problem," Titus paced around the room. "The buffoonery of our so-called security forces and mercenary charges baffles me and so yet again I come to you."

Lucien Ferrer moved like a snake, his body encased in an old decrepit black space suit. The helmet surrounding his head was an antique looking cosmonauts helmet with corrugated pipes emanating from it. The latches that contained it were securely locked, so as to contain the spirit of the old devil incarnate.

"Young Titus, I was dealing with these sort of people before your own clone father was even injected onto a petri dish. Forgive me if I sound conceited but I will confront these people like I always have done and terminate them effectively and efficiently. You have nothing to fear."

"Fear is not for me," replied Titus, "fear is for the people. We control the populace with fear, the fear of us, the fear of religion, the fear of faith, creed or colour, the fear of violence and ultimately the fear of the unknown...that is the greatest fear."

"So…you understand fear."

From within the darkened gloom of the room an artificial whimpering noise could be heard.

"I see you have brought a friend with you Lucien!" said Titus, rubbing his hands.

The silhouetted figure of Magnus Bowser appeared behind his master Ferrer.

"Magnus here will find Xavier Miro for us. He is a recent experiment of mine!"

"But Shadows do not exist, not in space, surely they are just Earth-bound?"

"Not any more Titus. Not any more!"

"Good. Then I have some work for you, I want you to find Xavier Miro for me and kill him. He is undoubtedly in hiding and making his way towards Earth. We lost him in Debris."

"Is this to protect your honeypot out there," Ferrer pointed in the direction of Zola.

"How vulgar you are sometimes, Ferrer," said Titus. "Age has not mellowed you, has it?"

"Titus, I may be older than I care to recall but I have never allowed the influence of a woman to misguide my judgement."

"I doubt highly, Lucien, that you have ever had a woman in your life."

Ferrer hissed at Titus.

"How did Xavier Miro evade you again? I thought you had engaged the services of that ruthless savage Torruk to take care of him."

"Torruk has always been good for me in jobs like this in the past. But alas, he is no longer with us. Word has reached me that he has been eaten alive by shamanic pirates of all things. This does solve the problem of payment though," Titus said, not missing a beat.

A sound not unlike a snigger came from Ferrer's helmet,"Bitten off more than he could chew. Marvellous!"

Titus shook his head. "And so yes, Miro is still at large," continued Titus, as he walked towards Magnus Bowser. "Maybe Magnus here could find our fugitive and give him the adventure he has so dearly yearned for."

The vessel of Magnus remained motionless and dead as Titus circled him.

"Ferrer, oversee this," Titus snapped. "Make sure this man Xavier Miro is captured or killed. I am tired of his antics."

"He obviously has admirers and people aiding him in his flight," Ferrer said.

"Get rid of them too if necessary. Miro is a pariah to us and needs to be dealt with using only the most extreme measures."

"Oh well...extreme measures are what we like most of all," snarled Ferrer.

"Lucien, you may be the most malicious creature in all the worlds but you had great integrity. You do what you say. Even when that meant the extermination of millions...You did it."

"I did indeed, myself and the resolute, unswerving, steadfast devotion of Kremer Gracian!" replied Lucien Ferrer, his mind cast back to the days of the Exodus.

"Ah! The notorious Kremer Gracian! Did you not recruit him to remove any human straggler left behind during the Exodus?"

"He was a devoted disciple to the cause. A man who took his duty very seriously and never wavered from the task."

"I would have loved to have met him."

"You might still."

Titus paused unsure of what Ferrer meant, "So...can we entrust the simple task of eliminating Xavier Miro with your protégé Magnus here?"

"I believe so."

"I worry what message he sends to the millions here in Genesis."

"*Fait Accompli*," Ferrer bowed his head and turned with Magnus, leaving the room and heading towards an unmarked shuttle being prepared for them.

Titus walked back through the corridor and into his private suites where he watched Zola swimming laps in the pool before him. His face showed no emotion as he entered the pool area and stood at the end as Zola approached him.

She looked up at him from the water plastering an ingratiating smile on her face. Titus stared down at her, momentarily lost in thought before he smiled back.

"I was recently on Earth for business. It really is a beautiful place," he said wandering off in contemplation, "Perhaps we should go there, you and I."

★★★★★

39
The Moon Is Not A Balloon

Magnificent desolation…Xavier recalled an Edu-Imp of the primitive pioneer astronaut Buzz Aldrin's description of the moon when he flew over it in the company of Neil Armstrong, the first man ever to set foot on the surface of another world. Xavier shared the same feeling as they flew over the illuminated silver-grey rock that dazzled his eyes from the reflected light of the sun. It was indeed magnificent. It was indeed bleak and forbidding. Yet it was a far cry from the world where Armstrong and Aldrin had first taken those memorable steps for mankind. The Moon was as much a part of the human soul as the Earth. Its pockmarked surface was the legacy of millions of years of meteor strikes.

Meteor strikes were still common on the moon and many of the colonies that had been developed were burrowed deep underground. Huge, labyrinthine caverns excavated into the lunar mines were in turn converted into living quarters. Incredible tunnelled cities replete with shopping malls and residential housing estates existed under the surface with sports stadiums and theatres that naturally filled small craters. An immense wave of immigration had taken place and saw the residents and colonists become very patriotic and proud of their new moon home. With the discovery of vast mineral deposits all over the moon and the advancement of lunar extraction techniques, a rapid change saw corporations lead the way in the very first factories and refineries. The expansion of human colonisation and industry saw the growth and construction of many colonies in the L5, even before the area had been named Genesis.

Flying over this desolate landscape, Aqua Terra hugged the lunar terrain with the tell-tale signs of man's occupation all around them. Mining colonies and settlements were dotted everywhere, discarded machinery and storage facilities, giant solar energy farms, mass drivers and launchers; each had the signs of man's infinite touch. The mass drivers seemed to be continually at work, flinging their consignments and cargoes into the depths of space to be collected when they were out of lunar gravity and taken to Genesis or beyond. Projectiles of lunar rubble flew high into the jet black void of space without a sound in the ghostly lunar landscape.

The seminal Trans-Lunar Express and Aqueduct connected the major conurbations and industrial hubs of the Moon. The flashes of light as trains shot along the tracks at breakneck speeds seemed like bullet traces shooting into the night. The illuminated tracks provided a guide for any craft lost or in need of refuge in this lunar wilderness. Four hundred years on from those early pioneers, the major cities of the Moon were now home to millions.

Ancient man had loved the moon from afar - Man still loved the Moon only now it was for a vacation. The most popular vacation destination in the entirety of the colonies was The Branson Entertainment Crater - a covered paradise and leisure complex, where families holidayed and played sports in the low gravity environment of the moon with the Earth as their spectacular backdrop. Thousands of people relaxed at the crater and its popularity never seemed to wane over the centuries. It was rumoured that the early private space pioneer, Sir Richard Branson, never shy of a photo opportunity was sometimes seen by vacationers dallying around the crater, after being kept in suspended animation for the last four centuries.

The far side of the moon was occupied mainly by military bases. It was the realm of covert forces, mining prospectors, radio telescopes and observatories looking into deep space, sending and receiving clandestine communications from surreptitious corporate operations that continued to flourish in the dark shadow of the Moon. Even if it was disinformation meant to stop people going there, it certainly did the trick. Nobody needed to go to the dark side of the Moon.

As Aqua Terra sped at low altitude across the surface, the odd prospector scuttling around their remote outpost would look up and wave to the craft, confirming that life did exist. Life pods were scattered all over the surface of the moon and acted as safe havens in the event of a breakdown. They were stocked with water, food and oxygen supplies in the eventuality of anyone getting lost in this bleak and forbidding land.

Xavier dialled in a local frequency on his communication system and made a call, "This is Aqua Terra calling Tranqualandia, Aqua Terra calling Tranqalandia, I have a passenger with me called Ray, Old Man Ray. He is gravely ill and needs urgent medical attention, over."

There was a pause, then the airwaves were broken, "This is Tranqualandia here, we have been expecting you Aqua Terra, you are free to enter our territory on co-ordinates one nine zero, eight four niner, over."

"I will set co-ordinates and be ready to arrive shortly please make sure you have a medical team ready for our arrival."

"We will have an emergency team awaiting your arrival Aqua Terra," the voice broke off, leaving Xavier to wonder who had notified them of his arrival with Old Man Ray.

He looked down at his friend, "Hold on now buddy, you are nearly home."

Tranqualandia was a collection of domes and settlements comprising of five interlinking craters. Most were over five-hundred meters deep underground and had been domed and sealed, with the land converted into hydroponic cultivation centres where vegetables, plants and fruits could grow profusely in the low gravity of the Moon. Some of the plants in the craters had turned into forests, growing in excess of one-hundred meters high. Havens and shelters had been built within these forests forming a perfect idyll within these craters.

The space hippies that inhabited these craters became known as Moon Dudes; hardwearing, hardworking pioneers who had harnessed the moon's resources and cultivated the land in order to bring life to a barren and inhospitable place. Being solitary, self-reliant people, they desired to be left alone and for the most part people respected their wishes. They were happy on the Moon, it was close to Earth and they spent their days harvesting their crops and their free time enjoying the life that they had created. It was their own paradise and from this crater they could gaze across the void of space towards the beautiful blue planet.

It was Old Man Ray's *alma mater*.

There had been episodes throughout history when a zealous *politico* or corporate henchman had tried to exert his control and influence over the fraternity of Moon Dudes banding together as one kept them strong allowing no-one to break them up.

"Friends in high places, that's what we got!" Old Man Ray would tell Xavier and he was probably right. His recent meeting with San Chun Li had shown him how high-ranking these friends were.

The Moon Dudes had definitely been able to harness the best from Earth and the best from the Moon to make their home, Sativaland, a unique domain that only very few people were lucky enough to venture to and explore. The inhabitants were not only great cultivators of flora and plants. It was said that after so many generations of living here, they had harnessed the forces of nature which ebbed to and fro to transport themselves within the universe. These transcend-ental experiences were real, but how they manifested themselves no one knew.

Old Man Ray would spend hours talking about Tranqualandia and Sativaland, jokingly referring to it as '*The Lot of Pot*'. He would talk about the old Moon Dudes, their community and neighbourly respect and what it meant to live in a world where your friends and neighbours mattered and everyone cared for one another. That spirit of togetherness was now lost. Old Man Ray mentored Xavier as much as he could. Xavier always recalled Ray being there, always close to him and keeping an eye on him. He would keep Xavier on a short leash, explaining the rights and wrongs and moral dilemmas that everyone faced. He would always reprimand Xavier if he got too lippy or his *braggadocio* became too much.

Ray would point out that, "It was nice to be nice," and that the murder of others in the pursuit of any ideal was wrong, the executions by the Air Authority were not justified and should not be tolerated.

"Well, why do you stay in The Hives you crank pot?" Xavier would shout at him.

"To keep an eye on you!" Old Man Ray would reply.

Xavier had never understood why Old Man Ray had not become a resident of Debris or returned to the Moon Dudes, whom he spoke about so passionately.

Now Xavier was bringing Old Man Ray back to his people.

They reached a long promontory rising from the flat basin. Xavier banked Aqua Terra and headed down an obscured gully whose sides dropped away by a kilometre into another valley. They followed the ravine for a hundred kilometres until they came to an oasis in the distant silver-grey of the Moon. The protective shield of the dome was laid low over the crater with the sides of the canyon obscuring the crater from above. At surface level there was very little to see of the canopy and it resembled a thousand hydro plantations that scattered the lunar surface. A row of blue lights welcomed the visitor down towards an entrance which led below ground.

As Aqua Terra slowed, Old Man Ray pointed slowly in its direction.

"Home," he said, before slipping back into unconsciousness.

Xavier guided Aqua Terra down towards the entrance and engaged the lunar skids and filters that allowed the craft to make a landing on the dusty grey terrain. Storage silos and solar panels encircled the crater and gas-filled spheres stretched out into the valley basin that contained hydrogen and helium 3 as well as many of the by-products that came from the plants inside the crater. There was a stillness about the area.

As Aqua Terra made her descent into the entrance hangar, a huge door closed behind them, sealing and balancing the pressure and oxygen levels. A service droid directed the craft to its bay in the hangar and Xavier promptly cut the engines. Within minutes a team of medics were inside Aqua Terra and checking Old Man Ray's vital signs. He was murmuring and managed to smile and mouth a thank-you to Xavier, before closing his eyes and drifting back into his deep sleep.

"Don't you worry about a thing," a tall and gentle-looking woman said.

"He is back where he belongs," said Xavier, whose face betrayed his concern for the old man's life.

"We will take care of him now. He will be fine. As for you, come with us and see the dome."

"He said he was poisoned."

"I think it would take more than poison to end Ray's life."

"I think you could be right," smiled Xavier.

Some of the craters that made up this community were over five hundred meters deep and had been domed and sealed centuries before, then filled with oxygen. The temperature inside these craters was not like the cold of the Moon. Air was circulated throughout the tunnels that connected the flora filled chasms. Houses were built along the sides of the craters to gaze down upon the forest below. Many of the first trees that had been planted were now so big that houses had been built within the branches with ladders connecting the assorted buildings to one another.

There was something mystical about the Moon Dudes; Xavier could see it in their faces. They seemed to glow, all radiating an energy that diffused amongst one another. They referred to it as their life energies.

Xavier felt a firm hand on his shoulder, he turned around to see who it was.

"My name is Horace Clunk, I am one of the elders of us Moon Dudes."

Horace Clunk was a rotund figure who had long white hair and a beard like Old Man Ray and had a rolled, spotted bandana covering his brow.

"Can you feel it, Xavier?" asked the host, "Can you feel the energy that surrounds us dudes? Incredible, isn't it? You have that energy too, Xavier."

Another old dude stepped forward, "Everyone has this energy. The problem is that it is repressed and restrained. The whole of mankind has this energy. It is very powerful when expressed."

"Everyone? Even in The Hives?" asked Xavier.

"Everyone's life force is unique and special. It is with us the moment we are born and leaves the moment we pass away," said a man who looked a lot like Old Man Ray.

"It is your spirit," said a tall red haired woman, "my name is Nana Lulu, I am an old time friend of Ray's, I have been here for many years." She had a kindly face and ushered Xavier through the tunnel and into a huge hydro forest, "Your aura is very strong Xavier."

"I'll take your word for it," said Xavier, turning to see the beautiful forest that had been created in the huge caldera, "but I'm pretty much of the humans as biological machines, school of thought."

"That is what they'd like you to think. We are all vessels crossing oceans and we all carry a precious cargo," said Horace Clunk.

"These vessels carry auras. When they are expressed, they can change everything," the benign tones of another dude joined in, "greetings Xavier. My name is Pete Casso, I too am an old friend of Ray's."

"When these auras are all expressed they can change society forever," said Nana Lulu.

"They can change the world?" said Xavier.

"Change the universe," smiled Nana Lulu.

"Change everything," grinned Casso merrily.

"The Powers are in control, Xavier. They do not want mankind to use their auras to their full potential. They use evil in the form of The Shadows to restrain and subjugate our spirits. You can do something different. You can send them a message by getting to Earth, Xavier...and we want to help you," continued Clunk.

"The people in The Hives need hope. They need to know that there is a future...on Earth," Nana Lulu declared.

"I need to get to Earth!"

"Xavier, you have to show the people now living in Genesis that one of them can get to Earth," said Pete Casso.

"When I was on The Cathay Wheel I was given what I believe to be an Edu-Imp that would get me past the Celestial Gate."

"We could show you how to get through the Celestial Gate...we are old timers!" laughed Horace Clunk.

"You are about to embark on a journey as momentous as the one made by the first men who came to the moon, Xavier," Nana Lulu's excitement was apparent in her voice.

"It has been a long time since man ventured back to Earth," Horace Clunk proclaimed solemnly.

"Well, at least…someone who is uninvited that is," added Pete Casso.

"Looks like I got the call, but I still can't work out why it's me," Xavier asked, scratching his head.

"You will find out soon enough," said Horace Clunk, "now you should get some rest."

*****

40

The Merry Loonsters!

For the first time since he had left Genesis Xavier slept solidly.

He had worried to himself if he would ever sleep normally again. It was his dreams that had led him on this wild adventure and he just wanted, if only for a little while to feel, 'normal' with 'normal' dreams. In the in-between moments before his eyes opened, when he thought himself awake but was still unconscious, Xavier felt a presence within the room.

His eyes opened and there framed in the doorway stood Pete Casso, "Xavier, I need to show you something," he asked.

Xavier blinked but said nothing.

"Get dressed and I will make you a beverage," Casso continued.

Xavier nodded gently, his eyes adjusting to the artificial light streaming in from outside the bedroom.

Xavier stretched his arms over his head before finally speaking, "Whatever you say," he said. He had become accustomed to this kind of thing now. This was why he was alive. He entered a kitchen area and was greeted by Nana Lulu, Horace Clunk and Casso all drinking a hot tea made from the sativa plants from their dome.

"Slept well?' asked Lulu, looking up at Xavier.

"Yes, yes, very well thank you," replied Xavier, taking a seat at the end of the table.

"Tea, coffee, water?"

"Whatever is easiest," Xavier said, "how is Ray?"

"Oh, he is fine," answered Casso promptly, pouring Xavier both hot tea and cold water.

"Responding well to treatment."

"Can I see him?"

"He still needs to be completely undisturbed, Xavier. He is rather an old man and his system will need extra time to heal," Casso said kindly, aware that Xavier really needed to see Ray.

"Poor old Ray," Xavier said quietly, "I am relieved he's better though!"

"Just doing what we do," Nana Lulu said.

"Wow! You Moon Dudes are pretty amazing!"

"Yes, we are," Casso smiled.

"You have to be careful don't you?" said Xavier, "When you live in space or on the moon the changes in temperature and gravity."

"Well, just like in Genesis or any other colony here on the moon, our pressure and gravity are set according to the norm of 101.3 kiloPascals for the air pressure and 1g for gravity."

"We do our best, but obviously from time to time we have problems. Most colonies do."

"Did you think you would be walking differently here?" Nana Lulu asked.

"Well, yes but I suppose that is because we are in these pressurised domes."

Casso beckoned Xavier towards him, "Here put this on," handing him a pressurised space suit to go over his other suit, "we will take the truck. I want to take you for a little ride and show you something."

Xavier finished his drink and began to suit up along with the rest of them and within minutes they were ready to go.

"I think you will find this of interest," said Lulu, as they made their way from the kitchen and out through an airlock into a garage. Before them stood an old lunar rover with a cabin attached.

"This antiquated old thing is over three-hundred years old," she continued.

"Nearly as old as you guys," joked Xavier.

"Doesn't come close," Nana Lulu smiled.

It had huge wheels and was painted, like most things the Moon Dudes touched, in a glorious technicolour swirl. There was a ladder leading up to the hatch and all the necessary apparatus required for embarking on a lunar exploration.

"This is The Merry Loonsters moon rover 'Farther' which criss-crossed the surface of the moon, dark side and light nearly three centuries ago looking for lunar enlightenment and boy did they find it Xavier!" Horace Cluck laughed.

"Is it safe?" Xavier enquired, as he looked over the chassis and viewing portholes.

"Oh quite safe, young man, this beauty is well-preserved and looked after by us all."

Xavier climbed the small ladder and entered into the confines of the rover, where twelve padded seats were set in rows before him.

"Belt up now Xavier, you will feel a change as we leave the confines of the dome, and put your helmet on just in case, these portholes are pretty old and creaky!" Nana Lulu guided Xavier to his appointed seat. Her confidence was not reassuring.

Xavier took his seat with trepidation, tapping the inside of a porthole.

In the drivers seat was another Moon Dude, again a white-haired gentleman called Goff, wearing an old spacesuit and helmet who turned and quietly nodded a greeting to Xavier, "Hold tight everyone, especially Xavier Miro."

The rover lurched forward as Goff engaged the engine and instantly the doors of the garage dome opened and the vehicle proceeded up a ramp and out into the silver-grey light of the lunar landscape.

"We lead a very solitary life here, we always have done. Nobody disturbs us and for that reason we do not disturb them," said Goff.

"Well, from what I can tell you have everything you need in Tranqualandia," said Xavier calming down, as the truck proceeded smoothly down a boulder strewn hill and then out onto a flat maria.

"We do indeed Xavier. We are totally self sufficient… always have been," said Horace Clunk. "It feels good to get out and take this beauty for a spin," he added.

"So why are we venturing out today?" asked Xavier

"Because we would like to show you some of the moon…not a lot, but some of it and also to show you something very special," Clunk continued.

"You might get an idea of our and the Earth's relationship as we are the closest of neighbours," added Casso

"There is a bond between us," Nana Lulu smiled. "A most definite bond. Without the moon, the Earth could not be the planet it is."

"They are entwined Xavier, ultimately and forever," said Goff who didn't speak much pointing to a ridge in the distance. "The moon gives Earth life, the Earth could not exist without the moon's help."

As 'Farther' made its way over the plateau of dust and small boulders towards a range of mountains in the near distance, Xavier gazed through the porthole next to his seat and at the screens from the cameras set around the rover which piped in images from all directions. The hand of man had not been kind to the moon, all manner of refuse had been discarded by corporate prospectors and itinerant settlers, from small tools to bulky containers which had been either left there on the surface or jettisoned by erstwhile prospecting parties in search of new mineral wealth amongst the barren lands. A fine dust hung like a fog over the maria, caused by the relentless churn of trucks crisscrossing and boots kicking. This continual agitation had caused a ghostly cloud to linger across the landscape. There was silence which seemed unnatural; only in the distance, the swish of the mass drivers, giant devices used to propel goods in the low gravity, catapulting their payloads into space resonated across the basalt plains. Every minute another consignment of goods was launched into the darkness, to be collected and ferried to the construction yards on ArkLight and Genesis.

A sudden flash of light caught Xavier's attention.

"Trans-Lunar Express," said Goff, motioning his hand towards the direction of the famous rail line.

"Everything goes by the Trans-Lunar Express," Lulu began humming a popular jingle from a television commercial.

"One of the great feats of human engineering," replied Xavier, "a hyper loop train system linking all the major cities and industrial zones of the moon built by the Musk Lunar Corporation at the beginning of the 22nd Century."

"Yes, it is…you know your facts!" Goff replied, "Used by nearly every citizen on this lump of rock."

"There are so many marvels of human invention and endeavour to mention Xavier, not only here but all over the solar system," said Casso. "Man has really excelled himself since he emigrated to space. The thousands of colonies throughout the solar system, Genesis, the Cathay Wheel, the great Mars colonies, the cloud colonies on Venus…the list goes on."

"It is as if humanity went into overdrive," said Xavier. As he looked through his porthole he could see in the distance

The Great Wheel of China which he had just left and the large strip of colonies that made up Genesis. Each one vast in size and home to millions.

"Sometimes you never realise your full potential in life. You cruise along, happy with your lot and quite content to remain where you are," said Pete Casso.

"And then…" said Goff.

"Boom!" exclaimed Xavier, "Yep. You've pretty much described my life."

"Why do you think this is happening Xavier?" asked Lulu.

"I always felt I was here for something other than just working on Arks in the Nu Humana dock. I don't know…but I'm sure I am not alone in thinking that I am put here to do something special with my life. Everyone thinks that to some degree…"

"Exactly!" the Moon Dudes spoke in unison.

As 'Farther' began an incline up a ridge Xavier noticed a rising excitement in him; he was the closest he had ever been to Earth…apart from in his dreams. A mere 384,400 kilometres was all that separated him from there.

The rover came to an abrupt halt at the top of the ridge. Goff stepped from his seat and motioned for everyone to secure their helmets and life supports. Nobody uttered a word disembarking via a ladder at the side of 'Farther' and onto the lunar dust. There was a gentle crunch as Xavier's boot touched the ground and finally Xavier could feel the low gravity of the moon.

"Here on the moon it is just one-sixth the gravity of Earth and all the colonies in Genesis," Pete Casso remarked, as Xavier gingerly made his way along the side of 'Farther'.

"You'll get the hang of it soon enough!" said Goff, skipping away.

"The standardisation of gravity throughout the Pax Humana colonies was made so that the transition and acclimatisation of people from one colony to another did not disrupt productivity," Casso continued.

"You've got to hand it to those scientists and engineers back in the day for overcoming the laws of gravity by creating an artificial one," Xavier replied as he began to find his rhythm of a hop and a skip.

"And an efficient one too!"

The ridge of the crater looked out towards the Earth, behind them the Seas of Tranquility and Serenity stretched for hundreds of kilometres. In the far distance the sprawl of Apollo, the metropolitan lunar capital that millions called home could be seen, its linear lights stretching out across the horizon.

"Apollo City, crazy huh?"

"You could never imagine that a city of that size could be built upon the moon!" exclaimed Horace Clunk.

"Yes, it's incredible really!" said Xavier, as he gazed at another Trans Lunar Express flash past in the distance, "And to think that the majority of the city lies underground."

"Underground, yes…but with the same rules as Genesis. It might be a little easier here but nobody gets cut any slack that's for sure!" said Horace Clunk, as he motioned everyone to follow him.

They made their way along the ridge to a giant rock boulder about seventy meters in length with a sloping ledge which they began to ascend. Clunk led the way followed by Goff, Xavier and Nana Lulu with Pete Casso following a little way behind. Xavier looked around at the grey terrain on either side of him and then above him at the crest of the boulder, the Earth came into full view.He had never seen it so large, so beautiful.

"Wow!" he cried.

"Isn't it just!" replied Nana Lulu.

From their vantage point they could see the distinct coastlines of the continents, the polar ice caps and the oceans with their weather patterns swirling above them. The wafer-thin atmosphere was no more than two hundred kilometres yet it protected the planet from everything space could throw at it. Even from where he was standing he could feel the vibrancy and the life on Earth.

"It is a glorious sight to behold is it not, Xavier?" said Horace Clunk, pointing towards the beautiful planet.

"You can never tire of watching this amazing view," murmured Goff, as he stared across to the azure globe.

"We are so close, yet so far," said Xavier, "Heaven…"

"Yes, a paradise that mankind has been banished from… forever."

Xavier gazed on silently. Overwhelmed by the emotion he was feeling. All at once, everything became perfectly clear to him. Turning to Horace he said, "So how do I get there, friend? How do I get to this Paradise before us?"

"You don't know?" asked Horace Clunk, his eyes twinkling.

"I was given an Edu-Imp while on The Cathay Wheel which I believe will allow me access."

"That is possible but trust your judgement Xavier and look for the signs that will guide you."

Xavier watched as the African continent passed in front of him and then the Atlantic Ocean, the weather patterns swirling before him.

"You see those lights twinkling midway from where we are to the Earth?" asked Pete Casso, "That is the Celestial Gate"

As Xavier followed where his finger pointed. He could make out a row of gleaming objects, like a ring of Saturn that radiated on either side into a finer mesh of smaller glinting spheres. It was a lattice of death, created by the Powers to stop anything they did not want from getting through to Earth, be that asteroids or human stragglers from the colonies of Genesis whose curiosity brought them too close. The defensive mechanisms that formed the mighty barrier sparkled and gleamed seeming almost inviting.

"Has anyone uninvited ever got through there?" Xavier enquired.

"Yes, of course they have," Nana Lulu replied, "Old Man Ray went there a number of times!"

"What?" Xavier was aghast, "I thought that crazy bastard was making that shit up!"

"It was a while ago, but he was a frequent visitor."

"A frequent visitor? He would say stuff like he'd been to Earth but no-one believed him or even cared. I just thought it was crazy talk."

"It was for you to find your own way here and make your own journey."

"You have learnt more about yourself and others by embarking on this voyage,"

Xavier shrugged in his EVA, "Even so, you would have thought he would have told me!"

"You jest Xavier, but Ray had his reasons, he told us to let you know that by heading in the direction of the Celestial Equator and following the line of Ursa Major on an axial tilt of 23.4° to the elliptical equator you will find a way in via an old space elevator."

"Oh that easy huh! Just follow the Great Bear and it will take me there right. Anyway I thought all the space elevators had been destroyed," Xavier couldn't help feeling a little pissed off. How could Ray have kept something so important a secret? Why had he never confided in him? Xavier felt perplexed the more he thought about Ray and this motley bunch of Moon Dudes. What exactly were they all about?

"That's what they like you to think," said Horace Clunk, "a lot of them were destroyed but some survived and are still in use, mainly by the Powers and their escorts."

"Look behind you and then towards the Earth, you can see how close you are now. The Edu-Imp you have may help you as you approach the Celestial Gate, then once you are through you will just head for where Ray told you."

Xavier shook his head, still in disbelief at how easy it sounded, "You make it sound so simple, like anyone can do this!"

"Not everyone...just you, Xavier!" said Goff.

They turned to look at the Earth rotating and the cosmic blackness that framed her. Xavier stood silently. His visions previously only in his dreams were staring him in the face. There were no words to describe it.

★★★★★

41
Bad Moon Rising

G iant steps are what you take when you walk across the moon.

It seemed every step Xavier took became more exaggerated and the moment of reflection which he had shared with the Moon Dudes was now replaced by simple acts of play as Casso, Clunk, Goff and Lulu cavorted and skipped across the lunar surface towards 'Farther' which was parked at the base of a large boulder. It was not unusual for clouds of dust to form and be seen on the surface of the moon but Xavier's attention was drawn to a billowing mass which seemed to be shifting at break neck speed towards them.

"Do you see that?" he asked, his voice crackling on the com-link.

"I see it," said Casso, as they approached 'Farther'.

"Over there!" exclaimed Goff, pointing in the direction of another dust cloud, "Looks like we have uninvited guests who wanna crash our party!".

"How many?" Casso called, fumbling with a latch below the old moon truck.

"Hard to tell, but I have a feeling they are not going to be friendly," Goff replied, hitting a panel on the side of 'Farther' and opening the hatch inside.

"What are they?"

"Who knows what they are, but without a shadow of a doubt they don't look good."

The mood changed in an instant. Pete Casso reached inside a cargo hatch and passed Xavier a hover board.

"Take it and head back to Tranqualandia."

"On this?" Xavier was bemused. He looked at the old hover board and couldn't believe of all the out-of-date things to have, the Moon Dudes had given him this for his escape.

"Seriously!" he said after a pause, "On this?"

"Xavier, this isn't the best but it will get you back to Tranqualandia and away from here pretty quickly. Just head over to the craters to the right of here and lay low."

"And what are you guys going to do?"

"We will be your decoy and give you a sporting chance," Casso patted Xavier and handed him some containers which he placed in a box. "This is more air which should last you for a while."

"A sporting chance?" replied Xavier, uncertain what Casso meant as he bundled the box of air canisters into a bag and attached it to his suit, "You will be all right won't you?"

"Don't worry about us we'll meet you back at the ranch!"

"You sure?" Xavier replied.

"Xavier, its time. We've taken you as far as we can it seems. It's now for you to make that journey on your lonesome. And don't worry kid we are rooting for you all the way."

Xavier placed his feet into the straps of the hover board and switched it on. There was a sudden kick and Xavier elevated a metre or so off the ground.

"Remember Xavier, follow the Bear, Ursa Major then down. Take the Edu-Imp you got from The Cathay Wheel and that will give you headings and access codes past many of the defences but trust your own judgement as well. Do not rely solely on the uploads."

"A pleasure meeting you Xavier!" Horace Clunk called, "Ray always spoke very highly of you!"

Xavier skimmed the surface with the hover board, holding his balance while heading towards the direction of Tranqualandia. Horace Clunk, Nana Lulu and Pete Casso all climbed into the multi-coloured Loonster's bus which stood out like a sore thumb against the dark and sombre terrain. Although he could not see them he could hear them through his com-link as they attempted to pull away before the arrival of the unknown intruders.

Through the com-link Xavier heard Pete Casso shout, "Put on some music dude!"

Suddenly the audio speakers inside 'Farther' blared out an old Earth song.

'...*I see the bad moon rising, I see trouble on the way, I see earthquakes and lightning, I see bad times today!*'

Xavier shook his head as he listened to the words and then a ripple of laser fire began to echo around the space bus. He turned to look but toppled to the ground. The board, still attached to his feet began to drag him across the gravel strewn plateau and into a shallow crater. He was hidden from view and eased himself up to take a look back at 'Farther'

The wonderful colourful little truck over three hundred years old had meant so much to so many when it embarked on its famous journey across the lunar surface filled with Moon Dudes all looking for a meaning to their life on the moon. It was now surrounded by three black trucks, devoid of any corporate markings but with enough weaponry and malevolence inside and out that Xavier knew the outcome was not going to be good. Xavier could hear the various traffic filtering through his com-link, a mixture of Intel-Security chat, Genesis Can-Com, Russian, Hinglish, Mandarin and Lunar patois.

From inside 'Farther' he could hear that the Moon Dudes were defiant until the last,

"I ain't going any further in 'Farther'" said Goff.

"Oh, well, let's see what these gentlemen want with us," Nana Lulu said.

"They can kiss my hairy butt!" laughed Horace Clunk.

The hatch opened and the Moon Dudes stepped down as the black suited and helmeted figures surrounded them.

"'Farther' forgive them, for they know not what they do," said Pete Casso, raising his hands like the rest of the dudes, "now go fuck yourselves!"

An intense barrage of fire opened up, spraying the Moon Dudes and Farther in a violent torrent of laser-fire ripping the suits and helmets of the Moon Dudes to shreds while shattering 'Farther'. Round after round seemed to hit the old moon bus sending splinters and fragments in all directions before the antiquated lunar truck decided enough was enough and exploded into pieces.

From his vantage point a kilometre away, Xavier could not bear to watch anymore. He slid down the side of the crater, overcome with grief. He could not control the sob that escaped him.

He took a deep breath trying to regain some kind of calm. He felt cold, intensely cold as if a jet-black cloud was breathing directly onto him. Raising his head slowly, something dark was staring down at him - the chilling figure of Magnus Bowser.

*****

42
Come And Meet My Little Friend!

"Who are you?" demanded Xavier.

"My name is Magnus Bowser, I have come to kill you," came the stark reply.

Magnus moved towards Xavier, slashing at him with a laser saw, forcing Xavier to raise up on the hover board to escape the hail of blows. Like a nightmare where the dreamer is stuck and cannot move himself, Xavier seemed unable to escape from the clutches of Magnus Bowser, yet he knew he was in a fight for his life. The more Magnus grasped, the more desperate Xavier became. He tried to counter the blows using whatever he could grab hold of, but the attack was relentless until Xavier managed to use one of his gloved hands to pick up a small boulder which he thrust at an airlock on Magnus's side and momentarily was able to break away from his grip. He began to hop away in a fast forward motion as he fumbled to get back onto his hover board. With a sharp turn, Xavier arced around and covered Magnus in a cloud of dust before grabbing his bag containing the air containers.

"Dust, moon dust, is that all you've got space boy?" Magnus snarled, brushing away the dark grey powder, then lurching forward and tossing Xavier from his board and into a pile of rocks scattered across the crater floor. Xavier's helmet hit the ground with such force his face pressed right up against the inside of the visor causing his nose to bleed and the air to be forced from his lungs. He immediately felt Magnus descend upon him and he struggled to get him off as Magnus took Xavier's helmet on each side and began to ram it into the rocks. Once, twice…there would not be a third time. Xavier lifted himself up using every last ounce of energy, his fingers fumbled inside his bag, delving to seize one of the air containers he had been given. Grabbing one, he lifted the catch inserting one of his fingers inside the valve and pushing it open. He quickly rotated his helmeted head to stop the visor making contact with the rock again. The tortured vestiges of a young man's face lay behind the visor, whose features were now in eternal pain.

Xavier pivoted his body around as much as he could without breaking his neck then gazed into the ghastly mist contained behind the visor which was the form of Magnus Bowser.

"Stop this. You do not need to kill me," screamed Xavier, as he slung the bag around his arms and then removed his finger from the open valve of the air container, instantaneously releasing the pressurised oxygen in a continual burst before driving it into Magnus's visor. Their bodies jerked apart before tumbling in opposite directions in the crater. The spent air container protruded from Magnus's helmet and the once full pressure suit now lay twitching opposite Xavier's feet. A safety leash attached to Xavier's leg and the hover board dangled limply and he began to draw the board towards him and placed his feet into the straps. He did not know whether Magnus was alive or dead, he did not care, he needed to flee and find Aqua Terra. Adrenaline was coursing through his veins, his heartbeat verging on explosive. The blood from his nose ran along the back of his throat forcing him to cough a spray of blood that coated the inside of his visor. The heavier he breathed the more oxygen he used. Silently, he thanked Pete Casso for the emergency oxygen canisters. At this point though, he knew he would last no more than an hour. However, he had no idea about the distance from where he was to Tranqualandia. Despair was edging closer, despite his determination to forge ahead.

The name of Magnus Bowser was banked for future reference and the savage murderers of the Moon Dudes would have his revenge exacted upon them…that much was certain. He made calculations for his passage back to Tranqualandia continually propelling himself forward on the hover board. Although, if he didn't make it back…there would be no revenge.

The destruction of 'Farther' and callous murder of Pete Casso, Goff, Horace Clunk and Nana Lulu had cracked through Xavier's soul. A warrior was born. Once reluctant to oppose the Pax Humana but now transformed by the brutal, senseless slaying of kind and gentle folk, Xavier swore vengeance.

Making sporadic stops to replace the old air canisters with the full ones, he felt with each kilometre the tiredness and fatigue slowly overcome him. He had not rested in hours and his body was sapped of all its energy. The loss of blood through his nose and the loss of liquid through him sweating and breathing in the confines of the suit were draining him. He needed air and water, the two staples so important to any human being, even more so to someone alone on a hover board a metre above the lunar surface. His eyes flickered and a feeling of serenity washed over him.

"Am I dying?"

He could sense he was close to Tranqualandia, in fact he could smell it, he imagined the sweet, fruity, pungent aroma of *Sativaland*. But all he could really smell was the congealed blood and fetid air in his helmet. He recognised a valley opening before him and directed the hover board down towards its floor before banking close to a small hilltop. He began to identify the topography again and distinct rocks he had seen on his journey out. He could just about make out the welcoming sight of solar panels and small domes which he knew belonged to Tranqualandia. Relieved they were intact and not smouldering ruins, he tried to contain his excitement and not use any further oxygen. He looked above him for the sight of any trailing drones but all he saw was the star-strewn darkness.

As Xavier clipped past a rock on the perimeter he felt his leg being clasped before being hurled to the floor. Exhausted, he could not move or even let out a gasp. He groaned as he felt himself being snared then dragged on his front towards an uninviting and hidden black hole.

His body was spent and he resigned himself to his fate. He had less strength than a newborn as his body disappeared into the hole. Xavier passed out, unable to fight yet unaware his life had just been saved.

★★★★★

43
Earth Calling Xavier

White light enveloped Xavier.

"I'm dead," the thought flashed through his mind.

He was going to meet his maker; the luminous glow his welcome into the afterlife. He could hear noises all around him, echoing and reverberating in every direction adding only to his disorientation. He was no longer on the cold grey lunar surface. His eyes flickered, adjusting to light and to the sounds that enclosed him. He could feel warmth for a change, the warmth of a hospitable shelter.

"Ssh, Don't say a word," a Moon Dude came into focus through his blurred vision. He was holding his finger to his lips. "You are alive but you will need to leave here immediately."

The outer pressure suit which Xavier had used on his ill-fated journey with Casso and Clunk had been removed and he was now dressed in a simple white smock. His legs and chest were throbbing relentlessly.

"K-O-K," Xavier groaned.

"Do not worry," said the Moon Dude, "we are well and no harm has come to the colony."

"Casso…," Xavier managed to mumble.

"Your journey must continue, Xavier," the Moon Dude said reassuringly, "Casso and the others are gone, but not forever. They will never leave us totally. They have gone on another adventure and you my friend are about to embark on yours."

"I need to rest."

The Moon Dude brought Xavier his clothes and placed them on the bed.

"Xavier, sadly there's no time for that right now. You have to go on. Your craft is ready."

"But I just want to…"

Xavier gestured to the Moon Dude for some water. He took a large gulp and sat up a little, groaning. Taking a deep breath he attempted to brace himself with what little energy he could muster.

"Ray…what about Ray?" he asked as the Moon Dude swung his legs over the edge of the bed.

"Ray is unable to make it."

"Is he OK?"

"Never better, but this is a journey you need to make on your own."

"Yeah, I've pretty much figured that out," he said as his whole body fought against him.

"You will meet with Ray again when your journey has been completed."

"When, not if ? " said Xavier, "You sound confident that I will make it."

"It is all in the mind Xavier. Stay positive and remain focused. You will reach your goal."

Xavier began to dress slowly, as he did so he felt a renewed passion and motive. He realised that nothing would finish or resolve itself until this journey was over. And it was down to him. He had followed his convictions and would see his odyssey through until the very end. He found he was no longer concerned about dying. After his experiences in the last few weeks…the things he had felt and seen - death no longer frightened him. He looked in the mirror for what seemed like the first time in months. He looked different - older somehow just in a short time.

He picked up his helmet and belongings and turned and grabbed the Moon Dude by the shoulders and planted a kiss on his forehead.

"Be safe. Be well, Godspeed!" said the Moon Dude.

"Alright then Moon Dude!" Xavier said, "It's time to fucking do this!"

The Moon Dude smiled, "Right on, Xavier! Right On!"

Xavier was led back to Aqua Terra, his faithful craft gleaming in the empty hangar. He put his hand inside his jacket pocket and placed the Edu-Imp in his mouth. He clicked his neck and cracked his fingers, then bellowed, "Earth calling Xavier. Come in Xavier!"

The engines erupted and Aqua Terra hovered up from the hangar floor and shot out as the large hangar doors slid open.

Aqua Terra was making its maiden voyage to Earth.

★★★★★

44
The Celestial Gate

The Celestial Gate was a formidable network of space stations connected to a ring of geo-stationary asteroids which acted as the last line of defence to Earth. This, combined with an immensely powerful force field used to protect the planet from stray meteor strikes from deep space, made this the most forbidding place to enter without express permission from The Powers.

Why did he always make such impetuous decisions? They were taught at the Academy *the consequences of choice* and how dangerous that could be when pursuing a career through the Pax Humana. He was now at the point of no return.

From a distance the defensive barrier of the Celestial Gate looked like a thin mesh but as Xavier neared he could determine each of the small twinkling dots was either a mine, a laser guided missile launcher or part of a more elaborate net protecting the atmosphere and deflecting any unwanted objects that might encroach. The Earth's atmosphere was no more than four hundred kilometres thick and looked like a thin piece of tissue paper wrapped around the planet. Against the vast blackness that surrounded the Earth it was hard to imagine that such a delicate and finite element could protect her so well. There was nothing for millions upon millions of kilometres that contained life such as Earth. The colonies of Genesis, the Moon, Mars, the solar system and the numerous mining operations out on the Belt did not even come close to the abundance of life on Mother Earth.

The Edu-Imp kicked in forcing Xavier's eyes to widen and take in a diagrammatic map as a myriad of patterns formed before him. The constellations were his guide and they began to take shape as he propelled towards the Earth. They formed technicolour valleys which he steered Aqua Terra through and guided him to what he believed was his ultimate rendezvous. They triangulated and formed a passage which he could follow, and he tapped away making adjustments to his flight path. A single purple line which originated from Ursa Major, down to a point where it seemed he would be landing. It was the old Galaxie Generale Space Elevator in Sector FR9. The Earth co-ordinates were four-north, fifty-three west.

"If I set those now, I should see the beacon ahead." Xavier busily tapped the co-ordinates into Aqua Terra.

"Get ready for your welcome party," Xavier muttered.

His arrival had not gone unnoticed.

An alarm sounded, its shrill tone reverberating throughout every corner and corridor of Fortress Mendoza. The human guards that manned this orbiting sentry post sprang from their various states of slumber. The alarm had never been set off before. They ran to their battle stations where they stared in disbelief as a lone spacecraft made its way without fear or reservation towards the Celestial Gate defences of Earth. The same alarm flicked an electrical charge that activated a battalion of ESP androids arming themselves in preparation for the approaching intruder, their red eyes shooting beams that cut through the darkness.

Xavier witnessed the planet getting larger and larger through the screen of Aqua Terra. As he approached, the blue of the oceans became more and more intense as Aqua Terra hurtled like a bullet towards the vast expanse. It would not miss, the co-ordinates were set. In his craft he had followed the Ursa Major constellation since leaving the moon. It seemed as if he was being secretly directed as an array of coloured shafts emanated from the stars and formed a pattern for Aqua Terra to follow.

Commander Piotr Kazinsky of the ESP looked in disbelief at his screen at what appeared to be a suicide mission. Normally barracked on the moon, he and his crew had been seconded to the fortress to overlook the remote firing systems and the android troops and drones held in reserve there.

"One solo occupant or life-form," a monitor blared.

"It is definitely from Genesis but what does he think he is doing?" said one of the guards.

"Fix target and alert android battalion for despatch. Fire warning volley then engage," barked the commander.

Xavier's controls suddenly awoke and began to whistle. He had been spotted by the ESP and was now the target of a multitude of defence systems. A com-link opened directly to Aqua Terra's computer and a voice of foreboding gave warning of what was about to happen.

"This is Commander Kazinsky of Fortress Mendoza Earth Security Patrol, you have breached the perimeter of the Celestial Gate. You are in violation of Rule 19; the illegal entry into Lower Earth Orbit and are ordered to immediately turn back."

Xavier did not respond.

"There will be one warning and no more," Kazinsky continued, "then I will order your immediate destruction."

Kazinsky shook his head. Interlopers were deterred - the Genesis propaganda machine ensured that. Who was this joker? In his entire career, he had never seen or heard of such a thing.

"Turn back now before you are destroyed. We will send an escort for you and take you back to the moon," Kazinsky spoke into a microphone headpiece. His voice echoed inside Aqua Terra. Xavier grimaced. He continued following the imaginary markings that were guiding him to a destination.

Kazinsky started to bite his upper lip, his attention never wavering from the small object on his screen. Did the person in this space craft realise that even if they got past the Celestial Gate, the Earth's atmosphere would incinerate the craft and whoever was inside?

Of the forty or fifty laser beams aimed at Xavier one was placed just in front of Aqua Terra. A flash alerted Xavier to the fact.

"Sorry guys…I gotta keep going. One way mission and nothing is going to stop me now!" Xavier braced himself. All he could see was reaching his final destination. He recalled a manoeuvre he used to do back in The Hives whenever he had been chased by the local cops while throwing up a graffiti piece. If Xavier could stop his trajectory and speed instantly then he believed he would be able to lose the tracking beams and slip through and drop down through the Celestial Gate. The warning shot had been received. There would be no more warning shots. He switched off all of the computers within Aqua Terra and screamed at the top of his voice.

"5-4-3-2…" Xavier counted down to the trick of the century… if it worked. He pulled back hard on the joystick slamming a switch on the side, "One!"

Aqua Terra did an inverted flip at such a speed that Xavier, even though harnessed to his seat was thrown against the ceiling, his stomach somewhere near his eyeballs. The craft jerked and screeched in every direction, beginning to spiral and twist uncontrollably. The density of the air pressure had him gasping for breath as the centrifugal forces pinned him to the side of the cockpit. The tracking systems ploy caused the missiles to momentarily lose their target allowing Aqua Terra to tumble violently away from the weapons systems towards Earth.

"They won't survive now, those G-forces will kill anything and he will burn up in the atmosphere," Commander Kazinsky sounded confident again that his quarry was as good as dead.

Aqua Terra was spinning out of control like a comet burning fast through the sky and Xavier, although barely conscious, managed to edge his foot to the side of his seat and with every last drop of strength he had left used it to draw down a lever just in reach of his boot. Aqua Terra juddered, coming into some kind of controllable spin before levelling as the auxiliary engines and safety drill were initiated. Lights flashed, alarms blared inside the cockpit as Xavier tumbled to the floor released from the severe G-forces.

"No...Nothing can stop me!" he mumbled, before momentarily blacking out.

★★★★★

45

Space Elevator Descent

T he interior of Aqua Terra was a mess with bits scattered
everywhere. Xavier could feel his head still spinning and
his internal organs felt like they were in all the wrong places
but he realised he was alive. In the distance behind him he
could see Fortress Mendoza and the Celestial Gate. He
checked his life support systems and switched on Aqua Terra's
reserve engine. He met with a voice of disapproval. Aqua Terra
was not happy.

"Come on! You can give me just a little bit more can't you?
We are nearly there."

As Xavier said this, a red beacon began glinting in the
distance. It was the asteroid counterbalance to the elevator
cable. The curvature of the Earth shone below him but still he
had a way to go. Xavier checked the navigation and flight
systems and tried to lock the controls of Aqua Terra onto the
beacon.

The azure atmosphere of Earth illuminated the planet
against the depths of pitch black space. He was still thousands

of kilometres above the Earth, but in all directions weather systems could be distinguished. The panels and dials of the dashboard flashed in front of Xavier a warning as they neared JK 59401, the call number of the space elevator counterbalance. Xavier was now able to distinguish the beacons call-sign and lock on the controls of his craft. Stretching out along the curve were the remnants of the disused and dormant space elevators, like solitary golden metal flowers glittering in the sun across the equator. They conjured up the time honoured folk tale of Jack and The Beanstalk, of new worlds way past the clouds which could be reached by ascending a carbon stalk; it was a revelation and revolution in science and space technology.

The Space Elevator had long been abandoned for regular commercial operations. The corporation of Galaxie Generale had interests as far away as the moons of Jupiter and out past the Kuiper Belt. This, for centuries, had been their elevation site in what was old French Guiana. The subtropical climate and its proximity to the equator had made it the perfect site to launch the lift.

The geo-stationary asteroid JK 59401 was over fifty-thousand kilometres above the Earth and had a carbon nanotube cable connected to it that led down to an elevator and space station platform some twenty-thousand kilometres below. The platform and reception area were huge. Held in geostationary orbit, they comprised of a large rotating reception area, docks and bays for craft to load and unload and tanks of water that were stored for distribution. It was a collection of solar panels, communication dishes, cranes, pipes, booms and towers, as well as a plentitude of platforms jutting in all directions.

Cylinders and spheres containing gases and liquids were at every junction and the platform had a number of other daises above and below, which were receptacles for the traffic that had once made this a very busy space port. The cable which transported the wares of Earth was like the trunk of a sequoia redwood now. Where there had once been only one cable there were now six, positioned around a hoop that held them in place. The carriages and cars that traversed the cables were aligned in a holding yard that had lain dormant for decades.

"Let's see if you can get a response from the guidance system here," Xavier said as he attempted to find a place to land Aqua Terra. There was no response.

"Maybe we can activate one of these cars? Or maybe I'll just have to break in and get it rolling myself."

Aqua Terra remained his silent partner.

Xavier manually steered the craft towards one of the vacant bays close to the carriages and docked the craft gently. The platform was gigantic, a testament to human ingenuity. A huge terminal for the arrival and departure of people and goods, the first port of call for millions to a life in space and their banishment from Earth forever.

An electronic message beeped into the cockpit, giving directions.

"They think we are a routine maintenance team," said Xavier incredulously, "they think we are a routine maintenance team." The computers and security systems responded to their arrival.

"Well done, Aqua Terra. What will I do without you, girl?" he said, patting the dashboard.

Xavier leant over a console, grabbed a small rucksack, his sidearm and whatever provisions he had that lay strewn throughout the cockpit. He began tapping at some keys to his side, "Aqua Terra, I have set a protocol here allowing you to shut down," he gazed around the battered interior of the cockpit, "what a journey we have had old friend? You will be safer here."

"I have accepted the protocol, Xavier," the voice of Aqua Terra answered, acknowledging his final command. Xavier smiled knowing his beloved Rod would be safer than he would. One by one the panels began to fade and the lights dim as his faithful craft shut down. Everything he was about to face was unknown.

Now, he was truly inside his dreams.

"Here we go, Xavier," he suited up, putting on his helmet, which was now on its last legs with cracks and dents to prove it.

Xavier made his way through the hatch and onto one of the platforms leading to the cable carriages. He turned to briefly glimpse Aqua Terra for one last time. He knew with the cloaking devices on and great deal of luck, Aqua Terra might be safe and secure for the foreseeable future.

Xavier, on the other hand, was not sure how long his adventure would last.

★★★★★

46
Ride On The Ribbon

T he space elevator groaned into life. No-one had used it in centuries.

It had been left sealed in pristine condition. As good a working condition as it had been the day the last person had boarded one of its many carriages. Xavier walked from the hangar into a huge terminal which must have acted as the arrival and departure lounge for the elevator's passengers.

A small galleria of shuttered shops greeted him, their signs still advertising their wares and services centuries later. The rows of stores that once sold trendy looking spacesuits for new arrivals by Snaaag & Co, the Scran-Quik synthi-meat restaurants and medication bars from Smilon Fi-lon all looked as if they could be open for business in the next few hours. There was something uncanny about how the stores had been left. Xavier imagined the throngs of people crowding these spaces before they left to make new lives on their respective colonies. He proceeded past a sitting room, its chairs and tables carefully stacked, then turned to his right where a children's play area still advertised its services. There was an eeriness pervading throughout the aisles and walkways of the terminal. It seemed immaculate for a place abandoned centuries before. The floors were polished, the shuttered stores and signs still seemed to welcome imaginary travellers. He continued down an escalator whose steps no longer moved towards a sign that stated: ARRIVALS

His attention was suddenly grabbed by a group of red lights at the far end of this walkway.

Twelve red pin point dots emanated from the darkness and he became aware his walk to the elevator carriages was not going to be as straight forward as he had hoped. His right arm reached down towards his sidearm and flicked off the safety catch. The row of red dots before him felt out of place, sinister and scrutinising. A flurry of flashes shot out from the darkness forcing Xavier to dive to his left and into an old shop doorway. A short barrage exploded above his head sending fragments of glass and steel in all directions and shattering the signage above him. He tried to shrink into the doorway as another volley erupted and then he saw the shapes of six dreaded android guards heading towards him. He had to fight, for his life. These droids were shooting to kill. Xavier took a deep breath then jumped up and levelled his firearm at the advancing targets and began to squeeze off laser bolt rounds in short bursts. He hit three with great accuracy, a clean round hitting them straight between the piercing red eyes.

Emergency lighting flickered overhead, then swamped the mall in a blue haze triggering a series of alarms, filling the area for the first time in hundreds of years.

Xavier began running as fast he could, then seeing a sign which read EARTH he ran as quickly as he could towards the glass security barriers and smashed his way through. The android guards kept up their pursuit, firing another volley which destroyed an entire wall of advertisement hoardings bringing them crashing down all around Xavier. Above him a warning flashed:

THIS WAY TO ATLANTERRA BASE
NO UNAUTHORISED PERSONNEL ALLOWED
BEYOND THIS POINT

Xavier winced in pain as he realised one of the bolts had clipped his bag and then ricocheted through his outer suit which immediately began to de-pressurise. Although not piercing his body, the flesh wound suddenly exposed to the elements began to throb incessantly and the pain grew. A searing burning sensation erupted from his side and a singeing smell quickly filled his helmet.

"That fucking hurts!" he yelled, as he continued running towards the security checkpoint counter. He fell over it and then lifted himself up to see if his android stalkers were still on the hunt. They were. He could see their eyes scanning the corridors. Xavier had one incendiary flare for emergencies and if ever there was an emergency this was it. The flare might distract the three droids if not destroy one or more. Loading the flare, he looked for the right target as they advanced. He noticed a pipe above them, firing the flare towards the pipe which exploded just in front of the three android guards and ruptured the pipe engulfing them in a cloud of gas and steam. Xavier quickly loaded his sidearm with his remaining ammunition then lined up each android before targeting each one with a true and proper shot between the eyes.

"Goodbye Junk! Nice knowing you!" he shouted, as they dropped one by one. Xavier did not know if there were anymore ESP droids on the space elevator platform. If there were, then without doubt they would be making their way to this location at the double. He staggered towards the sign and saw one of the carriages welcoming him, like a train of yesteryear. Xavier quickly dashed around the cabin of the carriage to assume control, which would allow him to descend of his own free will as opposed to being directed by the automated system that once shot supplies, goods and people back and forth like a fairground amusement ride.

"C'mon life support," Xavier muttered as he looked over a panel of controls before him. His Edu-Imps on life support systems came in useful as he hot-wired the unit, turning a few handles and punching buttons on the controls. The power kicked in from the emergency solar panels of the station stored for just such an eventuality. Xavier had been anxious about the operating systems but to his surprise, the air controls immediately sprang to life. Despite being untouched for an age they were functioning like new.

"That is some quality engineering," he chuckled, "can't fault them for that."

His eyes darted around the carriage, looking for anything that would help. He pulled at a first-aid unit on the wall and the contents spilled out. Rummaging through the medication and bandages he picked up painkillers, muscle repair, skin sealant and antibiotics. This was a quick fix, as he began to squirt and spray the different substances onto the wound on his side.

"It ain't too bad," he sighed, as he injected himself with a combination of painkillers and antibiotics. He hobbled over to another panel which closed the doors.

"Let's get this show on the road," said Xavier, as he collapsed into the first seat he found, tapping on the 360° clear screen which revealed the laser beams used for guiding the carriages as they travelled back and forth. The motors of the carriage came to life, and with a jolt they moved to a platform which tilted them in a downward trajectory. Xavier estimated that the journey would take approximately ten hours to cover the thirty-thousand kilometres from space to Earth, but he was not sure. All he could do was wait and see what would happen, he had no idea if the carriage would even make it down to Earth. Though the cabin was pressurised, he decided he would keep his tattered suit and helmet on. Old habits died hard. He pulled the harness and restraints over himself and secured all the buckles and straps ready for his descent. There was a whirring sound as the carriage connected to its leash. Without warning, a voice filled the cabin. It took him a few moments to realise that it was simply an automatic safety notice, explaining all the safety procedures travellers should take note of as well as the precautions and breathing exercises they should adhere to on the journey down.

Pod 16 began to lurch a little and the vertical drop was glorious.

From the small windows in the carriage he could see the drop towards the planet and the white clouds below him. Looking down made him feel as if he was standing upon a ledge, holding on tightly, pressed against a wall. Xavier listened to the safety warning then placed his hands across his chest. He thought about Jericho and the thousands of times they had spoke about the possibility of going to Earth. He pictured his friend laughing and joking. He then wondered if his compadre Old Man Ray was okay, but his emotions overwhelmed him.

"Need to keep it together…need to keep it together," he chanted mentally, but the floodgate was open. He thought about Keki Lascaux and her dancing in Debris. He could not save her. His journey to the Cathay Wheel and the fate of the Moon Dudes and Old Man Ray.

And what about Zola?

Zola, Zola, Zola…always putting him before herself.

"Keep it together, Xavier. Just keep it together."

If he went down that route, he may just not make it…for this, the trip of the century.

"Just get your ass down to Earth Xavier Miro," he commanded himself.

If he could just get there…perhaps everything would work itself out.

The carriage jerked forward. The vertical descent had begun as the momentum increased, gravitational forces began to compress his body. The old carriage, after years of inactivity, creaked and groaned forcing Xavier to squeeze his restraints.

There was no turning back now. The forces of destiny were set in motion. He was now on a free fall to Earth at thousands of miles per hour. The rapid acceleration of the craft rammed him into his seat. Gritting his teeth, he could see the blue of the Earth starting to fill the small window. With the atmosphere of Earth fast approaching, Xavier could only hope he would survive intact. Gripped by a mixture of fear and excitement like he'd never felt before, coupled with a cocktail of painkillers, Xavier could not escape the sheer thrill of the moment. He was loving every second of his perilous journey into the unknown. As the carriage entered the atmosphere and its beautiful haze, the vibrations increased.

Xavier felt a strong pressure upon his chest and began to go through the breathing exercises as advised by the safety voice. Earth's gravity was so incredibly strong, Xavier found himself battling to remain conscious as the carriage continued down the elevator ribbon. In an attempt to keep conscious, Xavier concentrated on the details of the carriage trying his best not to succumb. The pressure pipes within Xavier's suit expanded and began to harden around his body, instinctively protecting him from the forces surrounding the carriage.

In an instant, the blackness and cold of space was replaced by a brilliance which consumed the inside of the carriage in a dazzling and glorious light. Xavier adjusted his vision as the glaring sunlight of Earth penetrated every perceivable crack in the cabin. The vivid blues, whites, reds and yellows streamed through the small window and filled him with wonderment. The sensation as his body was enveloped in the beautiful radiance of Earth's energy was unlike anything he had ever experienced.

As the velocity of the craft grew more intense, Xavier gripped the restraints and used all his power to prevent him from passing out as he entered the vista of his dreams. The Earth's atmosphere was a thin blue line that had separated his dreams and those of others for centuries and now he was through it. It was unlike anywhere else in the near known universe. There was nowhere like Earth for hundreds of light years...nowhere!

He was trying to savour every moment in the struggle to stay conscious; the vast continents made of rock and soil were now clearly visible and the wonderful oceans below him seemed to be as infinite as the vastness of space. As the carriage entered the blue planet's atmosphere, Xavier blacked out, succumbing to the effects of the forces governing Earth.

★★★★★

47
Atlanterra Base

Xavier opened his eyes. An intense light was streaming into the carriage, blinding him in his current disoriented state. He had passed out, that much was certain and now…he was…on Earth? Could it be? He seemed to have little control over his faculties - his mouth had fallen open and his eyes rolled in his head. He removed his helmet, grunting at the exertion; his suit immediately deflated and opened up. One thing was for sure he was alive, and damn lucky to be so.

He grunted, unable to articulate at the moment and was seemingly immobile.

Taking a few deep breaths, he tried to gain his bearings. He looked down at his side where the laser bolt had scratched his skin to find a dark red wound. It had healed but it was still sore. He grabbed more of the painkillers which lay by his side and shot them into the wound.

The descent had caused more exhaustion and disorientation than he had bargained for. His strength, which he relied on, was sapped. The lurid light filling the carriage was more luminous than anything he had ever imagined.

A screen above him blinked the name of his location - 'Atlanterra Base…Atlanterra Base…Atlanterra Base…'

The words meant nothing to him. Until his body felt better he could not do anything.

"Fuck! This is some trip!" he muttered to himself. He had always imagined something more grand and eloquent as his first words, but for now this would have to do. Doing justice to Neil Armstrong would have to wait.

Slowly he felt his body revive. So what's the plan? He thought to himself. I have never had a plan. Not since this adventure began.

"Remember, Xavier," he said aloud, "you have to have a plan. They kept telling you that at the Academy. And look where it got you…Earth."

Xavier lifted himself up gently then paced along the carriage repeating, "I got to pee."

He stretched his body out and the muscles started to feel better after being cramped up for so many hours. Then just as he started to feel close to normal, Earth's gravity hit him like an asteroid hitting his body and knocked him to the floor. He shouted out as the pressure on his body became agonisingly intense. He suddenly felt disorientated as his legs turned to jelly and he started to flap his arms and legs as if being pulled by a set of invisible strings.

Xavier took a few moments to collect his thoughts and slowly but surely he pulled himself up and began to make his way to the door.

"Let's do this," he roared cautiously, finding his feet and picking up his helmet and outer suit before heading toward the exit of the carriage. He left the safety of the pod and walked through the door. He moved through a series of caged gantries and walkways that ran down to a service corridor and platform. Ahead of him was a set of double doors with a sign - WAY OUT.

"Well, if that ain't the understatement of the last few days," laughed Xavier as he pushed open the doors in one sweeping motion and suddenly he was overcome.

Before him lay the most awesome sight he could ever have dreamt up. The place he had for so many years looked out at as the blue planet in the distance from his trans-hab window. With the sun blazing down across an azure sky sweeping into the distance for as far as the eye could see. The ocean rippled gently for miles on end. The tips of the waves glistened white as they folded placidly into one another while the sun's reflection shimmered on the water.

The smell of fresh Earth air filled his lungs for the first time, the purity of this air unlike anything he had experienced. For a few moments it overcame him. It was a strange, alien feeling to be able to breathe air the way humans had done for thousands of years. Free of a life support unit or oxygen tank. Free oxygen, which could be inhaled into his lungs unencumbered by the constraints and evil controls espoused by the Air Authority.

Xavier had arrived at Atlanterra, a man-made island and elevator base a few miles from the coast of South America. He gazed in wonder at a row of palm trees moving to and fro and felt the gentle luscious breeze of the ocean across his face as it blew across the briny waves. Xavier surveyed the undulating coastline on the horizon. He could not stop himself from smiling at the sight before him. It was land…terra firma. He was so small in this majestic ocean, as insignificant as a grain of sand on a beach; but for him, the moment was one of exhilarating enchantment. He looked into the sky and guessed Genesis was somewhere in that direction, invisible for the first time in his life from his vantage point below.

"That's the sea!" yelled Xavier out loud to no-one in particular. He pointed to the waves rolling before him, "That blue is the blue I could see every day from the Hives!"

He felt like a child again.

There were times when he could have just given up. Not bothered about his desire to reach Earth. But the dreams which motivated him to leave his graffiti all over Genesis had been inspired by visions of this place.

He had a thirst like he had never felt before.

"First things first," he said to himself.

He realised if this base had been abandoned years before there would be little or no chance there would be water here. He had to try. He chuckled to himself remembering the words from an Edu-Imp of an old Earth poem called 'The Rime of

The Ancient Mariner' he had mind-loaded. Now in his present situation and seeing the oceans for himself it seemed all the more prescient:

Water, water everywhere and all the boards did shrink.
Water, water everywhere, but not a drop to drink.

And as for a plan…there still wasn't one.

He did not know where he was and how he was going to get off this disused and sealed elevator platform. He hoped in one of the many small rooms he looked into he would find some kind of refreshment. Coming across a small office, he forced the door open to find a sink unit.

"At last," he sighed, turning on the tap and closing his eyes while listening to the unmistakable sound of running water.

Placing his mouth under the water after he had let it run, he was ready to spit it out, fearing it was salt water or poisoned in some way, but with a simple motion he began to drink down the beautiful, cold, clean water; refreshing and rehydrating his body.

He gulped down the water until his belly was full and then looked for a container and filled it. He looked at the charts and maps on the walls. There was a chart that showed him their location. The maps showed the geopolitical system before the wars, the Exodus with the continent of South America close by, he could not help but think about all the old cities and their inhabitants who had populated them centuries ago and how they had become lost in history; a time when ships and planes traversed the oceans and skies, much like on Genesis and

Mars, taking goods and people to destinations and trading with one another.

And then they were gone.

A road and tunnel had once connected Atlanterra with the mainland but had since been demolished to prevent anyone using the elevator. The port which had shipped goods from space and taken supplies to be lifted had been blocked with old scuttled sea ships in the harbour. Aged photos lined the wall showing the base in its heyday, a launch pad for Galaxie Generale and other nations and corporations in their ventures into space. There was a great feeling of achievement, camaraderie and happiness on peoples' faces, the mood of a new beginning, the pioneer spirit that had set humans apart. Xavier scouted around looking for more information on how to get somewhere, anywhere. But where? The planet had long been abandoned. Now that he had reached Earth he was stranded on this base. He thought he should never have sent Aqua Terra away. He should have packed her into a crate and sent her down the elevator.

Xavier threw down his helmet and outer suit and found an old toilet and relieved himself. He no longer felt he needed his old clothes and for a while could not stop smiling and laughing about where he was. He gazed back up at the ribbon of the elevator which disappeared from view kilometres above and shook his head in disbelief, he Xavier Miro, had actually made the journey to Earth.

He started feeling hungry; this may be Earth, the heaven of the universe, but how do you get food here? He hadn't thought of that!

"Damn, I could do with a Geronimo Burger or some of Nish-kin's hot Zug O'Noodles, right about now!" he said to himself, "Even something from the ArkLight canteen or the Astral Apache would be fine."

There was no chance of finding anything resembling that in this uncharted land.

"So where do I get some food?"

He walked back outside and drinking the water from his container, found himself transfixed by the motion of the waves. An albatross squawked overhead, capturing his attention.

"It's a frickin' bird! A real bird," Xavier gasped. A pod of dolphins were breaking through the ocean. It was all Xavier could do to not actually jump with glee. There was no denying the magic and wonder of what was occurring all around him.

In the distance, something else captured his attention; an ominous addition to this spectacular morning. Xavier spotted specks on the horizon which grew as they moved towards Atlanterra. Three airships were headed towards him and they were headed fast.

Xavier stood up and viewed the approaching nemesis, "Looks like my ride has arrived. Maybe they'll have some food."

★★★★★

48

Let Me Take You To Your Leader

H e watched the craft approaching Atlanterra.
"Should I run?" he wondered, "Run where? I'm
surrounded by water!"

Besides he wasn't sure if he could physically run. Nope, he
was going to take his chances with the approaching ships.

He looked up at the carbon nanotube ribbons of the space
elevator stretching into the blue sky for miles before disappearing into the faint wispy clouds as they traveled into
space. It was an astounding feat of engineering that had built
this avenue to the stars and for the slightest moment, Xavier
wished he could whisk himself back up those wires to the
familiar safety of space. For a moment, he wished he could be
back with Zola eating Zug-O-Noodle and listening to Scun
Scum in his trans-hab, but he knew there was no 'back' to go
back to.

It was better to be just in this moment. This very moment.
As hairy as it may become he decided to take a seat and wait.
Things in space were very different from here on Earth. The

sun was bright, beaming down across the ocean making his skin look like he had never seen it before. The experience of natural heat on his body was worlds apart from his existence in the confines of the Hives.

And breathing! Real proper breathing... clean Earth air...Xavier needed some time to get accustomed to it. As the vessels got nearer he began to take in more of the free air and satisfy his craving for the oxygen. It felt incredible, he actually felt high on air! His lungs were inhaling and exhaling to the point he thought they may burst. As the airships pulled to the platform, the central one released pontoons that allowed it to glide across the water and make its way to where he sat.

"ESP guards," Xavier muttered, as he watched a squad disembark from inside the craft brandishing firearms.

"You are here illegally, which is punishable by death. Place your hands on your head and get to your knees," barked one of the troops. Xavier could not make out whether the voice was human or android but complied with orders by holding his hands above him.

A powerful voice boomed from inside the vessel, "Escort him aboard."

Within seconds, Xavier was surrounded by a group of uniformed troops who took his belongings and frisked him from head to toe for weapons. Within seconds they found his laser firearm, blade and trusty spray can. Xavier was placed in a prone position and scanned by a number of security wands, then escorted by the guards along a gangplank and into the flying ship. He could not make out any of the marking or insignia on the troops and was aware he was being scrutinised by every member of the crew as he was bundled along.

By the reaction of the people on board the vessel, his presence had obviously caused a major commotion. How could it be that somebody had breached the security of Earth? Xavier was then searched again before being taken into a large salon that opened onto a deck. Xavier could feel the craft beginning to move, yet he still had no idea who these people were.

"What is your name?" the voice said, from a loudspeaker.

It was the same voice that had commanded the guards to escort him from the Space Elevator platform.

He stood to attention, "My name is Xavier Miro."

"What is your purpose here on Earth?"

Xavier then paused and shrugged his shoulders, "I have no other intention but to see the planet Earth."

"Why do you want to see Earth?"

"Why?" replied Xavier, "It's simple, because I look at it every day and she is so beautiful and I wanted to know why I could not go there!"

"A straight forward, to the point answer to an incredibly complex question," came the reply.

Suddenly, Titus Haq stood behind him, resplendent in his military uniform with the emblem of The Shadows on his collar, cuffs and breast.

"Xavier Miro," Haq continued, "Miro, Joan Miro, the abstract Earth artist of the twentieth century was a scribbler too. He is your namesake. Are you aware of him?"

"Yes, sir. Of course I am," Xavier answered.

"You have been the cause of great consternation, Xavier," Titus said, "you, with your dissident doodling and lurid scribblings all over Genesis."

Xavier shrugged, smirking inwardly - nothing could bring him down.

He, Xavier Miro was on Earth, sure he was currently in a potential world of trouble...but hey! The guy seemed important but he did not know who he was.

Titus paced around Xavier scrutinising him, "I have been ordered to take you unharmed and untouched to meet with someone. You have protection from the highest of ranks and I have been charged with making sure you have safe passage. Relax, you will not be harmed."

"Oh yeah?," replied Xavier, confused for certain, but he was accustomed to this confusion.

"So..how was your journey?" said Titus, in oily tones.

"Eventful!" said Xavier.

"I have tracked you for a good while Xavier, I cannot lie," Titus could not take his eyes away from Xavier. "You do not know who you are, or do you?"

"Who I 'am'? Not sure what you mean," replied Xavier.

"You have been a topic of discussion for a very long time and I can assure you, your trip here will be, if hasn't been already, somewhat significant for you," Haq continued.

Xavier, unsure of what to reply, said nothing.

"Do you know who I am?" asked Haq.

Xavier shook his head.

"The inquisitiveness of youth, the tenacity and bravado; it's really quite admirable," Titus was indignant by Xavier's lack of recognition, "I am Titus Haq, I am the Governor of Genesis and Inquisitor of The Shadows. I believe you may have heard of me."

Xavier was genuinely surprised. The Shadows; the bogeymen children were told would come and visit them as they slept if they did not behave, or were unruly in class or failed to salute their team leaders correctly. Here he was, with the man who mastered them. Haq's hair was jet black and swept back, his hands clasped behind him with his angular, patrician features and bright blue eyes; crystal clear yet dark and murderous behind his gaze.

"I would have had you killed a long time ago actually Xavier," he smirked, "in fact I believe you may have come across some of my charges on the moon."

Xavier's blood began to chill as he recalled the events in the crater and the destruction of the Moon Dudes bus 'Farther'.

"You see, I grew tired of your nonconformist pro-clamations, the prolix of a madman, quaint and imaginative I give you that, but ultimately futile, not beneficial for the society I am trying to govern." Titus continued, "I was intrigued, I will give you that."

Titus was a devious and Machiavellian character, with a keen intellect. His polite manner hid a psychotic leaning which delved into the dark arts and felt no empathy for his fellow man. Xavier could feel his contempt.

"I've seen your 'hieroglyphics', animals, aliens, nature unsettling the populace. It is nothing but misguided angst. What does interest me is what is inside you...I am interested in what you are!"

"What I am?," asked Xavier, quizzically.

"Come with me," he beckoned Xavier onto a terrace. "Take in the view of this beautiful Earthbound paradise."

From the terrace of the airship they crossed over the coastline and the tributaries of a river flowing into the sea. Xavier watched as wave upon wave crashed on the shore of the white sandy beach. Sand bars broke up along the shoreline and the ruins of old properties could be seen covered in weeds and so overgrown they had, over time, reclaimed the buildings as their own.

As the craft banked inland they flew over green sweeping fields teeming with wild animals darting in all directions startled by the vessel travelling no more than a kilometre above them. Long feathery clouds streaked the clear blue skies and the warm sun streamed down on the deck, with only the movement of the airship providing a cool and soothing breeze.

"I have gazed through my window every night at this marvellous blue planet, just as other inhabitants of Genesis have done before me. I do not think there has been a single night I have gone to sleep without looking at Earth and dreaming of living there. I do not think there is a single person in Genesis, not one person in Debris, not a person on the Moon who does not dream of being on Earth," said Xavier.

"And you, Xavier," countered Titus, "are the only person who has made it back here."

Xavier nodded.

"Do you think of yourself as special, Xavier?" enquired Titus, picking up an apple from a dish laden with fruit.

Taking a bite, Titus Haq walked towards Xavier.

"Do you think yourself special, Xavier?" he asked, again.

"No," replied Xavier, "not really."

"Different?" Titus questioned.

"I've never thought about those things."

"You lie. You know you are different and I will tell you why," Titus roared.

He took another bite of the apple, the sweetness of it filling his mouth. He closed his eyes and savoured the exquisite taste, then turned, offering Xavier the apple.

"You should try one, Xavier. Fruit grown on Earth. Fruit from Heaven. The forbidden fruit."

Xavier held up his hand, now was not the time to eat, no matter how hungry he had been.

"You think that you are somehow better than me?" said Haq, turning towards the millions of trees that now stretched across the vast land, "I am the Governor of Genesis and Inquisitor of The Shadows, I have personally come to Earth for a graffiti artist. Are you mad? If I tell you to eat an apple…you will eat an apple!"

He threw one at Xavier who managed to catch it. He took a bite. "Damn it was good," he thought.

"Do you think you are the only person who has ever tried to get to Earth, Xavier?" Titus seethed, "Because many have tried and many have died, but apparently someone, somewhere likes you…a lot!"

"So I've been told…sir," replied Xavier, beginning to tire.

Titus stepped to the edge of the balustrade and threw his apple core out into the forest below, then lamented, "This was once known as the Amazon Rainforest. This was once the lungs of the Earth until mankind turned a blind eye to the greed of landowners. Illegal logging scythed away vast tracts of land and let an area so rich in wildlife and natural history become a ravaged wasteland. With the rainforest gone, the oxygen it created was depleted, signalling The Great Suffocation of 2108. It was the start of the end of our planet."

For a moment, Titus Haq seemed genuinely overcome by sorrow. Xavier joined Titus at the rail as he continued.

"Three hundred years after man has been banished we still find ourselves here. Visitors to a strange land. Have you heard of The Loyal Order of Android Monks?" Titus asked.

Xavier wasn't sure. At the moment he felt he was sure of nothing. He was standing in front of a forest of trees with a psychopath for a host, who said he wasn't going to harm him - things were just too damn weird.

"They were commissioned by The Powers," Titus continued, "to ensure the Amazon Rainforest was returned to its full size and capability. There were rumours that many of the indigenous tribes had escaped the Exodus and the death squads, and were still living as they had done for thousands of years in the depths of this enormous tropical rainforest. For some reason I have always liked to think that those rumours are true."

"Really?" replied Xavier, uncertain what Titus meant by this strange declaration.

"Of course!...I may be a clone but I am human!"

"What happened to this planet, Titus? Why were we really banished from here?"

"That Xavier is something you will have to find out from somebody else I am afraid," Titus paused and turned back towards the salon, "I think it is time we introduced you to a couple of people. One of whom I believe you know and the other who is incredibly excited to make your acquaintance."

"What are you on about?" Xavier asked. Titus' games had only just begun.

"Don't worry old boy! They won't bite...much!" Titus laughed, a high pitched, maniacal sound not unlike a giggle, "Xavier Miro, may I introduce to you..."

Titus placed his hand over Xavier's eyes shielding them and then turned him around so he was looking across the open deck.

"Hello Xavier," said the unmistakable demure voice of Zola Capello, who stood smiling in a long green flowing gown, "Welcome to Earth!"

Xavier's legs turned to jelly and he felt himself buckle. This, he had not expected. What was going on?

"Zola! You're...okay!"

"And she got here before you," snapped Titus, unable to contain his laughter, "How about that, on Earth before you and as my guest."

Xavier could feel tears well up in his eyes. He did not know if they were being caused by a mixture of relief, anger or happiness. Zola smiled back at Xavier, yet she seemed vague and the smile feigned. She left up her head and stared through Xavier, as if trying to not engage his stare. Xavier could not help but look at her. He knew something was not right and could detect a tear in her eye.

Xavier's attention was broken as Titus snapped, "There are some others who would like to meet you too Xavier."

Titus Haq moved his hand in a flourish, his fingers performing a gesture which summoned four Shadows to appear and immediately move to his side.

Titus smiled.

Xavier felt some kind of presence surrounding him, wrapping itself tightly around his body, until he was unable to move.

"Do not fear it, Xavier. It is merely a Shadow come to say hello."

Haq moved towards Xavier and placed a hand on his shoulder. The invisible Shadow briefly revealed itself, one of an army of tormented souls, before melting into oblivion again.

"The Shadows have been dying to meet you Xavier," said Titus, his maniacal giggle loose again.

Xavier struggled to speak, "Why?"

"You have disturbed them, your presence here on Earth has woken them."

Titus flicked his hand again and The Shadows disappeared into the ether. Xavier felt his body released - able to breathe a little easier.

"So…are you a Shadow?"asked Xavier completely disturbed by Titus, who was obviously a lunatic, but still curious of him.

"Oh no! I am very much alive," Haq declared, "I have not, as of yet, succumbed to the afterlife. There is an eternity for death and at this present moment I am happy in my life."

He turned and opened his arms, waltzing with an imaginary partner.

Zola had said nothing this whole time, and Xavier knew there was a game being played. He just hoped he could play it right.

"Do you not find it strange we find ourselves here on Earth together, Xavier?" asked Titus.

"I do," replied Xavier. "How could I not!"

"I, too, Xavier, have throughout my years dreamt like everyone else in Genesis of being here on Earth and through my position I am one of very few who is able to visit…and now I find myself here with you…a renegade."

Titus seemed genuinely enthralled by being on the Earth. It was strange to witness someone so threatening being so ecstatically happy. It was hard to look at a man like Haq as being human.

"Zola," Titus called, "come and join us."

Zola walked cautiously over to join Titus and stood by his side. Titus kissed her on the cheek. Xavier felt his jaw clench. Something stank.

"Isn't she beautiful," Titus asked Xavier, well aware of the tension. "Quite stunning! Don't you think?"

Xavier felt his fists tightening. He really wanted to punch Titus in the mouth. Zola was quiet, but Xavier could read the message her eyes were sending.

Xavier nodded, "Yes, she is."

"Mine now!" Titus sneered, his arm placed firmly around her waist.

★★★★★

49

A Family Affair

Centuries before, the city was known to its inhabitants as Rio De Janeiro. Now it was the playground to The Powers. An immaculate setting located on the east coast of South America, looking out onto the Atlantic Ocean. Islands and bays flanked by huge mountains and rolling hills, turquoise waters lapping at the shores. White beaches were covered with sand that had, over millions of years, become as fine as dust in the ruins of an ancient city. Titus explained to them that many cities had been demolished during the Exodus. Those remaining were now overgrown with dense vegetation. In Rio's case this extended towards the beaches.

On one of the hills that overlooked the abandoned city there was a statue that had been a focal point and a symbol of the city for centuries. It was a statue of a man dressed in a long robe with outstretched open arms, almost embracing the city. 'Christ the Redeemer' Titus had said. Xavier studied the magnificent monolith. Graceful but somehow out of place in its surroundings. The brilliant white statue was maintained by

The Loyal Order of Android Monks. The jungle encroaching into almost every corner of the old city had been kept at bay here.

Zola, too, was watching visibly in awe as they passed over in the airship. Rio, a city that had once been home to millions of humans, was brimming with monkeys, deer, pumas, birds - a cornucopia of wildlife. The noise of the monkeys and the birds was at fever pitch, abruptly subsiding, allowing a moment's respite, before starting up again with such intensity that Xavier covered his ears, laughing at how much noise came from the jungle.

"It's great but I can't help feeling something is missing from here," he said softly. Titus was out of ear shot.

"Yes, us, humans!" Zola managed to whisper back to him, her eyes filling with tears.

The air yacht swept right by the statue, before descending over a lush mountainside into the valley. The beauty and eeriness of an uninhabited city surrounded them. All the abandoned signs of humanity were now scattered throughout the jungle like unwanted toys. For the first time, Xavier grew curious as to their final destination.

"So...where are we going?" he asked.

Titus Haq looked at the graffiti artist.

"You will soon find out, I would have actually preferred to throw you out into the rainforest."

"Who is it?"

"You are to meet with them alone. When we arrive, you will be escorted to the main quarters and I will not be with you," Titus smiled, before turning and walking away from the pair then disappearing into the interior of the craft.

Zola and Xavier were left alone on the deck. Xavier placed his hand on Zola's and gave it a comforting squeeze. She pulled her hand away.

"You must not," she said, sternly.

Xavier stepped away, "I need to know if you're okay."

"I am fine," snapped Zola.

"What the fuck is going on here?" Xavier grabbed Zola's arm, "He hasn't touched you, has he?"

"Are you fucking crazy Xavier?" Zola was enraged, pulling her arm away, "Can't you see what has happened here!"

"I just wanted to know you were okay!" said Xavier.

"I am fine Xavier, I have to be fine. I have to look after my own shit!"

Xavier could see the deep upset in Zola's eyes, "Tell me he hasn't touched you."

"How do you think I am here?" Zola leaned in towards Xavier, "Did you think this was a free fucking ride!"

Xavier could feel himself about to explode with rage.

"Listen," Zola continued, "now is not the time or place for this. You have to be cool and we have to get ourselves through this, do you understand?"

"I am sorry for leaving you back in the Hives."

"Forget it, think about now and think about our survival Xavier," Zola held her finger to her lips kissed it then placed it on Xavier's lips and mouthed, "…I love you."

Xavier smiled and nodded, aware discretion was key to their survival in the company of Haq.

"We both made it to Earth!"

Zola shook her head, "The circumstances for us though have been quite different."

"This journey has been a trip!" Xavier smiled.

"Tell me about it," she replied, mockingly, "by the way you look like shit!"

Xavier laughed out loud. That was the Zola he loved, "Damn right. You look amazing though!"

"Like I said, I have never been better!" Zola smiled, sarcastically.

"Whoever we are seeing must have some influence to tell Titus Haq what to do?" he whispered.

"That's what frightens me, now you are really on your own," Zola answered, smiling a nervous smile, then moving away from Xavier as Titus returned to the deck pointing towards a mansion below them.

"We have arrived at your destination, Xavier."

A palatial residence lay in front of them. The air yacht came to a gentle rest on a strip at the side of the house and Xavier was escorted off by a number of personal guards. A few androids busied themselves with tethering the craft under the powerful rays of the sun. Titus and Zola watched from a large window onboard, as Xavier entered the residence. A wide marble staircase led to an imposing doorway where a droid was waiting, "My name is Benson and I welcome you to Rio De

Janeiro. Please follow me. You are quite safe and welcome here."

Benson whirred around, rolling through a magnificent reception room. Once inside, and out of the beating rays of the sun and the watchful eye of Titus Haq, Xavier began to feel a little more at ease in these surroundings. The polished black and white marble floors felt cool underfoot. They had a swirling pattern that spiralled out to every corner of the room and along the intricately detailed walls. Enormous fish tanks containing colourful fish swimming in all directions, much to his wonder who had never witnessed such creatures.

The luminous aquariums cast a strange light as he passed by them. They were interspersed with ornate Roman statues and old masterpiece paintings ostensibly taken from great museums once found in the cities of Earth. His Edu-Imp knowledge was being put to task, it was all true and pretty overwhelming thought Xavier, feeling a kind of disorientation returning.

He entered a towering room with floor to ceiling windows ten meters in height. It opened out onto a vast balcony overlooking a green and luscious garden, and the bays of old Rio stretched away into the far distance. Xavier looked up at the high domed ceiling with its cathedral-like majesty, the controlled lighting filled the vast expanse allowing the natural beauty of Guanabara Bay to contrast with the magnitude of the interior. The room was enormous.

Inside, statues by Michelangelo, Rodin, Henry Moore, Giacometti, Jacob Epstein and the ancient Greeks, Romans and Egyptians filled the room as well as artefacts that were out of place in this tropical enclave. Suits of medieval armour were scattered around the room alongside a mask of Pharaoh Tutankhamen. A giant golden Buddha sat in one corner and an Abyssinian war chariot in another. The Wright Brothers' Kitty Hawk, man's first endeavour at mechanical flight, hung from the ceiling as did the capsule of Apollo 11, which overlooked a Viking longboat with oars raised in salute. Cabinet cases filled with ancient artefacts and paraphernalia accrued from Earth's distinguished history were displayed for any infrequent guest to peruse at their leisure. These were relics tracing man's journey through time, a record of exploration throughout the ages. It was a museum of everything man had achieved.

"This is like a hobby room," Xavier muttered to himself. In truth it was. A hobby room for the most prominent, powerful human being in the known universe and yet, there was an emptiness, it had no soul or energy, a place with no heart. Everything was detached; there only to look upon but never to touch. Ornate doors opened revealing an ante chamber, its walls lined with leather bound books, a deep red carpet upon the floor, a leather Chesterfield sofa with a drinks trolley next to it. Here before him, Xavier laid eyes on the most powerful man in the galaxy.

Drax Kraldon wore a blue tracksuit and had his thick white hair swept back. He was tall and athletic in build, his face glowed from the fresh Earth air and he betrayed no signs of stress or obvious ageing; he possessed a healthy tan and his fingers were manicured. A large diamond sparkled from his pinkie finger, the only piece of jewellery upon his hands. He had a charming, self confident and commanding charisma that captivated you without him having to say a word.

Xavier felt at ease in his presence; in fact, he felt quite at home. There was a warmth about Drax that welcomed him even if this imposing figure also scared him too. He turned and opened his arms towards Xavier.

"I have been waiting quite a while to meet with you, Xavier."

Xavier looked a little bewildered by his host and surroundings.

"My name is Drax Kraldon, I run the galaxy!" he said chuckling.

"It is a pleasure to meet you," stuttered Xavier, struggling to believe this was actually *the* Power, Drax Kraldon.

"Let me get you a drink," Drax nodded towards Benson. "What will it be?"

"Water would be great!" exclaimed Xavier.

"Water!" a surprised Drax replied, "Water! Of course! Earth water tastes good…doesn't it? The best in the universe!"

Drax moved towards the terrace outside, "Come outside and take in the view."

The large terrace was filled with potted plants, bordered by small pools and waterfalls flowing into one another. Down a long terrace of small manicured trees, the ruins of the city lay before them and beyond that the ocean disappeared out into the horizon; a thin layer of ozone filled the bay as the waves lapped along the shore.

"So, what are you thinking?" enquired Drax.

"What am I thinking?" exclaimed Xavier, "It is the most amazing thing I have ever seen in my life!"

"Spectacular isn't it, Earth. So it has lived up to your expectations I take it?"

"Yes, it's incredible. I'm not even sure I know how I've reached it, but every moment is more majestic and inspiring than the next."

Drax turned to face him, "Xavier, I don't think you realise what we have been through to get you back. You do not realise who you are. We have been looking for you for years. We lost you and now you are back with us again. We have found you. Welcome home."

Drax embraced Xavier.

Xavier pulled away.

"Welcome home! Home? What do you mean home?"

"This is your home, Xavier. You were born in this very house twenty-three years ago."

Xavier shook his head in disbelief.

"You are my grandson," said Drax.

"How can I be your grandson?" asked Xavier, stunned.

"You are and this is your home. Your mother was my daughter, her name was Maya. You were conceived here, even spent your first years here."

Xavier stood in stunned silence for what seemed like an eternity.

From the opening bars of songs to obscure quotes from the twenty first-century, he realised that the vague, unverified memories floating around his mind had probably been memories of playing on a terrace like this. The images of swimming in a pool with a young woman as the sun reflected off its surface - much like the one he found himself walking by now, were now seemingly real. He had always thought of these visions as dreams. Vivid dreams like the ones he woke from every night; certainly not distant memories locked away in his unconscious mind and forgotten.

"Xavier, I am sure this has come as a great shock to you, my boy. You are my grandson and that means you are part of me, you are part of this family. You have the power I have. A power that was tempered in through strength and a power that allows us to dictate," said Drax, holding Xavier by his shoulders.

Xavier staggered back towards the pool before being grabbed by Drax.

"Xavier, please take a seat," Drax guided him to some chairs under an awning.

"What just happened?" Xavier cried.

Xavier Miro, of Hives tenement 19 J 15 unit 26 12 1739 CVT, a product of the Pax Humana, a rigger at ArkLight Docks, a graffiti writer, who throughout his life had always wanted to visit Earth but thought his destiny was on an Ark, now looked around in disbelief at the mansion in Rio De Janeiro belonging to his grandfather; Drax Kraldon - the most powerful man in the universe.

"We have all the time in the world, Xavier," said Drax, taking a seat next to him, "all the time in the world."